Epic Adventures

LITERATUR
Forschung und Wissenschaft

Band 3

LIT

EPIC ADVENTURES

Heroic Narrative
in the Oral Performance Traditions
of Four Continents

Edited by
Jan Jansen and Henk M. J. Maier

LIT

Front cover: Illustration from Babad Jipang, Leiden University Library, LOR 3186, p. 8. Jaka Penulup, the younger blowpipe hunter, dated 1255 AJ/1839 AD.

Layout: Vocking in Vorm, Utrecht

Gedruckt auf alterungsbeständigem Werkdruckpapier entsprechend
ANSI Z3948 DIN ISO 9706

Bibliographic information published by Die Deutsche Bibliothek
Die Deutsche Bibliothek lists this publication in the Deutsche Nationalbibliografie; detailed bibliographic data are available in the Internet at http://dnb.ddb.de.

ISBN 3-8258-6758-7

© LIT VERLAG Münster   2004
Grevener Str./Fresnostr. 2   48159 Münster
Tel. 0251-23 50 91   Fax 0251-23 19 72
e-Mail: lit@lit-verlag.de   http://www.lit-verlag.de

Distributed in North America by:

Transaction Publishers
New Brunswick (U.S.A.) and London (U.K.)

Transaction Publishers
Rutgers University
35 Berrue Circle
Piscataway, NJ 08854

Tel.: (732) 445 - 2280
Fax: (732) 445 - 3138
for orders (U. S. only):
toll free (888) 999 - 6778

TABLE OF CONTENTS

Hear! Hear! Epics are a booming business! Jan Jansen and Henk M.J. Maier	7
The emergence of oral epics in Bantu-speaking Africa – The Cameroon Littoral and Buhaya Ralph A. Austen	11
The birth of Jaka Tarub, a hero from northern Java Clara Brakel-Papenhuyzen	22
A school for epic? The école Willam Ponty and the evolution of the Sunjata epic, 1913-c. 1960 Stephen Bulman	34
Theodoric rescues Sintram – The epic hero in romanesque church sculpture Michael Curschmann	46
The dynamics of the epic genre in Buryat culture – A grave for shamanism, a ground for messianism Roberte N. Hamayon	53
Epic as arena – Models of statehood and the Kyrgyz Manas epic Nienke van der Heide	65
The adventures of the 'Epic of Samori' in 20th-century Mande oral tradition Jan Jansen	71
The narration of the Sunjata epic as a gendered activity Marloes Janson	81
The deification of South Asian epic heroes – Methodological implications Janet Kamphorst	89
The sleeping giant: Dynamics of a Bugis epic (South Sulawesi, Indonesia) Sirtjo Koolhof	98

An *epik* that never was an epic – the Malay *Hikayat Hang Tuah* 112
Henk M.J. Maier

The narrative potential of the *Mi'râj*: two contexts for its interpretation 128
Julian Millie

Demise and reemergence of 'Hikayat Seri Rama' – 140
The epic adventures of a non epic
Amin Sweeney

The emergence of Blackfoot storytelling in educational programs 171
Lea Zuyderhoudt

Works cited 183

Contributors 195

HEAR! HEAR! EPICS ARE A BOOMING BUSINESS!

Jan Jansen and Henk M.J. Maier

At the conference 'Emergent Epics' held in Leiden, May 2001, some of the speakers – this collection of essays tries to hold the echoes of their voices – suggested in their presentation that epics do not exist, and they did so with a grin. Neither suggestions nor grins necessarily lead to serious discussions: the audience did not react, and thus once more it confirmed the impression that the relevance of the epic as a distinct literary or artful entity has been demolished for good and that scholars tend to restrict themselves to descriptions and discussions of performances, contexts, storytellers and politics. However, those very same scholars passionately elaborated on themes and meanings of 'their' epic during the conference's informal conversations, next to presentations an essential element in every academic meeting. Deep in their heart, so it seems, they assume that epics somehow do exist, after all. Or perhaps they speak from the assumption that epics can be constructed. This collection of essays should show that epics tend to emerge (or disappear), visible and audible, somewhere in between those two assumptions.

The adventures of the 'epic' in modern times are a fascinating topic in themselves. The Romantics claimed that every self-respecting nation should once upon a time have had one, and they set out to reconstruct these epics for political as well as cultural reasons. Echoes of their writings may have resounded up to the present day, but the notion of the 'epic' gradually lost its prominence on the agenda of literary scholars and politicians: epics represented earlier stages in the development of nation-states and in this modern world they are, therefore, hard to appreciate.

The introduction of taperecorders in the 1950s, however, brought the epic back in the lime-light, with a vengeance. It became fashionable for 'Western' scholars working in far away countries to record long oral narratives, write them out, and present them as long written poems that reflected deeply ingrained ideas. In this process, the idea of the epic was revitalized, and Iliad, Beowulf and Kalevala were revoked to measure the relevance and beauty of these newly found and newly constructed 'epics'. Their findings and opinions could not but have an effect on the conversations among local intellectuals and politicians. Epics – the word was assimilated in many languages – are strong. Epics are wonderful. Epics tell us of the world in concise manners.

Taperecorders – a new technology – put oral traditions on the academic research agenda, so to speak, creating new issues for those who are interested in the dynamics of culture and society. Concrete case studies based on the recording of extensive orally presented narratives forced us to reconsider, among others, the question of how in so-called 'oral societies' and 'predominantly oral societies' knowledge is acquired, transmitted, and stored. They also created a new interest in their tellers. The most important effect of these reconsiderations was a new awareness of the dangers of operating in this world in terms of an absolute dichotomy between oral and literate, which had been, for instance, the starting point for so many literacy campaigns in the so-called Third World, often financed by international organizations such as UNESCO (cf. Van Helden 2001: 21 sqq.).

In the final decades of the 20th century, this dichotomy has been definitely refuted in academic circles, and the self-evidence of the superiority of literacy over orality has been destroyed once and for all (see the empirical studies of e.g. Street 1987 and the theoretical studies of e.g. Chafe and Tannen 1987); the growing interest in the oral and the audible in literate societies could be seen as another effect of the introduction of the taperecorder and its cousin, the transistor radio.

Obviously, taperecorders and transistor radios have had more and equally far-reaching effects on our efforts of making sense in this world. Sound carriers and sound recorders can now be found everywhere, and to stick to our topic: long narratives or epics have often become better known to local and faraway audiences via cassettes (cf. Newton 1999) than via live performances, or via text books, for that matter. The new technologies have brought 'oral traditions' closer to people who had been excluded for so long.

Oral performance, radio, cassette, video, book: these days epics and other oral narratives, constructed or not, can in various forms be presented to various publics in a variety of ways. In this variety of presentations, they can play an important role in people's self-esteem and self-respect: their tales are worth preservation, they are appreciated in many places, they are more easily available – and all of this can serve as tools in a community's identity kit. Epics can make every group of people who can claim to have one proud and self-confident.

The variety of presentations in the academic as well as the commercial world has made the ownership of narratives a problematic issue, more problematic than ever before. Not seldom serious conflicts emerge between recording and publishing researchers, on the one hand, and the community or the reciters who accepted these researchers in their midst, on the other (cf. Zuyderhoudt, infra). Conflicts about ownership can also exist within a community or society itself (Jansen 1998), conflicts in terms of gender, for instance (Janson infra, Sidikou 1997), and conflicts between ethnic groups or political elites in states (Van der Heide, infra, and Hamayon, infra). Yes, the ownership of discourse has always been the source of many contests.

So far the climax of the reevaluation of the oral and the audible has been UNESCO's 2001 proclamation of 'Masterpieces of Oral and Intangible Heritage of Humanity', a statement that implicitly claims that every form of culture – including oral lore – deserves to be safeguarded and (re-)vitalized, if necessary by way of international and national governmental protection programs (see Nas 2002). The proclamation is a perfect example of how local contests about the authority of narratives are taken up to the level of *national* politics: the question which endangered cultural expressions should be protected creates 'cultural brokers' who will articulate the issues involved in the political arena and create many a conflict by doing so.

On the 2001 UNESCO list, several intangible heritages are strongly related to oral narratives (those in Benin, Ecuador/Peru, Georgia, Philippines, Russian Federation), and even to oral epics (the Guinean Sosobala project, for instance, is related to the conservation of a mythical instrument described in the Sunjata epic). Most essays in this collection more or less directly demonstrate that the narratives in this world which could be moved towards an 'intangible preservation' are numerous. The fact that individual nation-states, mediators to the UNESCO, can play a crucial role in the process of making their own epics 'intangible heritage of humanity' is telling. Such attempts show that artistic work can easily be appropriated by a government, become a substantial element in a state ideology – and then the construction of an epic is near. Curschmann's essay in this collection – how to the images and statues of the pagan Theodoric, the hero of early medieval narratives, were in the 12th century attributed the symbolism of a Christian ruler – should remind us that these political activities of the UNESCO to create and preserve particular tales are nothing new. A corresponding process of appropriation is described by Bulman (infra): Sunjata was given a 'Shakespearian' interpretation by West African schoolteachers, paving the way for a breakthrough in 1960, when Niane published his version of the tale of Sunjata, now the Sunjata epic.

A discussion about an epic is not only a discussion about narrative, aesthetics, and morality. It is also a discussion about politics. And perhaps equally important: it is business. People can be employed to record, collect, publish, broadcast and propagate the epic-to-be, and the books and other paraphernalia can make these intangible epics a booming business indeed.

The growing attention for oral traditions in the second half of the 20th century did not only lead to the demolition of every possible notion of 'epic', but also to its 'inflation' and the reconstruction of the notion of 'epic'. Scholars appropriated the term 'epic' so as to attract an audience or to get 'their' work published. Jansen's essay (infra), for one, sheds an eerie light on this process in his study on the so-called 'Epic of Samori', which hardly meets even the flimsiest definition of an epic. Inflation of the term continues: we recently spotted the publication of an epic of 67 lines (Oyler 2002 on the Guinean teacher/linguist Souleymane Kante). And Janson (infra) criticizes Sidikou for upgrading a narrative to become an epic in order to prove that also women can tell an epic, an example of how the door can be opened to a broad variety of social groups and categories who want to appropriate an epic for political or commercial reasons...

Research by scholars has been of major importance in the process of constructing and canonizing new epics. Unintentionally, Austen's essay offers us wonderful phrases about the first step of this: 'The Bantu-speaking regions (roughly everything south of a line drawn across the middle of Cameroon, the Central African Republic, Uganda and Kenya) have been relatively neglected. (...) Despite the relative neglect of Bantu Africa, there is material on many traditions from Cameroon, Gabon, the two Congos, the Central African Republic, Rwanda and Tanzania which could be drawn upon to illustrate the full range of epics in this large region.' Is it, for instance, mere coincidence that the recently published anthologies of African epics written by Mande specialists have such an impressive list of Mande epics (Dieng and Kesteloot 1997, Johnson, Hale and Belcher 1997)? Or is it the result of activities by a group of scholars at the University of Indiana (cf. Hale 2002)? Cases of active interventions by local scholars and western academics can also be found in Southeast Asia, witness the essays of Koolhof, Sweeney and Maier – and it is tempting to believe that sooner or later the narratives described in the essays of Millie about Malay storytelling, Kamphorst about Rajasthani oral tradition and Brakel about Javanese storytelling will be made into epics as well.

The contributors to this volume have been actively involved in the efforts to foreground the oral heritage and to reconsider the importance of the oral and the audible in contemporary life. 'Epic Adventures' sounds like an appropriate title of this book, referring to our intellectual adventures and our often heroic struggles with long narratives as well as to the adventures of the narratives' antagonists themselves. It also seems like an appropriate way to make sure that this book, a little dot in a huge field, will appear on the computer screens of students and scholars who are in search of the noun 'epic'. No doubt, most of us are driven by the conviction that scholars are morally responsible for the way a particular culture or community is represented. However, it cannot be denied that epics are not only a matter of literature and ethics, but also of politics and money; '(...) it should be noted that it is scholars such as ourselves at seminars such as this who have been keeping those manuscripts on a life-support system simply by writing about them' (Sweeney, infra). The construction, preservation, and discussion of epics has become a booming business indeed. And it is good to be aware of it.

Finally, a short note on the essays. Janet Kamphorst was 'in the field' with her taperecorder at the time of the conference; her essay is an echo of her experiences in Rajasthan, and not of a presentation. Curschmann's contribution is based on a lecture he gave at Utrecht University; we are very grateful that he agreed to have it published here. It shows that the European Middle Ages is an 'area' that offers insights which most of us, interested in the world outside of Europe, tend to overlook. We feel very grateful that most participants of the conference have taken the time to rewrite their presentation. Perhaps the epic has never been more alive than in the beginning of this new century. Hear! Hear!

THE EMERGENCE OF ORAL EPICS IN BANTU-SPEAKING AFRICA – THE CAMEROON LITTORAL AND BUHAYA

Ralph A. Austen[i]

While the study of African epics has received considerable attention in the last few years, within the continent the Bantu-speaking regions (roughly everything south of a line drawn across the middle of Cameroon, the Central African Republic, Uganda and Kenya) have been relatively neglected. Thus in two recent anthologies (Johnson, Hale and Belcher 1997; Kesteloot and Dieng 1997) and one analytic survey (Belcher 1999) the majority of texts published or commented upon come from West Africa and particularly the Mande region in West Africa.

Bantu Africa is included within what John W. Johnson (Johnson and Sisòkò 1986: 60-62) refers to as an 'epic belt' but recordings of narrative performances from this region have circulated less widely than such works as the Mande Sunjata epic (cf. Bulman infra). There is also some dispute about whether some of the available material (particularly from Rwanda and Zululand) should be considered epic.[ii] As will be seen below, at least one Bantu language repertoire which seems quite clearly to meet the criteria has been omitted almost entirely from the currently established African epic 'canon'.

The present tasks is thus as much to identify epic traditions of this subregion as to engage in the more difficult task of discussing the conditions of their 'emergence.' However, in working toward the latter goal I will first indicate what I see as the two major categories of epics found here. My definitions are based upon textual content rather than performance mode. The first category consists of epics which refer to the accepted historical past (whether outsiders consider it empirically valid or mythic) of the communities among which they are shared. The second set of epics deal in what may appear as freefloating fantasies or at least motifs which make no claim to historicity (even when outsiders may see connections to local developments). These distinctions, as will be noted, are not absolute but nevertheless appear relevant. Historical epics seem to be more associated with the experience of centralized states while avowed fantasies are linked to acephalous or highly segmentary societies.

I do not wish to argue that epics are ever a major or reliable source of history. In most cases (including the Haya one discussed below) there are independent and less formal oral traditions (and sometimes written sources in West Africa) which provide far better information to the historian and appear to be the inspiration for historical material in epics. What epics tend to do is condense events or beliefs about the past around the elaborated deeds of a few (often only one) figures from such an era. The aim is not so much to reconstruct the past as to use it as a heroic site of cultural values, social structures, moral dilemmas and even folkloric motifs which remain relevant in the present. It could be argued, of course, that even the most scholarly western historiography does much the same thing, but in epics the exemplary (or counter-exemplary) uses of the past are openly avowed and played upon to the greatest possible dramatic effect.

What I will call fantasy epics evoke an alternative universe not related to any recognizable time in the past. It is thus easier to find in them universal motifs, although they inevitably employ behaviors, values, social categories, landscapes and narrative tropes derived from the world in which they are produced. In the Cameroon case to be discussed here, local informants vigorously denied any historical references which I sought to identify and we have to take such responses seriously.

Despite the relative neglect of Bantu Africa, there is material on many traditions from Cameroon, Gabon, the two Congos, the Central African Republic, Rwanda and Tanzania which could be drawn upon to illustrate the full range of epics in this large region. I have chosen instead to focus upon two areas of which I have first hand knowledge (although, as will be seen, to very varying degrees as regards epics). They conveniently provide examples of the two categories discussed above. The Cameroon Littoral,[iii] where I have actually studied the epic of Jeki la Njambè (Austen 1996), represents the fantasy variant of this genre. The other tradition to be discussed, the *enanga* epic ballads of Buhaya come from a region of Northwest Tanzania where I did my first fieldwork (Austen 1967) although without any awareness at the time of local epics.[iv]

In reviewing the Cameroon Littoral and Haya epic traditions three issues will be stressed: the textual content of the narratives and its local meaning; the emergence of the epic from other genres; and the contemporary status of epic performance.

Cameroon: Jeki la Njambè
In the original program of the conference at which the papers in this volume were presented 'Jeki' was announced as a 'model' for the emergence of Bantu epic. In intention, if not perhaps in execution, my own work on this epic does constitute a relatively rare effort to study the emergence of an epic,[v] thus fulfilling the mandate of this collective project. However, in other regards 'Jeki' is hardly the richest example of even ahistorical African oral epics. Alone in Cameroon (and neighboring Gabon) the Beti-Fang *mvet* has justifiably attracted greater attention from both scholars and recording teams (Boyer).

The Jeki epic is performed within various communities in the Littoral (northwest coastal zone) of Cameroon.[vi] The subsistence and local exchange economies of this region are based on fishing and forest agriculture. However, since at least the 17th century the area has been linked to European oceanic trade, mainly through the present-day port of Douala, which enjoys access to the interior via a series of local rivers and creeks. The African side of this commercial system was dominated by the Duala people, who resided at the point of coastal contact and sent their canoes inland to purchase not only such 'legitimate' export goods as ivory and palm products (oil and kernels) but also large numbers of slaves, both for sale to Europeans and for local deployment. The Duala never developed any centralized political system, dividing themselves into a number of competing (often violently) trading chiefdoms. From 1885 onward, under first German and then French colonial rule, they gradually lost their economic role but maintained a privileged position as cultural intermediaries which has continued up to the present.

Because of their well-recorded role as middlemen, the Duala have attracted considerable attention from historians. More recently the Jeki epic, whose emergence appears to be linked with Duala prosperity, has also been recorded and studied by a number of scholars (Austen 1996, Bekombo, Kesteloot, Tiki a Kouellé 1987, 1991, 2000) and included in all the major recent anthologies and surveys of the African epic.

The Jeki epic narrates the career of a heroic figure with a marvelous array of magical powers and weapons.[vii] Its central episodes deal with a series of 'missions impossible' on which Jeki is dispatched by his jealous father, Njambè, who desires his death. Jeki is given major support by the women of his family: his mother, a scorned first wife of Njambè; and an older sister, kidnapped before Jeki's birth by spirits of the underworld from where, in most versions, she is eventually rescued by him.

The story is often said to 'have no end' and the number and variety of episodes varies considerably from one version to another. If there is any resolution, it involves a final confrontation between Jeki and Njambè but this is often omitted and when present, takes many different forms. The common motif is clearly the tension between father and son and its link to conflicts between spouses and half-brothers.

The narrative content of Jeki has no relationship to Cameroon coastal history, although the settings and structure clearly evoke elements of this region's physical and social landscape. Most significantly, many versions refer to two Njambès, one associated with the coast or sea (Njambè Manga) and the other with the interior (Njambè Pindi or Tindi). To anyone familiar with the history of this region such a dichotomy echoes the advantageous role of the Duala middlemen as well as their equation of free and slave status with coastal and inland origins. Likewise, the name 'Njambè' echoes the widespread West Central Bantu term for God or a primal ancestor: 'Nyambe' in Duala and other Sawa Bantu languages; 'Nyambie', 'Anyambe', or 'Nzambi' elsewhere in this wider zone. Many versions of the epic also make reference to *miengu* (sing: *jengu*) water spirits, who – like related 'mamywata' figures elsewhere on the West African coast- are the objects of extensive local beliefs as well as cult associations.

Despite this rich set of resonances, local understandings and uses of 'Jeki' remain resolutely modest. The story itself is often referred to by the generic term for tales of any kind (*munia*), thus linking it to much shorter narrative forms which abound in this region but show little connection to the content of Jeki. There is a special term sometimes applied here to 'Jeki' and other long narratives, *masomandala* ('marvels'); but this refers only to their scale and the wonderment of their episodes rather than any deeper significance of either the texts or their performance. The performance contexts (of which more later) are not very revealing either. There are no formally designated bards among the Sawa Bantu although some individuals have become known as virtuoso performers and appear with an entire entourage of instrumentalists and chorus singers, who punctuate the main narrative with musical set pieces. Sometimes these elaborate performances take place at funerals, but there is no general sense of why (or even whether) this is appropriate. The common denominator seems to be the need to mark an event as celebratory although more casual, unaccompanied narrations may also occur in normal domestic settings.

Most informants resisted any explication of the references in the text. Njambè is the chief of a village but he lacks all the trappings and activities of a Duala 'King' organizing long-distance canoe trade. Nothing is explicitly said about slavery and links to Europeans come up casually, usually as anachronisms, rather than in any historical context. Likewise the more spiritual aspects of the text go unrecognized. Almost everyone I spoke to insisted that Njambè was *not* Nyambe or any figure of similar stature and the jengu figures in the text are presented in casual, folkloristic terms rather than as (in other contexts) forces with significant control over social status, wealth or disease.

This absence or denial of historical or deep cultural meaning to the epic provides a clue to the conditions of its emergence. The narrative content and structure seem to derive not from the region around Douala but rather from the 'South Coast' of southern Cameroon, Equatorial Guinea and northern Gabon. It is in tales from this area (and particularly the southern Cameroon region of Batanga) that the primal ancestor/divinity is called Njambè and usually divided into a maritime and an inland figure. In this region such a dichotomy does not have the same hierarchical implications as farther north since there is no system of rivers which provides coastal middlemen with access to the interior. Moreover in Batanga, probably the immediate source of 'Jeki,' slavery (whether for trade or local use) was almost entirely absent. Thus the texts make more immediate sense here and many stories even contain references to the major historical development of the immediate pre-colonial period, the inauguration of trade with Europeans.

Even if we accept the hypothesis that the origin of the Jeki narrative was on the South Coast, we still have no direct documentation of how it moved to the Sawa Bantu region and was transformed from a set of disparate tales into a more narratively coherent, but less culturally resonant, epic. The movement can be traced through the Sanaga river region which extends to the coast between Douala and Batanga and contains variants of 'Jeki' which are closer to the Batanga tales (including allusions to historical contacts with Europeans) than to Sawa Bantu 'classic' versions. We know that there have been long-standing contacts (through trade and the sharing of fishing camps) between Batanga and the Bakoko and Malimba peoples of the Sanaga and between the latter and Duala merchants although little or no direct contact between the Duala and Batanga. Thus the Sanaga appears to be the zone of transmission for this narrative into the Littoral.

The development of a set of tales imported from the south into an epic tradition can again only be speculated upon. However, from what we know of performance practices in the early 20th century we can assume that it was the rise of wealthy merchant households among the Duala which initiated this elaboration of the earlier narratives as acts of patronage, although the epic also seems to have taken on a life of its own throughout the Littoral. The almost deliberate emptying from the epic of the cultural and historical references which accompany the originary tales on the South Coast can be related to the extremely unstable manner in which the Duala and their inland trading partners adapted to their middleman position. The epic evokes a village world in which all the issues which caused so much disorder in the 19th century are absent: political relations among rival trading lineages, slave-freeborn tensions, European partnership/domination, and missionary efforts to translate figures such as Nyambe/Njambè into Christian theological terms. Much of the fantasy of Jeki's adventures has no reference at all to these matters but the epic as a whole may be seen as an anti-history, intended as an escape into a past which – unlike more historical epics – is less about now-diminished heroism than (for all its violence) about now-lost innocence.

In the contemporary Littoral the Jeki epic seems to be dying out, as few competent performers still survive, but it is a death accompanied by considerable efforts to recuperate the narrative for more modern projects. None of these efforts have had lasting appeal, perhaps because they draw more upon an abstract idea of the epic than its textual and performance tradition. This clash is most obvious in the effort during the 1950's to incorporate a long version of 'Jeki' into the celebrations of the Ngondo, a pan-Sawa 'traditional council' revived/invented immediately after World War II (Austen 1992). However the epic, which certainly represents the regional cultural heritage which the Ngondo sought to evoke, was never taken up by the new organization probably because its content bears little relationship to the political issues of the decolonization era.

At about this same time, some local Christians seized upon the otherwise suppressed notion of Njambè's divinity and interpreted the epic as a parable of Jesus Christ ('Jeki son of God'); but their interpretation has found little audience. Somewhat later, two Duala intellectuals, a Negritude poet of the 1950's generation (Epanya Yondo 1976: 48-63. Kesteloot: 41-46; Kesteloot and Dieng: 499-504) and an Afrocentrist of the 1970's and 1980's (Dika Akwa 1978, 1981: 91f.) each molded a Jeki in his own terms; but again, neither has enjoyed much success with these efforts. In 1989 the Cameroon pop singer Tom Yoms released a cassette which contained two songs inspired by the published Tiki a Kouellé version of 'Jeki' (Yoms n.d.). Although this bonding of traditional oral narrative and modern popular music was celebrated by a number of Cameroonian commentators, it is fairly clear, especially from the text and reception of the hit number on the album, 'Pona-Pona' (one of the 'Jeki'-derived songs) that neither Tom Yoms nor his Cameroonian audience had a very strong sense of the content of the epic.

Indeed, it is unlikely that if Tom Yoms had not been a native of the same small inland town as Tiki,[viii] he would have read the published version of 'Jeki' since the two-volume work, despite a very low price, has not sold well in a Cameroon wracked by economic difficulties.[ix] This edition and the far more expensive Classiques Africaines version published by Manga Bekombo may represent the form in which the epic now survives – as a kind of academic museum piece rather than a still living aspect of Cameroonian culture. Such preservation of the epic at least allows possibilities like that of Tom Yoms, so the obituary of 'Jeki la Njambè' may be premature.

The Haya Enanga[x]
The Haya people of Northwest Tanzania form part of the East Central African interlacustrine region, famous for its major kingdoms such as Buganda, Rwanda, Burundi and Bunyoro-Kitara. The Haya themselves were historically divided into a series of six or seven relatively small states, the best known of which were Karagwe, Kiziba and Kyamtwara. Within each of these polities could be found the same hierarchal social order which characterized – in varying forms – the region as a whole. At the base were 'autochthonous' Bantu speakers, engaged in agriculture or fishing (sometimes perceived as a hyper-autochthonous occupation). The ruling elite represented themselves as cattle-keepers who had migrated into the region from outside and subsequently adopted Bantu languages. The dynasties ruling Buhaya at the time of colonial conquest, the Hinda or Bito, traced their ancestry to invaders who probably entered the region from Nilotic-language portions of Northern Uganda or the Southern Sudan in the about the 16th century.

The oral traditions of the region refer to pre-Hinda/Bito figures called Cwezi who are sometimes represented as earlier pastoral rulers but more universally seen as the spirits of shrines linked to the local environment and maintained by mediums/priests descended from local cultivator clans. The Cwezi (also referred to as *mbandwa*) provide the basis for claims of autochthony as well as cults of possession and affliction, thus paralleling in many respects the Jengu water spirits on the Cameroon coast. But in Buhaya, as will be seen, these figures have a much closer relationship to the content, and possibly the historical emergence, of oral epics.

The earliest notation of Haya epics appears to be their recordings by the South African musicologist Hugh Tracy in 1950 (Tracey n.d., 1952). The analytic study of Haya epics began some decades later with the research of Mugyabuso Mulokozi (1983, 1986, 1997) and Peter Seitel (1999, n.d.). The work of Mulokozi and Seitel's book have focused on three major narratives, all of which deal with mythic-historical themes that have great resonance in other oral traditions and continuing social and cultural issues.[xi] One of these epics, 'Mugasha' focuses on a Cwezi spirit associated with water, fertility and particularly the major local body of water, Lake Victoria.[xii] Mugasha is presented in this account as simultaneously a powerful semi-divinity and a lowly fisherman. He comes into both conflict and union with another Cwezi figure, Wamara, who appears as a terrestrial personage of ruling status, although not associated with cattle.[xiii] The source of conflict is Mugasha's desire to marry Wamara's daughter, a quest which is first rejected but, after much violent struggle, ultimately accepted.

The second of the 'classic' *enanga*, 'Rukiza' is told from the perspective of a Hima (pastoral) warrior who is also in an ambiguous relationship with a Haya king, this time Ruhinda, the alleged founder of the conquest states established around the 16th century. Rukiza's sister (in some versions, daughter) is married to Ruhinda and when the two men come into conflict, she first reveals the secret of her brother's power to her husband and, after this results in Rukiza's death, herself kills Ruhinda. Here again the epic depicts tensions between major social groups (in this case different categories of pastoralist elites) but it also introduces a more agentive female figure and also includes an autochthonous male commoner who, as a spy or messenger, links the two major protagonists.

The other major epic studied (and particularly admired) by both Mulokozi and Seitel is 'Kachwenyanja', the story of a pastoral warrior so loyal to his king that he abandons a newly won bride for military duty. Kachwenyanja is killed and sexually dismembered by the commoner he was sent out to subdue and his wife then journeys forth to avenge him. She does so by first marrying the killer, and then slaughtering him as well as his entire kin group. The characters in 'Kachwenyanja' are not major figures from myth or history, although the titular hero does represent the generic noble warrior of the Haya precolonial past and the values which motivate his action. However, the central role of marital life and sexuality in this epic and especially the emergence of the wife as the restorer of her husband's public honor draws less from the oral traditions surrounding courts or (apparently) shrines than from two other Haya oral narrative genres, 'love ballads'[xiv] and folktales. It is thus not possible to see an absolute division between the Haya epic tradition and a narrative like 'Jeki la Njambè', which avoids all cultic and historical themes. It is rather the blending of the historical and the folkloric motifs, as well as public and domestic spheres of action which gives epics such as 'Kachwenyanja' (and, in Mande, 'Sunjata') their special appeal.

The available evidence on Haya epic does not provide much indication of how old this genre is, to say nothing of the circumstances which gave rise to its emergence.[xv] The absence of any references to epics in 19th and early 20th century travel and ethnographic literature on the Haya (Mulokozi (1983: 290-91)[xvi] suggests that its development may be relatively recent, although such silence may simply be an artifact of the European and indigenous observations which happened to be recorded during these times.[xvii] Mulokozi (1997: 160-61) and Seitel (n.d.: 26 f) provide biographies of two major bards, Habibu Selemani (born c. 1928) and Abdallah Feza (born 1915). Both men learned their craft from bards who were already in their prime by the 1920's so we can at least trace the tradition to the turn of the 19th century.

Whenever the Haya epic actually emerged, we are fairly safe in assuming that it is derivative of other poetic and narrative genres which were not only recorded earlier in this region but can also be found (without any epic traditions) in related cultures of Uganda. The relevant form of poetry is panegyric (praise poetry) and the relevant narratives are the oral traditions associated with both Cwezi shrines and royal courts.

Praise poetry can be recited about almost any animate object in the Haya world and many variants of it are incorporated into the *enanga* epics. However, the forms most relevant to the epic itself are again those linked to Cwezi cults and royal courts. Cwezi mediums performed (and still perform) elaborate paeans to Mugasha, Wamara and other figures (Berger: 19-20; Pennacini: 267-74 et passim). The praises of warriors in Haya royal court settings are called *eby'ebugo* and usually performed by the subjects themselves (Seitel: 122).

The oral traditions of both Cwezi heroes and ruling dynasties have no specified performance context, although they are credited to the same sites as the praise poetry. It is thus at least reasonable to assume that, as in other better documented African cases (Austen 1999: 71), much of this prose serves to explain the allusions contained in the non-narrative panegyric. It does not matter for this purpose whether the panegyric functions as a mnemonic device for fairly stable (and thus presumably accurate) historical memory or its opacity allows for new interpretations (such as the insistence on early Cwezi kingship, which Berger and Chrétien see as a response to 19th-century Ganda expansion and colonial European racism). The story of Mugasha and Wamara's daughter may, as Peter Seitel suggests (personal communication), have no direct relationship to Cwezi praise poetry. To pursue this question further, however, it would be necessary to have a better collection of this poetry than is presently available.

Epic emerges in these circumstances as a 'secularized' synthesis of panegyric poetics, oral tradition narratives and folk tales. Why this should happen in some parts of Africa and not in others (e.g. most of the Interlacustrine region) is not clear, at least from the limited evidence at hand. In the Haya case, unlike that of the Mande griots/*jeliw*, the *enanga* bards are not an identifiable – to say nothing of hereditary – social group which has a more general function of performing panegyric.[xviii] Like the Cwezi/*mbandwa* mediums, Haya bards are usually commoners, but the former are normally women, whereas the known bards are all men.

In the colonial era (and possibly well before) *enanga* performances did take place in royal courts, which were also the site of warrior panegyric and at least some Cwezi rituals. The abolition of chieftaincy shortly after Tanzanian independence has been cited as an explanation for the decline of *enanga* bardic practice (see below). The other major occasions for performances were weddings of clan commoners and the reason for the loss of such settings is not clear. The performances recorded by Mulokozi and Seitel mostly seem to have taken place in private homes and bars.

Enanga, as an art form, cannot therefore be tied to a specific context although it obviously draws its materials from the same discursive universe which has produced the elaborate cult practices and historicist narratives of the entire Interlacustrine region. However, as indicated in the brief accounts of three *enanga* narratives, Haya epic also incorporates erotic and folkloric motifs which are not so apparent in court and Cwezi performances. It is in this sense that it differs from the only other known Interlacustrine epic tradition, that of Rwanda, which remains very close to court narratives of warrior deeds and political intrigue. Indeed, given the degree to which they stress tensions between social groups *enanga* narratives actually seem more appropriate to the 'civil society' of homes and bars than they do to the ceremonial spaces of rulers.

As in the Cameroon Littoral, the Haya epic appears to be dying out simply because – as Mulokozi amply demonstrates – there are few competent performers left and all of them are fairly old. From the 1960's many *enanga* performances were recorded on cassettes (Mulokozi 1997: 161-162) but, with the exception of research by university professors and their students, there seems to be little effort among the Haya to adapt the epic to more modern projects. Mulokozi (1986: 41) notes that *enanga* have been composed (sometimes in Swahili rather than the Haya language) to celebrate contemporary personages and events but admits that they do not have the appeal of the earlier versions. The loss of chiefly patronage may be a factor here but at least as important seems to be the competition of other musical and literary media and the emergence of new social issues to which the *enanga* narrative tradition cannot effectively address itself. Buhaya has been particularly victimized by AIDS, and it is not clear whether even the Cwezi/*mbandwa* mediums can provide any comfort in such a situation.[xix]

Conclusion
A good deal of the argument in this essay has been speculative since the history of oral literature is, by definition, difficult to document. However, I hope that I have at least demonstrated the value of such an effort. Epic is not necessarily the most significant genre of African verbal art but its monumental character and selective presence do imply that it 'emerged' in some specific times and places. Even if we can never locate the circumstances of such developments with any precision, the process of seeking them at least acknowledges the

historicity of precolonial Africa and allows us to identify the relationships between elements of recently recorded African culture that are most relevant to change in the more distant past.

NOTES

[i] I received considerable help with this paper from Aldin Mutembei, Peter Seitel, and Brad Weiss although, needless to say, none of them are responsible for the results.

[ii] Kesteloot and Dieng (1997: 560-603) include selections from both these societies but the Rwanda material verges on the prose recitation of court chronicles and oral traditions while the Zulu texts are modern written compositions drawing on a combination of praise poetry and oral traditions rather than anything which could be recognized as oral epic.

[iii] The ethno-linguistic term for this community 'Sawa Bantu' ('Coastal Bantu'), seems less useful for present purposes than the more geographical/administrative 'Littoral'. As will be seen, there are other Cameroon coastal regions relevant to the epic under consideration but 'Littoral' is the official term for its main site. The best known of the Sawa peoples are the Duala, but it would be misleading to identify the epic with them.

[iv] 'Jeki,' through the work of myself and others (Bekombo, Kesteloot, Tiki a Kouellé), has received recognition in the various anthologies and surveys cited above but the Haya *enanga*, except for brief mentions in Johnson and Sisòkò (1986: 62,75), has not.

[v] For some similar attempts with regard to the Mande Sunjata epic, see Austen 1999, Wilks 1999.

[vi] The background material here is presented in greater detail in Austen and Derrick 1999.

[vii] What follows, unless otherwise indicated, is drawn form Austen 1996.

[viii] They are both from Dibombari and speakers of Pongo, a Sawa language closely related to Duala. Tom Yoms recalls that Tiki, whose formal career was in the Catholic education system, had taught him as a child and introduced him to Jeki at that time.

[ix] It can be obtained in North America from the Seminary Cooperative Bookstore in Chicago (texts@semcoop.com).

[x] The term (sometimes written *nanga*) refers to the instrument (a zither/harp) which is used to accompany the performance of texts. The full technical designation for Haya epics is *enanga y'emanzi* ('heroic *enanga*').

[xi] Some of the epics which Mulokozi (1997: 170-71) cites but does not quote deal with 19th and early 20th century politics and warfare and presumably resemble Rwandan court recitations (see note 2 above)

[xii] For an account of Mugasha throughout the Interlacustrine region see Schoenbrun (1998: 204-06).

[xiii] There is also an epic of Wamara but it has not, apparently, been recorded (Mulokozi 1997: 164); on the historical and religious significance of Wamara see Schoenbrun (1988: 237-43).

[xiv] Seitel's unpublished manuscript presents an analysis and translated transcription of three such texts. He considers them to be 'epics' but this is not the place to pursue what should become a very interesting comparative discussion.

[xv] Mulokozi (1986: passim) insists that the epics all derive from the historical periods to which they refer. He gives no empirical evidence for this and the very notion of successive Cwezi, Hima and Hinda/Bito regimes in this region is highly questionable (Chrétien). On the other hand, the social tensions which Mulokozi ascribes to this history are quite real and, as indicated above, critical to understanding the issues within the epics.

[xvi] Mulokozi has probably understated this situation since the one source he credits with at least mentioning the *enanga* narratives but does not cite specifically or entirely accurately (Césard 1927, 1936) gives separate accounts of Haya oral tradition and bardic performance but never establishes any textual connection between them.

[xvii] Other African epic traditions (e.g. 'Jeki' and 'Sunjata') were strongly noted by at least the first decades of the 20th century. The best Haya ethnography from this period contains vague references to 'Heldenlieder' ('heroic songs') and a rendition of 'Mugasha' in prose form by a later prominent Haya figure, Clemens Kiiza (Rehse 1910: 329-30).

[xviii] Feza told Seitel (n.d.: 28) that, like several categories of craft specialists, precolonial bards had tributary obligations for service at royal courts but, in contrast to these other groups, 'were not associated with a particular clan.'

[xix] There is no reference to these spirits in Weiss and the author insists that *mbandwa* 'were not relevant to the scene by the late 80s' (private communication). Another researcher did find considerable *mbandwa* practice in the Buhaya of the 1990's, although political changes, AIDS, and conversion to Christianity and Islam clearly undermined its vitality (Pennacini 1998: 243-245). Seitel's love ballads do make reference to venereal disease and the materialism of women but not AIDS or (except in one poorly received narrative) prostitution (a major issue in Buhaya since the early 20th century). Mutembei (2001) cites and analyzes a wide variety of oral poetry which addresses AIDS and related issues of sexual behavior, but none of it is in an epic mode or makes reference to mytho/historical themes.

THE BIRTH OF JAKA TARUB, A HERO FROM NORTHERN JAVA

Clara Brakel-Papenhuyzen[i]

Introduction
The great Old Javanese epic poems, which over the centuries have been transmitted in written or dramatic form and, in the words of Pigeaud, 'exercised a lasting influence on the development of belles-lettres up to the 19th century in Java' (Pigeaud 1967: 15), are largely of Indian inspiration. However, besides these epic tales of Indian inspiration or origin, there are also indigenous tales in Java. They are primarily found in oral traditions, which have not been studied with the same care as written literary works, in spite of the fact that in Javanese society written and oral traditions have been existing side-by-side for centuries.[ii]

During my fieldwork in Java in the 1980s I made several trips to areas on the northern coast of the island, where I could witness and record the rarely investigated art of Islamic Javanese storytellers, known as *dhalang kentrung*. Their repertoire includes, besides epic and romantic themes of Middle Eastern origin, tales that deal with local history and mythology, often connected with Islamic legends. As this rare art of storytelling is presently giving way to the pressures of modernization, its form, repertoire and social role urgently need to be documented and studied in comparison with other genres.[iii] To start off the process, I have selected a famous tale in the *dhalang kentrungs*' repertoire, named the tale of Jaka Tarub. It was recorded in July 1983.

Dhalang kentrung, the Islamic Javanese storyteller
Unlike the performers (*dhalang*) of the Javanese shadow play (*wayang kulit*), Islamic Javanese storytellers (*dhalang kentrung*) are hardly known outside their own region and receive little or no attention from tourists. They are mainly active in small towns and villages along the northern coast of Java, in East Java and on the island of Madura, performing for predominantly Muslim communities, which have existed there since the 15th century. In accordance with the rules of Islam, these (male or female) storytellers do not use any visual means to support their recitation; their sober performance is embellished only by rhythmic patterns played on one or more *terbang*, a single-headed framedrum of Middle Eastern origin which is associated with Islam,[iv] sometimes supported by a (double-sided) Javanese drum (*kendhang*). Usually the storyteller is seated on a large sofa (*ambèn*) which is found in most traditional Javanese houses and on this occasion functions as the stage. The *dhalang* is not always performing on his or her own; he or she may be supported by one or

more helpers who play *kendhang* or *terbang*, and may enliven the performance with encouraging shouts (*senggakan*), improvised popular verses (*parikan*) and Islamic exclamations (*ya la illaha illolla*).

Dhalang kentrung are often invited to tell stories which originate in Islamic countries, such as the Ménak Amir Hamza, the Stories of the Prophets or the Serat Yusup; their repertoire may also include indigenous Javanese stories and legends connected with Javanese history. Even if a purely Islamic story is performed, such as the birth of the Prophet Muhammad or the story of Déwi Pertimah (Fatima), in the Javanese language it cannot but acquire a strong Javanese flavor.

In his study of *kentrungan* in the area of Tuban, North Java, Suripan Sadi Hutomo explains that these storytellers are not merely secular entertainers; usually they are invited to celebrate a special occasion in the family, such as the approaching birth of a child (*tingkeban*), the dropping of a baby's umbilical cord (*pupak puser*), or a wedding (Suripan 1993: 32). In each of these cases a story is chosen with a theme that matches the occasion. At a *tingkeban* ritual, for instance, the *dhalang kentrung* will select a birth-story, and then can select a story about the birth of an Islamic prophet (*nabi* Musa, *nabi* Yusup), or a story of the birth of a local Javanese hero such as the Jaka Tarub story, discussed here.

While usually related to rites of passage, an evening of *kentrungan* may be arranged for other reasons as well, such as redeeming a pledge (*ngujari kaul*), exorcism (*ruwat*) or the annual village ritual which is connected with agriculture and the worship of ancestral spirits (*bersih desa*). Moreover, the celebration of Indonesian Independence Day on the 17th of August is one of the secular occasions at which *kentrungan* may be performed.

Apart from occasions where the storyteller is invited to perform against a previously arranged fee, less fortunate artists wander from place to place offering their performances at random (*ngamèn*) to whoever wants to pay and listen. In this case the storytelling is not connected with a ritual, the arrangement is less formal and the story is told per section or chapter (*babak*); if the storyteller succeeds in pleasing the audience, he is asked to continue.[v] This type of performance may not be highly esteemed, yet the audience may actually be more attentive here than during a more formal and complete nightlong recitation where most people come to oblige the host.

Most of the stories told by the *dhalang kentrung* also exist in a written literary form, yet the art is primarily oral: it is not only composed in performance but also learned by frequently attending performances.[vi] Apparently, some *dhalang kentrung* cannot even read or write.[vii] This does not mean that their performances are haphazard: the *dhalang* usually deal with a story that is widely known, and they must be able to perform in such a way that they will keep the audience's attention for hours. Moreover, like the authors of written texts, the storytellers must be able to structure the story in an orderly way, and they must be able to make musical embellishments and crack jokes as well

(Suripan 1993: 39). In short, *kentrungan* is a complex and sophisticated form of storytelling, even without the accompaniment of a gamelan orchestra or the employment of visual aids.

The story of the birth of Jaka Tarub

The story of *dhalang kentrung* Sutrisno which I recorded in a village near Blora in July 1983 was organized as an entertainment for all villagers in the house of the headman, Bapak Sastro Soekarno, whose guest I was. In fact, to the host and many people in the audience, listening to the recitation meant more than just entertainment, as is evident from the fact that the session was closed by the recitation of a *mantra* to ward off evil from all directions, each with its particular protecting prophet: Adam in the East, Moses in the South, Abraham in the West, Rasul(ullah), i.e. Mohammed in the North, Joseph up high, the seven angels in the centre. Blessings were invoked for the owner of the house and his family.[viii]

The *dhalang* arrived just after sunset and he performed without any assistance for approximately four hours,[ix] accompanying himself on a set of three *terbang*. The audience consisted of local villagers, men and women, and many children. Snacks and drinks had been prepared for the *dhalang* and the main guests, the atmosphere was festive. The choice of story had been left to the *dhalang*, the only stipulation being that it should be a Javanese tale. In his opening lines, Sutrisno qualified the birth-story of Jaka Tarub (*Lairipun Jaka Tarub*) as history (*sejarah*) and fairy-tale (*dongèng*) at once.[x]

Sutrisno situated his tale at the court of Tuban – a coastal town northeast of Blora – ruled by Adipati Wilatikta and his vizier Jaya Sekati. The presence of Islamic preachers in the tale indicates that the story is situated in the period of transition to Islam, when the coastal town of Tuban was still under the dominance of the Hindu-Buddhist kings of Majapahit, for whom it functioned as an important port. As indicated by the title, the story mainly deals with the hero's antecedents; it explains how Jaka Tarub came into being.

Unknown to himself, the hero Jaka Tarub belongs to the highest nobility as princess Rasawulan, daughter of Adipati Wilatikta of Tuban, conceives him out of wedlock. His father is a foreign preacher named Sèh Maulana Maqribi,[xi] who has come to Java in order to convert the people of Java to Islam. Sèh Maulana Maqribi is doing ascetism in a banyan tree overhanging the pond in which the princess is taking a bath. After having been conceived and delivered in a supernatural way, the baby is left in the care of the father, who abandons his son in the vicinity of Tarub. When the widow Asiyah finds the little boy, she takes him and brings him up as her own child. One day hunting in the jungle, the boy of Tarub sees seven heavenly nymphs (*widadari*) bathing in a pond. He snatches the clothes of the youngest fairy, and thus he succeeds to obtain her for himself and marries her. Eventually she leaves him and flies back to heaven.

Performance of the story Lairipun Jaka Tarub
In a formal prose opening the storyteller introduces himself and mentions the sponsors, the occasion for and the location of the performance.[xii] He then states that, having been asked for a historical tale, he will 'tell the story of the birth of Jaka Tarub which has come from the ancestors' (*nyejarahaken sejarah kentrung naluri nènèk moyang jaman kala rumiyin*). Then the performance starts with a musical overture played on three frame-drums, followed by a pious salutation. The story as a whole is structured as a sequence of different scenes, each change of scene being indicated by a special formula, such as 'the music is changed, [but] the story is the same' (*séjé gendhing tunggiling kandha*).

The framework of the performance conforms at least in the first part to a structural pattern used in most traditional theatrical performances: the first scene is an audience-scene at the court of Tuban, where the ruler and his vizier (*patih*) discuss the problem of the ruler's succession, since his son Raden Said has left Tuban. When his daughter Déwi Rasawulan arrives, she is told to become her father's successor. The girl replies that she must first perform ascetism (*tapa*) as a deer in the forest. This is granted, and her name is changed. Then *patih* Jaya Sekati is ordered to collect all the soldiers of the land and to go to the jungle in order to protect the princess. In this scene the *dhalang* cleverly inserts the obligatory political propaganda, without interrupting the story line. The following jungle-scene still conforms to the classical Javanese *wayang* tradition. It introduces the foreign Sèh Maulana Maqribi, meeting on the crossroads in the jungle with Sunan Bonang, the famous Islamic Javanese saint (*wali*). The two men decide to share the task of colonizing the island of Java and spreading Islam: Sunan Bonang will colonize and Sèh Maulana Maqribi will spread Islam. After they have parted, Sunan Bonang is confronted by princess Rasawulan's brother Radèn Said, prince of Tuban, who is roaming around as a brigand and wants to rob him of his sandals. The prince demands and obtains wealth from the saint in a miraculous manner so that he repents and is converted to Islam.

In the middle of the jungle at the Maérakaca pond, Sèh Maulana stops and decides to perform *tapa* by hanging upside down in a banyan tree. Nearby, Rasawulan is performing *tapa* as a deer, surrounded by the animals of the forest. As her *tapa* causes a heat wave, she goes to refresh herself in the pond. With her beautiful appearance she so much excites Sèh Maulana that his 'sweat' (sperm) drops into the water, and enters Rasawulan's womb. When she finds herself pregnant, she first blames the pond, but then she perceives Sèh Maulana hanging in the banyan tree, mirrored in the clear surface of the water, and she asks him to tell her who he is. He answers that he has come from Arabia in order to convert people to Islam. She immediately throws herself at his feet and asks him to help her giving birth, which he is willing to do on condition that she is able to solve four riddles. Rasawulan doesn't give the right answers, yet Sèh Maulana gives her some mystical instruction, and then tells her to bare her left side so that the baby can be born from it. Rasawulan asks him to hold the baby while she goes off to clean herself in the pond – then she leaves the jungle and returns to her father in the palace of Tuban. Sèh Maulana tells the baby that he will find someone to look after him, and predicts that he will marry a nymph once he has grown up.

On seeing the wound on his daughter's left side, the ruler of Tuban sends his *patih* Jaya Sekati out to find a medicine. The *patih* asks the 150 years old hermit, Pandhita Purnama Sejati, for help to cure Princess Rasawulan's illness. When the old man tells him that the illness is God's punishment and that he does not know its cause, the *patih* returns to Tuban and reports the ruler that the Pandhita cannot give medicine to cure the illness. Then the ruler sends his daughter back into the forest; she decides to try and find Sèh Maulana Maqribi. Meanwhile Sèh Maulana is carrying the baby in a scarf singing and talking to him in (pseudo)Arabic, until he reaches the hamlet of Segaluh in the village of Tarub where he leaves the boy, his heirloom weapon at his side; after telling him once again that he will marry a nymph, he returns to the pond to perform *tapa*. Rasawulan, too, returns to the lake and asks him to help her, offering her apologies for having run away. Again Sèh Maulana gives her four riddles to solve – this time about the mystical terms *makripat, kakékat, taukid* and *saréngat* – and when she knows the answers he tells her that he has been sent to Java by his father to spread Islam, and that she must convert in order to be cured. Rasawulan becomes a Muslim and then takes him to her father in Tuban.

A widow from Segaluh, named Asiyah, finds Rasawulan's baby with the Sèh's weapon. Taking him to be her husband's reincarnation, she adopts the baby and organizes a ceremony for the dropping of his umbilical cord, to which all her neighbors make rich contributions (as predicted by the Sèh). The boy is named Radèn Bagus Jaka Tarub.

Back in Tuban, Princess Rasawulan brings Sèh Maulana before the ruler. Asked about the identity of this foreigner with his yellow sandals, she tells her father that this Arab has come to spread the pure religion. The ruler asks him to explain the meaning of the twenty syllables of the Javanese alphabet, which he does.

Thinking of the baby that he left in the village of Segaluh, Sèh Maulana goes into meditation, changes into a white pigeon, and flies off southeast to the village, where he finds the boy attended by many servants. He lands on the boy's head, causing great wonder, and then flies away. The boy fetches his heirloom blowpipe, and follows the bird into the forest. Eventually he finds it in the banyan trees near the Maérakaca pond, but as soon as Jaka Tarub tries to shoot it, the pigeon disappears. Then he sees eight heavenly nymphs bathing in the water; the first one is named Bethari Nawangwulan. When he sees their beautiful shining clothes, he decides to take the smallest pair of clothes and hides them in the barn where the rice is stored, in his village Segaluh. Meanwhile, the nymphs put on their clothes and fly off to heaven, leaving Nawangwulan in tears near the lake. There Jaka Tarub finds her, and she

Dhalang kentrung Sutrisno in July 1983 in the house of Bapak Sastro Soekarno, in a village near Blora.

reveals him her identity and explains that she cannot find her clothes. The boy offers to bring her hand-woven clothes from the village, an offer she accepts. He brings her a scarf, a skirt and a blouse from his mother's chest, and tells her that she must now remain on earth, under the influence of sun, moon and stars. She agrees to follow him to the village and meet his mother. In Segaluh, Jaka Tarub introduces Nawangwulan to his mother, Asiyah, who tells him that he must now look after the rice. The boy suddenly realizes that she is a rich woman, as the rice-barn is very full. The closing sentence says that later Jaka Tarub will be separated from Nawangwulang.

The tale closed off with a *mantra* to ward off all evil: '*Nabi* Adam in the East, nabi Musa in the South, *nabi* Ibrahim in the West, *nabi* Rasul in the North, *nabi* Yusuf up high, the seven angels in the centre. May the owner of the house and his family be blessed.'

The Jaka Tarub legend in Javanese culture
Variant versions of the legend discussed here can be found in many Indonesian cultures. In fact, the motif of a young man who marries a nymph after he has stolen her clothes so that she cannot return to heaven, is known all over the world and is considered to belong to the 'world fund of folktales, which Indonesia shares with Asia and Europe' (Brakel 1976: 5; for a similar theme, see Kamphorst, infra). Versions of the story about Jaka Tarub, the 'young man from [the village of] Tarub', are known all over Java. Contrary to the customary plots in the dramatic tradition inspired by the Indian epics, this story does not end happily with the hero's marriage to the heavenly nymph Nawangwulan. Instead, events take a sad turn when the nymph discovers her heavenly clothes, hidden by the hero on the bottom of the rice-barn. Until that moment, the hero's union with the heavenly nymph has been blessed with prosperity, as there is never any shortage of rice when they are married, but the prosperity ends when he breaks her spell by lifting the lid of the rice steamer which is on the fire while she has gone off to wash clothes, and discovers that the pot only contains one ear. From that moment on, Nawangwulan has to pound rice every day to feed her family, like an ordinary human being; gradually the rice-barn becomes empty, and when she finds her clothes hidden on the bottom she puts them on and returns to heaven, leaving her husband and baby behind.

The connection between the Jaka Tarub story and the cultivation of rice has been discussed by Djajadiningrat in 1913 in his study of the history of Banten (*Sejarah Banten*),[xiii] and although the modern species of rice that are grown by villagers no longer require extensive rituals, recent research has shown that in many villages on the North coast of Java the story of Jaka Tarub still functions as one of the main rice myths. Particular prescripts for the care of rice and child which are transmitted via the story are still maintained there, such as the taboo for men to lift the lid of the rice steamer while it is on the fire (Heringa 1997: 366). The story (or perhaps the term myth is more appropriate here) also functions as the basis for a particular ritual at the court of Surakarta in Central

Java where once in eight years the ruler performs a rice steaming ritual in the middle of the night, using an ancient, ceremonial steamer named *Kyai Dhudha* ('Venerable Widower') to secure prosperity for the realm, as part of the celebrations for the prophet Mohammed's birthday (see the photographs in Veldhuizen-Djajasoebrata 1984: 81).

From Jaka Tarub to Kyai Gedhé Tarub
For many Javanese people, the hero Jaka Tarub who marries the heavenly nymph Nawang Wulan is more than a mythological figure. Versions of the story about him are often incorporated into historical compilations (*babad* or *sejarah*) of the royal courts in Central Java, most of which were composed during the 18th-19th centuries. These historical Javanese texts may function as chronicles or history-books, yet they do not usually give an accurate account of historical events arranged in chronological order. Instead, they contain historical information mixed with myths and legends from various sources.

Javanologists have pointed out that *babad* texts developed from 17th and 18th-century books of stories (*serat kandha*) (Pigeaud 1967: 130 ff). Such 'compendiums of mythology', first composed by scholars in centers of Islamic learning on the North coast of Java, are still used as sources by storytellers and performers of the shadow play (*wayang kulit*). In his authoritative 'Synopsis of Javanese Literature', Pigeaud suggests that the authors of *serat kandha* and the performers of shadow plays 'probably used the same fund of traditions pertaining to mythic and epic history' (Pigeaud 1967: 140). Ras gives the following explanation on the connection between *serat kandha* and *wayang* stories: 'These *kandha* books contain summary outlines of *wayang* stories. These outlines are strung together in such a way as to provide a pseudo-historical account of events supposed to have taken place in Java in the distant past' (Ras 1992 [1987]: 243-258).

Javanese historiography is not unique in this respect. Taib bin Osman's remarks about Malay historiography suggest a correspondence with the way Javanese interpreted their island's history: 'Historical writing (...) in the past was not meant only to be a recording of events, but also a form of literary art (...). The most common feature of Malay historiography is the genealogy of the dynasty traced to its origin. Usually the origin of a dynasty is shrouded in mythologies involving mythic kings of the past.' The purpose of these dynastic myths is, 'to give an aura of divinity to the Sultanate. The *rakyat* or the common people were thus imbued with a sense of respect and worship towards their kings' (Taib bin Osman 1976: 127-29).

In many historical Javanese writings Jaka Tarub is an important ancestor who is clearly located in time and space. Thus, the *Babad Tanah Jawi*, the main history book of the Central Javanese court of Surakarta which, completed in 1836, is considered as 'the official chronicle of the kingdom of Mataram' (Ras 1992[1987]: 243), describes the young man from Tarub as a grandson of Kyai Gedhé Kudus, leader of the Islamic northern town of Kudus (Olthof 1941:

25(24)ff). As the child has been conceived out of wedlock, the mother, who is here the daughter of the headman of Kembang Lampir, flees to the jungle where she dies while giving birth. The baby is picked up by a hunter and left behind in the hermitage of a deceased spiritual leader, the headman of the village Tarub, where he is found and adopted by his widow. Following in the footsteps of the parents who adopted him, the hero from Tarub becomes a spiritual leader after the nymph's departure, and is then referred to as Kyai Gedhé Tarub.

According to the *Babad Tanah Jawi*, this Kyai Gedhé Tarub becomes the teacher and father-in-law of a son of king Brawijaya, the last king of the Hindu-Buddhist Majapahit kingdom. This son has been removed from the court at a young age because of a prediction that he would bring his father's kingdom to an end (Olthof 1941: 24(23)). Thus, in the main history book of the syncretistic Islamic House of Mataram, the hero from Tarub forms a connection between the Hindu Buddhist rulers of East Java and the leaders of the Islamic towns of the northern coastal districts. Later, his descendant Ki Ageng Séla serves as the spiritual guide to the ancestors of the Surakarta rulers (Olthof 1941: 37-38 (35-37)).

Jaka Tarub in the history of Jipang
The Jaka Tarub legend often functions as an origin story in local histories of noble families of the northern coastal districts, as pointed out in Djajadiningrat's analysis of the *Sejarah Banten* (Djajadiningrat 1913: 291).[xiv] A clear example of this is found in an illustrated manuscript of the History of Jipang, dated 1255 AJ/1839 AD, which is kept in the Leiden University Library (LOr 3186). This history of the ruling family of Jipang (*Sejarah Jipang*), a place north of present-day Blora, is composed in metrical poetry (*macapat*). Written in popular cursive Central Javanese North Coast script and idiom (Pigeaud 1968 (II): 110), it has a popular flavor.

In the first verse of the *Sejarah Jipang* the author specifies the time when the book was written according to the Javanese and Islamic calendars.[xv] Then he (or she) mentions the location of the writing as a place named Bandayudan to the south of Karanganyar. Preceding the story proper, instructions are given for the way in which the work should be read – or rather: recited – to an audience, to old and young, men, women and children. There is a warning not to keep the manuscript too close to the oil-lamp, and specific kinds of food are mentioned which must be offered: bananas, tea, and a tasty chicken-dish for the reciter.

The *Sejarah Jipang* proper begins in the residence of Kyai Gedhé Tarub, a local headman who, at the commencement of the story, has passed away a year ago; his faithful, childless widow regularly goes to worship at his grave, keeping restrictions such as abstaining from food and sleep on that day. She encourages her servants to do the same. This is rewarded when she finds a beautiful, 'shining' baby at the graveside, whom she adopts as her child. At his mother's instruction the boy named Jaka Tarub also goes to worship at the grave of Kyai Gedhé Tarub, where he finds a golden blowpipe. One day, when he goes hunting birds in the forest, he finds the fairies bathing in the pond, and takes away the clothes of one of them. Then he offers her human clothes and she follows him to his mother's house, where their wedding is celebrated. The story ends as usual with the nymph's departure. The *Sejarah Jipang* continues with events concerning king Brawijaya, the last king of the Hindu-Buddhist Majapahit kingdom and his son Bondhan Kejawan who marries Ki Gedhé Tarub's daughter.

Although there is no clear explanation of how the foundling has come into being, in this history of the noble family of Jipang the young man from Tarub is called 'the son of a king' (LOr 3186, p. 11: *sang rajapinutra*); he is classified as a member of the nobility (*satria*), the nymph as a goddess (*déwi*), a term which is also used to address a female person of noble birth (LOr 3186, p. 12, verse 27). In the view of the author, the very fact that Jaka Tarub is able to marry a heavenly nymph proves that he is of royal descent. This is expressed in the deliberations of the nymph during their first encounter at the sacred pool in the jungle, when she says to herself: 'No human being is strong enough to enter the pond where the heavenly nymphs are bathing; this man who has come to the forest, can only be of royal descent, in my opinion' (LOr 3186, p. 13a, verse 32).

Illustration from Babad Jipang, Leiden University Library, LOr 3186, p. 15. Jaka Penulup and Nawangwulan.

Conclusion

Both the *Sejarah Jipang* which was put into writing in 1839 AD, and the *kentrungan* story of the birth of Jaka Tarub, which was composed in performance in 1983, are meant to be recited in front of an audience and thus they are part of a tradition which is based on public performance. It is clear that they belong to a historical tradition that transcends the legendary and personal levels. Parallels in structure and content may be connected with the fact that in several respects both versions conform to the conventions of the *wayang* tradition, e. g. by their typical opening with an audience-scene (respectively in the court of Tuban and the residence of Kyai Agung Tarub).

On the other hand, there are many differences of form, style of performance, content, and context. While both versions consider the story of Jaka Tarub as part of the history of Java, they are at variance in the way they situate it. In the *Sejarah Jipang* the tale of the foundling from the village of Tarub is connected with the rulers of Jipang. To *dhalang* Sutrisno and his audience, the story belongs to the history of Tuban;[xvi] however, his attitude is somewhat ambivalent, as he also qualifies the story as a 'fairy-tale' (*dongèng*) in his opening lines. In some recent Indonesian publications the story is labeled as a folktale (*cerita rakyat*) (Affandi 1984, Sugiyo 1984). But the *dhalang*'s aim goes further than telling tales of historical or mythical origins, as is clear from the way in which the hero is contextualised. Rather than presenting him as a fatherless foundling of unknown origin, the *kentrungan* version provides the Javanese hero not only with an aristocratic Javanese mother, but also with an Islamic father of 'foreign' origin, thereby integrating the foreigner and his religion into Javanese society. This is not surprising, as apparently one of the aims of this narrative genre is to proselytize and instruct.

To western scholars the significance of Javanese historical texts is primarily 'as documents revealing how Javanese courts saw their own past and their own place and significance in Javanese history' (Ricklefs 1972, Ras 1992: 176). Accordingly, the *Sejarah Jipang* may be expected to contain the dynasty's genealogy and history as seen from that family's point of view. In his study of the history of the court of Banten (*Sejarah Banten*) Djajadiningrat gives another, significant reason why the story of Jaka Tarub is often linked with the origin of noble families when he states that the myth is connected with agriculture, especially with the cultivation of rice (Djajadiningrat 1913: 291).

Ultimately, as L. F. Brakel stated in his 1980 article on Indonesian historiography,[xvii] the clue to the lasting popularity of Javanese epic and historical tales lies precisely in the function that they have in their cultural context. Thus, the vitality of the story-telling tradition springs from its effective contextualization. In my view, both *dhalang* Sutrisno and the author of the *Sejarah Jipang* have been very successful in this respect.

NOTES

[i] A first version of this article was presented at a seminar on Islamic oral traditions, Tel Aviv University, 7 December 1995. The material was used later while lecturing at the Hebrew University of Jerusalem.

[ii] This question has also been discussed in Brakel-Papenhuyzen 2000.

[iii] The only scholarly researchers of the genre known to me are the late Suripan Sadi Hutomo who published a text with comments and several articles in Indonesian, and Jack Body with Yono Sukarno, who produced a cd with fragments of different storytelling styles.

[iv] In Java, ensembles of *terbang* usually play in accompaniment of Islamic songs of praise.

[v] This practice is not restricted to *dhalang kentrung*, it is also common practise for other roaming artists such as wandering mask players (see Brakel and Moreh 1996: 42).

[vi] Personal information from *dhalang kentrung* Sutrisno, see below.

[vii] This does not hold true for *dhalang* Sutrisno.

[viii] This is not unusual, see Suripan 1993: 137 and 185.

[ix] With just some short stops for changing the tapes and having a drink.

[x] The storyteller first states in his introduction: 'Well, as you requested history (*sejarah*), I will relate the history of the birth of Jaka Tarub.' In the opening lines of the recitation he says that he starts telling a folktale (*dongèng*).

[xi] De Graaf and Pigeaud (1974: 28-9): 'Tome Pires... vermeldt, in het begin van de 16e eeuw, dat er na het ontstaan van Moslimse vorstendommen aan de Noordkust van Java (...) 'Moulanas' uit het buitenland zijn gekomen; zij vestigden zich bij de inmiddels gestichte moskeeën.'

[xii] Performed on 21-7-1983 by *dhalang kentrung* Bapak Sutrisno in a village near Blora, in the house of Bapak Sastro Soekarno.

[xiii] Djajadiningrat states that the myth is connected with agriculture, especially with the cultivation of rice (Djajadiningrat 1913: 291). A variant version of the story from the Babad Demak is given in Arps 1992: 139-144, 220-231.

[xiv] Djajadiningrat remarks that the story of Jaka Tarub is often linked with the origin of noble families (Djajadiningrat 1913: 291).

[xv] The writing started on the days Rebo-Kliwon, on the fourth day of the month Sawal, at nine o'clock, in the Hijra year 1255.

[xvi] The word *sejarah* used by the *dhalang* is a bit ambiguous as the Indonesian noun *sejarah* means history, but in Javanese the noun *sejarah* means: family tree, the verb *nyejarahaken*: to tell a (long) story.

[xvii] 'Ultimately, the historical 'reliability' of a text will largely depend on the character, the structure and the function of that text' (Brakel 1980: 41).

A SCHOOL FOR EPIC? THE 'ECOLE WILLIAM PONTY' AND THE EVOLUTION OF THE SUNJATA EPIC, 1913 - c.1960

Stephen Bulman

Introduction
In this paper[i] I want to highlight what I see as the important role of the elite French West African Ecole William Ponty in encouraging and facilitating collection and publication of oral traditional materials by west African scholars in the first half of the 20th century. This encouragement and facilitation operated through the curriculum of the school – which, at points in the 1930s and 1940s, included in-depth studies of traditional African culture based on fieldwork, and transcription and translation from African languages to French – and beyond the curriculum, where school staff encouraged the production of plays based on traditional African themes or historical events, and fostered research and publication of oral-traditional material by ex-scholars in colonial journals. I explore in a small way the French colonial context for these developments – a project to develop a so-called 'Franco-African culture' – and something of the African responses to these trends. I then focus in detail on the impact of the school on the evolution of the Sunjata epic from an oral to a literate entity.

The epic of Sunjata is in effect a group of more or less similar oral traditions, including numerous narrative episodes and songs, the preserve of bards or *jeliw* of the Maninka of Mali, Guinea, and surrounding west African states, which tell of the establishment, in the 13th century, of the empire of Mali out of a contest for power between the Susu and their leader, Sumanguru (or Sumaoro) Kante, and the victorious Maninka, led by Sunjata Keita.

I think the school was a significant site for the development of the Sunjata tradition through its encounter with literacy and modernity: the school staged a drama based on the Sunjata story in 1937; at least three Ponty graduates produced written versions of the epic; while the school's influence – via the 1937 play – is clear in one further early literary version of Sunjata.

I also argue that the transformation of the Sunjata epic into a stage-play in 1937 – which might be seen as a sort of half-way house between the oral and literate modes – inaugurated what may have been the most influential modern re-working of this oral tradition in west Africa in the 1940s and 1950s, before the production of the novelistic accounts such as those by Niane and Camara Laye.

Before these issues can be addressed directly it is necessary to sketch where this particular oral-to-literate transition – for I think there were a number – fits into the wider scheme of the evolution of the epic. The epic of Sunjata is currently available, both in Africa and the West, in a plurality of forms: in performance, on paper, on the radio and TV, and on audio and video cassette.[ii] Before the 19th century – in fact in all probability up to the last decade of that century – I assume that this epic was only available as an oral performance (although the existence of Arabic manuscript versions of Sunjata along the lines of those produced at Nioro du Sahel early in the 20th century is not impossible). The process of evolution whereby the completely (or overwhelmingly) oral epic became a tradition existing simultaneously in a number of diverse media in about one hundred years is one whose outlines are becoming clearer but about which there is still much to learn, and to which this paper seeks to make a contribution. So far, the outline of development can be described thus:[iii]

1) An Arabic literary traditional history, including the Sunjata legend, was either initiated – or most probably appropriated by – French colonial officials from 1891 in the form of French literary translations, published from 1904.
2) From the last decade of the 19th century European colonisers – often military and administrative staff and almost all French – collected versions of Sunjata which were published in French and German translation from 1898.
3) Western-educated West Africans produced literary versions of Sunjata, mainly from the mid 1930s, but including at least one (Tounkara 1988) from the first decade of the 20th century.
4) From at least the early 1960s jeli performances of Sunjata were tape-recorded and transmitted on the radio.
5) The first line-by-line transcription of the epic was made in 1967.[iv]

So far, I have no reliable dates for the first broadcast of the epic on TV or use of cassette, although both dates are likely to be in the 1970s.

What I will focus on in this paper is stage three, when western-educated Africans started to produce literary versions of the oral performances of Sunjata. What might be called the high points are well known: Djibril Tamsir Niane's 1960 *Soundjata* and Camara Laye's *Le Maître de la Parole* (1978). Niane's version of the epic initiated a broad interest in the tradition and helped spawn many more literary versions in the 1960s and 1970s and has been seen as the start of contemporary interest in the epic. This paper will examine what literary versions were produced prior to 1960 and focus on the period 1913-1960; it will look at the period between the early colonial versions and the flowering of interest that was nourished by Niane's book. I will argue that the period 1913-1960 was in fact a significant time in the development of the epic towards the multi-form product of today and not in any sense a hiatus between the initial period of colonial collection and later time of broader scholarly and popular interest. I aim to demonstrate that the William Ponty school at and then near Saint-Louis, Senegal, was a key site for this evolution, and that the period witnessed a transformation of the epic less from an oral performance piece to a literary narrative of the Niane model than to a stage-play.

The William Ponty School

The Ecole William Ponty, and its role in educating the elite of French Africa, is well known and needs only a brief resumé here.[v] The prestigious school[vi] was established in 1903 – although not under that name, which came only in 1915 – as a normal, or teacher-training, school at Saint-Louis, was re-sited to Gorée in 1913 and then to Sébikotane in 1938. It existed to train teachers alone between 1903 and 1920, and then after 1950; in between, its graduates were groomed for medical training, administration, engineering, etc., as well as teaching. A snap-shot of the school in the mid-1930s, when Inspector-General of Education Albert Charton called it 'the most important of the schools of French West Africa' (Mumford and Orde-Brown 1936: 109), reveals an establishment with a staff 'almost entirely European' (ib.: 45), taking less than one in every 545 boys who went to primary school in French West Africa,[vii] with a 3-4 year course, from which most graduated aged between 20 and 22, from which half went on to be teachers and the others into a variety of careers or to further training, e.g. medicine.

Although in the mid 1930s the school was said to have a curriculum largely comparable to similar French schools, there had, since the 1910s, but particularly in the 1930s,[viii] been various moves to integrate the study of African cultures and history into the activities of the scholars and, at some points, into the curriculum itself. It is through these policies that the school became associated with the Sunjata epic.

In 1913 the new Inspector-General of Education Georges Hardy (1884-1972) wrote to the school 'to suggest that educated Africans could be used to explore their own local history' (Sabatier 1977: 84). Nothing came of his proposal at the time, but he did go on to found a periodical for the education service in French West Africa in the same year, the *Bulletin de l'enseignement de l'Afrique Occidentale Française* (which later changed its name to *L'Education africaine*) in which many ex-Ponty scholars (known as 'Pontins') published articles.

The idea of Africans researching their own cultures as part of their activities at the Ponty school was revived in the early 1930s under Governor-General Jules Brévié and his Inspector-General of Education, Albert Charton. Brévié was keen to develop what he called a Franco-African culture which would draw 'its inspiration from the purest French tradition while plunging its roots in native life (...) We must develop an African culture which will reveal to the native his country and his soul in order to make him accede gradually to the ideal of Franco-African culture'.[ix] Brévié wrote as early as 1932 of the need to 'encourage indigenous studies' (Sabatier 1977: 126) and in a circular written in 1935 he called for a programme of collection and analysis of historical documents relating to West African history and colonisation, including oral traditions, which he noted might disappear in the rapidly changing colonial situation. He went on:

'C'est dans ces traditions, dans ces récits, parfois romancés, poétiés ou transposés en façons de légendes épiques, que s'est déposée toute la substance historique des peuples indigenes.'ˣ

The publication of this circular in the teaching journal for French West Africa seems to indicate that Brévié saw the teachers of the federation as key workers in this policy of historical investigation. Brévié appears to have wanted to give Africans a stake in what was still overwhelmingly an alien culture that French education sought to inculcate but also to ease the burden of control via the knowledge that such a programme would throw up. Writing in 1931 he said: 'We expect the educated natives to reveal to us some of the secrets of their peoples' soul, to guide our action...' (quoted in Conteh-Morgan 1994: 51). More prosaically, moves to make the curriculum of the elite schools of French West Africa more reflective of the African context may reveal the concern that an education too divorced from African realities might create 'rootless' – and therefore dangerous – intellectuals, who could no longer relate to the immediate world around them (Sabatier 1978: 247, 255).

Brévié's policy was implemented at the William Ponty school in two separate but related innovations of 1933. Firstly, the school changed the curriculum, which henceforth required scholars to undertake study of an aspect of their own indigenous culture during the months of the summer vacation which was to be written up as a major element of the third year of study. As Sabatier (1977: 138) describes it:

'At the end of their second year at Ponty students were given a choice of topics (such as indigenous food, hunting, religion, medicine, etc.) and a list of questions around which to structure their research. They were to restrict their investigation to a specific area, such as their home village...'

This element of study is the origin of the famous 'Cahiers William Ponty' now held at the archives of IFAN in Dakar. From a 1967 catalogue we learn that almost eight hundred of these studies were recorded (although some have now gone missing), including over a hundred from Mali and over eighty from Guinea (Afanou and Togbe Pierre 1967).

Alongside Hardy and Brévié, Maurice Delafosse may have been an early influence for the collection of oral traditional material via Ponty scholars. Delafosse's three volume study *Haut-Sénégal-Niger*, published in 1912, was based initially on questionnaires on local culture and traditions sent for completion to the colony's officials from 1908. Did French-trained school teachers appear suitable proxy researchers for the colonial administration, as its own *cercle* officers had before?

The second significant development of 1933 was the encouragement of students to research, write and perform dramas in French based on indigenous traditions, stories or history. While the cahiers were part of the curriculum these plays were to form part of the pupils' leisure time. Charles Béart, the war-time director at Ponty, whose name is most closely associated with the plays, claims the idea came from Albert Charton (Charton 1934; Sabatier 1977: 179). The first recorded performance of such a play was in June 1933 at the annual *fête scolaire* when a group of Dahomean students acted out 'The last interview of Béhanzin, King of Dahomey, with the French Resident, Bayol'. Bakary Traoré (1958, English translation 1972), himself a Pontin, who graduated in 1950, explains how:

> 'In the same spirit [of the cahiers] it was suggested to the students [by the school authorities]... that they should write indigenous plays, in French, to be performed at the festival which marked the end of the scholastic year. So, during the holidays the students interrogated old men and village sages and made a collection of legends and traditions. On returning to school they argued, in groups of 2 or 3, about the subject that would be "closest to European taste".'

The first indigenous performance was apparently well-received (Moran 1937: 574); one witness to the 1936 'fête' performance – they became annual events from 1933 – of a play by Guinean students called it a 'gay and accurate historical reconstitution' (quoted in Warner 1984: 182). *L'Education africaine* 1935 (24) includes an announcement for the fête which includes 'L'élection d'un roi au Dahomey: pièce indigène en 3 actes et 4 tableaux composée et jouée par les élèves Dahoméen'.

The same journal also published the scripts to the plays, which tended to be historical dramas and comedies. The school even sent a troupe of thirty scholars to the Colonial Exposition in Paris in 1937 where in August performances of a tragedy ('Sokamé') and a comedy ('Prétendants rivaux') were staged at the Comédie des Champs-Elysées. Robert Delavignette recorded the plays as a great success and a signal of the achievement of 'une grande et profonde colonisation' (Delavignette 1937: 471).

In 1940 Béart introduced classes in transcription and translation of indigenous texts – presumably many of them collected from oral sources – for students at Ponty, although the novel discipline did not outlast the war. Plays apparently continued at Ponty school until 1948 when introduction of the baccalauréat reduced the time available to students for such activities (Kerr 1995: 38).

Clearly some of the impetus to stage African themes as plays came from the students at Ponty themselves. Nicholas Hopkins (1972: 220) notes that the opportunity to write and stage African plays 'struck a very responsive chord among the students' and Sabatier (1977: 179) writes that most students at the school joined in, although there was no compulsion to do so. One Pontin gives an interesting insight into the attitude of Africans at the school to the plays when he introduces a production from the 1930s thus: 'This production, which is an occasion for re-living a few moments of the much-loved native village life, constitutes also a pleasant relief from the monotonous life led by the students here at Gorée' (in Traoré 1972: 74). Charles Béart himself attributed the theatre tradition at least in part to a spontaneous theatre of satire that developed at the French school at Bingerville, Côte d'Ivoire, in the early 1930s, where he had been a teacher (Sabatier 1977: 180).

The William Ponty School and Sunjata
What, then, is the link between the Ponty cahiers and plays and the Sunjata epic? There are in fact several links. Although no cahier treating Sunjata is extant (and there is no evidence that the epic or person of Sunjata was ever the subject of a cahier by a Pontin), one of the surviving plays from the 1930s is based on the Sunjata epic, and at least three Ponty graduates were the authors of literary versions of the epic.

The theatrical version of Sunjata was performed at the annual fête of the school at Gorée in 1937. Entitled 'La ruse de Diégué' (Diégué being Sunjata's sister who discovers the secret of Sumanguru's strength),[xi] it has three short acts and begins at the point where Sunjata has failed repeatedly to defeat Sumanguru. It goes on to describe how Sunjata's sister discovers Sumanguru's power and ends with the triumph of the hero. It contains several songs and dances with words both in Maninka and French translation.

The seduction episode is present in accounts of the epic from many parts of the Mande world, making it impossible to deduce the origin of the play's traditional information. According to Bakary Traoré the play was the work of two (unnamed) students from Mali (then Soudan Français) (Anon. 1949; Traoré 1972: 45-46). Consideration of the name Diégué for Sunjata's sister might suggest a northerly tradition, specially from the Nioro du Sahel region. Accounts from the Mande heartland mention Sogolon Kolonkan as Sunjata's sister and Nana Tiriban as his half-sister. A reference in the published script of the play to the septennial re-roofing ceremony in Kangaba (Anon. 1949: 796) indicates some familiarity with the Kela/Kangaba tradition, but the play itself is unlikely to have been based on information garnered from this source, as the seduction episode is absent from this tradition (Jansen 2000b: 139; Jansen 2001).

The school's policy of encouraging Africans to explore their own past helped develop interest in and knowledge of Sunjata in West Africa during the first half of the 20th century; it may also have influenced the way the epic altered over time. The ways in which school, and broader colonial cultural, policy impacted on the epic can be considered under three heads:

1) provision of a spur to investigate oral traditions such as Sunjata, to accord them significance as historical documents;

2) provision of a means for the dissemination of knowledge of and interest in traditions such as Sunjata across West Africa;
3) suggestion of the stage-play as a mode of re-coding the Sunjata epic for modern audiences.

Turning first to the way in which I suggest the school's project may have encouraged the collection and publication of oral traditional history, the periodical founded by Hardy in 1913, by the 1930s called *L'Education africaine*, along with other colonial journals such as *Outre-Mer* and the *Bulletin du Comité d'Etudes Historiques et Scientifiques d'Afrique Occidentale Française* became frequent publishers of collections of oral tradition and other articles on aspects of traditional Africa by African school teachers, products, one might claim, of Brévié's programme of collection of African oral material and of Hardy's encouragement that preceded it. For example, Ibrahima Bathily, an *insituteur adjoint* in Bougouni, Soudan Français, published oral traditions collected at Djenne, Ségou and Nioro in *L'Education africaine* in 1936 (Bathily 1936). And a teacher from Oudoussébougou school, near Bamako, Paul-Emile Namoussa Doumbia, published in 1936 extensive traditions of the Kante and other blacksmith clans in the *Bulletin du Comité d'Etudes Historiques et Scientifiques d'Afrique Occidentale Française* for the same year.

One individual who particularly exemplifies this trend is Mamby Sidibé, perhaps the key figure in the transition of the Sunjata epic from the period of colonial collectors to that of indigenous writers. The long-lived Sidibé (1891-1977) was born near Kita of Fulani stock, and an early Pontin, graduating in 1913, earning him the title of 'patriarch of Pontins in Mali'. Trained as a teacher, his early promise is shown by the fact that he received an 'honourable mention' in 1918 from the government – one of only eight African teachers so noted (Sabatier 1977: 273). Sidibé began publishing on African culture and history in 1917. His first contribution on the Sunjata epic came in 1937 when he was a school teacher (published in 1959). His piece is a detailed account of the epic, including songs and associated lore, which notes variant traditions – such as how many wives Sumanguru had or different names for Sunjata's mother – indicating a long and painstaking study of epic traditions. Although it has been claimed that Sidibé employed Kele Monzon Jabate's father, Bolin Jigi, as his source (Diabaté n.d.: 684), it is clear that he had listened attentively to many different versions of the epic. At the time, in 1937, Sidibé's article on the epic was not the most detailed or lengthy account of a performance of Sunjata (cf. Bulman 1999: 235-236), but it was the most scholarly treatment, and the one with most evident knowledge of the epic as a series of variant traditions.

The Sunjata epic received what can claim to be its earliest literary re-telling in French by an African from the writings of another distinguished early Ponty graduate, the Senegalese Abdoulaye Sadji (1911-1961).[xii] Sadji graduated in 1929 and became a school teacher in Saint-Louis. He was one of only three Senegalese to gain the baccalauréat in the 1930s and went on to a successful career as a teacher, school inspector, and novelist (Bulman 1990: 450-457). In 1936 he published a version of the epic in *L'Education africaine* as part of a collection of traditional stories for children (Saji 1936; 1985). Sadji's version is at times confused and unusual (for example, Sumanguru is Sunjata's brother) and does not suggest a wide knowledge of the epic, although his informant, the jeli Bakary Diabaté of Khasso province – that bit of Mali closest to Senegal – claimed descent from the bard of Samori Touré.

It is of course hard to determine if Sidibé, Sadji, and the other teachers whose work dots the pages of these journals, were influenced by Georges Hardy's original call for western-educated Africans to research their own past, or subsequent French colonial projects to stimulate research announced by Jules Brévié, or by the cahiers and plays at Ponty School – or by the annual prize announced by Charton (1934: 202) for indigenous inquiries into geography, ethnography and history – or whether they simply proceeded to employ French literacy, and the openings provided by colonial periodicals, to document traditional African culture spontaneously, as it were. Certainly I would not claim that the colonial project for a Franco-African culture in any way encompassed Sidibé's work or that of his near-contemporaries in the schools of French West Africa: however, that it may have aided and influenced their beginnings is, I suggest, highly probable.

Turning now to the way in which the William Ponty school may have provided a means for spreading knowledge of Sunjata through West Africa, the journals already mentioned must by themselves have spread awareness of the epic, at least to others in the intellectual elite who one imagines read them. Beyond this, though, there is evidence that the plays performed at the school from 1933 spread knowledge of the history and traditions of west Africa. The school, via the plays, acted as a point of cultural exchange for the pupils who hailed from all parts of French West Africa, and beyond. We can note that, in the words of Sabatier (1977: 179): 'It soon became the custom [at the school] for each group to learn the plays and songs of others to increase their vacation repertoire in their home territory.'

In the case of the Sunjata epic, there is clear evidence of the 1937 production 'La ruse de Diégué' being a source for at least part of an early literary rendition of the epic. The author in question was Maximilien Quénum Possy Berry (b. 1911), from Cotonou, Dahomey. Quénum published 'La Légende de Fama-Soundiata' as one of three *Légendes africaines* in 1946, a book aimed at children which won an award from the Académie Française. There is no evidence that Quénum was a Ponty graduate, but he may have been, given that he indicates as a source for his Sunjata legend 'la fête annuelle d'Art Indigène organisée par les Elèves-Maîtres de l'Ecole W. Ponty' (1946: 65n). Alternatively, he may have come into contact with the Pontins who had written or performed the piece or subsequently learnt it. Either way, it is a proof of the way in which the school disseminated knowledge of the Sunjata epic.

Sunjata as a stage-play
I shall now turn to the third area in which I think that the William Ponty school had an impact on the evolution of the Sunjata epic. The encouragement to stage histories, traditional legends and stories as plays at the school may be partly responsible for the development of a lively theatrical sector in French Sudan in the 1940s and 1950s and in Mali in the 1960s, which included in it productions of Sunjata as a drama.

Nicholas Hopkins states (1972: 220): 'By the 1950s the 'Ponty Theatre' had spread widely in French West Africa, carried by former Ponty pupils.' The most famous West African ballet company of the time, Fodéba Keita's *Ballets africains*, had in fact begun in Paris in 1949 as *Théâtre africain*, where Keita, a Ponty graduate himself, included some plays performed at the school in his repertoire (Traoré 1972: 37f). In Bamako a group of Ponty graduates formed a theatre group called *Art et travail* to perform Ponty plays and new material in the town. We know that the company put on three plays in Bamako's Maison du peuple in 1938 and toured regional centres in French Sudan during 1945-46 (Cutter 1971: 253). In the late 1940s regional theatres developed in Bougouni, Sikasso, Mopti and Ségou, inspired by *Art et travail*. In the mid 1950s the French authorities inaugurated a theatrical competition within each colony of the federation. This competitive tradition survived into independent Mali where an annual youth festival included a dramatic tourney (ib.: 253-273; Hopkins 1972).

'Sundjata,' writes Charles Cutter (1971: 254), 'was of course a great favorite of *Art et Travail*', based perhaps on a version of 'La ruse'. Unfortunately, to my knowledge, no other text survives of an early play based on the epic. One title is mentioned by a number of sources: 'Mali ou Soundiata' which Hopkins saw in a 1962 performance by a troupe from the Kita area but which he writes (1967: 170) 'is apparently a standard version often played in various places in Mali but particularly by the troupe in the national capital.' Sidibé is certainly a likely candidate for author of a play about Sunjata for a Bamako theatre troupe, given his links the town, reputation as an early Ponty graduate, and wide knowledge of the tradition from the mid 1930s (cf. Hopkins 1972: 220). Certainly by his death in the 1970s Sidibé was better known as a story-teller than a school teacher.

In many ways the Sunjata epic has a natural affinity to the stage-play. The theatricality of jeli performances is as obvious today as it was to Frobenius and Delafosse early last century; and Hopkins (and others) have seen the traditional Bamana *Koteba* performances as another source – along with the Ponty plays – of contemporary Malian theatre.

Although the novelistic literary re-telling of the Sunjata epic became conventional after Niane's 1960 version it is probable that before this date, during the late 1930s and through the 1940s and 1950s, when considered outside of its traditional setting, the epic was imagined more often as a stage-play than as a novel or literary narrative. It is certain that the Sunjata epic was *witnessed* by Malians more often on stage that in literature: in the form of a drama the epic was able to reach more of the illiterate mass, and indeed was closer to its oral traditional roots. Theatre, rather than the novel, may be a more natural response for oral tradition, when confronted with literacy and modernity. Niane himself wrote plays, including one for school performance, while even in the 1970s and 1980s theatrical versions of the Sunjata epic were produced, including one by a Ponty graduate from the late 1930s, the Malian Sory Konake, whose *Le Grand Destin de Soundjata* won a radio award in 1971 (see Blair 1976: 107).

Conclusion
This paper has argued that the William Ponty school and the colonial education authorities behind it acted in the early decades of the 20th century as a key agent in the encouragement of Africans to record oral traditions and African history, specifically via the cahiers and plays of 1933 and beyond, but before that through the founding of a journal for teachers; that the school helped spread knowledge of traditions such as Sunjata via the plays and the journal; and that the plays themselves helped foster a theatrical tradition which flourished in French Sudan/Mali during the 1940s, 50s and 60s.

It might be argued that *L'Education africaine*, the school's policy on cahiers, plays and Brévié's project for collection of oral traditions were unnecessary or irrelevant: that simply through bringing together a diversity of talented Africans and educating them in French, thereby providing a common language, the scene was set for a spontaneous development of African research into African culture and history. This may have been the case – though even then the school and French colonial education policy would be recognised as an important factor – but the evidence suggests that it is more likely that the school and the educational authority's encouragements to research were a key factor in creating a body of research into oral traditions of which the Sunjata epic was a beneficiary.

In what ways did the school's influence affect the evolution of the Sunjata epic? Putting Sunjata on the stage was probably the most crucial development for the epic at the time, although today that legacy is somewhat hidden by the impact of Niane's *Soundjata* and what came after. Recovering the full history of the theatre tradition of 1940s to 1960s French Sudan/Mali will help answer questions about the way in which theatrical performances of Sunjata by stage companies may have influenced the form of that epic as it is known today, and allow us to determine what impact, if any, such a theatrical tradition had on the generation of 'novelistic' Sunjata's by Niane, Camara Laye, and others.

What type of Sunjata – if I can put it that way – did the school produce? Certainly the dramatic and literary versions of the epic that can be associated with the William Ponty school are not reducible to a single type; nevertheless, several interesting trends can be isolated. The first is a tendency to find parallels in the epic traditions for European legendary or mythic themes. The focus of the 1937 stage-play about Sunjata, 'La Ruse de Diégué', is the seduction episode, where Sunjata's sister discovers the secret that can kill Sumanguru after becoming his lover. Is this the sort of subject 'closest to European taste' that Pontin Bakary Traoré claimed the students would choose for the dramas they performed? It is certainly close to some familiar Biblical and Greek stories, and indeed Mamby Sidibé, in his 1937 written version of the epic, says as much, comparing the episode to Hercules and Diana or Samson and Delilah (Sidibé 1959: 44). Such points of reference are to be expected, given the education the school provided. Was this Franco-African culture in practice?

Both Abdoulaye Sadji's and Maximilien Quénum's literary accounts of Sunjata can be linked to the Négritude or Pan-African tendency of this period. Naturally enough for authors who came from another linguistic and cultural tradition from the Maninka, what they saw in the Sunjata story was less its local import than its universal messages. Both appear keen to stress the mysterious, even anti-rational, elements of the story; for Quénum, Sumanguru's disappearance into the rock at Kulikoro is a cue for a critique of the Western worldview he characterises as 'arid' and 'mechanical', in contrast to the 'African spirit' for whom 'the universe was alive' and natural phenomena reflected the souls of the departed great (Quénum 1946: 70-71).

The wistful, nostalgic mood in Sadji's and particularly Quénum's prose contrasts strongly with Mamby Sidibé's treatment of the epic. Sidibé's approach is scholarly, detailed, precise and comparative – that is to say between variants of the corpus of traditions about Sunjata, as well as with European counterparts. His account of Sunjata, I think, inaugurated the comparative study of the epic as a collection of variant traditions; he was aware of the topographical particularities of the traditions, and the importance of the seven-year cycle of ritual performances at Kangaba (1959: 47). While implausible elements of the story are by no means elided, the whole is treated as a more or less historical recollection.

How influential were the versions of Sunjata produced or inspired by the scholars at William Ponty school? Sidibé's direct influence is hard to measure, and was probably limited by the fact that the article in question was not published until 1959.[xiii] Serious attempts to use Sunjata traditions as a *historical* source had of course been attempted before – most notably by Maurice Delafosse (1912) and Charles Monteil (1929). There is no evidence that either Niane or Camara Laye used Sidibé's work; Sidibé or Sadji's early work of collecting oral versions of Sunjata may have inspired them, but we lack evidence of a direct debt.[xiv] More likely, the tradition of an interest in oral material and local history, encouraged at the William Ponty school and fostered through publications such as *L'Education africaine*, was one which they could emulate.

From a literary point of view, however, the work of Sidibé, Sadji and Quénum did have a legacy. There is a sense in which Niane's *Soundjata* is a direct descendant of Sidibé's: both emphasise the historical, the believable, and both document variants; while Sadji and Quénum's universalising tendencies lived on in Camara Laye's *Master of the Word* with its talk of 'Black soul, African soul' and its contrasting of European rationality with African awareness of mystery and 'the hidden depths in every existence' (Camara Laye 1980: 13).

NOTES

[i] I offer my thanks to Ian Grosvenor and Paulo Farias, who commented on an earlier draft, to the conference organisers, Henk M.J. Maier and Jan Jansen, for inviting me to contribute, and to Jan Jansen (again!) and Ralph Austen, for helpful comments on the conference presentation.

[ii] Audio cassettes include both professionally-produced recording by musicians and jeliw and the amateur recordings of jeli performances described by Robert Newton (1999) and David Conrad (1999). For a near-complete listing of all extant written versions of the Sunjata epic see Bulman 1997.

[iii] See Bulman 1999. Of course, underpinning and running alongside these changes was a continuing oral tradition of performances on which presentation of Sunjata in other media drew.

[iv] A version of Sunjata by Tiemoko Kone of Mourdiah (Kone 1970).

[v] In an interesting parallel to my thesis of the school's role in disseminating knowledge of the Sunjata epic through west Africa, Eric Charry writes that the school 'had a major impact in disseminating European-based dance music in the 1940s and 1950s' (Charry 2000: 245).

[vi] One pointer to its prestige, noted by Sabatier, is that, at Independence 'the presidents of Mali, Niger, Dahomey (now Benin), and the Ivory Coast, as well as the prime minister of Senegal, were graduates' (1978: 266).

[vii] Sabatier (1977: Introduction) writes that in 1935 43.100 boys went to primary school in French West Africa and 237 scholars attended the William Ponty school, making one year equivalent to 79 pupils. the ratio of 1: 545 over-estimates the number who attended from French West Africa as the school also took pupils from French Equatorial Africa, Cameroon and Togo.

[viii] When, Sabatier notes, the overall curriculum of the William Ponty school became 'less 'French'' (1978: 261).

[ix] Warner 1984: 181, quoting a piece written by Brévié in *L'Education africaine* 1934.

[x] Brévié, Circular 175, 2 May 1935, in *L'Education africaine* 24 (1935): 131-133.

[xi] The seduction episode itself, in which Sunjata's sister seduces Sumanguru and tricks him into revealing to her the secret of his invulnerability, is found in most written accounts of the Sunjata epic. See Bulman 1990: 3710384 for a detailed treatment of the episode. See also Belcher 1999: 94-95.

[xii] Sadji's version is challenged for this position by Monzon Tounkara and Père Barrie's collection *Le Monde Malinké de Kita des Années 1910*, which contains a short account of Sunjata. It names no source, though, and may not have come directly from a jeli performance of the epic.

[xiii] However, his *oral* influence may have been significant, given his reputation, in Western Soudan/Mali, and the fact that he worked for a time in 1944 at IFAN in Dakar.

[xiv] I have yet to confirm if Niane himself was a Ponty pupil; Camara Laye certainly was not (Sabatier 1977: Ch. V). Camara Laye's own interest in oral traditions began in 1956 on his return from France.

THEODORIC RESCUES SINTRAM –
THE EPIC HERO IN ROMANESQUE CHURCH SCULPTURE

Michael Curschmann

Introduction
Theodoric the Great, King of the Ostrogoths and ruler of Italy from 497 until his death in 526, stands at the center of the most widely disseminated and most durable cycle of heroic legends known to us from the southern hemisphere of the Germanic world.[i] There he is known as Dietrich of Bern – Germanic for Verona – the city that the legend substituted for his historical residence, Ravenna. Medieval historians like the monk Fruotolf of Michelsberg around 1100 paid reluctant tribute to this oral tradition by defining it as another kind of historiography, an indigenous way of representing the past that was at variance with their own, but common among 'the people' even in the 12th century.[ii]

The historical Theodoric had been an Arian christian, and the catholic church – which considered arianism to be a heresy – used both word and image to demonize him and vilify him as a *rex stultus*, a foolish king. But there were of course also more constructive ways for the clergy to engage the cultural memory along with the visual imagination of the laity. Five examples from the period of around 1140 to the early 13th century have survived, four of them in

Figure 1
Basle, minster, relief on a choir capital: Dietrich rescues Sintram. Photo from Das Basler Münster, *ed.* Die Münsterbau- kommission *(1982), fig. p. 131.*

Figure 2
Rosheim, St. Peter and Paul's, relief atop the south transept facade: Dietrich rescues Sintram.
Photo from D. Bretz-Mahler, Rosheim *(1979), fig. 23.*

the German-speaking South-West of the Hohenstaufen empire, and it is those four that I shall discuss. They form a thematic group, at least in the sense that in every case the same particular episode from the popular legend of Dietrich was incorporated into the picture program of local churches, in the form of sculpted stone reliefs in various architectural settings, some marginal, others prominent, but usually in full public view. The one exception to this is a capital in the dark recesses of the choir in the minster at Basle (figure 1).

It nonetheless represents the basic situation very clearly: a helmeted warrior with his sword raised above his head attempts to pull another warrior from the jaws of a winged, biped dragon. The rescuer's escutcheon, a lion rampant, designates him as Dietrich of Bern, in accordance with the legend.[iii] Arguably the most public representation of this heroic moment occurs atop the south transept of the parish church in Rosheim, further down the Rhine valley, in Alsace (figure 2). Surmounting the pillar at the west side of the facade, we see the dragon's head and (more imposing here in proportion) the two warriors. The larger of the two appears to have been swallowed, at least in part, while his rescuer, as the local guide book maintains, thrusts his sword into the dragon's mouth (Poinsot 1997: 25).

About half-way between Basle and Rosheim lies the abbey church of Andlau (figure 3) with an extensive stone frieze on the outside, also high above the ground (Will 1988: 323-336). It begins on the north wall of the nave and runs all the way across the west façade. What we are interested in is a segment from the north side where this scene is paired with the figure of another warrior on horseback who holds the reins of a second, riderless horse. I shall have to skip this addition and concentrate on 'our' scene. It looks somewhat different again: this dragon lives in a cave, his victim still holds on to his shield, and the rescuer

Figure 3
Andlau, abbey church, segment of an outside frieze, north wall of the nave: Dietrich rescues Sintram and returns his horse.
Photo Michael Curschmann.

Figure 4
Altenstadt, St. Michael's, tympanum relief above the west portal: Dietrich rescues Sintram. Photo Rupert Neumayr

is portrayed with two swords: one that rests in its sheath by his side, while he seems to manipulate the other precariously between the victim's chest and left arm, close to the dragon's mouth. The gesture strikes one as counter-intuitive and will require further comment in a moment.

One hundred and eighty miles to the east of Andlau, as the crow flies, lies the village of Altenstadt in southern Swabia. Here, in the parish church of St. Michael, our scene appears prominently in the tympanum above the only door of the west portal, as the only figural decoration of the whole west façade (figure 4).[iv] And here the artist has made this curious motif of the two swords even more explicit: while the hero wields one of these weapons above his head, as he does in Basle, another one has fallen (or is falling) to the ground.

No one has so far considered these images as a group, but a number of scholars have suggested the thematic connection with Dietrich in individual cases. Others have denied such a connection and explained these pictures as anonymous, generic variations within a much older paradigm of Christian iconography devoted to the eternal battle between good and evil. The latest verdict is that the identification 'remains uncertain' (Heinzle 1999: 142). I have already indicated my own conclusion that these pictures were indeed designed to evoke the legend of Dietrich, but my main interest is in the argument itself. How can this kind of argument be made in ways that are both methodologically sound and historically plausible, in view of the fact that it involves two essentially unstable traditions: oral legend and a pre-existing iconography that was itself highly variable? The question is ultimately: how is identity constituted and maintained in these visio-verbal contexts?

The verbal accounts that survive are much later, circulated in different parts of the Germanic world and differ considerably from each other. I shall refer only to one, the Old Norse *Saga af Thidrek af Bern* which was put together from continental sources for King Haakon of Norway around 1250. The saga relates that Dietrich and his companion of the moment, the giant Fasold, come across a large low-flying dragon weighed down by the body of a man whom he has 'taken off his shield' while he slept and swallowed up to his armpits. But the man is still alive, and, heeding his pleas for help, Dietrich and Fasold attack the dragon with their swords. It turns out, however, that the dragon's skin is too hard for these weapons and the man instructs Fasold to retrieve his own sword from the dragon's mouth. This sword has magic powers and Fasold and Dietrich manage to subdue the beast. The man they have thus freed is called Sintram, the three men become friends and ride off together.

Looking again now at Andlau (figure 3) and Altenstadt (figure 4), one notes that these visual accounts disagree in a number of important details with the *Thidreks saga* narrative. But there is a common core as well, a motif in which verbal and visual representation overlap: the success of this operation depends on a second sword that has to be extracted from the dragon's own mouth. The Andlau artisan offers a comparatively stylized version of this key moment: with his own sword safely back in its sheath, the attacker secures the magic weapon from Sintrams side. In other words, the second sword in the picture is Sintram's sword, and it is actually being withdrawn. The Altenstadt artist chose to portray the same constellation a little more vividly and at a slightly later point in the epic succession: In the light of the verbal account, it seems that the sword that drops is the attackers own sword; the one he swings is the one he has just acquired.

The most conspicuous difference between the verbal and visual accounts of this episode is that the surviving text also features two rescuers. On the other hand, that is the sort of arrangement that could readily be absorbed by the pre-existing iconographic tradition.

That tradition displays a considerable variety of ways in which humans or superhuman beings do battle with the forces of evil in the shape of large beasts, dragons in particular. In general, there are those that are swallowed, usually headfirst,[v] and those that prevail, and these two generic types could easily be combined and converted into a direct ad hoc response to a particular text. Thus

Figure 5
Ipswich, St. Nicholas', relief on a dislocated slab, now in the chancel wall: St. Michael attacking the dragon. Photo from K.J. Galbraith, Proceedings of the Suffolk Institute of Archaeology, 31 (1967-9): 24.

the example traditionally cited as particularly close to what we see in Altenstadt or Andlau is a historiated initial in the *Psalter of St. Albans*, from the early part of the century, which illustrates the words of the sixtieth psalm, *dominus, in adiutorium meum intende*: Christ in the cloud above rescues a human from the jaws of a winged dragon.[vi] Actually, the resemblance in this case is mostly thematic not iconographic. The specific iconographic framework that was best suited to accommodate an act of *armed* intervention was the one associated with the archangel Michael of the Apocalypse. A 12th century relief from Ipswich (figure 5) shows one of the two basic forms in which this motif occurs: Michael wielding a sword. A miniature in an Italian prayerbook of around 1000 (figure 6) shows the other form, and in addition a rather interesting iconographic variant: while Michael here transfixes the dragon with a lance, as he does most of the time in continental art, he also pulls a human soul from its jaws.[vii] That is the kind of iconographic perspective from which Dietrichs legendary feat could be seen as a secular analogue with the potential for visual integration into ecclesiastical picture programs. The question remains whether under those circumstances the secular subject would or could retain its identity.

Another example of this process of vernacularization may offer additional suggestions. In the Germanic north, another dragon-slayer, Sigurd, entered church art as a highly distinctive figure.[viii] From 10th century memorial crosses on the Isle of Man to Romanesque wooden church portals in Norway he is always seen killing 'his' dragon, Fafnir, from below. After all, everyone knew that Sigurd dug himself a pit in the ground and when the serpent-like Fafnir crawled over it Sigurd thrust his sword through the soft underbelly into his heart. That moment became the hallmark of this particular dragon fight in visual representation, so much so that it is clear whose dragon fight this is even where the motif appears in extreme shorthand, as it does on an earlier Norwegian picture stone that shows only a dragon with a sword stuck in his belly.[ix] Not unlike the oral tradition that gave rise to the image, the artists who shaped and established it focused on special, distinctive details around which narrative could cluster.

The same thing appears to have happened in the case of Dietrich. A similarly defining motif imparts identity to Dietrich's dragon fight in visual representation: the need for the magic

Figure 6
London, The British Library, Ms. Egerton 3763, fol. 104v: St. Michael transfixes the dragon and rescues a soul. Photo from P.M. Johnston, Proceedings of the society of Antiquaries of London, 24 (1911-2), fig. 3.

Figure 7
Altenstadt, St. Michael's, baptismal font, relief scene: St. Michael transfixes the dragon. Photo from H. Karlinger, Die romanische Steinplastik in Altbayern und Salzburg (Augsburg, 1928): 171.

sword in the verbal account generates the duplication of weapons and the potentially ambiguous gesture we have observed in Andlau. Other details of this negotiation between two very different, open-ended systems of signification must remain obscure. But this is the one significant constant and as such it also explains what we see in Rosheim (figure 2): adjusting to the exegencies of space this artist offers a drastically foreshortened version of the whole scene and in the process shows only one sword. But anyone familiar with the Dietrich story would recognize it as this second, magic one that is not thrust into, but being pulled from the dragon's mouth. Visualization of an heroic moment had introduced a significant variant into the received pictorial code, and, even in extreme shorthand, that variant signals the identity of the new subject. By the same token its absence means loss of identity unless the artist compensated in some way. That is what the artist did in Basle, my very first example: he took a somewhat more distant view of his subject and 'named' the rescuer in chivalric fashion through his coat of arms.

Such decisions are related as much to programmatic context as they are to format, and to do them justice requires a different approach. As long as the goal is to reconstruct their relationship to the verbal tradition, these images need to be considered as a group. But when it comes to purpose and function, we need to consider them individually, case by case. Allow me in conclusion to say just a few words about one of these cases, Altenstadt (figure 4), a parish church dedicated to St. Michael.[x]

A parishioner who entered here, say, in the year 1200 and took with him this image of a famous act of deliverance in secular narrative might procede to the beautiful baptismal font inside (figure 7), and here, on one of the four reliefs that grace this quatrefoil form, he would encounter the patron saint of the church in analogous action: The archangel Michael defeating the dragon of the Apocalypse, *ille magnus serpens antiquus,* whose satanic soul escapes to the left, in poignant and perhaps even intended visual parallel and contrast to Sintram's exodus. Thus the familiar story re-sonates in the not-so-familiar. Here in Altenstadt a synergetic relationship has been created in which the sacred and the profane, the memory of oral culture and the precepts of scriptural culture are reconciled through visual experience.

NOTES

[i] The following is the text, essentially unchanged, of a paper delivered at the Third Utrecht Symposium on Medieval Literacy in December, 2000. An expanded and copiously annotated version of this paper is Curschmann 2003b. I want to thank Marco Mostert and Mariëlle Hageman for their kind permission to reprint my original remarks. For a full discussion of my topic, bibliography and much of the pictorial evidence I refer the reader to this essay and to Curschmann 2003a. For the present purpose I have added only a few essential footnote references and confined myself to the necessary minimum of photographs.

[ii] The best and most recent concise introduction to the matter of Theodoric/Dietrich is Heinzle 1999.

[iii] For examples from 13th century written sources, see Grimm 1957: 156-157. For *Thidreks saga*, see below.

[iv] For the latest research on Altenstadt see Exner 1998, especially 521 (for the date).

[v] A splendid example is the abbacus relief on the south portal of Verona cathedral from the middle of the 12th century. For a recent photograph, see Curschmann 2003a, figure 4.

[vi] Hildesheim, Domschatz, Ms. G1: 207. For a recent photograph see Curschmann 2003b, figure 8.

[vii] The British Library, Egerton 3763, fol. 104v.

[viii] For recent research on Sigurd, see Curschmann 2003b, n.38.

[ix] For recent photographs of this Tanberg picture stone of circa 1000 and the late 12th century door jamb from Hylestad, see Curschmann 2003b, figures 11 and 13, respectively.

[x] This case is being argued in considerably more detail in Curschmann 2003a.

THE DYNAMICS OF THE EPIC GENRE IN BURYAT CULTURE – A GRAVE FOR SHAMANISM, A GROUND FOR MESSIANISM

Roberte N. Hamayon

The epic as a 'model': a vehicle for ideology
The Buryats are not a homogeneous ethnic group, but a set of related tribes that live around Lake Baikal in Southern Central Siberia and use languages that belong to the Mongol linguistic family. These tribes, some of them autochtonous, other emigrated from Mongolia, were integrated, first as an ethnic minority into the Russian Empire, then as a national minority within an Autonomous Republic into the Soviet Union. Nowadays, in the post-Soviet context, just a little bit more than half of them live in the Republic of Buryatia.

This article is based on a series of previous studies on various aspects of Buryat epics; all conclusions point to the intrinsically ideological properties of the epic genre in Buryat culture. This ideological character is suggested by their very name: epics are called *üliger*, which means 'model, example, pattern'. Elsewhere I have extensively argued that the ethnography of Buryat epics confirms the assumption that the notion of a 'model' aims not at reflecting reality but rather at becoming the ideal reference; a model is both exemplary and inimitable since only heroes may conform to the ideal reference – and as a result the epic model may remain foreign to social practice. In this respect, it is significant that epic heroes are not considered ancestors but imaginary characters that embody ideal values.

In the following the property of epics to carry ideological values will be explored; determining the logic of the genre's dynamics, these values account for the place of epics in a society as much as for their changes in time and context. I shall first give a sketch of the 'traditional' situation, up to the 20th century (in some areas up to World War II), then I shall dwell on the innovations that appeared in Buryatia since the end of the Soviet regime.

In the first part, devoted to the 'traditional' context, I will argue that the epic genre emerges from the shamanic ritual genre and then develops to its detriment. This change is connected with changes in society and in the local ways of life, concurrent with the development of pastoralism (instead of hunting) and of segmentary or clan organization (instead of moieties or dualism). From a formal point of view it is possible to recount how epic performances progressively replace the most important shamanic collective rituals or, in other terms, how narrative progressively replaces gesture in a ritual performance.

Secondly, I will deal with events related to the most famous Buryat epic, the epic of Geser, in post-Soviet Buryatia. They suggest another type of change that has affected the epic genre. The epic narrative and its contents do no longer matter; emphasis is on the figure of the particular hero. Although one may wonder whether it still makes sense to speak of 'epics' in this context, the role assigned to the hero can be analyzed as potentially derived from the epic's intrinsic property of carrying ideal values, in connection with modernity at a national level.

I will attempt to characterize the logic that leads from one mode of expression to the next: shamanic ritual action, epic narrative performance, the hero's portraying – and I will try to bring to light similarities as well as divergences between the shaman, the traditional epic hero, and Geser as ideal figures.

The 'traditional' situation of epics among the Buryats
The epic tradition is not homogeneous in Buryatia. Moreover, differences do not strictly correspond to different groups; variations in the epics' structure and ritual function can be correlated, instead, with variations in social organization and ways of life. Precisely the analysis of these correlations will help us to understand how epics both derive from and gradually supplant shamanic rituals.

The Buryats are currently divided up into two types, the Western type on the West side of Lake Baikal, the Eastern type on the East side. Schematically, East and West are opposed in several ways. The Western type is represented by the Ekhirit-Bulagat, who are held to be the only autochtonous Buryat tribe, initially seen as hunters in a forest environment who adopted horse-raising to further large-scale hunting. The Ekhirit-Bulagat have maintained a very strong hunting ideology although they developed stock breeding. The Eastern type is represented by the Khori(n), who emigrated from Mongolia and Northern China mostly in the 16th and 17th centuries; they are associated with pastoral nomadism in a steppe environment. As a matter of fact, the Khori primarily live on extensive stock breeding although they also occasionally hunt.

The Ekhirit-Bulagat are organized in clans that maintain their rivaling relationships by way of marriage and revenge, while the Khori form a union of eleven clans held together by a tendency to centralizing hierarchy.

The Ekhirit-Bulagat retain a strong shamanic tradition although they have been christianized, while the Khori have been deeply buddhicized, with the result that shamanism among them is marginalized both as an institution and as a practice. More precisely, while as a rule Siberian shamans were traditionally male and still are males among the Ekhirit-Bulagat in the post-Soviet period, they are mostly female among the Khori, even though patrilinearity and patrifocal ideology are equally strong among both.

The epics: a paradoxical distribution
The relationship between epics on the one hand and types of culture and ways of life on the other hand is characterized by several paradoxes in the Buryat

pre-Soviet context. A first paradox derives from the fact that epics are only found among pastoral groups and that the groups of the Eastern type, who are the most addicted to pastoralism, tend to give epics a very small role in their culture. Another paradox lies in the fact that these epics primarily relate to hunting, whereas, as a rule, hunting societies do not have epics. These paradoxes ask for an explanation.

In the descriptions of the Eastern groups in the pre-Soviet period mention is made of several epics, yet none of these has been recorded in its full length and no mention is made of their ritual function. Many accounts stress that the Buddhist clergy of Buryatia prohibited people to perform the epic of Geser, the most famous epic among all Mongolian peoples; this prohibition may have hold for all epic performances and it may account for the decline of the epic tradition as a whole. We shall see below the peculiar motives for the prohibition of Geser, unique in the cultural history of the Mongol peoples.

The epic genre seems to be more developed among the Ekhirit-Bulagat than in any other group and that should be surprising: they are the ones with the strongest hunting tradition and the weakest (and most recent) pastoral tradition. This is even more surprising given the fact that the small neighboring societies who live primarily of hunting in the Siberian forest *(taiga)* do not perform or relate of heroes in epics in their versified and ritualized form but only have short tales about them; meant to make hunting a success, these tales are preferably recounted at night during the hunting season and they are not submitted to strict performing rules. By contrast, according to traditional rules of the Ekhirit-Bulagat the epic performance is absolutely mandatory before going on a hunt and absolutely prohibited outside of the hunting season. Highly ritualized and clearly defined in terms of rules and purpose, these performances take only place at night; they are forbidden in the daytime. The hero's story must absolutely be recounted in a singing voice[i] until its complete ending. Bard and audience should refrain from falling asleep, and the audience should encourage the bard unto the end.[ii] As a rule, these epics are not written down; recording them is either radically forbidden or submitted to drastic restrictions. People expect the performance to be symbolically efficacious.[iii] To their mind, the epics would be harmful instead of helpful to those who transgress the rules of performance.[iv] In addition – and here is another paradox – the epic narratives only incidentally describe the hero's hunt as hunting is not of primary relevance to him and his heroic course: it is not one of the hero's fixed goals.[v] In short, the performance of epics pertains to hunting but their content does not reflect this activity.

From shamanic ritual to epic performance
How do hunting societies prepare for the hunt? These preparations belong to the category of 'life-giving rituals' as Hocart calls them. They are extremely sophisticated rituals, meant to obtain promises of game from game-giving spirits that, themselves, are seen as animals. Focused on animals and their

spirits, they are mainly based on ways of singing and dancing in imitation of animals; no reference is made to the tales and their heroes.[vi] In most societies of the Siberian *taiga*, they are performed under the ritual leadership of shamans.

Shamans are the ones who prepare the hunt in these societies, and the way they function is strictly checked by the community, which puts them in charge to lead the ritual and keeps them under control during their performance. If the hunting season is not successful, the shaman will not be asked to perform again and in his place another one will be invited. Thus, taking part in the shamanic rituals is as mandatory in hunting societies as attending an epic performance is among the Ekhirit-Bulagat: it is a condition for membership of the community.

It is significant that in groups with a mixed hunting and stock breeding economy like the Ekhirit-Bulagat the preparations for hunting are ensured by epics instead of shamanic rituals. On the one hand, it suggests a change in the very conception and practice of hunting and, as a matter of fact, the Ekhirit-Bulagat have been able to develop a large scale mode of hunting big game (mainly reindeer and elks) since they raise horses. On the other hand, the replacement of shamanic rituals by epics may throw some light on the question of the correlation between epics and pastoralism, which can be epitomized by a famous formula Lawrence Krader used in a half-joking manner: 'no epics without milk, no milk without epics'.

For all these reasons together, I shall continue to focus on the Ekhirit-Bulagat tradition, which will also prove to be of determining importance in the section devoted to recent events in post-Soviet Buryatia.

Several types of epic poems are found among the Ekhirit-Bulagat. All of them are entirely versified (by way of alliteration) and must be sung on extremely low notes and with a strong and deep voice until the very end. Varying from about two thousand to twelve thousand verses, the poems stage several heroes, indicated by the fact that they are called different names; the stories are similar and likewise abound in stereotyped formulas.

As for the ideological relevance of these poems' contents, previous analyses have led me to select kinship relations as the main determinant and to distinguish two main types, depending on the hero's kinship situation. Both types define the hero's search for his wife-to-be as his main duty;[vii] they differ, in the first place, by the fact that the hero has either a father but no sister or a sister but no father (he is therefore an orphan), and secondly, by the varied implications of this. As for Geser, whose specificity in all versions is his celestial origin – he comes down to the earth to be reborn at his adoptive parents' home – outside this specificity he mostly conforms to the type I labeled 'with-a-father' in the Ekhirit-Bulagat version, where he is called *xübüün* 'son'.

I shall not dwell here on these differences which I have examined elsewhere. I would only stress that the very existence of different types of heroic models suggests that the epics represent the principle of an ideal norm of a society or community rather than a particular ideal norm, since the details of the norm may change from one type to another. Here I concentrate on the relation between the contents and the purpose of the epic performance, in other words: on the relation between a quest for a wife and a preparation for the hunt. On a first level, this relation incites to parallel a son-in-law and a hunter, a wife and a piece of game, a father-in-law and a game-giving spirit. Taking a wife is paralleled to taking game, and the hero's position is a taker's. On a second level, the relevance of this parallel is suggested by the way the search for a wife is depicted: one may only marry one's predestined wife and this marriage is compulsory. In other words, only the one who is legitimate to undertake an action can effectively carry out this action. Applied to the hunter, the lesson of the epics is not only that marriage and hunt are two faces of every man's duty, but also that the hunter must be legitimized as such on the model of the hero: the hero must be a rightful husband in opposition to being an abductor to finally take the woman, that is: the hunter is allowed to take game only insofar as he obeys an agreement similar to a marriage alliance.[viii]

Then, the parallel indicates that an agreement must be concluded with a game-giving spirit, for this is precisely the purpose of collective shamanic rituals aimed at obtaining promises of game. The agreement that is reached in this framework is also expressed in the shape of a marriage: the shaman, who is supposed to marry a game-giving spirit's daughter, dramatically represents a hunting campaign that unfolds in a context of alliance relationships and finally sets up a married couple.[ix]

Marrying goes along with fighting (entailed as a joint deed) in shamanic rituals and epic songs as well. The shaman must repel rival shamans to have access to his spirit-wife – which somehow mirrors a hunter's attitude with respect to game. In the same way the epic hero must overcome trials imposed to obtain the bride and triumph over other suitors. In the second type of epics (with-a-father) he must also carry out the duty of revenge against those who have disturbed his father. Thus the notion of a marriage alliance is always closely associated with that of self-defense in a perspective of legitimate perpetuation.

This similarity shows a continuity between shamanic rituals and epics. It makes the substitution possible although it does not account for it. Besides, the emergence of epics and bards is not directed against shamanism as such and it does not mean its disappearance, although it reduces the scope of its function.[x] It is rather to be analyzed as a part of a process of hierarchization and specialization that in particular amounts to remove the shamanic institution from its central place in the community.

Firstly, the main periodically performed collective rituals are no longer aimed at obtaining good luck at hunting although they may still be characterized as 'life-giving rituals'. Shamans still play a part in them, but clan elders now have the leadership,[xi] and the clan institution rather than the shamanic institution is in charge of the main collective ritual. The shamanic institution is henceforth subordinated to clan authorities in this framework just as a younger is with respect to his elder. As to individual shamans, their activities tend to be more and more directed at healing, hence to become private, depending on circumstances and paid for. In the process, their attitude becomes more and more subversive with respect to clan power. Gradually shamanism evolves in a plurality of counter-powers in society.[xii]

Secondly, although the epic performance is highly ritualized and aimed at preparing for the hunt, it does not provide bards with a central institutional place in society.[xiii] More precisely, the bards do not have, it seems, a specific relationship to any type of social institution, even not to their clan or lineage. Neither do they form a social category of their own. On the other hand, their performances are subject to strict social control and they are not paid for.

Thus, in order to prepare a hunt, the shamanic ritual is replaced by an epic performance, both being compulsory. This calls attention to the respective type of ritualization and entails to parallel the shaman and the bard. A ritual based on miming animals is replaced by a narrative recounting human stories, gestures and sounds by speech, dramatic representation by verbal evocation.[xiv] Things pass from a gesticulating shaman to a lying or sitting bard, from daytime to nighttime and from springtime to fall, from a hut built on purpose in the forest to a yurt in a camp, from miming a hunt turning into a marriage to recounting a marriage quest portrayed as the most difficult campaign.

As for the symbolic contents, the shaman is to be paralleled to the hero. Things pass from an emphasis on hunting as a metaphor of marriage in the shaman's ritual action to an emphasis on marrying as a metaphor of hunting – hunting meaning livelihood in general – in the hero's destiny. This change in the symbolic contents can be tied to the above-mentioned change in the way of life, from a simple mode of hunting to an elaborate one that implies pastoralism along with appropriate changes in the social organization. The shamanic ritual that addresses animal spirits is aimed at acting on 'nature', the epic performance is aimed at imposing strict social rules to human society.[xv]

Despite these differences, shamanic rituals as well as epic performances convey the ideal values of alliance and self-defense that, together, ensure legitimate perpetuation at the level of the individual and the community at once. The variations in the ways of achieving these ideal values in the two types of epics do not affect the general principle of legitimate perpetuation of the social self.

The emergence of the hero Geser as a national emblem in post-Soviet Buryatia
Now I will deal with the process that unfolded during the last decade in post-Soviet Buryatia. I shall start with a short reminder of the events that I have examined in previous papers (Hamayon 1998, 2000 & 2001). Although these events were initially intended at celebrating a particular version of the epic of Geser and formally remained attached to that version, the whole process appeared to be in fact focused on the single figure of the hero Geser.

The process was set in motion by the Russian-dominated government of the

Buryat Republic, when the republic proclaimed its sovereignty in 1990 and it was taken over by the mainstream Buryat intelligentsia.[xvi] The Supreme Soviet decided to create a special section called Geseriad at the Ministry of Culture on the 15th of November of that year and place the process of organizing festivals under the aegis of the President of the Cabinet. The Ekhirit-Bulagat version of the epic of Geser (that had been recorded by Zhamcarano from the bard Emegenej Manshuud-Manshut Imegenov and published in Russian spelling-in 1906)[xvii] was proclaimed a thousand years old, and, more importantly, the only genuinely Buryat version of the epic, notwithstanding the fact it is widely known in its lands of origin, Tibet and Mongolia. Large-scale commemorations of its millennium were planned for 1995.

Before turning to this particular epic and its hero, I would like to stress that these events were launched and performed by representatives of the highest official level of the Republic that, by doing so, proved to be nationalistic with respect to culture and realistic with respect to politics. The Buryat branch of the Russian Academy of Sciences and the Buryat Union of Writers managed to jointly organize, first, the conference that initially asserted the millennial age of the epic and, then, the festivals, press campaign, publications and other manifestations that followed.

The whole process can be analyzed as a pseudo-commemorative movement.[xviii] Its pretext is related to Buryat culture but its actual relevance extends beyond the frame of Buryat ethnicity and relates primarily to the national identity of the post-Soviet Buryat Republic: Geser is to be a national cultural emblem for the Republic of Buryatia, not related to the ethnic identity of the Buryats but, instead, to an overall recomposition of identities on a territorial basis. As a commemoration, the conference and subsequent festivities fully conformed to Soviet stereotypes. As a millennial commemoration, it acquired a quasi-messianic role in the political context of post-Soviet Russia. The heroic figure of Geser is well suited to this quasi-messianic role.

As early as 1990, a series of events dedicated to both the hero and the epic were launched to punctuate the five-year preparation of the commemoration planned for 1995: both popular and academic books were published,[xix] cultural and artistic manifestations were set up. Festivals called 'Geser's Games' (*Geserei naadan* or *naadam*) were organized every summer from 1991 to 1995; taking place in the homelands of traditional bards of the 19th and early 20th centuries, famous for their way of performing this epic, they combined elements of shamanist and Buddhist traditions, along with national ritual 'games', their itinerary symbolically outlined an area encompassing the three Buryat-inhabited territories dismantled in 1937.[xx] The banner of Geser was carried ceremoniously from one selected place to the next; it was 'animated' the way a shaman's drum used to be. Moreover, a visit was made to a Buddhist sanctuary, and traditional wrestling and archery contests (*sur xarbaan*) were held. The great celebration of the hero and his millennial epic story took eventually place in the framework of an international Forum-Festival that was organized in the capital Ulan-Ude in July 1995, in the vicinity of which sacred poles dedicated to the hero and his horses were erected.

Meanwhile a national natural reservation park called 'Geser's Land' (*Geserei oron* in Buryat, *Kraj Gesera* in Russian) has been inaugurated in the heights of Oka valley at the intersection with Tunka valley, a seismic and volcanic mountain area, abounding in valuable mineral resources,[xxi] with many geographical features (peaks, rocks, etc.) that are named after Geser's deeds.[xxii] The construction of a sanctuary devoted to Geser was begun near the village of Khuzhir. In the minds of the organizers, the whole park is intended to foster ecological and moral education among young people (*Kraj Gêsêra* 1995). It is significant that the sparse local population does not belong to the Ekhirit-Bulagat (who mostly live outside the autonomous republic), but to the Khongodor, who emigrated from Mongolia. The epic narrative is hardly known among them and no specific Khongodor version was ever recorded.

Somehow these multifaceted celebrations have been going on until today in several forms; publications and conferences have continued.[xxiii] A jubilee dedicated to Manshuud Imegenov, the bard whose version was proclaimed millennial, was held in December 1999 in Ulan-Ude, and there are now at least thirty Geser sanctuaries in various Buryat-inhabited areas. Moreover, the construction of a large 'ethnico-cultural' Institute with a Buddhist center and on top of it a sanctuary dedicated to Geser has been officially planned.[xxiv] The fact that this sanctuary is to be built on top of the Buddhist center questions the relationship between the hero and Buddhism, and may serve as an indication of how the government and Buddhism are related.

It is worth to emphasize here that the glorification of Geser and the epic about him remained essentially confined to Buryat intellectual and artistic circles; the hero has not become popular among the people in rural areas. Although the scarcity of information makes it difficult to really appreciate the situation, it seems that the average Buryats do not adhere to the Geser movement (if they ever supported the very idea, to begin with) and that there was no echo of it even in the Tunka region where millennarian trends not related to Geser were recorded at the very same time, i.e. 1994-1995 (Stroganova 1999).[xxv]

A borrowed figure

It is worthy of note that the very decision of assigning a politically important function to an epic hero was not a specific innovation of the Buryat Republic. Independently of the properties of Buryat epics that were highlighted in the first part of this paper, it is well known that epic traditions have had (and still have) a prominent ideological – and therefore possibly also a political – role in the history of Central Asian nomadic communities. The ritualization of epic performances and their symbolic efficacy account for the fact that epic heroes rather than, for instance, mythical ancestors and historically famous leaders are selected for the role of cultural national figures.[xxvi] The epic tradition, it seems, is in principle the appropriate base to ensure the legitimacy of the ideals it carries.

Similar commemorations of epic heroes had been held previously. A politically important one was decided upon already under the Soviet rule, that of the Kalmyk epic called Zhangar of which the five hundredth anniversary was celebrated in 1940. A festival was devoted to its 550 years in 1990, just after the change of regime. Other peoples of Central Asia also celebrated the millennium of their respective heroic epics in the 1990s.

As for Geser, he had been made into an emblem of the Buryat national culture during and after World-War II as a reaction against the enforced Russification of the 1930s. In those years the hero and his epic were objects of acute debate,[xxvii] in 1948-1949 they were condemned as tools that glorified Mongolian nationalism and feudalism, in 1953 a conference was held for their rehabilitation. The proliferation of works (editions of several versions, records, studies and comments of various kinds) published almost without a break during the decades that followed suggests that Geser was a famous figure in Buryat intellectual circles. Geser, in other words, may have become a ready-made national figure, but this does not account for the fact that he, a borrowed figure, was selected from amongst Buryat epic heroes such as Alamzha mergen.

I shall argue that it is precisely because Geser is a borrowed figure that he could be promoted as a national emblem. And it is not coincidental that the hero's story varies from one version to the other. Borrowing makes it possible to claim a tradition but also leaves room to free interpretation since this tradition is unknown. A borrowed character can be used in many ways.

The name Geser was adapted long ago from the Latin Caesar (as were the German word Kaiser and the Russian Tsar). It was adopted as the name of an epic hero first in Tibetan (Stein 1959), and passed to Mongolia and from Mongolia to Buryatia. The name apparently left no trace on its way through Central Asia, although Turkic populations living there also have strong epic traditions with powerful heroes.[xxviii] The Buryats are aware that their hero is shared with the Mongols and Tibetans, but seem to be unaware of the Latin origin of his name.

In Tibet, Gesar is the only epic hero, and through the centuries he has become the champion of Buddhism. In Mongolia and Buryatia, by contrast, Geser is merely the greatest among many heroes. The Mongol Geser supports Buddhism in a very similar way the Tibetan hero does,[xxix] while the Buryat Geser is either indifferent or outright hostile to Buddhism, depending on the version. Thus, the Ekhirit-Bulagat version makes no reference to Buddhism, while the hero victoriously fights against lamas and Buddhist deities in all other versions known among the Buryats. For this reason, the epic of Geser has been violently opposed by the Buddhist clergy among the Eastern Buryats. In all areas, it is held to be the most powerful, and it is also the most submitted to prohibitions and rules.

These differences illustrate to what extent borrowings result from selective strategies implemented by borrowing cultures: the Buryats borrowed Geser and made his figure the reverse of its Tibetan and Mongol models. Reverse, that is, with respect to Buddhism: the absence of Buddhist elements in the epic's Ekhirit-Bulagat version was seen by the official Buryat intelligentsia as evidence for authenticity and historical precedence over every other version. It served as a powerful argument for proclaiming it millennial.

At a first glance, the differences between the versions and the selection of the Ekhirit-Bulagat version do not really matter for our purpose, since its narrative contents are ignored or forgotten, except for the very general idea that the hero is a warrior fiercely defending the independence of his people against all kinds of domination and invasion. Moreover, the narrative as a base for performance is insignificant: no attention is paid to the story of the hero and his deeds. So we may think that the reason for selecting this version is that the Ekhirit-Bulagat are held to be the only native Buryat tribe.

What seems to support the idea that it could serve as a national emblem is not the performance of the epic, but the way the hero is pictured: only the hero's figure matters. Precisely the insistence on his image alone and the very way it is pictured allow us to assume that the whole process was primarily aimed at building a national emblem as such, that is, so to speak, a purely emblematic figure. The fact that the hero is mainly portrayed as a medieval warrior[xxx] precludes any interpretation of his figure as foreshadowing that of an actual leader, and the image of a medieval warrior could be seen as the personification of the ideal of self-defense: it is rooted in ancient times but is ideally valid, thus potentially (re-)actualizable – which are the characteristics of a messianic figure. Basically this type of joint reference to history and myth makes the process similar to the development of 'messianic expectations', according to the current understanding of this expression. As defined by Gerschom Scholem, for instance, 'messianic expectations' consist in making 'appeals to an idealized past to draw an idealized vision of the future from it'. Applied to Geser, he had to be imagined or portrayed as living in the past so that he could be expected to eventually appear in the future. His ability to defend his people in a distant past had to be demonstrated so that they might eventually benefit from him again – and in order to increase the strength of this memory in popular consciousness the memory of his heroic values had to be rooted as far as possible in the past. All this also suggests that what matters in such a process is expectation as a symbolic construction.

Thus we may state that the Buryat intelligentsia very aptly strove to combine old events with a utopian mythical figure and grant the hero's figure with quasi-messianic features. However, was the hero as depicted in epic narratives likely to be granted such features? In most versions spread among the Buryats Geser himself has messianic features from the very beginning. Different from all other Buryat epic heroes whose whole life unfolds on earth, Geser is initially sent from heaven by his father in order to (re)establish peace and order on earth. Hence a touch of Christian influence has often been suspected.[xxxi] However, Geser's celestial father is given a name derived from Ahura Mazda and the initial situation that accounts for his descent to the earth reproduces the main features of Mazdean cosmology.[xxxii] No doubt the epic of Geser is permeated with a variety of influences – and this is consistent with the borrowed origin of the hero as well as with the above-mentioned general idea about the very fact of borrowing. In the process of the millennium, however, the hero's figure is only portrayed as a warrior. That appears to be the price Geser had to pay in order to acquire national fame.

NOTES

[i] Recounting an epic poem by way of a speaking voice *(üliger xelexe)* would deprive the performance from symbolic efficacy. The expression *üliger böölexe* – an active verb derived from *böö* 'shaman'– is used for respecting the right way of performing.

[ii] The audience must sing an 'invitation' to the bard at the beginning, and a 'farewell' at the end of the performance (Hamayon 1990: 175).

[iii] Preparations for hunting are the only 'official' reason for performing epics, the only reason to be ideologically acknowledged since they determine seasonal restrictions. In practice, the epics are supposed to be efficacious also on many other occasions, in particular against cattle's diseases. Fragments of epic songs are thought to be helpful to someone who is lost at night in forest, etc.

[iv] In particular, the performance of an epic in order to record it may entail disaster for the bard and his family (Heissig 1973: 469; Hamayon 1990: 181-183).

[v] On the contrary, the hero is said to possess large flocks and enjoy pastoralism; he criticizes the hunting way of life that characterized his enemies, in the second type of epics mentioned below, those with-a-father.

[vi] Nevertheless telling tales is thought to be indispensable on the eve of the hunt on the very place where the hunt will take place, although it remains an informal activity and is not held to be a part of the rituals aimed at preparing for the hunt.

[vii] Epics do not have to be (and are not) performed during weddings.

[viii] Heroism is not directly attached to the hero's person and behavior but to reaching his goals; more than his so-called martial virtues, it is the hero's situation and achievement that are exemplary. The hero is permitted to employ any means as long as they serve his ends, because these ends are totally and absolutely legitimate (since determined by the ideal norm) and his predicament is the worst imaginable. Conversely, anyone who opposes these ends is a *mangad*, rival, traitor or enemy (whether he behaves as intruder or aggressor, grabber or abductor). This is an ideological framework where new *mangads* can be included: Russian colonists, Daniel (as a saint representative of the Christian Church), lamas, Ungern-Sternberg or Hitler. The hero is a normative figure as the founder of social ethics. The way he carries out the ideal is exemplary, not his magical capacity which is also possessed but misused by his enemy.

[ix] In hunting societies marriage is marked primarily by bringing home a wife. Weddings as such are not ritualized.

[x] Also Russian influence may have favored their emergence. In the context of colonization, Russification and christianization, shamans were criticized, bards were not. Among the Kazakhs in Central Asia, the word *baksy* refers to the shaman as well as bard, and there are many overlappings between the activities, the techniques, etc. of the two. Both make use of the musical instrument *qomus* in their respective rituals.

[xi] Their legitimacy as ritual leaders derives directly from their position as clan elders and not from personal qualifications. They are not sanctioned in correlation with the symbolic efficacy of the rituals.

[xii] This is the topic of a previous paper (Hamayon 1993).

[xiii] The name for bard is derived from the term for epic: *üligershin*.

[xiv] Obviously the tales recounted on the eve of the hunt in hunting societies also played a role in the emergence of epics.

xv I would like to suggest that speaking of a mutual implication of epic and milk may be a way of asserting a mutual implication between extensive pastoral nomadism and a type of clan organization characterized by an ideological emphasis on patrilineality and patrifocality, insofar as these social options require the glorification of martial values. Of course, this is only a part of an explanation.

xvi On the whole, the post-Soviet intellectual elite is the heir of the Soviet intelligentsia. Previously dissident trends remain marginalized.

xvii It was first published in Cyrillic transcription by Zhamcarano in 1930, then adapted to contemporary Buryat and published along with its Russian translation by Khomonov in 1961.

xviii As a commemoration it fully conforms to Soviet stereotypes.

xix See bibliographical references at the end of this and previous papers.

xx At the beginning of the Soviet regime, Buryat tribes and territories were brought together for the first time; they were granted an autonomous republic of their own in 1923. Created as a component of the multi-ethnic Soviet state, it was named Buryat-Mongolia. However, this was a short-lived situation: in 1937, at the end of a decade that was marked by compulsive Russification and purges against presumed nationalisms, the Buryat territories were dismantled and the size of the autonomous republic sharply reduced. After the war, in 1958, it was renamed Buryatia instead of Buryat-Mongolia. The reunification of the dismantled territories of Ust'-Orda and Aga with the Republic of Buryatia may have been a reason for the government's initial decision. And the celebration of the Buryats' most famous epic hero may have been aimed at obtaining the support of the Buryat minority in order to better assert land rights and claims. Significantly, the dismemberment of the Buryat territories achieved in 1937 was declared illegal by the Supreme Soviet of the Republic in June 1993 (Stroganova 1999: 120, n. 30).

xxi Namely gold, molybdenum, graphite, bauxite, asbestos etc. (Dugarov in *Kraj Gêsêra* 1995: 5). Tracks of lava are identified with the ruins of the castle of the fiercest enemy of Geser (ib.: 17). An independent ecological fund 'Akhalar' was created by the lama Fedor Samaev also in the beginning of the 1990s; its aim was also to transform some territories of Oka and Tunka into a parcel of World Heritage (Zhukovskaya 1997: 11). I have no idea about the possible initial connection between the two projects.

xxii Such interpretations of the landscape were already mentioned at the end of the 19th century.

xxiii The epic of Geser was the topic of Khundaeva's Doctoral dissertation and her two books published in 1999.

xxiv Part of this information comes from Isabelle Charleux (CNRS, Paris), another part from Elizaveta Khundaeva (the Buryat Institute of Social Sciences, Ulan-Ude). I express my thanks to both of them.

xxv In her paper, Stroganova insists that millenarist ideas were found before in this area, and she mentions that similar events had been recorded by Vampilon in 1919 and Zhigmidon in 1933 (Stroganova 1999: 114, 119).

xxvi Actually, to support the construction of a national figure for Buryatia, the official Buryat intelligentsia in charge of the process did not address the figure of Bukha Nojon, Lord Bull, the founder of the Ekhirit-Bulagat, the main native Buryat tribe, nor did they address Gengis Khan, the great unifying figure of the medieval Mongols and the emblematic reference of post-communist Mongolia. The fact that Mongolia has long been centralized and is an independent state is enough to account for the erection of this historical figure as the emblem of the nation-state. Let us note that through the millenium of the Ekhirit-Bulagat version, the epic of Geser was made more ancient than the emergence of Gengis Khan as a world's emperor in history (end 12th-13th century).

xxvii 'L'obstacle majeur dans la campagne contre le nationalisme culturel bouriato-mongol pendant l'après-guerre n'était pas cependant un écrivain ou un poète vivant mais le héros légendaire des Mongols, "Geser" ' (Kolarz 1955: 163).

xxviii Alexander the Great is another ideal figure in Central Asiatic narrative traditions; this borrowed figure is associated with the propagation of Islam in Central Asia (see Aubin & Hamayon 2002).

xxix He is the leader of the campaigns aimed at propagating Buddhism in 'all ten directions'.

xxx While his feats were 'historicized' (assigned a place in space and time), his figure was kept mythical: on banners and posters he is dressed in full armour, brandishing a weapon, riding a winged steed jumping over clouds.

xxxi In addition, Russian orthodox Christianity has long been imbued with messianist ideas.

xxxii The events that occur in the sky and provoke the hero's coming to the earth can be analyzed as a version of the struggle between elder and younger. Geser is the heavenly elder's second son. More generally, a younger's position seems to be characteristic of messianic figures in a number of cultures (see Trigano 1997: 17, Hamayon 2000: 240-243).

EPIC AS ARENA –
MODELS OF STATEHOOD AND THE KYRGYZ MANAS EPIC

Nienke van der Heide

Introduction
Although few people have ever heard of the Kyrgyz Manas epic, many Kyrgyz think the epic is famous all over the world and widely recognized as one of the highest achievements of mankind in the realm of story-telling. Moreover, among the *Manaschi*, the tellers of the Manas epic, there is a wide-spread belief that the Manas is the last epic in the world to be recited orally: they do not know of epics outside the former Soviet Union. But then, conversely, who knows about the Manas epic outside of Kyrgyzstan? This mutual ignorance merely shows that the former Soviet Union and the 'capitalist countries' have been living in almost complete isolation from each other, with gossip, rumors, and prejudices filling in the gap of actual contact and exchange of information.

The epic
The Manas epic is an ancient epic, recited in Kyrgyz, a Turkic language spoken mainly by ethnic Kyrgyz in Kyrgyzstan. This republic was a part of the Soviet Union and is bordered by China, Kazakhstan, Uzbekistan, and Tajikistan. The population of the republic is multi-ethnic; its ethnic composition has undergone major changes since independence in 1991 as a large proportion of the Russophone (Russian, Ukrainian, German, Belorussian, etc.) population has left the country for economically more prosperous places, such as Germany, Israel, North America, and Russia.

Since *perestroika*, the state language of Kyrgyzstan is Kyrgyz. However, the official policy to replace Russian as a language of public communication among the people of the republic has been a failure. People from ethnic groups other than Kyrgyz often look down on Kyrgyz (an 'uncivilized' language) and prefer Russian in official settings, as do many Kyrgyz. The Manas epic functions as an arena for fighting out these issues. But let me first introduce the historical, literary and ethnographical background of the epic.

The Manas epic recounts about the hero Manas, his birth, childhood years, his heroic actions, his feasts and his death. Manas was a Khan who managed to gather the forty Kyrgyz tribes and lead them back to their homeland that they had been driven out of by Kalmyks. When peace was restored, Manas decided to fight the other big enemy, the Chinese, and organized what is called the Great Campaign. Together with his forty *choro*s (knights) he invaded Beijing, but there they were defeated. Manas was fatally wounded but he managed to return home, to his wife, before he died. Manas' wife fled to Samarkhand with their son, Semetei. The second part of the epic tells of the life and deeds of Semetei, the third part of the adventures of Semetei's son Seitek.

The Manas epic is full of elaborate descriptions of fighting scenes, of horses, of feasts where sheep are slaughtered, of supernatural events such as foretelling dreams, of the main characters' magical skills, of visits of angels, of laments. It is recited by *manaschis*, bards who have specialized in telling the tale. Each *manaschi* will develop his or her own style of reciting in a slightly melodic form with a strict rhythm. Some of them recite on the accompaniment of musical instruments, many others claim this is not allowed. The epic is presented in the form of verse; usually the end of the lines rhyme, and alliteration is used extensively. One of the main characteristics of the Kyrgyz language is vowel harmony which means words can only have vowels from matching pairs. This rule determines the sound of the numerous suffixes, which makes the language perfectly fit for long and melodic recitals. Moreover, many words in Kyrgyz start with a 'k' which makes alliteration easy; the extensive use of gerunds makes end-rhyme easy. Altogether, a translation of the epic into a non-Turkic language inevitably means the loss of its poetic effects: either the alliteration and rhythm are lost or the use of plain daily language of the epic is turned into artificial use of archaic words. As is the case with most epics, the text of the Manas epic is not fixed. In fact, improvisation by individual *manaschis* is even an official part of reciting and serves as a way to judge their competence.

In Kyrgyzstan, the Manas is referred to as an 'epos', the Russian word for epic. However, before Russian presence made itself felt, Kyrgyz referred to the Manas as *jomok* (tale, folk tale) and a *Manaschi* was a *jomokchi*, and therefore it could be argued that the term *epos* is closely related to notions of ethnocentrism and cultural imperialism. Be that as it may, the use of the word *epos* is presently not under discussion in Kyrgyzstan; it has been adapted and internalized in the literary classification of Kyrgyz reciters and audience alike.

In 1995, the thousand-year existence of the epic was celebrated in nationwide festivities (cf. Hamayon, supra; Abydalek 1995). 'One thousand' is obviously a symbolic number; even the official brochure of the festivities explains that opinions differ on the exact date of birth of the epic. Some Manas scholars date it back to the 6th century (during the time of the Great Kyrgyz state in Siberia), others to the 11th (a second golden age of the Kyrgyz) or the 17th (during the struggles between the Kyrgyz and the Oirat-Kalmyk), and the *manaschi* Kaba Atabekov even claims it is five thousand years old. The founding myth of the epic is based on the story of Manas' musical knight who composed a mourning song after Manas' death, and over time this song grew into the enormous epic it is today. The version of one of the latest *manaschis* has half a million lines in writing, and in every book or article on the Manas one can read that that is twenty times longer than the Odyssey and the Iliad taken together.

As is the case of the figure of King Arthur, there has been – and still is – a lot of discussion about the historic existence of Manas. In a 15th-century Tajik text, *Madzmu at-Tavarig*, Manas is mentioned as a historic figure, but many scholars take this merely as an indication that the epic was very popular in those days, and prefer to see Manas as a compilation of a number of historical figures, turned into a mythical hero. *Manaschis*, however, have a different approach of verifying the existence of Manas. They do not turn to ancient written records but, instead, rely on their own personal experience: they see their encounters with the Spirit of Manas in the form of dreams, visions and unexplainable events as evidence that Manas really exists.

The profession of *manaschi* has many resemblances to that of a shaman. Just like shamans, *Manaschis* are called to their profession by a dream or a vision. Usually around the age of twelve, young boys (and some girls) dream of a *yurta* (a round felt tent) into which they are invited by the wife of Manas. They are offered something white to drink (milk or *kymyz*) and are asked by the epic's main characters to start reciting. From that moment on they will feel both the urge and the ability to recite. However, some youngsters are hesitant to become a *manaschi*; too shy to perform or too afraid of the spiritual forces that are involved in telling the epic, they may refuse to recite – but then they will fall ill time and again until they give in to their vocation.

The dreams don't stop from coming after the calling dream. Talantaaly, a 29-year old beginning *manaschi*, who became a close friend of mine, often recites in his dreams. I witnessed this twice when I stayed with him and his family. As we were all asleep on the blankets and pillows laid out in the living room, suddenly Talant burst into chant. We woke up while Talant himself remained sound asleep and kept on reciting for half an hour, with a melody and words even more beautiful than when he recites awake. Eventually he fell silent after a funny, gurgling sound and we went back to sleep. In the morning, Talant told us of his dream and his wife told him that this was exactly what he had recited about. Another time he dreamt about the funeral feast of Manas, an episode never performed before in public. He recited this in a *Manaschi* competition, but the jury was so appalled by the cheek of this young man to recite an episode that had never been heard before that he ended up losing the contest.

Manaschis receive their inspiration and knowledge of the epic through recurrent dreams and visions. When they recite they usually get into a kind of trance and see the story happening in front of their eyes, as in a movie. The epic and art of recital is of course also learnt by practice and guidance from older *manaschis*, but as the belief in inspiration by the Spirit of Manas himself is so strong, training is hardly talked about. There are also *manaschis* who are not dream-inspired; they learn parts from books by heart, and although the ability of these people to recite extensive parts by heart is admired by the audience, the 'Real *Manaschis*' see them as lesser artists.

The question whether the Manas epic is dying out is a topic of many discussions. Documentaries and articles called *'The last manaschi'* (always about different 'last' *manaschis*) keep popping up, and many Manas scholars inside and outside Kyrgyzstan claim that it is disappearing indeed. It is tempting to assume that the Manas epic is always on the verge of dying out because folklore is always seen as dying out and disappearing – and this is what makes it attractive and worth collecting.

The *manaschis* I met claimed that the epic will be recited as long as the Spirit of Manas calls people to recite. The supernatural is a driving force behind Manas recital for reciters as well as audience, a force more important than nationalistic ideas or entertainment. Contrary to what is suggested by several contributors to this volume, I suggest we take tellers' claims seriously.

Epic as arena
As I indicated in my introduction, the Manas epic functions as an arena where the important issues of ethnicity and statehood in Kyrgyzstan are fought out today. The epic may have had this function in centuries past, but it surely did in Soviet times, when every cultural expression was subject to close ideological examination (cf. Brubaker 1996; Bremmer 1997; Tishkov 1997).

As the epic describes how Manas became Khan with many wives and subjects, the main protagonist was regarded as a suspect representative of the old feudal order and the epic as a superstructural form of feudal art. Protectors of the epic working in the Kyrgyz Academy of Sciences have argued that Manas was chosen by his people because of his courage and that he always acted in close consultation with knights and elders; therefore his rule does not reflect the feudal order but rather the historic period of 'military democracy'. With this ideological dilemma explicitly solved, there was another problem to be dealt with: the ambivalent attitude of the Communist Party towards folklore. On the one hand, folklore was seen as a backward relic of pre-socialist days with the danger of evoking nationalistic sentiments. We all have seen examples of how folklore could be made a major catalyst in uniting an ethnic group, and the Soviet leaders were clearly afraid of this. On the other hand, however, folklore became a central focus of the Soviet's 'Nationalities Policy'. Folklore festivals were organized to prove that in the Soviet Union there was no suppression of ethnic groups, as there was in capitalist and colonized countries; instead, ethnic groups had the right of self-determination and self-expression. Folklore festivals meant to show how in the Soviet Union the hundreds of ethnic groups lived peacefully together, and how the solidarity of the proletariat had overcome the ethnic divisions in the socialist state.

This ambivalent attitude haunted the fate of the Manas epic during Soviet times. On the one hand, the epic received a lot of attention and underwent a transformation from a purely oral epic to an epic that was both orally performed and written down. Moreover, it was the subject of research of many members of the Academy of Sciences. It is fascinating to see how much effort was put in explaining the magical elements of *manaschi*-hood in a materialistic and rational way: their dreams, for instance, were no longer seen as messages coming from the Other World but as psychological phenomena. It was also during Soviet times that the Manas epic was given the pompous labels that are still found in almost every article, book or brochure on the Manas today, such as 'Manas is a Treasure of World Art Heritage'. It is also worth mentioning that in World War II nationalistic sentiments were consciously raised with the use of folklore so as to mobilize people for the War; Kyrgyz regiments had tanks called Manas, and Kyrgyz soldiers used 'Manas!' as their battle cry. On the other hand, the epic was subject to repression as well. Written versions of the epic had to pass censorship, certain elements were changed, and the Russians were given a part in the epic. In this connection it is telling that in Soviet times the plans to celebrate the thousand-year existence of the epic were twice rejected. And at the time the *epos* was elevated to the status of an Important and Extraordinary Work of Art, the people in the street lost contact with the epic and forgot about it.

When the Soviet Union fell apart and Kyrgyzstan became an independent republic, the Manas epic became an important symbol of national unity. In search of a new ideology, president Akayev found in the Manas a non-religious historical text that was still so close to the Kyrgyz heart that it could be used as a new ideological point of reference. Streets all over the country were named after Manas; a stylized image of Manas on a horse was sprayed on all the kiosks in the capital; Coca Cola used it for its advertisements; numerous books about the Manas were published; special teaching programs were developed and used at all education levels – and Akayev published a book with the Seven Principles from the Manas that were to be the new ideological guidelines for the republic. At the climax of this propaganda offensive, the festivities of the Manas' thousand years of existence were organized.

In this way, the choice for the Manas epic expressed the paradox that underlies the models of statehood in Kyrgyzstan: the simultaneous existence of the ethnos and the demos model. In the ethnos model, Kyrgyzstan is the country of the Kyrgyz, and all other inhabitants are guests or immigrants. The demos model holds the idea that Kyrgyzstan belongs to all citizens of Kyrgyzstan, to all Kyrgyzstani. These models are the extremes between which the positions of the people in the republic of Kyrgyzstan fluctuate.

In the Seven Principles that president Akayev distilled from the Manas, the paradox becomes clear once again. Whereas the epic is quite clearly a Kyrgyz nationalistic epic, the Principles are so carefully defined that the other ethnic groups in the country are not excluded. One of them is 'patriotism', another 'national unity', and a third 'friendship between all peoples'. Against the background of the character of the epic itself, these Principles sound very artificial. It should remind us of the remark by one of the Conference's participants that epics are often violent stories about sex, drugs, and rock and roll: it is not very convenient to take such stories to be the basis for a state ideology.

Of course the tension between ethnos and demos can be found in every nation-state, but it is particularly strong in the states that were part of the Soviet

Union. In Kyrgyzstan, it plays a predominant role in political life, and therefore also in the two topics of my research: the language policy and the use of the Manas epic as a symbol of national unity. In the first ten years of Independence we have been able to detect a clear shift in the arena of the Manas epic; a concurrent shift can be found in the arena of language. Whereas in 1995 the Manas had reached its climax as a representation of the nation (the celebrations, posters, conferences, references in nearly every speech by president Akayev), in 2000 interest for the epic had faded. The Direktia responsible for Manas propaganda had been closed, thus bringing the Manas hausse to an end. In the arena of the language policy, the attempts to make Kyrgyz the major language in Kyrgyzstan was dealt a heavy blow when Russian was formally given the status of 'official language'. Thus, the government, or rather president Akayev and the people who pull his strings, made a shift from a more ethnos-oriented approach to statehood to a more demos-oriented approach.

The Manas *epos* is used in political conflicts, but then it is still a form of art, embedded in supernatural forces – and very much alive. Life for the *manaschis* is not easy, since there are very few ways in which they can make a living with their performances these days. But thanks to his passion and commitment to the Manas, the young *manaschi* Talantaaly whom I mentioned earlier, is managing slowly, step by step, to build up a career as a *manaschi*, finding the ways to give expression to his calling.

THE ADVENTURES OF 'THE EPIC OF SAMORI' IN 20TH-CENTURY MANDE ORAL TRADITION[i]

Jan Jansen

Introduction
Samori Toure (d. 1900) is a celebrated figure in the West African countries Mali and Guinea. In both written history and oral tradition he is lauded for founding an empire and fiercely resisting the French, who sought to colonize the region. Recently published anthologies of African epics (Johnson, Hale, and Belcher 1997; Kesteloot and Dieng 1997; Belcher 1999) even attest to the existence of an orally transmitted Samori epic in these countries. Despite these claims, however, I believe that a Samori epic does not yet exist... but it may be in the making.

The texts hitherto presented as the epic of Samori (in the abovementioned anthologies) are basically oral narratives that have been produced more or less in agreement with 'official' written history. They have, moreover, been performed in quite specific contexts. Hence, these texts may not be representative of the present-day oral traditions on Samori. I believe that if ever a Samori epic comes into being and takes the form of a standardized oral narrative, it might deal with issues different than those found in these texts. In this article, I will compare these texts – the ones presented in the abovementioned anthologies as the 'epic' of Samori – to some oral sketches about Samori which I recorded during two years of fieldwork conducted in southwestern Mali and northeastern Guinea.

Samori
With the invention of quinine and the subsequent conquest of malaria by the Europeans, the previously impenetrable interior of Africa was opened up to European occupation. The so-called 'partition of Africa' followed in the 1880s. This is not to say that the European occupation of Africa was systematic. Yves Person – who wrote the standard work on Samori (1968) – compared the future French West Africa to the American 'Wild West' (1977). It was a frontier region where ambitious French army officers, often outside of the formal control of their superiors, attempted to fulfill their dreams. The French occupation of present-day

Samori Toure in 1898

southwestern Mali was impeded by the fact that the region was part of a huge polity ruled by Samori, whose superior tactics would have made him victorious, Person argued, if he had had the same arms as the French.

The first setback Samori suffered was in the mid-1880s, when his empire crumbled because of the rise to power of Kenedougou (present-day south Mali), whose walled capital Sikasso he unsuccessfully besieged in 1887-1888. Samori had also, meanwhile, signed treaties with the French. Notwithstanding these treaties, however, after the French decided to penetrate and occupy the entire 'Soudan' in the late 1880s, Samori became their enemy, and he moved southward, to the present-day Ivory Coast. There he subjugated the population and established a second empire, this time as a 'foreign' ruler. By the mid-1890s, Samori had become France's principal enemy in West Africa. His persecution was of national interest, reported in French newspapers and magazines nation-wide. Samori was captured in 1898 and sent into exile to the island of Missanga (Gabon), where he died in 1900.

Samori's regime was violent; the 'collaboration' of local rulers was not voluntary. For example, the ruler of Kangaba, a politically and strategically important town south of Bamako, was forced to hand over some of his sons as hostages. When Kangaba fell to the French in 1887 – Samori had withdrawn his troops from the region – the sons were killed by Samori. Moreover, Samori built a strong fortress at Degela, a few kilometers north of Kangaba, in order to keep a close watch over his 'partner' (Bâh 1985: 172). Documents from the Malian National Archives (Koulouba, Bamako) and the National Colonial Archives (Aix-en-Provence, France) attest to the fact that many villages in the Kangaba area were burned down at least once, and that the villagers became refugees during the period 1885-1888 (cf. Person 1968), although they quickly resettled after the French occupied the area.

The epic of Samori in academic tradition
In spite of his oppressive regimes, Samori is intensely and often positively re-imagined in oral tradition. As discussed at the beginning, anthologies of African epics attest to a Samori epic, which, interestingly enough, is evaluated in various ways. Each anthology attributes a different prestige to it. Analyzing the epics of 'Afrique Noire', Kesteloot and Dieng include the epic of Samori among the five *épopées mandingues* (1997: 192-200). (The other four are the Sunjata epic, the Gabou epic, the Ségou epic, and the hunters' epics.) As an example of the Samori epic, they cite a few pages of an unpublished and un-dated text from Conakry,[ii] which deals with Samori's siege of Sikasso. As additional illustrations of Samori's fame, Kesteloot and Dieng mention playwrights who have written about Samori and announce the publication of a text by David Conrad.

Johnson, Hale and Belcher's anthology (1997) of oral epics from Africa presents twenty-five epics, nine of which have been classified as 'Mande'. Compared to Kesteloot and Dieng (who identify five Mande epics), Johnson,

Hale and Belcher have included more 'epics', such as the 'Fa Jigin' or 'Sarah'. The notion that there are important, although not yet (fully) recorded, story cycles about a particular hero seems to be their rationale for including unpublished or relatively short texts. However, they do not discuss the criteria they use when classifying an oral text as an 'epic.' The Samori text they have chosen to include in their anthology is the text from Conrad's unpublished volume (mentioned by Kesteloot and Dieng); other versions of the Samori epic are not referred to.

Belcher (1999) – one of the authors of the anthology mentioned above – is more critical concerning oral narratives such as the epic of Samori. According to Belcher, Samori, along with El Haji Umar Tal, is one of the two 'terrifying great men from the 19th century' (1999: 113). Belcher goes on to say (ib.: 114):

'In addition to the epics of these heroes, a wealth of localized historical narrative lends iself easily to epic singing in the hands of *jalilu* [bards or *griots*]. As recording, rather than textual publication, becomes more widespread, a great deal more material from this fertile homeland will become available.'

Although Belcher accepts the existence of an epic of Samori, he touches upon one reason to assess the texts presented as African epics critically: 'epics' are constructed by those who manage the means of communication.[iii] I would like to include and emphasize the role of the researcher – who is also a manager of the means of communication – in this 'upgrading' of (African) oral narratives to 'epics'.[iv]

In the 1960s, Ruth Finnegan (incorrectly) argued that there was no epic in Africa. Her claim was refuted a decade later by, amongst others, Isodore Okpewho and John Johnson. These researchers collected and published texts of long narratives, and undermined the Homeric hegemony in epical standards by establishing revised literary standards for 'epics', thus proving that the epic exists in Africa. But a word of warning. A fascination for a particular oral tradition, in combination with either a lack of training or a modest appreciation of the criteria used in the literary sciences, may easily inspire researchers to see an 'epic' in a long oral narrative.[v]

The published oral narratives about Samori have certainly been molded by Mande literary models to represent warfare, hunting, gender relationships, and labor differentiation. Samori's younger brother, army leader Kèmè Brèman, is an important figure in many of these narratives. For example, the well-known praise song (*fasa*) on Samori is entitled 'Kèmè Brèman fasa'. Hence, the texts presented in these anthologies may convince us that an 'epic' of Samori exists.[vi]

Regarding the oral traditions about Samori, I believe that the process of categorizing more or less standardized texts on wars and conflicts as the epic of Samori is questionable. Although the two texts of the 'epic' of Samori (presented in two of the anthologies) both deal with events that allegedly occurred during Samori's siege of Sikasso, each 'epic' narrates a completely different event. One would expect that *the* epic of Samori would deal with a unique event or set of events, with different versions of the epic classifiable as variants. By adding some stories collected during my fieldwork to these two texts, I want to illustrate that the narrative tradition on Samori – interesting though it is – must not (yet) be labeled an epic.

Samori in Mande oral tradition: some examples
Local lore about Samori depicts what he did to the local population and how he personally communicated with them. For example, when I once passed through[vii] the village of Nafadji (northeast of Siby), a man whom I greeted said that his village was famous because Samori had once spent a night there. This 'fact' may have been inspired by another village of the same name in the Mande hills, where Samori defeated a French army in 1886.

Often the events concerning Samori are more 'narrative' and are not recounted as simple historical 'facts'. For example, Seydou Diabate from Kela, a village famous for its *griots*, told me in 1996 that Samori appeared one evening at the *tata* (dried mud fortress wall) of Kela, intent upon destroying the village.[viii] Samori was so impressed by the brilliant replies to his threats, however, that he decided to spare Kela. Nevertheless, this story, which was told to me by a young *griot*, must be apocryphal. Despite the reference to verbal skill and the evident esteem for the spoken word – verbal artistry is much appreciated by the Mande people – contemporary French documents indicate that Kela was an agricultural hamlet of about a hundred people until the 1880s, without a *tata* and without *griots*.

The following story, told to me by Daouda Nambala Keita from Narena on 3 October 1996, sheds a different light on Samori's relationship with *griots*:

'Samori had invited the Keita [the ruling group in Narena] to partake in the drinking of *dègè* [porridge] with him. A refusal was tantamount to a declaration of war, so a delegation was selected. They set off to fulfill their commission accordingly. When it was their turn to drink the *dègè*, a *griotte* [female *griot*] among the delegation suddenly started to sing that they [the people of Narena] had never been subjugated by anyone. One of the delegates then said that they had forgotten their commission. Samori asked: 'Where are you from?' 'From Narena,' the delegate replied. 'Isn't that over there, in the hills?' Samori wanted to know. 'Yes,' the delegate replied. 'So close to here,' Samori said, 'and your commission already forgotten! Go back to Narena and ask about it.' The delegation then returned to Narena and Samori ordered to kill the *griotte*.'

This is a story of an agreement between two 'gentlemen' who considered the intervention by the *griot(te)* as an impediment, although male and female *griots* have been exercising diplomatic functions in Mande for centuries.

Again, the story does not refer to an actual historical event. Narena was – just like the other villages in the region – demolished by Samori's armies sometime between 1885 and 1887. (When Samori withdrew his armies from the left bank of the river Niger, he applied the *'terre brûlée'* strategy.) When I told Daouda – himself a member of the local ruling Keita clan – this, he was astonished: 'That is not what we recount about Samori.'

But what kind of stories do people tell about Samori? I once suggested to M. Keita – a lawyer from Bamako who was at the time a visiting scholar in Leiden – that research on the oral tradition about Samori would be interesting. He, however, objected and said that the only stories collected would deal with babies taken from their mothers and pounded to death in mortars, and the construction of defense walls using living humans as building material. These are indeed stories that I have heard quite often. In fact, I recorded old Bala Kante from Farabako, where I conducted half a year of fieldwork, recounting these stories.[ix] Bala was a well-informed blacksmith who often talked to me about blacksmithing technologies and other subjects from the past. His tale about Samori illustrates some of the methodological problems related to the 'epic' of Samori.[x]

'... In the meantime, the French arrived. They made a nice city of Dakar. You saw cars passing your compound, and the paved roads which connected the compounds, with vehicles being driven around everywhere. They [the French] constructed a very decent Dakar, along the sea.

After leaving Dakar, Jolo [the ancestor of the Wolof, the dominant ethnic group in present-day Senegal] met Samori and told him that he had a huge army. Samori replied that he too had a huge army, and that since he was an army leader (*kèlètigi*), they weren't the same; if he [Jolo] was a benefactor (*jigitomògò*), he would allow him to pass. Thus, Jola and his men passed.

In some of the villages that he passed through, Samori made walls of the inhabitants. He forced them to dig holes and to put their feet into the holes. He also ordered women to be imprisoned and forced them to pound their children in mortars. Samori did that all.

Samori went to Cèba of Sikasso. He [who?-JJ] told him that something bigger than him was going to come after him. He said that this must not happen.[xi] Then Samori left, saying that this thing that would happen would be his problem. Biton also arrived at Cèba's place and informed him of his intention to attack Samori. Cèba replied: 'Something will come that won't save Samori. But that is far away in the future!' A year passed, and the French arrived the following year.

Samori went to the French and made sneaky proposals to them. He told them that he had proposed an alliance with Cèba who refused, saying that no living creature could beat him. 'Really?' 'Yes.' Someone went to Cèba and told him this. Cèba confirmed that he had an army. The French also had an army. Samori sent the French a message. He wrote: 'You may have an army. Well, I am also the leader of an army. But first catch the scum who told you those lies.' So they went to Sikasso, but failed to take the fortress (*jin*) there.

The French encountered Samori on the road: 'It is you who put us in conflict with Cèba – God's will is your will[xii] – you put us in conflict with Cèba of Sikasso.' They had a long discussion. Samori destroyed all the villages he passed. In the end, his army was starving. But again, Samori and his army went to Sikasso despite that fact that Samori knew, that acting this way, he risked being captured by the French.

They argued that he himself was partially responsible for his own arrest, because he had gone *politiki*.[xiii] *Politiki* is a bad thing. They consulted each other. Samori's army was in trouble; his troops were starving and there was a famine.

There was a huge manioc field. At sunrise Samori went there, seeking refuge. The ancestor of the Wolofs informed the French that Samori had fled into the manioc field. He went to the French to tell them. They said it was okay. Then they sent two guardians to search for Samori. When they found him, he said: 'Ah, hunger ruined me.'[xiv] 'Really?' 'Yes.' 'That's it; when you think hunger is killing you, that is only the beginning!'

The French recorded his voice. He was put in chains and at the moment of his arrest, he said: 'Ha-an-an-an-an, selfish people!' His voice was recorded and taken with them. That was the way he was arrested. The people of Mande made a song of it: 'Samori was caught in a manioc field / This year things happened in the absence of certain people / A manioc field ...,' that is the way the song goes. They took him to 'an island in the French sea' (*Faransi kògòji kan*).[xv] I don't know whether it still exists. They built a train, and put on it the thing on which they had recorded his voice. Every Sunday the French gathered together in huge crowds to listen to Samori's voice. When everyone had arrived, they put 'it' (*a*) in the machine. The train howled: 'Ha-an-an-an-an, selfish people!' – the words of his arrest. His words are in France, over the sea, if they haven't destroyed that train.[xvi] It is there.'

This is neither an epic, nor a well-narrated or historically accurate story, but it *is* a fascinating text with some interesting historical layers. The historicity of 'facts' such as walls being constructed from living humans and mothers pounding their babies to death in mortars must be doubted. People who tell such stories locate them in their own particular regions or villages. Moreover, the French – who documented Samori's cruel and violent deeds extensively – did not record these types of atrocities.

With regard to Samori and his adversary Cèba, they were indeed contemporaries, and Samori did lay siege to Sikasso in the 1880s. However, Samori was captured to the south of Sikasso in 1898, the same year Sikasso fell to the French. Moreover, Biton Kulibali was a famous 18th-century king of Ségou (a region 250 km. east of Bamako), the most powerful polity in the area that is now present-day Mali. The joint appearance by Biton, Cèba, and Samori – three heroes of different ethnic and temporal origins – in this oral narrative may be evidence of an ongoing process of nation-formation in present-day Mali.

Themes that seem bizarre at first, appear to be references to major issues in Mande society. I have already mentioned *griots* and the high status of the spoken word in Mande culture. It thus makes a certain kind of sense that the French are perceived as wanting to preserve Samori's voice.[xvii] The recording of Samori's voice is paired with the construction of a train, both major technological achievements. The train, moreover, is a vehicle that appeals to people's imagination.[xviii] The reference to the French listening to Samori on Sunday is an allusion to the seven-day week that had been introduced by the French.[xix] Could the fact that on Sundays the French go to church and listen to a priest – and this is mere speculation on my part – be the reason why Samori's message appears to be so 'Christian' (i.e., Samori accuses the French of being selfish, an accusation often made in Africa, suggesting the whites are unwilling to share their richesses with the Africans)?

The manioc field is an allusion to a potential wartime scenario. At the time, the Maninka, an agricultural people, used to grow millet and maize, manioc being an additional crop. Manioc, however, is also the first crop that refugees grow, since it is easy to cultivate, has a relatively short growing cycle, and can be grown in the middle of the bush. Thus, it is not a coincidence that Samori's capture is imagined to have taken place in a manioc field. The scenario represents the hardship people suffered during times of war and famine.

Bala Kante's account cannot be used to reconstruct the past. Moreover, it features Samori himself; the usual emphasis on Kèmè Brehman is absent. Bala Kante's tale does not resemble the texts presented as the 'epic' of Samori in the anthologies. (Both these texts feature events on the battlefield, thus meeting the Homeric epical standard, as well as the criteria for Mande epics such as the Sunjata and Ségou.) Bala Kante's story, however, does reveal the impact of the French upon daily life in Mande society. It is a story about modernity and its inevitability. That is why, I believe, the ancestor of the Wolof has been made responsible for Samori's treason. Living along the Atlantic coast, the Wolof surely were 'impregnated' by the French way of life earlier and more intensely than the Maninka.

Some reflections
Samori's empire was, from the French perspective, a frontier zone where French colonial administrators attempted to realize their personal ambitions and dreams; hence, Person's metaphoric comparison to the Wild West. This same metaphor may be useful with regard to understanding the epic of Samori. I believe that many academics use oral narratives about Samori to demonstrate the greatness of West African oral tradition in order to realize their own personal ambitions and dreams, e.g., professional distinction, and career advance-

ment. These scholars thus construct their own epic adventures. However, as we have seen, oral traditions about Samori are not limited to the epic, the genre hitherto used to present Samori's oral heritage to academic audiences. Here too, academics are in a frontier zone in which things are in flux, in the process of creation. One should not create too many *a priori* epics in the frontier zone which is African oral tradition studies. Although sketchy and not the result of systematic investigation (which is, as we have all been taught, a prerequisite for sound scientific research), the material I have presented on Samori gives me reason to think that more data collection on this topic will certainly contribute to a better understanding of the dynamics and variety of Mande oral tradition.

APPENDIX

Alu ye t'o dò, o tuma tubabu sògòra yen de fòlò ma. A ye Dakara baara. An sigilen lu kònò, mòbili bè tèmè e la lu kuntò. An sigilen lu kònò, mòbili gutòròma be tèmè lu kuntò. A ye o baara, ka ko bèè kè ka na kògòji ye.

Jolo, ka bò yen ka na, a ni Samuru waara nyògòn ye: ko ale min ye min di, ale ka jama ka ca. Samuru ko k'ale ka jama ka ca. Ko bali ale ye kèlètigi ye, a ko ne ni ile tè kelen di. Nin ya jigitomògò tò di ko ale ka tanbe. O n'a ya mògòlu tagara. A mana se yòrò dòlu, a bè hadamaden dugu sen ka waa, ka hadamaden dò nyògòn nò k'u sen jòsò k'o kè kòlòkò ye. Olu bè bò yen, a bè taga hadamaden ma. A mana hadamaden mina, o tuma a bè muso, muso bila o k'a den susu kòlòn kònò, a b'o kè. Samuru tun b'o kè.

Sikaso Cèba, a tagara o diya. O ko, ko fèn ye kòfè ka na, k'o ka bon ile fana ta ye. A k'o kana na dè. A dèsèra o la. Samuru ka jèn ka taga. Ko bali fèn dò natò ye, ko i la fèn y'o ye dè. Cèba fana, Sikaso Bitòn nara ka w'a yira Cèba la k'ole b'a fè ko ka Samuru kèlè. Ayiwa, ko fèn ye kò, ko Samuru kèlèbaga le nato ye. K'o ka jan dè! K'o san dama bila, o san filanan, tubabuw k'i kunbò.

A waala mafaniyafòli kè, ka waa a yira tubabulu la k'ale waalen ko Sikaso Cèba bannen. Ko nimafèn si tè s'a la. Ko ahan? Ko uhun. Mògò ye waa o fò Cèba ye. Cèba ko ale ye kèlètigi ye. Tubabulu ye kèlètigi ye. A b'a sèbèn. A y'a sèbèn k'a ban: ko ni e ye faama ye, n fana ye faama ye. Ko bali nafigi min waala fò la, a k'i bè o mina. A tagara o le tò o tuma, ka waa dèsè Sikaso jin ma.

A ye i muru ka na, ka na se Samuru ma. Ko Samuru ko ile ye ne ni Cèba bila nyògòn na. Ala sago i sago. Ko Sikaso Cèba an nò bila nyògòn na. Alu ye o kuma fò, k'o yira nyògòn na. Samuru a mana se dugu min tò, a b'o ti, a mana se dugu min tò, a b'o ti. Bòn, kòngò nara ka n'a ka kèlè minè. Kèlè minèna, ko Sikaso, alu selen yen, ko bali fèn min nanen nin di, ko tubabuw b'ale minè nin sen in.

Ò ko n'u bè ile minta, i fana nò y'a di, pasèkè i waalen politiki k'alu ni nyògòn cè. Politiki dun man nyi. Ali waara ka waa nyògòn ye. Ko Samuru a ya kèlè bara tinyè, a bara kònònafili. Kòngò kèlen i k'a k'a fan haliki.

Banankuforo belebele lalen, a banankuforo Samuru solita ka taga. Samuru solilen ka waa bananku fè dò. Wòlòfòlu bènba, o waara yira hali bi tubabu la ko Samuru ye banankufè rò. A tagara ka waa o fò. Ko nin tèbasi ye. A nara wuruuuu ka garadi cè fila bila ka n'a kama. A manen a kama. Aa, ko, yo, ko kòngò bara ne haliki. Ko òhòn. Ko basi tè! Ni kòngò na e haliki, a k'a ma se fòlò. A y'a kan ta. A nara ka na nègè k'a kan. Samuru minètuma, a ko ko han-an-an-an-an-an nyangow. Alu y'o kan ta ka taga o di bolo. Samuru wara ka na minta. A minèlen Mandekalu y'o le la la donkili tò. Ko Samuru minènen banankufè dò. Ko nyinan ta tè kè bèè nyèna. Ko banankufè o, k'a tògò don o donkili tò. Ko tanbe ka taga ko waa a ka nin ta Faransi kògòji kan. U nò na k'a dabila sisan, o ko, ali waara ka waa tèrèn do dila. O kurun dilanen o tuma ka kan bila o la. Dumansi ni dumansi tubabu bè yen falen ka n'i lajè a kan bolo. A mana na o tuma, alu bè a bila mansin na. A bè karoon ko han-an-an-an-an nyangow, o y'a minètuma ye. O kan bè fansi, kògòji n'alu nò ma k'a tèrèn tinyè. O bè yen.

NOTES

[i] Research for the period 1999-2002 has been financed by the Royal Netherlands Academy of Arts and Sciences (KNAW). During the period 1988-2000, I have conducted more than two years of fieldwork on several topics related to oral tradition in the region south of Mali's capital Bamako (in Kela, Kangaba, Narena, Siby, and the Monts Manding). This area is known as the Mande heartland. Mande, or the Manding, was originally the region around Kangaba, the presumed capital of the famous medieval Mali empire founded by Sunjata. Nowadays, the term is used to describe a much broader area, culturally as well as geographically. As Belcher writes: 'The Manden (or Mande) is a space, in some way perhaps a time, and for many, an idea. The space is roughly defined by the headwaters of the Niger and its affluents, and lies in western Mali and eastern Guinea; it is occupied by the Malinke, for whom it is a symbolic heartland from which the more widespread branches of their people have departed [or claim to have departed-eds.] at various times to take on different names (Mandinka, Dyula, Konyaka, and others). As a time, the Manden looks back to its period of unification and glory under the emperor Sunjata. [...] To speak of the Manden is, of necessity, to evoke the time and space of Sunjata's rule: thus, the Manden is also an idea spread across Africa' (1999: 89).

[ii] Kesteloot and Dieng present this text as a Bamana epic, although it was recorded in Kissidougou (northern Guinea), a region dominated by the Maninka (Malinké). I suppose that this is a typo.

[iii] As Newton states: 'Most students and teachers outside Mali have experienced Mande epics only in printed form. [...] The vast majority of Malians experience these epics aurally, not as live performances, but as audio cassettes, played on local and national radio stations or on their own cassette players' (1999: 313).

[iv] The following anecdote may illustrate this process. When I asked Stephen Belcher to write an introduction for a book – provisionally titled *L'Epopée de Nankoman* – that I had co-edited with the Malian historian Seydou Camara, Belcher convinced us that the versions of the Nankoman narrative that we had prepared for publication were only variations of a 'local' family history, not an epic. Accordingly, the book was published as *La Geste de Nankoman-Textes sur la foundation de Naréna* (Leiden: Research School CNWS, 1999). Trained as historians, Camara and I had clearly not been very critical in elaborating epical criteria before we pronounced Nankoman an 'epic'; we just liked the term 'epic'. I suggest that this is often the case with historians who work on African oral tradition.

[v] See previous note. Texts presented as West African epics often give insight into groups other than non-African academics and publishers who have an interest in the existence of these epics. These groups include (African) audio cassette sellers in need of an attractive commercial product

and local scholars. A good example of this complexity is the Musadu 'epic' (in Johnson *et al.* 1997: 80ff), which is illustrated by a narrative told by a history professor at the University of Kankan in North Guinea. Another text of this epic (Geysbeek and Kamara 1991) is narrated by a retired schoolteacher. Since these storytellers are all literate men, the evidence for the existence of a narrative tradition on Musadu is not convincing, and is in no way comparable to the texts used in the 1970s as proof of the existence of epics in Africa (the Sunjata epic, the Ségou epic, and the Mwindo epic).

[vi] An important factor in the distribution of knowledge about African epics must be attributed to Indiana University Press, publishers of almost all the literature in English on African epics (works by Johnson, Hale, Belcher), as well as several texts of African epics.

[vii] My usual mode of transportation is a bicycle.

[viii] Unfortunately, I did not record this anecdote in my diary, hence, the absence of detail. I doubt if the story was about Samori, or even about one of his officers.

[ix] I am privileged to have worked with Bala Kante. When I read the villagers of Farabako my transcription of the Sunjata epic (Jan Jansen, Esger Duintjer, and Boubacar Tamboura, *L'Epopée de Sunjara, d'après Lansine Diabate de Kela [Mali]* [Leiden: Research School CNWS, 1995]), Bala was very happy to have found a young man who was still interested in their traditions. He often complained about the lack of attention to the past shown by the local young.

[x] I am much indebted to Muntaga Jarra (DNAFLA, Bamako) for help with the preliminary transcription and translation of the Bala Kante interviews. We are currently at work on the publication of a selection of these interviews. Unfortunately, I have not been able to consult with Mr. Jarra about the minor changes I have made in both the Maninka text and the translation included here. The Maninka transcription has been appended to this article.

[xi] Tentative translation by JJ.

[xii] Often used expression which has no particular significance to the story.

[xiii] Translated by M. Jarra as 'escroquerie'.

[xiv] Jarra gives this translation, which I do not understand, but which was probably inspired by the rest of the narrative: 'Aa, egoïstes, la faim m'a ruiné.'

[xv] The literal translation of this phrase is 'on the French se'.

[xvi] Tentative translation by JJ.

[xvii] Adversaries are often highly esteemed in Mande oral tradition. For example, Kante blacksmiths, who are descendants of Sunjata's adversary Sumaoro, are respected members of society. Hitler, too, is often appreciated as the man who almost defeated De Gaulle, though this appreciation is certainly loaded with anti-colonial bias.

[xviii] Bala Kante, a blacksmith, often expressed to me his admiration for the railroads; he thought the iron was strong and durable.

[xix] In this region, a five-day week was the norm, although a seven-day week was known from Islam, a religion that had long been present in the region.

THE NARRATION OF THE SUNJATA EPIC
AS A GENDERED ACTIVITY

Marloes Janson

Introduction

Transmission is crucial for the existence of oral epics. Hence, attention should be paid to who is allowed to narrate epic and in which contexts. In this article I will focus on the transmission by bards of the Sunjata epic, the most famous epic of West Africa (see Bulman, this volume). In the past decade, scholars working on the West African Mande[i] cultures started to address the question as to whether women are able to narrate the Sunjata epic (e.g. Durán 1995a; Jansen 1996; Johnson et al. 1997: 114-123; Hale 1998: 226-232; Belcher 1999: 91). However the ethnographic data presented in their discussions are scarce.

This article attempts to redefine the issue of epic narration by women, by providing ethnographic data collected during my field research conducted among Mandinka bards in eastern Gambia between 1996 and 2001[ii] as well as by demonstrating that the concept of gender has hitherto been used too rigidly in the debate on women's participation in the domain of the epic. I will argue that narrating the epic of Sunjata is not so much a question of gender, as is often assumed in the literature, but rather a question of age. In old age the axes of male and female intersect, and gender differences tend to dissolve. It will appear that although the public performance of the epic seems delimited to men, women may recount the epic in less formal contexts. Furthermore, I will show that because of socio-political changes in Mandinka society and beyond, the cultural appreciation of modes of transmission (the song mode versus the speech mode) has become highly relevant in the discussion about women's participation in the epic tradition.

It has been generally assumed that there is a division of tasks between male bards (*jalikeolu*; griot men) and female bards (*jalimusoolu*; griot women),[iii] whereby the former narrate oral traditions and play musical instruments and the latter sing. Most authors follow the format outlined by Johnson (1986: 25):

'The wife will often sing the songs in her husband's epics. Also popular is the musician who accompanies his wife's singing. A full ensemble ... includes a mastersinger who only narrates, a woman who sings praise-poems and songs, a female chorus, a male naamu-sayer [the narrator's assistant – M.J.], and several male musicians.'

This format suggests that women do not narrate the Sunjata epic: griot women may only sing the songs in the epic narrated by griot men. It struck me that all the people whom I met during my field research, adults as well as children, could tell about Sunjata. Given the familiarity of people with the Sunjata epic – his endeavours are discussed at school and on the radio – we may ask ourselves why griot women are largely excluded from analyses of the epic. Why have they not been studied as transmitters of the Sunjata epic? Indeed, several scholars have even completely neglected griot women (see Hale 1998: 217-223; Janson 2002).

The gendered task division between griot men and women has been remarked in passing by many scholars, but is usually not further analysed (cf. Durán 1995b: 127). According to both Jansen (1996: 184) and Hale (1998: 228) women do not narrate the Sunjata epic although they know the contents quite well and are experts in singing the songs of praise that form part of the epic. Both authors, however, do not elaborate, for instance by providing ethnographic data, on the knowledge of epic they attribute to griot women. The case study by Sidikou (1997: 254-304) to prove that women have knowledge of epics is not convincing either, as it does not meet the literary standards for an epic (for these, see e.g. Kesteloot and Dieng 1997). Nevertheless, I firmly agree with Sidikou that theory on epic is male-centred and needs to be redefined.

Griot women narrating the Sunjata epic
Several griot women with whom I worked told me that they have knowledge of the Sunjata epic, called *taarikoo* by them,[iv] because they tune their songs to the narrative recounted by their husbands. When griot men recount the epic, griot women have to sing the right songs on the right moment. A praise song (*fasoo*) that griot women usually sing during recitations of the Sunjata epic is the *Sunjata fasoo*, in which Sunjata is compared to a lion because of his strength.[v]

However, I observed that griot women do not only sing about Sunjata. One day I was interviewing Naantassa Kuyateh, an older griot woman whom I had followed over a long period in order to record her life story. She was sitting on a mat in her room, shelling groundnuts, when I asked her to tell me something about the origin of *jaliyaa*, 'griotism' (i.e. the profession of griots). My informants usually answered that *jaliyaa* had been created by their ancestor, centuries ago. They saw it as their duty to undertake *jaliyaa*, as this is what their ancestors did. However Naantassa related that *jaliyaa* was founded by Surakata, the Prophet Muhammad's 'griot'.[vi] Her answer to my question demonstrates that she was well informed about narratives that have been described as men's knowledge, and that she had the skills to recount them:

'Initially, Surakata was the Prophet's enemy. He did not believe in God and he wanted to kill the Prophet Muhammad. Surakata pursued him on horseback. The Prophet, who was helped by God, looked back and shouted a special formula. At that moment the earth burst open and Surakata fell with his horse into the earth. When he promised to convert to Islam, Muhammad released Surakata and his horse. However, Surakata did not keep his promise and the same happened a second and a third time. After the third time, Surakata was convinced that Muhammad was not a liar and that God existed and finally he converted to Islam.

Henceforth, Surakata followed the Prophet. They travelled together and everywhere they went to, Surakata announced the arrival of Muhammad and exclaimed his praises. Upon hearing these praises, people came out of their houses to greet the Prophet. They treated him with respect and they offered him gold, silver, cattle and other valuables. The Prophet always gave Surakata the largest share of these gifts when he praised him. The Prophet's followers were jealous and they asked the Prophet why Surakata always received the lion's share. The Prophet told his followers to prepare for a journey and Surakata to stay at home. They visited many villages, but nobody gave them presents and they did not even get water and food. The Prophet explained to his followers that because Surakata did not exclaim his praises, nobody recognized him. Then the followers understood why Surakata always received more than them. From that time, Muhammad always travelled with Surakata. We [the bards] stem from Surakata. When we undertake *jaliyaa*, we do it for the sake of God and His Prophet.'

Jeneba Kuyateh, another griot woman, also narrated a passage of the epic of Sunjata. Shortly before, her husband had told me how *jaliyaa* had come into being by telling a tradition featuring Nyankuman Duka, Sunjata's griot. Elaborating on a theme known in large parts of West Africa, he explained to me that this Nyankuman Duka – who was later named Balafasiki Kuyateh – was the grandson of Surakata, the Prophet Muhammad's bard.[vii] Jeneba's account stressed different episodes than her husband's, and emphasized the origin of the griot woman:

'The first griot woman in Mande was Tumu Maniyang Kuyateh. This lady sat on the ground and cried because she did not have anything to eat. The blacksmith king Sumanguru Kanteh ordered her to come to his palace. He asked her why she was crying. He decided to help her by giving her a *neo* [an iron percussion rod – M.J.].[viii] She started to play the instrument, while she sang Sumanguru's praises. He was so happy when she praised him that he rewarded her with a seven-year-old cow.

When Balafasiki Kuyateh heard Tumu Maniyang sing, he decided to marry her. When they were married, they performed together: Balafasiki played the *balafong*[ix] and Tumu Maniyang sang praises and played the *neo*. When she was not performing with her husband, Tumu Maniyang sat on a stone, carefully looking around her. When somebody behaved well, she announced it in public by praising him. When somebody was a coward, she also broadcast it. This is how the profession of griot women started. Tumu Maniyang was the first griot woman who played the *neo* and sang. Other griot women soon followed her.'

It is common knowledge that Balafasiki Kuyateh (whose original name was Nyankuman Duka) is considered the griots' ancestor. Less often it has been documented that Tumu Maniyang is the Kuyateh matriarch and that she is considered the first griot woman in Mande.[x] Jeneba's account informs us about marriage patterns: the first griot man married the first griot woman on earth so that they could perform as a couple.[xi] Tumu Maniyang Kuyateh accompanied her husband by singing and playing the *neo*. What is interesting in this account is that Tumu Maniyang Kuyateh did not only accompany her husband, but also performed independently of him: she acted as a kind of commentator by broadcasting the good and bad deeds of people. During my field research it became obvious that griot women hold positions independent of their husbands, the griot men, while in the literature the role of griot women is usually diminished to supporting their husbands (see below).

New perspectives on the intersection between gender and genre
Naantassa Kuyateh and Jeneba Kuyateh were the only griot women I met during my fieldwork in eastern Gambia who narrated parts of the Sunjata epic. How can we explain their knowledge of the epic? Both griot women bear similarities: they are esteemed 'good' griot women with a profound knowledge of their profession and they are classified as 'old women' (*musu keebaalu*). Naantassa is in her fifties and Jeneba in her sixties. Characteristic of a *musu keebaa* is that she has passed menopause. An older griot woman who herself has reached the status of *musu keebaa*, defined this concept as follows: 'A *musu keebaa* has grey hair. Because she is old, she has fewer activities than younger women and therefore she has more time to worship God. Furthermore, her children are married and have children themselves.'

Typical of a griot woman with the status of *musu keebaa* is an extensive knowledge of her profession. Naantassa Kuyateh explained to me that an old griot woman with knowledge, a *jali kotoo*, cannot be compared to a young apprentice, a *jali dingo*. She stated: 'Even if a *jali dingo* has more knowledge than a *jali kotoo*, she cannot express this in public, otherwise the elders will make her life a misery. A *jali dingo* has to respect a *jali kotoo* and she has to behave in a correct way towards the latter.' Their status of *musu keebaalu* may explain why Naantassa and Jeneba Kuyateh were not only able but, more importantly, also allowed to relate parts of the Sunjata epic. In addition to quoting from the epic, singing the songs of praise related to the epic is restricted to senior griot women. One of my informants was shocked when I asked her if every griot woman is able to sing the songs about Sunjata. She exclaimed: 'Of course not! After all, griot women below 45 years old are only children.'

Naantassa and Jeneba's status as postmenopausal women makes them in a sense 'sexless', and this may explain why they are allowed to narrate the epic and sing the corresponding songs. In their position as *musu keebaalu*, they represent an accumulation of authority which enables them to perform a role forbidden to younger women (cf. Freeman 2000). In this light, I follow Herbert's argument that gender is a fluid concept which transforms itself and evolves through the life cycle (1993: 219-220).

Just like griot women, the griot men who narrate the epic of Sunjata have to meet certain requirements and just like griot women the griot men who are able and allowed to recount the epic are few. In the course of my fieldwork I concluded that narrating the epic is not so much a question of gender, but rather a question of age and also of personal skills. In addition to old age, griot men and women who concentrate on relating the epic need certain personal qualities, as it requires special verbal skills to hold the attention of an audience, and courage to talk for a large crowd. My informants noted that – in the context of a performance – griots need to be shameless (*malubali*). This quality is related to age: young griots are usually more ashamed to perform in public than older ones. The training of apprentice griots is focused on getting rid of feelings of shame (*malu*). Griots are taught that being ashamed of or being embarrassed by their behaviour is inappropriate for a griot: 'They are thus taught to be *ashamed* of being ashamed' (Hoffman 1995: 37; Hoffman's emphasis). The shamelessness of a griot is, of course, confined to the context of the performance; in daily life bards, just like anyone else, have to show feelings of shame (CF. Jansen 2000a: 58-60).

Another quality of griots that was mentioned by my informants was intelligence (*hakilidiyaa*). Griots who narrate the epic should remember the words by heart and this is not granted to everybody. It requires a lot of practice. Usually those griots who have attained the honorific title of *ngaaraa*, master bard, may relate the epic.[xii] My informants used this term for outstanding griot men and women who have reached a certain age and 'really know their profession'. A griot woman who, according to her colleagues and patrons, had reached the status of *ngaaraa*, explained to me: 'A *ngaaraa* is a bard whose words have a meaning.' She emphasized that such bards are few. *Ngaaraayaa*, the state of being a *ngaaraa*, is the basic yardstick by which ability and achievement are measured (Durán 1995a: 201). The ability to perform the epic is the ultimate test of *ngaaraayaa* (op. cit.: 202). *Ngaaraayaa* is both inherited and a skill. A middle-aged griot woman told me that one can develop it by training, but it is God who decides whether one becomes a *ngaaraa*. She interpreted *ngaaraayaa* as 'a gift from God'. We should note that the term *ngaaraa* is not only applied to griots who have a whole series of musical attributes, but also moral attributes (cf. Knight 1984: 74). My informants explained to me that a *ngaaraa* needs to live according to the pillars of Islam.

From the above-mentioned we may conclude that within Mande there is a hierarchy, not only of knowledge but also of the expression of knowledge.

Knowledge depends on the prestige of the generation to which a griot belongs. In addition to age and generation, individual skills are necessary to give the spoken words a meaning and to embellish them.

The value of the spoken word in relation to the value of the sung word
As mentioned earlier, most authors take it for granted that women sing songs of praise in the epics narrated by their husbands. In the literature on epic the women's singing usually plays a supporting role: griot women are portrayed as vocal backing to male narrators. This suggests that the song mode is less appreciated than the speech mode (cf. Schulz 2001: 135). Referring to a case in which a griot woman sang a long praise song, Hale asks himself: 'If they [griot women – M.J.] sing a song for two hours, does that constitute an epic or simply a form of panegyric, or praise?' He then states that he cannot answer this question since we do not have enough long texts by women at our disposal (1998: 228). From my observations described above, we may conclude that it is fairly easy to record long texts by griot women, if only one makes some efforts.

First of all, we have to rethink our definition of griot women. Instead of describing them as vocal backing to their husbands, an approach by which the male is taken as norm and starting point, we should study them as social actors in their own right. Taking this course, an end may be put to the male-biased view in which griot women are excluded from the domain of the epic. Secondly, the prejudice against the griot women's song mode of performance needs to be brought up for discussion. The griot women with whom I worked themselves attached much value to their singing. A middle-aged griot woman who was generally considered a good singer said: 'Singing is very, very difficult. When I sing, my throat becomes painful. It also gives me a headache, since I have to think hard to remember the words of the song. Because everybody listens to me, I can sing only those words that are true. A good singer has to be intelligent.' The griot women's husbands also underlined the significant role of the song mode by women. They noted that without their wives singing, their profession would not be 'sweet'. Mawdo Susoo, a famed griot man in The Gambia, told me that he married his two wives because they were good singers. He asserted that 'a good instrumentalist does not feel complete unless he has at least one wife who is a good vocalist' (cited in Jatta 1985: 25).

These positive remarks on the griot women's singing can be interpreted in the light of the recent empowerment of griot women in the Mande – particularly Malian – music scene (cf. Durán 1995a: 198, 204-207; Diawara 1997). With changing social and political circumstances, the emphasis in the griot's music has shifted increasingly away from epic towards praise song and entertainment. In this griot women have had a crucial role to play (Durán 1995a: 205). Therefore Diawara speaks of a 'feminization of the artist's profession among griots' (1997: 43). It seems that nowadays Mande peoples attach less value to the rare occasions during which elderly griot men narrate (parts of) the Sunjata epic, and tend to appreciate more the art of singing. Singing has turned into a women's genre on its own, separate from the genre of the epic. While epic narration and the singing of praise songs in the epic are restricted to a few elderly, talented griot men and women, the younger griot women feel out the market of the new forms of popular singing.

Concluding remarks
In this article I attempted to differentiate the common notion that the ability to narrate the famous Sunjata epic belongs to the domain of griot men. It is generally assumed that griot women may only sing about Sunjata. I brought this supposed task division between griot men and women under discussion by arguing that older, expert griot women may narrate the epic without harming social conventions. Besides I argued that contrary to what is often suggested in literature, among the griot men only a few senior talented ones are actually able and allowed to narrate the epic. Moreover, I called the common negative picture of griot women as vocal backing to their husbands into question, by exploring the appreciation of the song mode. With the changing socio-political circumstances in the Mande world, the griot women's singing seems to make headway to the epic narration by griot men.

It appeared that some elderly griot women know well how to narrate the Sunjata epic and that they may even offer us new interpretations and perspectives of the epic by highlighting other fragments than griot men. I concluded that in old age the axes of male and female intersect, and at the point of intersection gender differences tend to dissolve. Thus, narrating epics is not so much a question of gender but rather of age. In addition to age, personal qualities are also significant. Usually those griot men and women who have attained the title of *ngaaraa*, an honorific term which refers to the bard's musical and moral attributes, may recount the epic. This suggests that instead of underscoring the differences *between* griot men and women, we should pay more attention to the differences *within* the categories of griot man and woman. If we want to understand more fully the genre of the epic, we should study it first of all from a transgender perspective.

NOTES

[i] The term 'Mande' (sometimes 'Manding') refers to a set of culturally and linguistically related West African ethnic groups that live in Mali, Guinea, Guinea-Bissau, Senegal, The Gambia, and parts of Ivory Coast, Mauritania and Burkina Faso. The Mande peoples bear marks of a common identity by tracing descent to Sunjata Keita, who is considered the founder of the Old Mali empire, one of a succession of empires which rose and fell in West Africa in the Middle Ages. The ethnic group on which I focus in this article is the Mandinka, who comprise the majority in The Gambia.

[ii] This research was funded by the Research School CNWS. The results of the research have been published in my PhD thesis (Janson 2002).

[iii] Griot is a gender-neutral term, corresponding to the Mandinka term *jali* (plural *jaloolu*). Male bards can be called *jaloolu*, as can female bards. A distinction is made between the male and the female by means of the suffix *keo* (man) or *musoo* (woman). Due to the male bias that marks social

science research, the word 'griot' is often assigned to men in the literature. In this article I will use the terms 'griot man' and 'griot woman', as they are closest to the local terms.

[iv] *Taarikoo* (derived from the Arabic *tarikh*) means 'history', or 'story', and refers to something that is conveyed through the spoken word (cf. W.E.C. 1990: 316).

[v] For published versions of this song see e.g. Jansen 2000a: 84-87; Janson 2002: 226-228.

[vi] Versions of the well-known tradition on Surakata, which forms part of the Sunjata epic, are also recorded in Zemp 1966 and Conrad 1985. Surakata is the Mandinka form of Suraqa ibn Malik ibn Ju'shum, in Arab tradition an enemy of the Prophet Muhammad who became an early convert to Islam (Conrad 1985: 43).

[vii] Charry argues that there appears to be a two-tiered ancestry among griots: that of their profession in general, which is projected back to the time of the Prophet Muhammad, and that of bards in particular, which goes back to the time of Sunjata (2000: 104). This indicates that we have to distinguish between a global (Islamic) tradition in which Surakata plays the leading role and a local Mande one in which Balafasiki Kuyateh is central (op. cit.: 103). By stating that Balafasiki was Surakata's grandson, Jeneba's husband telescopes both traditions.

[viii] The term *neo* refers to the material of which the instrument is made: iron. The *neo* is composed of an iron tube that is twirled in one hand while striking it with an iron rod held in the other hand. It produces a ringing sound which accompanies the singing and dancing of griot women. Only griot women are allowed to play this instrument; it is the only instrument played by them.

[ix] This instrument resembles a xylophone.

[x] Tumu Maniyang plays a role in a few published versions of the Sunjata epic, among which Johnson's (1986: 129, 145, 168) and Jansen et al.'s (1995: line 396ff).

[xi] Intermarriage between griot men and women is still common.

[xii] The use of the term *ngaaraa* is debated. Johnson claims that only griot men can reach this highest level of achievement (1986: 25). Knight (1984: 74) and Jatta (1985: 25), on the other hand, define a *ngaaraa* as a superior female singer. According to Durán (1995a: 203), Charry (2000: 96), and Hoffman (2000: 268 n.7) gender does not count, but ability. I heard the term being applied to both griot men and women, but in particular to outstanding singers. Because singers are usually female, the concept of *ngaaraa* is mostly used for griot women. Elder griot men do sing sometimes, but the women's voice is preferred.

THE DEIFICATION OF SOUTH ASIAN EPIC HEROES – METHODOLOGICAL IMPLICATIONS

Janet Kamphorst

Introduction
My research is focussed on the written and oral epic traditions of the people in the Thar Desert of western Rajasthan on the Indian border with present-day Pakistan. I am particularly interested in the written and oral Rajasthani tradition of Pabuji, a fivehundred year old epic tradition about the 14th-century Rajput (warrior) Pabuji Dhandhal Rathaur. The written Pabuji tradition is part of the medieval manuscript tradition of Marwar, a former Rathaur Rajput kingdom in the Thar Desert. Contemporary oral versions of Pabuji's story are part of the epic Rajasthani tradition, transmitted by performers of various caste backgrounds. In the course of the last five centuries, Pabuji has evolved from a historical Rajput warrior into one of the many folkgods or *lokdevtas* of Rajasthan. Presently, most peoples of the Thar Desert worship the Dhandhal Rathaur hero in one way or another. In addition, two distinct folk religious cults have his story at the core of their beliefs: the *par* (story-cloth) epic and the *mata* (drum) epic cults of western Rajasthan.

An important theme of my research is the manner in which the Rathaur hero has become deified in the course of time. In the following, I will sketch some of the lines along which my research is evolving through a short survey of the written and oral sources I am using, followed by an exploration of the process of deification that Pabuji went through. By way of conclusion, the methodological implications of my findings will be discussed.

Written and oral sources
The written and oral traditions of Rajasthan know a great number of variant versions of Pabuji's story as it has been told and re-told by numerous performers for centuries. The medieval manuscript tradition of *virkavya* (heroic poetry) has been the starting point of my research. This particular form of poetry was composed by, among others, members of the Charan caste, the poets of the region. It is written in so-called Dingal, the poetic or bardic language of Rajasthan. A careful study of several kinds of manuscripts, varying in length and dates of composition, has given me an idea of the 'chain of transmission' of the story of Pabuji from its possible beginnings in the 16th century until the present day. The oldest available manuscript version is the 16th century *Pabuji ro chand Meha Vithu ra kahi*, 'Pabuji's verses as told by Meha Vithu', by a Charan poet of the Vithu lineage. The *chand* is an epic poem of which several

versions, differing in length and content as well as form, have been handed down. Here we will briefly discuss manuscript 5470 (*Rajasthan Oriental Research Institute*, Jodhpur), a composition of 375 verse-lines which glorifies Pabuji's heroism as well as the brave deeds of his companions, the tribal Bhil archers.[i] In Meha's poem, Pabuji is essentially portrayed as an exemplary Rajput warrior, a brave wielder of spear and sword who protects family honor and cattle. The poet does not ascribe magical powers or divine status to him.

One century later, in the first decades of the 17th century, Pabuji's story was again versified, this time in the *Pabuji ra duha* ('The couplets of Pabuji') and in *Pabuji ra parvara* ('Pabuji's heroic deeds').[ii] These poems were put to paper, and perhaps also composed, by Ladhraj, the *diwan* (minister) of the 17th-century ruler of Marwar. Retaining Meha's poem's war theme, the *Pabuji ra duha* added various elements to Pabuji's heroic actions. Whereas the *Pabuji ra parvara*, a short poetic appendix to the *Pabuji ra duha*, deals exclusively with Pabuji's godly qualities and seems to represent a medieval rendition of the present-day oral tradition of the Bhils of western Rajasthan.[iii] But first, let us study Ladhraj's *Pabuji ra duha* that tells us that Pabuji was a man with special qualities, a valiant fighter who rode out to protect the weak, the progeny of an insignificant Dhandhal Rathaur warrior and a celestial nymph. The story focuses on the rivalry between the two Rajput brotherhoods, the Dhandhal Rathaur Rajputs and the clan of Jindarav Khici, Pabuji's brother-in-law and enemy. The conflict between the two was caused by Jindarav Khici's demand for Pabuji's horse Kalavi in dowry during a marriage ceremony. When Pabuji refuses to meet his demand, Jindarav robs the cattle of a cattle-herd, Deval, a woman of Charan parentage. As Pabuji had promised Deval his protection in times of need – she was the one who gave him the black mare Kalavi – he comes to Deval's rescue. In the final battle Pabuji is slain, giving his life in battle and thus fulfilling his Rajput *dharma*.[iv] The last episode tells the story of Jhararo, the son of Pabuji's half-brother Buro. The day the boy learns of the fate of his uncle Pabuji, he immediately sets out to meet Jindarav Khici and beheads him. The concluding four verses of *Pabuji ra duha* sing the everlasting fame of Pabuji and his nephew.

Those are the main constituents of the story of Pabuji. The oral folk-epic of Pabuji contains many additional elements to which I will return in my discussion of the oral sources that I collected. In the *Pabuji ra duha* the hero Pabuji emerges as a protector, a warrior-hero with a semi-divine status. His divine qualities are generally ascribed to the fact that he was born from the union of a celestial being and a mortal warrior. The poem relates how, at the age of thirteen, Pabuji starts his search for martial experiences so as to fulfil his Rajput *dharma* by fighting neighbouring kingdoms and combating rival warriors. The outstanding feature of his heroism is the fact that he keeps his word to Deval and offers his life to protect her cattle. Apart from the celestial character of his mother, this medieval *duha* does not yet directly refer to Pabuji's divine or magical qualities.

This does happen in the *Pabuji ra parvara*, a shorter poem that is often attached to the *Pabuji ra duha*. Literally *parvara* means 'episodes of war' or 'heroic deeds'. This medieval poem commemorates the miracles that are performed by Pabuji after his ascent to heaven, for instance in the tale of the marauding Rajput landlord who steals the drum of one of Pabuji's Bhopo devotees. Coming to the rescue of his follower, Pabuji curses the Rajput landlord with a severe stomach-ache,[v] and soon enough it becomes clear that no cure will be able to relieve the Rajput of his stomach-ache until he returns the drum to the Bhopo. On returning the drum, Pabuji cures the Rajput who then becomes his true follower.

Since the 16th century the continuous recollection and retelling of the deeds and miracles of (semi-)historical warriors and cattle-keepers has given rise to a pluriform Rajasthani tradition. The medieval hero Pabuji, for one, is now at the heart of diverse folk religious cults; he is worshipped as a local or regional *lokdevta* (folk god) by, among others, his Rajput, Bhil and Charan devotees. The performance of Pabuji's epic is the core ritual of their regional belief systems. The extant Pabuji tradition has a more truly epic length than the medieval manuscript tradition; the longest version of the oral epic of Pabuji, the *par* epic tradition as recorded and transcribed by John D. Smith, has about 4000 lines of prose and poetry and takes 36 hours to perform (Smith 1991: 27-34). Presently, the *par* epic tradition is the most well-known version of Pabuji's story. However, during my two fieldtrips to the Thar, it became clear that not only the *par* Bhopos, but also other performers transmit Pabuji's story, both orally and in writing.

The following survey of the oral data collected by me should give an impression of the many versions in the contemporary tradition. Firstly, the *mata* (drum) players perform the oral Pabuji epic in the main Pabuji temple of Kolu (district Phalaudi). Their patrons are from the agrarian and nomadic communities in and around Kolu as well as the Rajput priests of the Kolu Pabuji temple. Secondly, present-day Charan poets not only keep the Pabuji tradition alive through written texts but also transmit his story in oral presentations.[vi] The recitation of poems about Pabuji and the performances of devotional songs (*cirjaem*) dedicated to him and Deval are part of the rituals of the Charan *shakti* cult of Rajasthan.[vii] In addition, the contemporary Pabuji tradition also includes poetry dedicated to Pabuji by the Rawal genealogists of the Charans, prayers performed by Dhola drummers, poems chanted by poets of the Motisar caste and hymns of Dhadhi singers, who all belong to the *gayak jati* or 'singing caste-groups' of Rajasthan.

Like the medieval manuscript tradition, the oral epic tradition has a multiform character. Here I want to focus on the *par* and the *mata* epic performances of the Bhil Bhopos. The *par vancana*, or the reading of the *par* (story-cloth), is carried out by Bhil performers who travel through the Thar Desert, visiting villages and *dhanis* (semi-permanent settlements). Their main patrons are the traditional camelbreeders of the desert, the Rebari, who worship Pabuji as the hero-god who brought a herd of reddish she-camels to the Thar and appointed their forefathers as the keepers of these camels. The Bhils who stage the *par* epic refer to themselves as 'Nayaks' or 'Bhil Bhopos', priestly performers of the epic.[viii] They read the *par* during nightlong performances containing different narrative episodes or *parvaras*, the performance of which varies according to the extent of the bard's knowledge as well as to the public's preferences for certain episodes. The central points in the story are the battle between Pabuji and Jindarav Khici, the return of the stolen cows to Deval, and Pabuji's death at the hands of Khici. Other popular episodes relate Pabuji's wedding, the adventures of the Rebari Harmal, a member of Pabuji's retinue, and Pabuji's journey to adjacent Sindh to steal the camel-herd of the powerful Sumro ruler in that region. The Bhopa and Bhopi (male and female performer) render the different episodes in *gav* (song) and in *arthav* (prose) sections. During the *arthav*, the Bhopa points with an oil lamp to the painted pictures on the seven-meter long story-cloth to illustrate his narrative. The Bhopi usually performs *gav* sections in unison with her husband; the *arthav* sections are, as a rule, performed by the Bhopa alone.[ix]

The other religious cult of Pabuji focuses on the performance of the *mata* epic during devotional ceremonies in the Kolu Pabuji temple. Here, the Bhil *mata* players call themselves Bhopos as well, but prefer the designation of 'Thori' to that of 'Nayak'. They hold that Pabuji himself appointed their forefathers, the Thori archers in his retinue, to sing his praise and perform the *mata* epic.[x] The Bhopos of Kolu narrate how 140 Bhil bridal parties, after being fed by Pabuji, accompanied him in battle and died at his side fighting Khici's army.[xi] The Bhil performers keep Pabuji's memory alive during all-night *jagrans* (religious wakes) when, like *par* Bhopos, they commemorate Pabuji's heroism in *parvaras*.[xii] In addition, the *mata* epic has *'sayls'*, prayers or petitions, that are dedicated to Pabuji. The narrative pace of the *mata* is slow as the episodes and prayers mainly function to glorify the present miracles and past deeds of Pabuji, Deval, and the Thori archers. The *mata* epic is performed during daily temple rituals and during celebrations for Navratri, the festival of the mother-goddess in Asoj (September-October). It is commonly regarded as a rite to appropriate Pabuji's benevolence by commemorating his protective qualities.

In the extant oral performance traditions, Pabuji is ascribed two roles. On the one hand, he is depicted as a true Rajput warrior who gives his life for the protection of others and, on the other hand, he is portrayed as a Rajput hero with magical qualities and a divine status, an *avatar* (incarnation) of Lakhsman, the brother of Ram, the hero of the Sanskrit *Ramayana* epic. This *avatar*-linkage mainly presents itself in the contemporary stories about Pabuji as told by the low-caste performers of the Thar Desert.

Deification
As the study of the different versions of Pabuji's tale exemplifies, in the process

of expansion common to the development of oral epic, numerous episodes, details, and story-elements have been added to the story. The main difference between the oral epic and the medieval tradition is the emphasis on the magical birth-story of Pabuji, in the extant tradition, which gives him a semi-divine origin. Another consequential addition is the fact that Pabuji is now worshipped as a folkgod, an *avatar* of Lakhsman.

This brings us to the deification of the historical warrior Pabuji that eventually sets him apart from other historical Rajput warriors. As we already saw, his godly status is not yet manifest in the earliest description of his heroism. Although the addition of the birth-story to *Pabuji ra duha* traces his parentage back to the union between a human warrior and a celestial nymph, this story-line has not been accorded much importance compared to the other episodes of the *duha*. The 17th century *Pabuji ra parvara,* however, seems to have been written solely for the purpose of extolling Pabuji's divine and magical qualities.

As the work of, among others, Stuart Blackburn (1989) has shown, the deification of warriors is a recurrent subject in South-Asian oral epics. Blackburn proposes a 'nucleus model' of epic development that proceeds by joining separate stories with the core story of an epic or by the addition of motives (ib. 21-30). He holds that at a local level these oral epics usually originate with the story of the violent or undeserved death of a village hero; such a story then evolves by assimilating motives, and assumes different forms as it spreads geographically. Once a story extends to the sub-regional level of epic telling, the birth of the hero is described in supernatural terms to impress the hero's divine origin on the public – and that possibly explains the addition of the magical birth story to the historical nucleus of the epic of Pabuji as well.

According to Blackburn, local heroes are identified with pan-Indian epic figures to cater to the tastes of a larger public as soon as epic stories gain a wider regional distribution. This process could explain the *avatar*-linkage of Pabuji with Lakhsman. But then, the study of the medieval versions of Pabuji's story show that the developmental stages do not necessarily follow the development that is outlined by Blackburn. From the brief discussion of the content of the medieval *chand, duha* and *parvara* that are dedicated to Pabuji, we may conclude that not only Rajput martial lore, but also poetry about Pabuji's magical qualities formed a source of inspiration for the medieval Rajasthani tradition.

The addition of *Pabuji ra parvara*, in which magical qualities are ascribed to Pabuji, to the *Pabuji ra duha*, a text which extols Pabuji's martial qualities, seems to suggest that the developmental stages of these particular versions of the story are not necessarily the result of a larger regional spread. It seems more likely that the development of these versions is the result of the dispersion of the story among different caste-groups, most notably the Charans and the Bhils.

My findings also contrast with the definition of the medieval Pabuji tradition as being a part of the written Rajput 'Great Tradition', commonly defined as a Charan heritage that established the legitimacy of Rajput rule by linking the martial values and deeds of forefathers with contemporary Rajput lineages.[xiii] Working in such a definition, scholars have ignored the fact that, alongside Rajput chronicles, the heritage of tribal Bhil Bhopos has formed a part of the Rajput 'Great Tradition' since at least the second half of the 17th century.

Methodological implications
In addition, the study of the Pabuji tradition also results in some reservations about the interpretation of the final stage of epic development, that is when local heroes are identified with pan-Indian epic figures. That stage is usually described in a derivative manner: the underlying thematic similarities are seen as a result of a Sanskritization or Brahmanization of folk traditions, a process that is best understood as a general 'universalization' of Hindu culture in which classical Brahminical values and traditions are integrated by tribal, nomadic or other forms of regional cultures.

Thus, for instance Smith interprets *avatar*-linkages and similarities between classical Sanskrit epics and the Pabuji folk epic in the light of the 'existential drama' at the heart of Sanskrit epics (Smith 1989; Smith 1980). In this view, the philosophical plot of the folk epic now centers upon the tension between human choice, *paurusa*, and *daivam*, the will of the gods, a tension which Smith has coined the 'existential drama' in South Asian epics. An interpretation of Pabuji's epic in terms of human existence seems like a late addition, Smith (1991) suggests, and I would like to add that during the performances by the Bhopos and other castes that I have witnessed this interpretation is not prominent at all.

My understanding of both the written and the oral Rajasthani Pabuji tradition has made me question Smith's interpretation of the *par* epic of Pabuji. If one tries to explain the content of Pabuji's tradition from a historical point of view, not the classical Sanskritic values stand out, but the continuities between medieval and contemporary versions of the story.

Thus, apart from *avatar*-linkage with epic heroes from the Ramayana, the reworking of the structure, themes, and subject matter of the classical Sanskrit epics is not very straightforward in either the medieval or extant Pabuji tradition.

First, the classical Sanskrit epics are eminently didactic works that impart moral doctrines and religious *dharma*, but neither the written nor the oral versions of Pabuji's tradition explicitly restate the classical teachings of the primary epics, neither in the medieval tradition nor for the present audience.

Second, the tradition about Pabuji mirrors a rather different socio-political context than the Sanskrit epics do. Pabuji's battles, for instance, are fought for the protection of cattle and not, like in classical epics, to uphold a rightful claim as the successor to a throne. Moreover, Pabuji and his allies have a different caste-status than the heroes of the Sanskrit epics: Pabuji comes from an insignificant Rathaur lineage while his associates are low-caste tribal Bhils and nomadic Rebari.

Another difference with Sanskrit epics is the fact that in the medieval and contemporary tradition of Pabuji, there is room for social mobility; individual status is often seen as achieved rather than ascribed. Present-day followers of Pabuji invariably stress his role as a 'social reformer', and this role is underlined through tellings of the story about the bloodstreams of slain Rajput, Bhil, Charan and Rebari warriors flowing together on the battlefield. At the moment when Charani Deval starts to build barriers between the bloodstreams to stop them from coming together, Pabuji's voice comes from heaven and tells her to let the different streams become one. The story is told to illustrate that Pabuji ascribed an equal status to all his retainers. Other contemporary and medieval tales also illustrate the claims to higher status by the nomadic people of the Thar. Thus it is said that, formerly, all Rajputs were Maldharis (cattle-keepers) (Westphal-Hellbusch 1975: 123) or, vice versa, it is asserted that all nomadic peoples have Rajput *ansa* (essence) in their veins.

By arguing in favor of a linkage between the medieval and the present-day epic tradition I do not want to deny the influence of Sanskrit classical epics altogether. Rather, I suggest that the Pabuji tradition is mainly concerned with the medieval Rajput ideal of protection and self-sacrifice and not with the philosophies of the Sanskrit tradition. The fact that Pabuji gives his life in order to rescue cows clearly points to different interests at the heart of this folk-epic, namely the concerns of a nomadic society in which violent deaths, especially while protecting cattle, form a recurrent theme.

Pabuji's heroism as well as the manner in which the socio-political aspirations of different caste-groups are voiced are readily recognized by present-day audiences. The interest that these audiences take in the Pabuji epic seems to lie in the fact that the medieval, nomadic and egalitarian standards still inform the current ideals of the peoples of the Thar. The fact that the pastoral-nomadic lifestyles of the camel-breeders and other mobile groups only very recently became subject to change further accounts for the ongoing appeal of Pabuji's adventures in Rajasthan.

In other words, the process of Sankritization does not help to fully explain the addition of epic story-elements. In order to understand them, we should, instead, carry out a historical reading of the context in which the tradition grew. If we saw the different tales about Pabuji as only a re-telling of certain story-elements of the classical epics, we would ignore the influence of daily life and of Rajput martial ideals on the epic as well as the 'lived past' of the largely nomadic population of West Rajasthan. The composite character of the epic of Pabuji points to a mixture of classical and folk poetry discourse and allows us to describe the oral and written Pabuji tradition as the product of a historical process of story-telling that was equally inspired by Rajput martial ideals, folk motives and avatar-linkage with heroes of the classical tradition.

Conclusion

By way of conclusion, I would like to propose that the developmental stages of South-Asian epic be best described in terms of a multi-layered process. For the Pabuji tradition, we may distinguish three layers. One, a medieval written manuscript tradition of heroic and epic poetry with an evident affinity with folklore or popular oral culture. Two, a contemporary oral folk-tradition, still very much embedded in the 'remembered historical time' of the medieval world of Rajput martial lore and nomadic survival-strategies. And, three, the classical, Sanskrit influences, which, at this stage of my research, seem mainly perceptible in the contemporary tradition.

A helpful approach to the different layers of South-Asian classical and folk epics is A.K. Ramanuyan's vision of 'three-hundred Ramayanas' (1991: 22-46). He argues against the hierarchical classification of epic that presents Valmiki's *Ramayana* as the ultimate rendition of Ram's exploits and other tellings as deviations of this 'primary' narrative. Instead, Ramanuyan charts the multiform, at times 'oppositional', traditions about Ram as expressions inspired by a common, aggregated set of sources or 'a pool of signifiers' (cf. Brakel-Papenhuyzen, supra). This common bank of story elements includes plots, characters, names, geography, and incidents that inspire the classical as well as the folk tradition of epic.

'Diversity' is central to Ramanuyan's discussion of epic. He makes clear that a heroic narrative is influenced by a diversity of oral and written traditions in different periods, circumstances and regions. Along these lines distinct narratives are parts of a 'series of translations clustering around one and other in a family of texts' (Ramanuyan 1991: 44). The idea of a common imaginative pool can also be applied to the concept of genre; such an approach should enable us to see the many forms of the Pabuji tradition as part of one 'multi-layered' and collective narrative construction of different Rajasthani performers, transmitted in oral and written forms.

NOTES

[i] The ancestry of the Rajputs, Bhils and Charans is shrouded in clouds of Rajasthani myth-history. Traditionally, the Rajputs are portrayed as the warriors and rulers of Rajasthan, they claim *kshatriya* status, the second class or caste (*varna*) of Hindu society. The Bhil are most commonly described as tribal hunter-gatherers. In the medieval manuscript tradition of Rajasthan they are also portrayed as accomplished archers. From the 12th century onwards, the Charans have been depicted as the poets and chroniclers of Rajput rule in Rajasthan. They claim a high ranking status similar (but not identical) to the priestly caste of Brahmans. However, numerous Charans were, in the past, horse-traders and cattle-keepers as well. At present, the occupational identity of Rajputs, Charans and Bhils has been diversified and the larger part of these communities are now farmers or landowners.

[ii] *Rajasthani Research Institute* (Chaupasni), Ms. 402. This 18th-century handwriting contains the *duha* (260 verses) and the *paravara* (83 verses).

[iii] Presently, the priestly Bhil performers (Bhopos) stage epic performances in the main Pabuji temple in Kolu (Western Rajasthan).

iv Rajput *dharma* refers to the socio-religious set of laws that rule a Rajput's life. The realization of his *dharma* enables a Rajput to sustain or increase his status within the caste hierarchy or to attain spiritual salvation.

v In the 17th century prose-chronicle of Marwar, Pabuji's magical powers have developed further. Magical feats that are attributed to him include the crossing of a river without bridges or boats. According to the contemporary tradition, Pabuji donates daily gifts of gold to some of his present-day devotees. Sakariya 1984: 58-79.

vi Based on the tradition of Charan communities around Jodhpur, Bikaner and Jaisalmer settled in the villages Deshnok, Khemn, Rama, Shiv, Sarvari and Marhwa and Charans settled in villages around Ajmer and Churu (Pabusar, Bobasar, Borunda).

vii The *shakti* goddesses of the Sanskrit tradition embody the female energy of gods; this energy is usually personified as their wife. Charan *sagatis* (*shakti*) are seen as the incarnation of the Puranic mother goddesses, in particular the goddess Hinglaj. However, Charan *sagatis* are customarily portrayed as historical Charan women with special powers as well. Presently, the Charan tradition counts at least five living *sagati* goddesses, most notably Suva Uday of Udaipur. Bhanvar Pritviraj Ratnu, *Suva Uday Samsara* (Dasauri 1996).

viii 'Nayak' literally translates as 'leader', 'headman' or 'skilled musician'. The Rajasthani title 'Bhopo' holds different meanings and may also refer to 'seer', 'reader of omens', 'medicine-man', and so forth. The standard Hindi usage 'Bhopa' refers to a 'kind of ascetic', 'magician' and 'idiot'. Sitaram Lalas (n.d.); McGregor 1993; Saxena 2000; Sharma 1998.

ix Based on *par* performances by Sarwan Bhopa and Durga Bhopi from village Kalmi (Thar Desert) in Chaupasni (Jodhpur), 1999.

x Thori was traditionally a term used for hunters. With the establishment of Rajput rule in the area, the title probably gained a derogatory meaning, namely 'thief'. The Bhopos of Kolu, however, use the title as a honorific, next to titles like 'Sanvala' ('Black'), a name which is also used for the blue god Krishna, hero of the Ramayana epic. Cf: 'Kavi Punjoji Barhat harvecam vircarit Chand Pabuji Rathaur rau' *Visvambhara* (1997) 29-3: 25-29.

xi Tales of Thori heroism are often linked to the assertion that the Bhils of Kolu, like the Rajput temple-priests, have warrior-blood running through their veins as well. Outside the earshot of the temple-priests, the *mata* players of Kolu claim descent of the Bhati Rajputs of Jaisalmer.

xii It is not clear how many episodes the *mata* epic generally contains. The Bhopos in Kolu hold different opinions on this matter. Moreover, the number of episodes listed often referred to a symbolic figure and not to the total of episodes that the *mata* players could actually perform. During fieldwork in Kolu, I recorded four *paravaras*: the *Byas ro paravaro*, *Jalam ro paravaro*, *Jhararaji ro paravaro* and the *Vahat ro parvaro*. The performances of the four episodes by the three brothers Khumbha Ram, Rupa Ram and Jetha Ram usually continued from sunset to midnight.

xiii Such definitions are often based on descriptions of Dingal *virkavya* in the colonial period by, among others, James Tod, the 19th-century British administrative officer in former Rajputana. Presently, high-caste Charan and Rajput scholars voice similar opinions that seem to be based upon perceived caste-distinctions between literate and illiterate poets, singers and other performers. Kaviya 1997: 29-31; Tod 1829 (1972): 111.

THE SLEEPING GIANT: DYNAMICS OF A BUGIS EPIC (SOUTH SULAWESI, INDONESIA)

Sirtjo Koolhof

This essay has its origin in an invitation by one of the organizers of the conference that stood at the base of this book. He invited me to prepare a paper for a conference about 'Death of the Epic'.[i] Having worked on a corpus of epic texts, called *La Galigo* which, from the moment of its first reference in (western) publications in the early 19th century has been seen as being in decline, if not dead, I was certainly interested in his proposal. However, when some time later a formal invitation fell on my doormat, – lo and behold – the conference's theme was 'Emergent Epics'.

Both of these themes evoke a process, a development. 'Death', 'emergence', 'loose authority', 'demise', 'rise', 'fall' are the words used in the invitation letter; they suggest that at some time in the past people's attitude towards epics was different from today. Epics once went through a Golden Age that has come to an end – or, on the contrary, that very Golden Age is coming closer. And of course the question could be asked whether particular epics have ever been more popular, more widely known and respected than they are now. Or, in correspondence with the metaphor above: was epic ever more alive or vital?

As for *La Galigo*, the epic to which I will restrict myself here, there is no way to prove that it was more vital in the past than it is now. Since the earliest reference to it in western sources in the early 19th century, the people who have understood its language or could give information about have always been very few. Of course, this does not necessarily mean that *La Galigo* never enjoyed a huge popularity; on the other hand, there is no indication that it ever did.

Let me first provide some information about the epic *La Galigo* and about the Bugis, the people who created it. The Bugis are the largest ethnic group on the south-western peninsula of the island of Sulawesi, formerly known as Celebes, in Indonesia.[ii] The Bugis now number around 3.5 million people, comprising nearly two per cent of the total population of Indonesia. In the past they were organized in kingdoms of which the borders roughly coincide with those of the present Indonesian regencies (*kabupaten*). In the early 17th century the rulers of these kingdoms adopted Islam as their religion. In the 20th century Bugis were generally regarded as strict Muslims, although they have retained certain elements of traditional religion. The Tolotang, a group of some 25.000 people, who mainly live in the regency of Sidenreng, adhere to a form of traditional religion. Formally, however, they are adherents of the official

Hindu religion. Hierarchy is very strictly followed in Bugis communities; at the same time there is a fierce competition between individuals.

The *La Galigo* begins with the myth of origin of the Bugis people. It tells the story of how the earth is populated by human beings originating in the Upper World. The first human being, Batara Guru, descends to the earth after his father, Lord of the Upper World, has been convinced by his servants to send one of his children down to earth, which is still empty, saying, 'How can you be a god, if there is no one to worship you?' (Salim et al. 1995: 58). Batara Guru's descent sets in motion an extremely long story, covering the adventures of the first six generations of humans. The main hero is Batara Guru's grandson, Sawérigading, whose son, I La Galigo, has given his name to the epic. Taken these adventures together, *La Galigo* is one of world's longest epics with a length of approximately one and a half times that of the Indian *Mahabharata*.

The *La Galigo* has been transmitted in manuscripts written in the Bugis *lontaraq*-script. Each manuscript contains only a small part, usually one or two episodes, of the story as a whole. The *La Galigo* is not the only written 'genre' in Bugis society. The written heritage of Bugis consists of histories of the various kingdoms, diaries, manuals, heroic poems based on the life of historical figures, legal works, and ritual texts – to mention just some categories. It is not always clear how these texts were read, but most likely *La Galigo* manuscripts were usually performed before an audience by an individual or a group of reciters.

The *La Galigo* is composed in a language that the Dutch Bible translator B.F. Matthes (1818-1908), the first and still authoritative western scholar to study the Bugis language and literature in depth, labelled 'Old Bugis'. The Bugis themselves nowadays refer to this language as *bahasa asli* 'original language', *basa kuno* 'ancient language', *basa to ri olo* 'language of the ancestors', *basa alusuq* 'refined language', or *basa galigo* 'galigo language'. Perhaps the qualification 'literary' is more appropriate than 'old' since there is no indication that 'Old Bugis' represents an older stage of the language spoken at present. It is characterized by its strict pentasyllabic metre and an abundant use of words and expressions that do not occur in everyday spoken Bugis; many of these words are also found in other poetic works as well as in the liturgical songs of the *bissu*, transvestite priests at the former courts of the Bugis.

Although primarily known to us in the form of manuscripts, *La Galigo* texts show characteristics of what is usually called an oral tradition: they are highly formulaic and repetitive, different texts of the same episode showing considerable variation in wording and length, with abundant parallelism. This is not to say that at some point in time, very long ago, the *La Galigo* was a 'pure' oral tradition which was then put to into writing, keeping some traces of its oral origins; rather, in its written form it has features that are usually regarded as being characteristic of an oral transmission. For example, the fluidity, the variation between manuscripts containing the same episode, and the permanent re-composition of episodes. It is not clear when the composition of *La Galigo* was initiated; given the fact that its language shows extremely little Arabic influence in its lexicon, contrary to the spoken language, Bugis literary language must have been established before the south-western part of Sulawesi was islamized in the late 16th century.

To investigate how vital the *La Galigo* tradition is and was, and in what respects it underwent change, I differentiate three different, albeit not always inseparable, aspects of the tradition. First is the production and transmission of texts in the form of manuscripts. Second is the presentation of these texts to an audience, or performances. And third is the use of themes, motifs, and persons from the epic in other settings. Before elaborating on these three points, I will present a short, more or less chronological account of references to the *La Galigo* in western sources.

The poet and linguist John Leyden was the first European who referred to the *La Galigo*, in 1811. Although he does not use the term *La Galigo*, in his article 'On the languages and literature of the Indo-Chinese nations' he gives a list of 53 titles of Bugis texts that bear the names of characters appearing in the *La Galigo*. He writes that 'The greater part of these compositions [...] celebrate the deeds of their national heroes', and offers a strikingly accurate translation of a few lines from an episode ('the only *Búgis* story in my possession') (Leyden 1811: 195-7). Six years later, his good friend Thomas Stamford Raffles wrote the following:

> '*La Galíga*, the reputed son of *Sawira Gáding*, is considered the author of the history of *Sawira Gáding*, which is a kind of heroic poem, and is read in a chaunting voice, with a pause at the end of every fifth syllable. The measure consists of a dactyl followed by a trochee [...]. He is the only author whose name is commonly known; and all books, even the most modern, which are written in the same manner, are called after him *Galíga*, although, properly speaking, the term should only be applied to the history of the heroes who are supposed to have lived previous to the seven generations of anarchy which subsisted at *Bóni*. (Raffles 1817: clxxxviii)'

Raffles and Leyden never visited Sulawesi; they must have gathered their information from Bugis who had migrated to the western part of the Archipelago, or from visitors returning from Sulawesi. Their contemporary John Crawfurd, another English civil servant did, however, pay a visit to Sulawesi. In 1820 his three-volume study entitled *History of the Indian archipelago* was published, in which he states:

> 'The Bugis are said to be possessed of a recondite and ancient language parallel to the Kawi of Java and the Pali of the Buddhist nations; but the knowledge of it is confined to a very few, and I have met no specimens.' (Crawfurd 1820: 61)

Although Crawfurd does not mention the *La Galigo* by name, it is likely that his 'ancient language' refers to the epic's 'literary language' already mentioned. Twenty years later, James Brooke, the famous 'white raja of Sarawak', mentions a small island in the north-eastern part of the Gulf of Boné:

'April 20. [1840] – Crossed over to the eastern bank, and made it out to be an island, called Pulo Paloèh (or separated mountain), which is bold and wooded, being divided from the main by a moderate channel. Tradition says Sawira Gading anchored on the coast; and cutting down a tree, it fell and divided this island from the shore.' (Mundy 1848, I: 159.)

This is clearly a reference to the *La Galigo* episode in which Sawérigading fells a huge sacred tree that he needs to build a ship to sail to the country of his bride-to-be, and although no specific geographical references are found in the texts, (oral) tradition has it that the Wélenréng, the name of the tree concerned, stood on the mainland in the vicinity of Malili. When it fell down, it split the island of Buluq Puloé in two.

The Dutch scholar Matthes who spent almost forty years in South Sulawesi (from 1848 to 1886) was especially keen on collecting information about the *La Galigo*. In his reports to the motherland he time and again complained about the fact that almost nobody was capable of explaining the meaning of the texts to him. So as to be able to ask the *bissu*, the transvestite guardians of the regalia, about the 'old language' of which they seemed to know more than almost everybody else he had to overcome his disgust for these examples 'of how low human nature can sink'.

A 19th-century philologist, Matthes was of the opinion that at some time in the past there had been a long, consistent epic that over the years or centuries had later fallen apart – which is how he came to realize that collecting a 'complete' version of the epic was even more difficult than obtaining the correct information about the contents of the manuscripts he collected.

'That is why it is to deplore that nowhere is to be found a complete copy of this poem. The natives content themselves with – from time to time, especially at the occasion of feasts – rattling off small parts of it, either written on palm leaf or on paper. I spent many years collecting as many as possible of those fragments that each count as a separate manuscript. [...] I do fear, however, that I will never succeed in collecting all the parts into one coherent whole again.' (Matthes 1872: 251)

Matthes's fears were justified. At his request, Colliq Pujié, the queen-mother of the kingdom of Tanété, set out to write a 'complete' version for him, but she produced no more than approximately one-third of her (imagined) 'complete' text. As well as these 2853 folio pages in writing,[iii] she presented Matthes with a summary of what she thought to be the full story, which reads like the main story line, leaving out many of its branches. Perhaps Colliq Pujié did not know these branch episodes, or perhaps she thought they did not really belong to the *La Galigo*. Matthes, who usually based himself on Colliq Pujié's opinion, took a clear stance in this question: in his catalogue he characterized these side stories as 'stories written in the metre of the *La Galigo*'.

More than a century of scholarly research of oral and written epic traditions should make us aware of the dangers of talking about the 'demise' and the 'disintegration' of a once glorious narrative. In the case of *La Galigo*, it is quite conceivable that the reverse process of what Matthes mentioned has taken place and that the epic has been growing from a longer or shorter core story that has been expanded and ornamented by a long series of poets who created new episodes and incorporated already existing narratives not directly related to the themes of *La Galigo*. Raffles seems to support this idea of growth when he talks of 'all books, even the most modern, which are written in the same manner, are called after him *Galíga*'.

'Growth' instead of 'demise' perhaps, but how this process took place is hard to tell, as Matthes' confusion witnesses. Very few of the manuscripts are dated, and from most of them it is unknown where and from whom they were obtained. It is not clear, either, if these manuscripts were newly composed or copied from other manuscripts, or a combination of both. Was the epic expanding in the sense that new episodes were added, or that existing episodes were elaborated and extended, thanks to more widely available writing paper? And, if the latter is the case, was a more or less pure oral tradition (if it ever existed at all) losing its authority to writing? Unfortunately there is no way to know an answer on any of these questions.[iv]

Matthes, like us, was a product of his time. Not only did he think in terms of a complete epic, a narrative of the adventures of a hero that summarizes and reflects the values and ideas of Bugis society, he also worked from a clear distinction between, on the one hand, 'high literature' of which the *La Galigo* was a good example, and, on the other hand, folk stories, legends and fairy tales. Of course, this 'high literature' could, in his eyes, only be produced by the Bugis nobility. Matthes was convinced of the fact that not noble men – who according to him wasted their time gambling, hunting, and smoking opium – but especially noble women were very much involved in the transmission and production of *La Galigo* literature – the earlier mentioned Colliq Pujié is a good example. However true this may have been – Matthes' contacts were almost exclusively with members of the nobility – doubts have to be expressed regarding this opinion, although noble women have played a significant role in the transmission up to the present day. An example is the late Andi Séngeq, a woman of the highest noble descent in Luwu, unmarried and well-known for her interest in Bugis traditional literature in the final decades of the 20th century. She, too, was very knowledgeable about the *La Galigo* and produced manuscripts for her own use or that of her family. When I asked her nephew if she ever performed before an audience, however, he answered that this would be something inconceivable to do for a person of her status; at the most she would recite a manuscript in her own house in a very soft voice, and when a performance for a larger audience was needed, for example during wedding ceremonies, she would invite people from outside her own circles to perform and provide them with a manuscript. Another example is taken from a manuscript containing a *La Galigo* episode copied in 1972 at the request of the late H. Andi Ninnong, a former (female) ruler of the kingdom of Wajoq. A note on the fly leaf states:

> Received from the Datu [ruler] on 3-4-1972. The copying began on Tuesday 4-4-'72 at our house in EmpagaE, Tanasitolo sub regency, Wadjo regency. Consists of 296 pages.
> The copying was finished on 27-4-1972
> The copyist, a civil servant of the Wadjo Cultural Office,
> Sengkang, [signature]

Although she was the head of a noble household, Andi Ninnong obviously asked (or ordered) an outsider to copy a manuscript for her, either because none of the household members was capable of doing so or because none was expected to do so. In her memoirs Andi Ninnong noted that in her youth 'from time to time someone who could read *lontaraq*-manuscripts was summoned', an indication that in those days it was not a member of the royal household who performed the recitation. When I interviewed her daughter Andi Muddariah in 1995, she told me that she herself had never been involved in either producing or reciting *La Galigo* manuscripts, although she owned quite a few of them. If I was interested, she would be all too happy to summon someone well versed in the tradition to her house. Such examples seem to suggest that the nobility, and foremost the women, played an important role in the transmission and production of the tradition. But then, that role could perhaps better be described in terms of patronage than of direct involvement in the production of manuscripts.

Do we know very little about the ways of production and transmission of *La Galigo* stories, even less is known about the circumstances under which the (written) texts were brought to life. By whom, how, and when were they read? Matthes' observation that 'The natives content themselves with – from time to time, especially at the occasion of feasts – rattling off small parts' of the epic is, together with Raffles' remark that 'it is read in a chaunting voice', the only direct reference to the way *La Galigo* texts were presented in the 19th century. The 20th century has not made the question of presentation very much clearer: no information can be found where, when, how often, by and for whom performances took place.

It is assumed that poetical texts were recited or read aloud (*massureq*, 'to read *La Galigo*') before an audience. This assumption is confirmed by what we know of what is done in most manuscript traditions, in particular those in

Indonesia. Handwritten texts were often called to life during social events, usually ceremonies or rituals, but not exclusively so. Andi Ninnong remembers how people were summoned to the palace to read manuscripts, and nowadays many people have stories of how their grandmother was sitting somewhere in the house reading *La Galigo* episodes in a soft voice, sometimes just to her self, at other times to her children or grandchildren. I myself remember an occasion in 1996 when I went with a Tolotang community leader to one of his houses in a remote village in the regency of Wajo. He was especially interested in *La Galigo* literature and did all he could to collect photocopies of manuscripts. During our visit we managed to borrow a manuscript from one of the villagers, and in the evening we had long discussions with them about the *La Galigo*. After I went to bed, I heard him chanting in his room from the manuscript he had borrowed; when I fell asleep after an hour or so, he was still reading and when I woke up the next morning I heard him reading again (or still?).

When people are asked on which occasions *La Galigo* texts are or were read, they usually answer that they are read at wedding ceremonies. This should not surprise us, as weddings are the most elaborate and most important ceremony in Bugis culture. Their importance is reflected in the *La Galigo* itself: the main event in a large number of episodes is the wedding of one of the characters, and in many other episodes, the adventures (such as long journeys to one's prospective bride or fights between two rival lovers) are usually related to a wedding. Other occasions where *massureq* takes place, I have been told, are the moving to a new house and the beginning of the planting season.

During my fieldwork in South Sulawesi in 1991, 1996 and 1999 I never witnessed a spontaneous performance for an audience of a *La Galigo* text,[v] people would tell me, instead, that such readings had been 'very popular in the past' or 'in other places', or 'among other groups'. My research was focussed on the Tolotang, a group of Bugis who are not Muslims but adhere to what is regarded by most as the original Bugis tradition or religion, and is officially categorized by the national government as being part of the 'Hindu religion'. Other Bugis used to tell me that they are the people who not only follow the religion of the *La Galigo* but also perform episodes of the epic during their rituals. Apart from this view being erroneous regarding the religion of the Tolotang, it is also incorrect concerning the performances. Of course, I was often told, in the not too distant past the *La Galigo* had been very popular and was performed regularly. But, if I really wanted to know more I should better look among a sub-group of the Tolotang who were still regularly performing episodes at their ceremonies. Even names of the performers were mentioned. Unfortunately... But, these people told me, in the village of Cerekang in Luwuq (see below) ... And so on.

As it turned out, *La Galigo* was not recited. I found some comfort in the fact that I was not the first one who was confronted with such 'misfortune'. Some 140 years ago, in 1856, Matthes had undertaken a trip to same village and reported as follows:

'The next day we walked to nearby Amparita [...]. The main purpose of this trip was to track down a complete collection of the *La Galigo* poems. I had imagined I would surely find them here, because here are various people who ascribe supernatural power to these writings. [...] But, like many times afterwards, I searched here in vain for an – even more or less – complete collection of these poems. Nothing more than a few bits and pieces were to be found here and there, and even then people were reluctant to give them on loan to me. This was a great disappointment for me.' (Van den Brink 1943: 180)

More comforting to me was the fact that it was easier for me than it had ever been for Matthes to borrow manuscripts. Moreover, I could have photocopies made of them whereas Matthes was forced to copy a manuscript by hand in the house of the owner 'ten days on end from early in the morning to late in the evening, to the amazement of a bunch of lazy natives' (Van den Brink 1943: 180-181).

I had already spent some six months in the village of Amparita, talking to people about the *La Galigo*, collecting manuscripts, and especially telling everyone that I was even more interested in performances than I was in manuscripts; then someone informed me that some days later one of the community leaders would move to a new house and there would be a ceremony at which a *La Galigo* episode was to be read. The performers were a group of women and men, of whom two were experienced and five others were doing it for the first time. Moreover, two days later someone else was organizing a ceremony in his house for the starting of the planting season. He had invited a group of friends, among them a man whose name was regularly mentioned to me as someone who 'often recites manuscripts'. When I asked the latter, he told me that it had been at least fifteen to twenty years since he had last recited a *La Galigo* text.

At the first ceremony the performance attracted the attention of an audience of about sixty people. However, within half an hour most of them started doing other things, and after two hours most were asleep. After four hours only three old men, the performers and a western researcher were still awake. The second performance, which was essentially organized for one household, attracted but some interest of the organizer's children and their friends for the first hour or so. After that, they remembered that I had made video recordings of the *massureq* two days before, and so they asked me if they could watch these. This created the somewhat strange situation: the children were (attentively) watching a video of a *massureq* performance in the front room, while at the same time in the backroom a live performance was going on. Marshall McLuhan would have loved it.

The main incentive behind organizing these performances turned out to be my presence as a researcher in the community for some period of time. Some people felt sorry for me, and they thought that my time would be wasted if I were not able to attend at least one performance. On the other hand, my presence also influenced the view the people themselves had of the *La Galigo*. Through our discussions their interest was raised and manuscripts that had for long been hidden in a cupboard or on the attic, although always regarded as a valuable heritage, suddenly became the focus of attention. If someone was willing to travel thousands of miles to find them, they felt that they themselves should show more interest in them. People would start asking about and discussing *La Galigo* with others they regarded as more knowledgeable than themselves, both in my presence and when I was not there. And, although neglected for quite some time, performances could be called to life again.

So far I have described the *La Galigo* tradition in terms of production – transmission – and presentation. The third aspect that I intend to talk about is that of the use of *La Galigo* materials in other contexts than these two. In the first place it should be mentioned that it is unlikely that people obtained knowledge of *La Galigo*'s story by listening to the reciting of all or some of the episodes. Firstly, as Matthes experienced, there is no 'complete' *La Galigo* available anywhere, and it is most unlikely that it ever was. Secondly, the language of the epic is not comprehensible to most people. These two facts mean that the main story line must have been transmitted in much less formalized ways than by way of the performances at which manuscripts were recited. Maybe grandmothers used to explain stories to their grandchildren. Maybe every now and then a father would tell his son a story from the *La Galigo* to give him examples of how to behave or not to behave. Lately another medium has become available: an Indonesian translation (1989) of R.A. Kern's voluminous catalogues (some 1300 pages) of *La Galigo* manuscripts. Published in Dutch in 1939 and 1954 the two catalogues contain detailed abstracts of the contents of manuscripts kept in public collections in the Netherlands and South Sulawesi. Furthermore, the streets in South Sulawesi towns named after *La Galigo* characters, such as Sawérigading and I La Galigo, might sometimes provoke a question of who they were. Perhaps some people knew the answer – but then, when I asked younger people in Palopo, the capital of Luwuq, who were the people the streets were named after very few of them could produce an accurate answer. The most common answer was that they were *pahlawan*, '(national) heroes', since of course heroes have streets named after them in Indonesia.

La Galigo may well have been an important source for the ideology, world view, and religion of the majority of Bugis before competition with Islam pushed it to the margin. Nowadays, only small communities directly relate their customs and beliefs to the *La Galigo*. The clearest instance of this I found in the remote north-eastern corner of South Sulawesi.

Cérékang, a small village alongside the main road to one of the world's largest nickel mines, situated some 60 kilometres east of it, is regarded by those people who know about its existence as the area where according to the *La Galigo* the first humans descended to earth. The village is situated at the eastern border of Luwuq, the kingdom that is widely regarded as the cradle of Bugis civilization,[vi] forms a small pocket of Bugis speakers amidst an array of other languages. Various sacred sites that are directly linked to events in *La Galigo* are close to it; the most important one, close to the village, is the hill of Pénsi Méwoni where Batara Guru arrived on earth in a golden bamboo. This place can only be visited by members of a small religious group called the Tossuq (from *to*, 'man, human', and Ussuq, the name of a village close to Cérékang). Only villagers of Cérékang and their relatives can be members of the Tossuq; they are not very keen on providing outsiders with information about their beliefs and rituals, and are even obliged to tell lies about these matters (Christian Pelras, personal communication).

The Tossuq are organized around two *puaq* (cognate to Bg *puang* 'lord m/f'), the *puaq makkunrai*, a woman, and the *puaq oroané*, a man. Both of them are assisted by five *paréwa* 'assistants': a Head (*panngulu*), a head (*ulu*), a shoulder (*salangka*), a hand (*lima*), and a foot (*ajé*). Local people told me that the two *puaq* are substitutes or successors of the first human being, Batara Guru, and his wife Wé Nyiliq Timoq. A note made in the 1930s tells us that the *puaq* are the successors of Sawérigading and his twin sister Wé Tenriabéng.[vii] This would, at least in the current situation, seem more likely: the two *puaq* live apart in different houses, are not married to each other, and very seldom share activities, and this would be more in concordance with the image of Sawérigading and the 'incestuous' relationship with his sister than with the happily married couple of the founders of humankind. However, a note in the margin of KITLV Or 545/200b says 'they are not always man and wife, but may be', which would oppose the latter interpretation. The *puaq oroané* is not allowed to ever leave the village, while his female counterpart can only leave the place in specific circumstances, usually in connection with ceremonies of the Luwuq royal house in the regency capital of Palopo, some 200 kilometres west of Cérékang.

The function of *puaq* is not hereditary. When a *puaq* dies, a successor is selected on the basis of the *paréwa*'s dreams: these ten assistants have to dream of the same person who should become the next *puaq* before this person can be appointed, a process that may take years. The candidate should be of Cérékang descent, but does not have to live in the village. The present *puaq oroané*, for instance, was called to this function approximately ten years ago when he was in his mid sixties, and had lived the longer part of his life in the province of Southeast-Sulawesi, where he made a living as a trader and owned a small plantation, while also acting as *imam*. The process of electing a new *puaq* is said to be inspired by *wéré* 'divine inspiration' (Ind. *wahyu*). The *paréwa*, who are seen as the successors of the close companions of Batara Guru and his descendants, are elected in the same manner: they, too, are elected on the basis of *wéré* of the *paréwa* who are in function.

This way of selecting a *puaq* may have worked effectively in the past – something we do not know due to a lack of documentation – but it became a point of disagreement in the early 1990s. After the death of the *puaq makkunrai* it took some time before the *parèwa* were given the *wéré* to appoint her successor. The new *puaq* was a rather modern woman in her mid-forties; she used to watch television, read newspapers and she had a good command of Indonesian, the national language. For a group of villagers this was reason enough to question the correctness of this 'decision'. Of course they could not question the validity of the heaven-sent dreams of the *parèwa*, so they publicly questioned the validity of the selection procedure instead, allegedly on the instigation of a woman who had hoped to be the new *puaq* and organized the people around her to challenge the decision. Basing themselves on the discourse of the Indonesian state, they claimed that the way of selection was undemocratic, not in tune with the spirit of the times. The Tossuq should be called together (*musyawarah*) so as to choose a new *puaq* in a democratic way. However, no meeting took place, and the rift in the community exists until today.[viii]

A more serious incident took place in Cérèkang in May 1930 when one of the hamlet heads by the name of La Tangkeq incited a small scale rebellion against the Dutch colonial authorities. He claimed to be inspired by the gods of the *La Galigo*, and changed his name to Batara Guru, the first human being on earth, while his supporters took names of other characters in the epic. The group attacked a police station in the vicinity of Cérèkang and then retreated to Cérèkang. The military unit that was sent from the capital of Palopo, 'rendered them harmless', while 'in the other party two people were wounded by pistol shots' (*Patrouille-actie* s.a.). Later that year the Dutch came and took the sacred objects (regalia) that were kept in the village (*Detachement* s.a.: 1).[ix] Seventy years later this incident is still vividly remembered in the village. People told me that the great annual ritual at the top of Pinsi Méwoni had not taken place ever since, due to the absence of the sacred objects, a ban by the colonial authorities, and a lack of funds. Rather surprisingly they did not blame the Dutch, but La Tangkeq who had been too arrogant (Ind. *takbur*). When I suggested that the Dutch soldiers had robbed the sacred objects from Cérèkang I was corrected: La Tangkeq himself had handed them over, because he realized that his magic could not compete with the much stronger magic of the Dutch.[x] Although they were deprived of their most important ritual (at least, if not performed in secret), the tradition has been kept alive. The *puaq* are still in function, performing their main task, praying for the well-being of the whole world, and participating in the ceremonies of the former royal line of Luwuq in Palopo.

Bugis academics prefer to treat *La Galigo* as a more or less reliable picture of the glorious past of the Bugis, full of references to real events and real places. However, as it suits an epic, those real events and real places are subject to various interpretations. And while the *La Galigo* is an epic of importance to the Bugis people as a whole, discussions about it reflect the tough competition between various groups that can be classified in terms of the half dozen or so kingdoms that have competed with each other for centuries. One of the subjects of those discussions, to give just one example, is the exact location of the kingdom of Cina, where the hero Sawérigading travels to from his (and according to tradition all Bugis') home Luwuq to marry his cousin, a princess of that kingdom. The texts suggest that Cina, or Tanah Ugiq, 'Land of the Bugis', is located in the Bugis heartland, around the Lake of Tempe. For people of the former kingdom of Wajoq it is obvious that Cina is in their area, even though it now has the name of Pammana. For people of the kingdom of Boné the *La Galigo*'s Cina is the village Cina, which lies south of Wajoq. Both have to face claims of other regions that Cina refers to China for which supporters find proof in the fact that Sawérigading's journey from Luwuq to Cina takes about seven months during which he has to defeat seven enemies and their fleets. A journey by boat from present-day Luwuq to Wajoq would take at most two days, they argue, and that is why Cina must be the empire of China. This interpretation is favoured by those who want to see in the *La Galigo* concrete proof that the Bugis have been bold sailors roaming the Asian seas for at least a millennium. Whether such discussions about the location of the places mentioned in the *La Galigo* took place in the past as well, I do not know. It seems conceivable, since Matthes, for instance, repeatedly states explicitly that *La Galigo*'s Cina is not China, but a village in Wajoq.

Only a small group of people are actively engaged in discussions about *La Galigo*. What then, does it mean that a tradition is still 'alive'? How do we measure 'vitality'? One possible answer is given by the organizers of the 'International La Galigo Festival and Seminar', held from 15-18 March 2002 in South Sulawesi: the tradition should be 'revitalized' (*revitalisasi*), and Bugis cultural works should be returned to their 'owners' (*Festival* 2002: 2; *Minim* 2002). One magazine reported that the *La Galigo* tradition 'is only known in academic circles', and its 'spirit' had 'to be brought to life again' (Pareanom and Amir 2002: 69). The festival included all kinds of traditional and modern performances and games from fifteen regencies, including some non-Bugis areas. It brought thousands of people to the village of Pancana, some 100 kilometres north of the provincial capital Makassar, where Colliq Pujié, the noble lady who provided Matthes with the twelve-volume manuscript containing one-third of the complete *La Galigo* lived. The organizers efffectively made Colliq Pujié the real heroine of the Bugis cultural heritage. 'We can not imagine what the fate of La Galigo would have been without her' (*Festival* 2002: 2), 'she should be honoured by the local as well as by the national government representing the people of Indonesia' (Fachruddin Ambo Enre 2002: 9). The festival received much attention from both the local and the national press; two of the papers presented at the seminar were published in the national newspaper *Kompas* (Tol 2002; Pelras 2002). To make sure that the *'revitalisasi'* would continue, its organizers sent a recommendation to the Indonesian Department of Education proposing that knowledge about *La Galigo* be included in the national curriculum (*Naskah* 2002), while Hasanuddin University in Makassar has set up a Centre for the Study of La Galigo.

Will all this result in a vital or revitalized tradition, being brought back to its owners, the Bugis people? It may be telling that the festival's program did not schedule a reading of *La Galigo* (*Festival* 2002: 40-3),[xi] a fact that also disappointed a 42 year old woman from Barru who visited the Festival especially to watch *massureq* (Pareanom and Amir 2002: 70). And Asdar Muis RMS, theatre director, poet, and journalist, publicly expressed his doubts about what will happen now that the festival is over. Surely the memory of *La Galigo* was given a boost, he wrote. But why did the organizers ignore or forgot the real pillars of the tradition? The way the invited *bissu* were ignored was a good example of 'cultural exploitation'; why were they not publicly thanked for their contribution to the preservation of the heritage? And why were the Tolotang 'neglected'? Asdar ended his article with the following remarks:

> 'The festival is over. Nothing is left. There are no follow-up discussions. What will be done and to what end with the results of the seminar? Yes, there is a recommendation to teach La Galigo in schools, but how far will the struggle go and where are the proofs? Those questions do not need an answer. [...] The *bissu* do not care. Together with the Tolotang community they remain the last pillars to safeguard La Galigo.' (Asdar Muis RMS 2002b)

I began this paper with some remarks about the terms 'death', 'demise', 'emergence' and 'rise', metaphors for describing the fate of epics over time. What I have tried to show is that at least for the *La Galigo* such terms are not very appropriate. It is impossible to say whether a hundred years ago, two hundred years ago, or ten years ago, *La Galigo* was more 'alive' than it is now. Epics could be defined as narratives that depict an imagined (and thus long gone) Golden Age in which everything was better, everyone happier and the world near to ideal. We should be careful not to view the epic itself as a product of a historical Golden Age in which it was known by all the people, performed at every corner of every street, and a guide to everyone's life.

A giant epic such as *La Galigo* is alive, but like every other living being it sleeps sometimes deeply, only to be woken by a wild dream or two – either in the form of a 'giant festival' (Asdar Muis RMS 2002a), or in a more modest shape like a ten-minute performance at a wedding ceremony. Moreover, it is good to realize that death can turn up unexpectedly during such a good night's sleep. But then, the dead live on in the memory of their loved ones.

NOTES

[i] I like to thank Ian Caldwell for his useful comments on this article.

[ii] See for a general description of the Bugis, Pelras 1996.

[iii] The first two volumes are published in Salim et al. 1995, 2000. For Colliq Pujié and her activities see Koolhof 1995.

[iv] The oldest extant manuscripts containing *La Galigo* episodes are from the late 18th century. The majority of manuscripts date from the late 19th and 20th centuries.

[v] Neither did Christian Pelras during his visits to South Sulawesi from the late 1960s onwards (personal communication). Raymond Kennedy, who visited the area in 1949-1950 does not seem to have come across performances either (Kennedy 1953).

[vi] See Bulbeck and Caldwell (2000) for the most recent discussion of this subject.

[vii] KITLV Or 545/200b, notes on names and words from *La Galigo* by Noeroeddin Daeng Magassing.

[viii] My information is based solely on what people close to the present *puaq* told me, which undoubtedly has coloured the data.

[ix] I have not found any extensive report from the Dutch side on this incident. In the Algemeen Rijksarchief, Den Haag, only some short references are available: Groeneveld 1938; *Detachement* s.a.; *Patrouille-actie* s.a. An extensive hand-written account based on interviews with his older fellow villagers of Cerekang was compiled during the 1990's by Usman Daeng Matanang. He situates the events in the year 1928.

[x] This is not as strange as it may sound, because the Dutch are not regarded as outsiders. Like the people from Cérékang, and the other Bugis, the Dutch are descendents of Sawérigading, who begot their first ancestor by a woman in the Underworld (see Koolhof 1999: 381).

[xi] A performance under the name of *massureq* is found in the program; however, this concerns a reading of *Meong Mpalo Karellaé*, a story not being part of the *La Galigo* (*Festival* 2002: 40).

AN EPIK THAT NEVER WAS AN EPIC – THE MALAY *HIKAYAT HANG TUAH*

Henk M.J. Maier

In the textbooks that in the closing decades of the 20th century were used in the kingdom of Malaysia to inform students, young and old, about Malay literature, the word *epik* invariably comes up when mention is made of one work in particular: the *Hikayat Hang Tuah*, the Tale of Hang Tuah.

'The *Hikayat Hang Tuah* is the greatest and most important original Malay *epik*,' Taib Osman and Abu Hassan Sham tell their readers, for instance, in *Warisan Prosa Klasik* ('Heritage of Classic Prose', 1978), a book of fragments from older Malay texts for university students. 'It can be categorized as an *epik*, and more particular as an *epik rakyat*, a 'folk epic'. Almost every nation in this world has created its own *epik*'. And then these two well-respected experts of pre-20th century Malay writing offer their readers a number of characteristics that, they claim, hold for every *epik* in the world, including the *Hikayat Hang Tuah*: its hero has a very high position in the history of his nation and sometimes in the international world; the tale's background is very wide, its timeframe very long; its hero has extraordinary characteristics (strong, smart, faithful, generous, compassionate), he is not only known for his courage but also for his supernatural qualities; and the tale's author is very objective (*objektif*) in presenting the hero and his opponents. That is a clear enumeration, in clear language. However, not all of us will agree with the assumption that almost every nation has an epic, and also the so-called objectivity of the tale's author seems like a questionable characteristic, unless the Malay word *objektif* refers to notions of ambivalence and polyvocality and to the idea that the public is supposed to be able to identify with several heroes and worldviews at once.

Epik is a Malay word, and the confusing meaning of the word *objektif* should teach us that the semantic equivalence between the Malay word *epik* and the English word 'epic' is not so self-evident either. More often than not, the numerous Malay words that have their origin in Sanskrit or Arabic, Chinese or Thai, English or Dutch tend to conjure semantic fields that are deceptively different from the meaning of those words in the language from which they have been taken. Translation is a risky endeavor, and so is the claim that notions of genre have a universal validity. An *epik* is not necessarily an epic.

Kesusasteraan Melayu Tradisional ('Traditional Malay Literature', 1993), written by some leading experts of older forms of Malay writing and published in Kuala Lumpur, gives yet another authoritative survey of pre-20th century Malay writing; it is clearly meant to serve as yet another compass for textbooks and teachers. The book has a separate chapter about three *epik* in particular, *Hikayat Hang Tuah*, *Hikayat Amir Hamzah*, and *Hikayat Muhammad Ali Hanafiyah*. In an emphatic attempt to remove every possible form of misunderstanding, the chapter's introduction makes a direct link between *epik* and the English 'epic' by quoting a definition from J.A. Cuddon's *Dictionary of Literary Terms* (1977). 'Epic', Cuddon tells his readers, is 'a long narrative poem on a grand scale about the deeds of warriors and heroes. It is a polygonal 'heroic' story incorporating myth, legend, folktale and history. Epics are often of national significance in the sense that they embody the history and aspirations of a nation in a lofty or grandiose manner'. After that definition and a shower of names of European authors such as Carlyle, Goethe, and Raglan (most of them are Romantics, of course) and of European epics such as Beowulf and Iliad, the Malay experts offer us the three most prominent characteristics of the *epik*: the background of the tale covers a long period of time, its world is wide, its actors are many; it contains many supernatural events and beings; and the author is *objektif* in his characterization of the heroes (Zalila 1993: 250-279). The echoes of Taib Osman and Abu Hassan Sham are audible – and the next step is a self-evident one: *Hikayat Hang Tuah* is a national epic (whereas the other two epics they mention are characterized as 'Islamic epics' without a clear justification: since the early nineties discussions of the Malay heritage seem doomed to operate in a discourse in which Islamic elements have to be made visible everywhere).

When yet another version of the *Hikayat Hang Tuah* was published in the series *Karya Agung Melayu*, 'Great Malay Works', in 1997 (next to novel versions of the *Sulalat as-Salatin* and the *Hikayat Merong Mahawangsa*), Noriah Taslim wrote in her introduction: 'as an *epik*, the *Hikayat Hang Tuah* has the following characteristics: 1. the hero has a high position in the history of his nation and in the international world; 2. the tale's background covers a long period of time and a wide world; 3. the hero has superior characteristics, he is smart, courageous, generous, compassionate and far from hateful and greedy; 4. the hero has supernatural qualities that make it hard for his enemies to fight him' (*Hikayat Hang Tuah* 1997: xxix). Repetitions and echoes, it seems, were many in the descriptions of the *Hikayat Hang Tuah* in Malaysia in the final decades of the 20th century. Altogether, they suggest there was a kind of discursive consensus among contemporary Malay intellectuals that the *Hikayat Hang Tuah* should be read as an *epik* – and perhaps it should be read as a national epic.

It may come as a surprise that Malay literary scholars, while focusing on its formal features, have paid so little attention to the fact that the *Hikayat Hang Tuah* is written in prose and not in poetry as an epic is supposed to be, according to Cuddon. But then, they may have argued in silence that in older Malay writing not the contrast between prose and poetry but the contrast between non-stylized and stylized is the predominant opposition – and the *Hikayat Hang Tuah* is very stylized indeed and, therefore, as artful and memorable as every other epic could be. Moreover, Cuddon's generic definition touches not only upon the epic's formal features but also upon its function – and about this very function Malay scholars have remained surprisingly vague. The *epik*, we are told repetitively, is a narrative in which the hero has 'a high position in the history of his nation' – and that high position is of fundamental importance for a tale to be treated as an epic: the Tale of Hang Tuah, admiral of Malacca, obviously has a greater significance for the tale's public than other narratives such as the Tales of Rama, Arjuna and Panji, kings of never-never lands.

But then, these repetitive statements about *Hikayat Hang Tuah*'s function are lacking the elaboration that is needed to make them persuasive ones. Whose history and what nation are we talking about? And more precisely: for which public does (or did) this narrative function as an epic, as a significant narrative that reflects (or reflected) the history and aspirations of a nation in a lofty or artful manner? How do we know whether its hero has a high position? And how do we know that superior, if not supernatural qualities can be ascribed to him? In the most general terms: how, where, and when did this stylized narrative about Hang Tuah become an epic or a national epic?

The terms 'nation' and 'national' are problematic notions, to begin with. The Malay world – the areas where forms of Malay are used in speaking and writing – covers the coastal areas around the Strait of Malacca, the South China Sea, the Java Sea and the Banda Sea, and given its vastness and, concurrently, its pluriform and heterogeneous history and culture it seems more adequate to talk about Malay communities than about the Malay nation. In some of those communities, it seems, the tales about Hang Tuah have been more prominent than in others: on the Peninsula Hang Tuah is better known than elsewhere along the seas, and even more than that: Hang Tuah is an almost unknown persona in what is now called Indonesia, apart from the Riau area and the East Coast of Sumatra. The nation that has been created in the kingdom of Malaysia, in short, is of a very restrictive character – and so are the notions of nationalism that come with it. Malays on the Peninsula tend to ignore the heterogeneity of the Malay world. They tend to remain silent about every form of Malayness beyond the borders of the Malay Peninsula, seen as the core of Malaysia. They pretend to be oblivious of the historical and cultural differentiations within the Malay world. They ignore the problematic nature of Malaysia which comprises more than the Malays alone. Nationalism can be narrow-minded indeed. And very selective at that.

Also in literary terms it seems appropriate to observe more caution than the Malay experts with their Europe-inspired notions about the epic tend to do. Distinctions should be made between, firstly, the written or printed texts of a work now called *epik*; secondly, the tradition, that indistinct cloud of more or less fragmentary memories that have been floating around over one or more communities and beyond; and, thirdly, the performances of such fragments that sustain and create the tradition as well as the epic within a community and could move tradition and 'epic' to other communities (e.g. Flueckiger & Sears 1991: 6). That is to say, there is, firstly, the *Hikayat Hang Tuah*, the texts on paper, written or printed: the *epik*, the stylized narrative about a hero named Hang Tuah that has allegedly been of great significance for an ever shifting group of people, called the Malays. Secondly, there are the adventures of a certain Hang Tuah that, in the form of fragmentary memories, are floating around in Malay communities and beyond. And, thirdly, there are performances, the more or less artful enactments of those memories about Hang Tuah in written and oral forms, in poems, plays, movies, jokes, short stories and tales, embedded in rituals and other communal activities that are shared and perpetuated within and between Malay communities. In this interactive and dynamic process of performances, memories and writing, Hang Tuah has apparently acquired a central position in the history of one Malay community in particular: in the community of peninsular Malays the *Hikayat Hang Tuah* has been given the status of an *epik*, a work of great and exemplary significance, embodying this community's history and aspirations.

Based on these terminological precautions – the peninsular Malay community or nation is a speculative concept in itself as it ignores the cultural heterogeneity among the Malays on the Peninsula – the main contextual question remains the same: why, when, and how was this particular text, *Hikayat Hang Tuah*, made an *epik*, a narrative that centers around a superior hero, Hang Tuah, whose exploits are of great import for the members of the community of peninsular Malays?

A remnant of the past

It has been argued that the epic is, by definition, an antiquated form of writing, a remnant of the past (Bakhtin 1981: 13). Once experience and knowledge were substituted for memory as the most prominent compass in communal life, such an authoritative narrative was bound to yield to the popular novel while questions about the moral of the tale were to yield to questions about the meaning of life (cf. Benjamin 1968: 99). The epic was, so to speak, invented as a genre by those who, operating within the domain of the novel, were looking back at the inaccessible past in search of an exemplary and elegant tale that would summarize the most illustrious characteristics of that very past – and in how far such an ancient text still has a meaning in their daily life has remained a contested question to the present day. Preserved as 'great works', epics tend to create and confirm nostalgia about a past that is definitely lost and gone rather than offer directions to the future.

A descendant of the gods in heaven settles on the island of Bintan, and together with the local people who make him their ruler he later moves to the mainland to establish a new state, called Malacca. Still on the island, Hang Tuah, son of a merchant, comes to serve him, together with four friends. Strengthened by his ascetic exercises and tested in a series of confrontations, Tuah rises to great prominence in Malacca. He shows an absolute loyalty to his lord, the Sultan, who makes him an admiral, *laksamana*. Faithful is Tuah, and humble, and cunning, and smart. For his lord, Tuah confronts the Javanese more than once so that the Sultan can marry a princess of Majapahit; their son becomes the ruler of Java. For his lord, Tuah abducts Tun Teja from the kingdom of Indrapura. For his lord, Tuah kills his own best friend, Jebat, who had started a revolt to take revenge for the way the Sultan had treated Tuah. For his lord, Tuah makes long journeys overseas, to Rum, to China, and to every kingdom in between. At the time the Portuguese appear in front of Malacca, both the Sultan and Tuah become dervishes and disappear.

The adventures of Hang Tuah and his friends take place in a closed-off past, in a world of beginnings, a world of firsts and bests; sustained by memories rather than by experience or knowledge, they have been made distant personas in a very wide world. In the first fifty years of print capitalism and nation-building on the Malay Peninsula, beginning around 1900, *Hikayat Hang Tuah* has been made the tale that tells its Malay readers: this is how we were. Driven by nationalism (the strong desire to be a cultural unity) and its complement, nostalgia (the wistful longing for memories), local literates have seen to it that the *Hikayat Hang Tuah* now offers its readers memories of glory and fame, a distant world of exemplary behavior and admirable deeds.

That memorable picture perfectly served Malay intellectuals and politicians in the second half of the 20th century once they started to look for a comprehensive survey of Malay values and ideas that had been lost – and should be restored. The Tale of Hang Tuah was made a manifestation of nostalgia, a cluster of memories – and nostalgia and memories may be essential elements of nationalism, they are not necessarily the most effective tools to implement the cultural unification and the political integration nationalism is striving for. In practice the interest for the *Hikayat Hang Tuah* has been minimal. Maybe it is not to be an epic after all. Maybe it never was.

In the second introduction to the 1997 edition of the *Hikayat Hang Tuah*, Kassim Ahmad gives us a succinct summary of its present status: 'For us nowadays *Hikayat Hang Tuah* is nothing but a literary heirloom. General readers are probably unable to enjoy it in the way they enjoy a modern work. Only students of secondary schools and universities read it, for their exams. Scholars are interested in it because they want to study its literary features and also because they want to know the Malay world of thought in a time that has passed'. 'Many readers will say that the tale is boring,' Kassim continues, 'just like Western readers will feel bored with the ancient Greek epics, the Iliad and the Odyssey. These epics are too long, their techniques too uniform.' That is the way it goes: 'Every period has its own distinct writing habits. And yet, apart from all these considerations we can not deny that the feelings of humanity and the spirit of heroism that are pictured in the *Hikayat Hang Tuah* create feelings of admiration, enthusiasm, and respect in our hearts. Similar feelings must have been experienced by its readers or listeners three hundred years ago, and perhaps they will still be experienced by readers in three hundred years from now, because those are the universal feelings in these tales. They justify the Tales' title of "Great Malay Work". (*Hikayat Hang Tuah* xvii)

A history of the Hikayat Hang Tuah
The earliest references to the *Hikayat Hang Tuah* so far have been found in reports of Dutch scholars. The reverend Valentijn called it 'one of the finest Malay books' in his encyclopedic *Oud en Nieuw Oost Indien,* published in the 1720s, and the reverend Werndly repeated that honorary title some ten years later in his survey of Malay writing (1736) – and those remarks were echoed in later studies of Malay writing. The oldest now available manuscript of the *Hikayat Hang Tuah* is dated 1172 H/1758 AD; preserved in Leiden, it does not differ considerably from manuscripts of a later date that have become available, or from the various text-editions of those manuscripts that were produced in the 20th century, for that matter. The differences among these texts are small and sometimes worthy of consideration, but the similarities and correspondences are so much more striking that scholars have considered it justified to speak of 'the Hikayat Hang Tuah', a term that refers to the various manuscripts and editions together. This *Hikayat Hang Tuah*, fixed in manuscripts and available in printed versions (in the Arabic as well as in the Romanized script), is the work which textbooks such as Taib Osman and Abu Hassan Sham's are talking about in *epik* terms. We are told that the *Hikayat Hang Tuah* offers marvelous pictures of a Malay Sultanate in its glory days and edifying memories of the people who served Malay glory. Whether this *Hikayat* functioned in ways that could be described as 'epic' in the beginning of the 18th century, not too long after the fall of Malacca to the Dutch, is impossible to say. Or rather: it seems highly improbable that this particular work was of great significance for Malay communities three hundred years ago.

A survey of Malay literary life in which the Tale of Hang Tuah may have played the role of an epic is so hard to give that it is almost inconceivable to do more than produce a list of titles, a series of summaries, and a set of predominant themes – and the rest is speculation, necessarily based on an occasional remark by European visitors and a sentence or two in the manuscripts written by anonymous Malay scribes. Our ignorance is not only due to the fact that the question of what exactly we mean by 'literature' and 'literary' in the Malay context has to remain unanswered: they are concepts that are as historically changing as the term 'epic' – and it is telling that the notions of 'epic' and 'literature' (and their apparent Malay equivalents, *epik* and *kesusasteraan*) did not enter the Malay world until the 1920s, when British involvement became more intense at last.

Malay literary life cannot be described in any comprehensive manner for other, more material reasons, too. Many manuscripts are irretrievably lost. Particular cases of how manuscripts were produced and copied, traded and interacted are not concretely known – and the lack of such particularities makes more general statements about the world in which the Tale of Hang Tuah functioned unconvincing, to put it mildly. The interactions between oral performances and writing practices must have been numerous and varied, yet a more detailed picture, necessary for a better understanding of their dynamics, can not be given: descriptions of how singers of tales actually performed and scribes factually operated have never been found but in an occasional short reference in a manuscript or two. The names of singers and writers were, no doubt, known in the days they wrote, copied and performed, but they have been lost since then, apart from the names of scribes and scholars of Islamic treatises that formed a separate corpus with specific functions and contents in the Malay world. The political function or cultural authority of specific works or tales in the various Malay communities is impossible to determine. The movements and adventures of particular stories, narratives, memories, and manuscripts cannot be traced. And so on. And so forth.

Altogether, we will never be able to give a balanced survey of the dynamics of Malay writing and reading, performance and listening – and that also holds for the manuscripts of the *Hikayat Hang Tuah* and the tales about Hang Tuah. Such a misty situation may be the dream of every post-modernist in search of fragmentation, as yet it is certainly not the dream of Malaysian scholars who have difficulties to come to terms with the fact that every 'history of Malay writing' is bound to be a series of little dots and a long list of titles, surrounded by a great number of black holes.

One black hole is of particular interest for us here: direct references to the adventures of Hang Tuah and to the *Hikayat Hang Tuah* are rare in the 18th and 19th century Malay texts that have been preserved. This virtual absence suggests a certain ignorance or disinterest in Hang Tuah, in whatever form his name and persona were actually floating around in the Malay world by way of chunks of knowledge, performances, or complete manuscripts. He certainly did not have 'a high position', and the rarity of references in reports of European contemporaries only confirms that conclusion. The *Hikayat* certainly did not function as an epic.

Not until the first half of the 19th century the name of Hang Tuah comes up with a certain frequency in the work of British scholars of the Malay world, mainly active on the Peninsula. Marsden, Leyden, Crawfurd, and Newbold make mention of a text by the name of *Hikayat Hang Tuah,* and this frequency could serve as an indication, no matter how indirect, that their informants had enough respect for this particular tale to mention it to their European interviewers and masters. Given their disqualifications of it as being 'childish', 'unreliable', 'boring', and 'fantastic', we could assume that almost none of these British sojourners in the Malay world took the trouble to read *Hikayat Hang Tuah* from beginning to end, but it is obvious that they were intrigued by it, and not without a reason or two. In their attempts to position the local population on the scale of civilization and give depth to the history of the Peninsula, they were interested in the Malay nation for curiosity's sake as much as for good government's sake. Trying to construct a picture of the Malay nation on the Peninsula in its totality, they were looking for texts that offered them 'some outline of Malay history and of the progress of that nation' as John

Leyden formulated it in the 1820s. Performances of tellers of tales were ignored by him and his direct successors as being unreliable and fabulous, and so were Islamic texts: Islam had come to Southeast Asia in a later stage, and Islamic texts did only give a later if not distorted picture of the core of the Malay world. The *Sulalat as-Salatin*, a collection of tales about the rulers of Malacca and their courtiers, was more suitable to these scholars' aims: it offered pictures of the history of the most glorious period of Malay history as well as pictures of Malay society. As early as 1823 an English translation of *Sulalat as-Salatin* appeared under the titles of *Sejarah Melayu* and *Malay Annals*, and ever since the *Malay Annals* has remained the most quoted work of the heritage, used by anthropologists, literary critics, and historians time and again to define Malayness.

The *Hikayat Hang Tuah* was to become another major subject of 19th century scholarly attention: its hero was presented as a real Malay, his location was the *Sulalat as-Salatin*'s Malacca, and the tale seemed, in one way or another, to give an adequate picture of Malay notions of love, life and death in days of yore. Moreover, was the language of this particular *Hikayat* not of an extraordinary elegance? Among the numerous manuscripts one came to know, those of the *Hikayat Hang Tuah* were to acquire a special position, next to the *Sejarah Melayu*.

Dutch scholars were more positive about this *Hikayat* than their British colleagues. In 1860 the Dutch scholar-administrator Elisa Netscher, for instance, called it 'a very important novel' *(een zeer belangrijke roman)* as it gave him a detailed description of Malay society in the olden days; Netscher may have been the first who called it a 'novel' or 'roman', in itself an ambiguous term, at once an echo of the English term romance, the word that was used since Leyden, and an evocation of a new genre, the novel. An echo of this positive qualification (not only among Malays scholarship works with echoes) can be found in Den Hollander's textbook *Handleiding bij de Beoefening van de Maleise Taal- en Letterkunde* (a sixth edition of this book for future administrators and military in the Indies appeared in 1893): 'a novel which is very important for the knowledge of Malay customs and habits'. The term 'novel' opened it up to novel readings indeed, and in retrospect we can say that *Hikayat Hang Tuah* deserved this ambiguous name: if only because of its open ending and its apparent tendency to coherence, the Tale of Hang Tuah is an extraordinary text that does not fit in any of the genres that have been developed to organize older forms of Malay writing. In late colonial days Hans Overbeck, an honorary Dutchman living in the Indies, called it 'the most beautiful book of Malay literature', a phrase that sounds like an echo of Valentijn's words. Overbeck did more than giving it a place of honor within Malay literary life: he translated the text into German, an admirable endeavor as the *Hikayat Hang Tuah* is not only one of the most elegant but also one of the longest Malay texts.

While in European circles the *Hikayat Hang Tuah* was rising towards prominence, in positive as well as negative ways, it remained as yet a relatively unknown work among the Malays themselves. Had the Hikayat been regarded as a narrative of great significance, embodying the history and aspirations of the Malay nation, that is: as an epic, more manuscripts would have been available, more references found in other works or in other tales, if only by way of frequent interactions with singers of tales who, on their journeys through the Malay world, may have made an occasional performance about Hang Tuah's adventures.

The beginnings
When, then, did the Tale of Hang Tuah – or should we say: the performances or the floating memories about Hang Tuah – start its rise to prominence so as to reach its present-day status of 'national epic' among one particular community of Malays? An easy way out would be to say: the very moment the first manuscript, a fine performance in itself, was created – but even in that case we run into trouble: we do not know when it was created, let alone how it was created. Did floating fragments of the oral tradition precede the construction of this first written 'complete' manuscript, or did it work the other way around and did this 'complete' text produce floating fragments and memories? It is not known when the *Hikayat Hang Tuah* in its present written form was produced. The questions of where and by whom and how will never be answered either.

Scholars have pointed out that the *Hikayat Hang Tuah* as we know it now has a dual character: the first part is a description of the rise of Malacca where Hang Tuah plays a central role together with the Sultan and his prime minister, the second part is a description of the journeys of Hang Tuah to places as far away as China, India, Mecca and Rum, ending up in Malacca's downfall and Tuah's disappearance. The suggestion has been made that two distinct cycles of tales have been combined into one. It leaves the possibility open that this combination, undertaken by one or more anonymous scribal geniuses, was itself the final step in a more or less gradual process in which textual fragments, performances and memories about one or more heroes were gradually brought together under the single name of Hang Tuah. In this connection, a reference to that other 'Great Malay Work', *Sulalat as-Salatin* or *Sejarah Melayu*, has become a self-evident move: in this collection of tales about the rulers of Malacca mention is made of a courtier named Hang Tuah who loyally served Sultan Mansur, went to Java to confront the treacherous Javanese, and had a fight with his best friend – and then the conclusion is frequently drawn that this Hang Tuah must have been the starting point of the *Hikayat Hang Tuah* as a whole: all sorts of stories that were floating around in the Malay world about heroic exploits in Malacca were brought together in this particular man, who must have lived in the beginning of the 16th century if we assume that his Lord, Sultan Mansur of the *Sulalat as-Salatin*, was a man of flesh and blood who lived in Malacca around the same time

The *Hikayat Hang Tuah* covers the rise and demise of Malacca, that is to say: for some two hundred years Hang Tuah played a prominent role in its defense and glorification. Pictured as the faithful servant of his lord, the nameless Sultan of Malacca, descendant of the gods, Tuah undertakes every possible task to show his loyalty. He kills people who run amuck in the city. He abducts a woman for whom his Lord is lusting. He kills his best friend who starts a rebellion. He protects the name of Malacca and his Lord during several violent confrontations with Java. He fulfills diplomatic and religious missions to the corners of the world, as seen from Malacca. Altogether, it has been rightly argued that the very first sentence of all known manuscripts could be read as an apt summary of the *Hikayat*'s most comprehensive theme: 'This is the tale of Hang Tuah, the one who was very faithful to his lord and performed very many services for his lord.'

But did Hang Tuah really live for two hundred years? And what is the name of the lord he so faithfully served? Was Hang Tuah not rather a symbol or metaphor of the loyal servant in the glory days of the Malay world? Asking such questions leads us into discussions about fiction and reality, myth and truth, in which Malays have indulged ever since intellectuals on the Peninsula, in the wake of their British masters, began to substitute discussions about the conflicts between reality and fiction for ideas about the tensions between truth and lie. In these discussions (that start in the 1920s) the *Hikayat Hang Tuah* was to become a very prominent testing ground, primarily thanks, again, to the endeavors of the British masters: it is telling that local publishers in Southeast Asia, commercially eager to serve local taste and interest, did not think it worth the investment to publish a *Hikayat Hang Tuah* until the 1950s.

The publications of the Hikayat Hang Tuah
Early 20th century British scholars and administrators, literates bone and marrow, were of the opinion that the *Hikayat Hang Tuah* was an important work. It was a remarkable creation, they thought. It dealt with the glorious Sultanate of Malacca. It offered a wide panorama, no matter how contorted, over Malay customs and history. It evoked a world of chivalry. It contained a number of very gripping fragments, such as Tuah's abduction of Tun Teja to please his Lord; the fight between Tuah and his friend Jebat; the violent visits to Java; the journeys to China, India, Mecca and Rum; the disappearance of Tuah into the forests. It was written in exquisite and elegant Malay. It seemed to be an authentic Malay text indeed. Entertaining and intriguing, it offered readers and audiences many nights of exemplary fragments of how Malay commoners should serve their lord and how Malay culture should be preserved. That is why in the beginning of the 20th century the Singaporean educationalist, the reverend Shellabear, looking for suitable reading materials for schools, decided to have the *Hikayat Hang Tuah* published in the so-called 'Malay Literature Series' (1908); he had it printed in the Arabic script of manuscripts, thus connecting it with the heritage and tradition, as well as in the Romanized script of books, opening up to modernity and novelty.

Shellabear's decision had far reaching consequences in that the mere availability of the *Hikayat Hang Tuah*, a printed text that was used as a textbook in educational institutions, gave a powerful impetus to the emergence of Hang Tuah in the collective memory of the Malays on the Peninsula. Reading the adventures of a common Malay boy who, driven by intelligence and cunning, made it to the top of the great Malay Sultanate of Malacca, schoolchildren must have been in awe. They must have been excited by the multiple tales about the glory of Malacca, vague memories of which may have been floating around in the minds of some of them. They may have been seduced by the elegance of the Malay in which Tuah's adventures were presented on paper. They may have been reminded of Malay glory and courage.

The first concrete indications of the possible epicization of the *Hikayat Hang Tuah* could be traced back to the reverend Shellabear's days: references to Hang Tuah are beginning to be made in Malay newspapers and journals on the Peninsula (and not on Java, the central island of the Dutch Indies). Some adventures of Hang Tuah become popular material for *bangsawan* groups, a kind of vaudeville theatre that enjoyed a fluctuating popularity in the urban areas around the Strait of Malacca between 1910 and 1940. No doubt this use of memories of Hang Tuah was partly due to the knowledge its directors, just like some members of their public, had acquired at school from the printed texts (which they used for their scenarios next to the dramas of Shakespeare and the Tales of 1001 Nights); they may also have learnt about Tuah's adventures from the singers of tales, the kind of artists who, enacting adventures of heroes and heroines in oral performances, escaped the attention of scholars and other literates and maintained their own public. The romantic exploits of Tuah who, at the risk of losing his life, abducted Tun Teja from Indrapura for his Sultan and the fight between Tuah and Jebat became the most familiar topics in the *bangsawan*. Feelings of love are always rewarded, people were told in between songs and jokes. And commoners should be loyal to their masters, the Sultans, for the good of the community as a whole.

When in the 1930s the calls for a glorious past became louder – knowledge of history often serves a community to strengthen its identity, nationalism leads to the construction of roots and tradition – Hang Tuah would have become an even more common hero in these *bangsawan* performances, had this particular form of theatre not to compete with other, more 'modern' popular forms of showing and telling such as movies, radio, and records, and had the Japanese period not made an end to much entertainment in general. *Bangsawan* lost its attraction; it was considered old-fashioned and suffered from scathing criticisms. 'There are many ridiculous anachronisms in costumes and scenes, the strong bias for magic elements and fairy tales in the stories enacted, and the hybrid, often dull song interludes between the scenes' (Za'ba, quoted in Tan 1993: 50). This negative appreciation of tradition and memories in which Hang Tuah, echoing textbooks, tellers of tales and newspapers, had gradually been gaining a growing significance, did not stand on its own; similar remarks were made with respect to the tales and poems that had allegedly been transmitted by the singers and scribes since days of yore on the Peninsula. Heavy with magic and mystery those tales and poems were – and in the days of Malay misery they were not the most adequate tools to strengthen the Malay spirit and resist the colonial practices of the British as well as the incisive intrusions of Chinese and Indian immigrants. Realistic stories were needed that would show their readers in a recognizable way of how to act in real life, and *bangsawan* was replaced by *sandiwara*, a form of theatre that, modeled on Western forms of drama, offered realistic portrayals of humans instead of fairies and ghosts. Gradually but steadily, in spite of an occasional local revival due to government interference, *bangsawan* and its repertoire of tales about kings, fairies, ghosts, and princesses, including the memories of Hang Tuah, were pushed to the periphery where they are still being occasionally performed up to the present day in little pockets such as Bintan, the place where Tuah had been born in the Hikayat of his name.

The emergence of *sandiwara* in the 1940s should be seen as another proof of the expansion of print: plays were written out and then published so that they could be read, rehearsed, and performed in many places – but then this genre was confronted with stiff competition of the movies, yet another novel genre of performance which, together with television, were to subvert peninsular literacy until this very day. Next to theatre and movies in which Hang Tuah played a role, new forms of poetry were printed and recited in which an occasional reference to Hang Tuah was made as well, the symbol of Malay courage and dignity. And, as a matter of course, novels emerged, testimonies of the new structure of feeling that spread over the Peninsula – and some of these novels, too, made Hang Tuah the hero.

'After making a careful study of the *Hikayat Hang Tuah*, the *Sulalat as-Salatin* and schoolbooks of Malay history,' for instance, A. Samad Ahmad composed a novel about life and death of Hang Tuah, *Laksamana Tun Tuah* (1954) ('Admiral Tun Tuah', Samad's first tale in the Western script). Although this novel was widely praised and read, its subject matter did not escape the critical eye of Za'ba, still respected as the mouthpiece of many literates of his generation. In his introduction to the novel he wrote: 'We highly value the honest and sincere efforts of the author to bring Malay glory of the past to life again. But let us hope that another time he will write tales that picture the circumstances of Malay life as it really takes place around us, without forgetting new things such as bikes, cars, trains, radio, telephones, hospitals. The life of a state in which people run amuck, fight and kill each other by the dozens, that is not the life that we can show with pride to experts anywhere in the civilized world.'

Thus were the words of a leader of contemporary intellectuals and writers who no longer participated in the performances about Hang Tuah and no longer read the *Hikayat Hang Tuah*. They had but some fragmentary memories of the hero; obsessed with the self-imposed task to see to it that the Malays were given a distinct cultural or ethnic identity in order to survive on the increasingly multi-ethnic Peninsula, they questioned the relevance of the heritage. Was it not 'ancient' and out of tune with new demands? Even Hang Tuah's battle-cry which Samad Ahmad invented, *Takkan Melayu hilang dari dunia!* ('Never the Malays will disappear from the world!'), could not really soften their stance. It was not the past that counted, they claimed, but the future – and the past was not of great pertinence for the present. At the most, tales of the past could be an exemplary and nostalgic side-show, and an occasional tale about Hang Tuah could suffice.

Hikayat Hang Tuah and politics
However, for most peninsular Malays the memories of Hang Tuah had become strong enough to think that his marginalization was too much of a shortcut. Their hesitations to reject and ignore the past were primarily inspired by political considerations. The Malays should stick together against the threats of British colonialism and immigrants, and in order to authenticate their identity as a distinct nation, they foregrounded not only the Malay language and the Islam but also the Sultans, benevolent centers of power and authority. One of the most sensitive topics in the political discussions and activities that were eventually to lead to the independence of the kingdom of Malaya (later Malaysia) in 1957 was the position of the Sultans, symbols of Malayness: a majority of the Malay intellectual and social elite firmly believed that they were necessary to make sure that the Malays keep their position as the original and authentic inhabitants of the Peninsula, with all the privileges that were to come with that. In independent Malaya, the aristocracy managed to consolidate its prestige and authority in new forms; the relevance of feudalism was hardly ever questioned.

Obviously, the persona of Hang Tuah could be of great help in the maintenance and explanation of this policy. Exemplary in his dedication, he was the most loyal servant the Sultans and his relatives and supporters could imagine – and Hang Tuah was made, so to speak, the contemporary emblem of a powerful stream of thought within the Malay community on the Peninsula which had lost sight of Malay communities elsewhere in Southeast Asia. Samad Ahmad's novel confirmed the values of loyalty and faithfulness which were foregrounded in Tuah's fight with his friend Hang Jebat who had rebelled against the Sultan of Malacca out of loyalty for his unjustly punished friend and was eventually killed by Tuah himself. In contemporary terms, this fragment more or less directly suggested that feudalism was good for the Malays: Jebat the rebel was rightly killed and Tuah was a great and faithful servant, eager to preserve Malayness in this world. This message suited the political agenda of the political elite: feudalism could be retained and the glorious traditional past was to provide the modern Malays with pride and self-confidence under the leadership of the Sultans. This is what Samad Ahmad implied. This is what *bangsawan* evoked. This is what the new *sandiwara* about Hang Tuah suggested. This is what the movies that were made about Tuah intimated. Jebat was a sympathetic figure but in essence he was not good and he was politically incorrect – and that is why he was killed. Hang Tuah had seen to it that the Malays had not disappeared from this world!

Malay memories came at a crossroads: time and again the persona of Hang Tuah, symbolizing Malayness, floating around in fragments, was evoked to steer the political discussions as to how the Malays could strengthen their position on the Peninsula, whereas the *Hikayat Hang Tuah* was given a place of honor as the book that confirmed and expressed the values and aspirations the Malays needed in order to maintain their identity and defend Malay interests within a plural society. The *Hikayat Hang Tuah* was made the national tale, the national epic about a 'hero who had a high position in his nation' and 'embodied the history and the aspirations of the nation' – and hardly anyone took the trouble to read the text carefully, let alone make sense of it. Many fragments of the *Hikayat*, rich and polyvocal, could (and should) have incited the attention of modern readers, driven by questions of love, life, and death. The hero's conflicts with Java, for instance. His pilgrimage to Mecca. His search for Death. His loss of the state's magical kris in the fight with the white crocodile. His visits to China, Thailand, India, Mecca, and Rum. His becoming a dervish. However, only his fight with Jebat was relevant in the search of the novel literates and politicians.

The intellectuals at the Dewan Bahasa and Pustaka, a Government supported Institute for the advancement and defense of Malay culture founded in 1956, were eager to trace the 'original' manuscripts, testimonies of Malay tradition, 'within the framework of their struggle to give Malay a sovereign position as the national, official, and sole language of the Malay Federation (later Malaysia)', as Samad Ahmad was to formulate it (Samad Ahmad 1981: 292). Not only did they make it their task to help create a standard language and a new form of writing which was strong enough to make the Malays aware of their superior position on the multi-ethnic Peninsula; they also wanted to preserve and edit Malay manuscripts, the material testimonies of a glorious past, the basis of Malay superiority, the foundation of a glorious future. As it turned out, the second task was as hard to perform as the first one: manuscripts were hard to find. One of the first manuscripts that were purchased by the Dewan was, of course, a *Hikayat Hang Tuah* – but it took another five years to produce a text edition, a modernized form of an old but 'authentic' witness of the Malay past. Malay intellectuals and literates, very active in formulating and shaping a national or communal identity, made it the 'national *epik*'.

Hikayat Hang Tuah was printed in 1964 – and many times reprinted. It was not read. A boring text, too long, too slow. More printed versions were to follow. There were the abridged versions. There were the adaptations by novelists. There were the movies. There were the cartoons. There were the discussions. But who was still willing to be absorbed by the narrative itself, by the *Hikayat Hang Tuah*? More precisely, who would still take the trouble to read it? And what Za'ba had written of Samad Ahmad's novel *Laksamana*

Hang Tuah was repeated time and again: the book was not contemporary, not realistic, and not novel enough. Meanwhile tradition was perpetuated in that the floating memories of the fight between Tuah and Jebat kept playing a prominent role in the discussions.

Of course not all Malays were (and are) happy to see that feudal society was maintained, centered around the sultans and their relatives who have managed to retain so much of their traditional authority in the multiethnic and multicultural Kingdom of Malaysia. They are not happy either with the glorification of Tuah, the exemplary servant of the sultan. Already in the late fifties, some poets and writers decided to take Hang Jebat's side: not only had he shown humanity and personal feelings by choosing individual friendship over communal service to the sultan but also, more importantly, he was the one who questioned the validity of feudalism by his rebellion against the ruler, trying to show Malay communities the way to a new order, to new societal organizations. Jebat subverted cultural and social harmony but with a sensible purport: he is striving for modernization, democratization, justice.

'He rebels against the existing feudal order. He is the herald of the newer age. This age belongs to a completely different category. It is the age which, in relation to the last, represents a leap forward from the absolutist to the democratic phase. But Jebat's concept of democracy does not belong to the revolutionary thoroughgoing Marxist-Leninist scheme. It does not even belong to the democracy of the modern Western type. His democratic principle, it would seem, is meant to apply only within the body-politic to which he belongs. He is thus a rebel of the nationalist turn of mind. We may therefore term him a prophet and hero of Malay nationalism. His tragedy, then, serves to demonstrate artistically and concretely that nationalist ideals and aspirations are unrealizable within the feudal social scheme.' (Kassim bin Ahmad 1966: 33)

The discussions about fragment of the dramatic fight between Tuah and Jebat have flared up among Malays time and again, even so much so that people's preference for either of the two has become emblematic for their political stance: Malays should never rebel against their rulers, or Malays and their culture should not disappear from this world, or Malays should remain loyal to their rulers so long as their rulers rule over them in justice (Kessler 1992: 147) – and for each of these possibilities the stance in the conflict between Tuah and Jebat has been exemplary.

Tellingly, those discussions never refer to the *Hikayat Hang Tuah*, to the narrative that is. Rather, they refer to the tradition, that cloud of memories and fragments. In spite of the usually respectful references to the text, the persona of Hang Tuah kept on floating away from the *Hikayat*, becoming a two-dimensional character, so to speak. The *Hikayat* does no longer have serious readers. It has become a topic of discussion only within a very small circle of scholars who tend to read the Tale of Hang Tuah as an encyclopedia of Malay values and ideas in days of yore as well as a novel – and encyclopedias and novels are complementary genres in modern life.

Tradition and text
The adventures of Hang Tuah suggest that the tradition is still operative in the Malay community on the Peninsula: memories of the Malay hero keep floating around, occasionally giving rise to a novel performance, a new movie – and such a performance or movie then triggers new public discussions about the role of Hang Tuah in the modern world, be it no longer in connection with the Tale of Hang Tuah but with real life in which the position of the Malays and their self-proclaimed identity are allegedly under a constant threat of being destroyed. Contemporary Malays are doing what their ancestors already did: they are not interested in the *Hikayat Hang Tuah* from beginning to end. When they are watching a movie called 'Hang Jebat', reading a cartoon strip about Tuah and Teja, or walking through a Jalan Hang Tuah ('Hang Tuah Road'), most of them probably do not even know that these fragments refer to a tale called *Hikayat Hang Tuah*.

In retrospect it could be questioned if the *Hikayat Hang Tuah* ever functioned as an epic. In the 20th century, the fragmentary memories about Hang Tuah may have been of some significance for some Malay communities, the performances about Tuah may have had some echoes – but the *Hikayat* never was of central importance. Like everywhere else in the world, the term of 'Great Work' came in use for a text that no longer worked – if it ever did. *Karya Agung*: the term sounds like the death bell for a text that once upon a time was so brilliantly composed by one or more nameless Malay geniuses. It has been laid to rest, fossilized and frozen, before it could sweep its public away. The Tale of Hang Tuah is essentially denied any significance in these days of confusion and modernization in which no longer the moral of the tale counts but the meaning of life, as Benjamin once contextualized the demise of the epic and the rise of the novel.

Kassim Ahmad has suggested that the *Hikayat Hang Tuah* tells us a lot about human beings and their failures to solve the problems of love, life and death – and it certainly does so in an elegant and stylized form of Malay. The text's greatness now lies in the fact that it still deals with the meaning of life, and as such it could easily be read as a very strong novel which is well able to compete with other novels in terms of depth and elegance. However, nobody on the Peninsula takes the trouble to read it. Instead of opening up the Tale and interpret it as yet another effort to understand the meaning of life, the Malays have put it away in the cupboard of heirlooms. An *epik* perhaps, but certainly not an epic.

THE NARRATIVE POTENTIAL OF MI'RÂJ: TWO CONTEXTS FOR ITS INTERPRETATION

Julian Millie

Introduction

Epics live at the mercy of the interpretations applied to them. With the passage of time, the contexts which shape interpretative approaches experience change, and the epic is thereby subjected to reappraisal in accordance with this process of change. In this paper, I choose to view the 'contents' of an epic narrative, understood to be the more or less distinctive 'events' by which it is constituted, as offering a storyteller or author a set of options; these are the potential of that particular narrative. The author/storyteller interprets this potential in constructing a text, and the manner in which he interprets it is determined to a large degree by the context and genre in which he operates. When his text is interpreted outside of that context, a contrasting mode of interpretation may be applied to the textual materials.

The narrative with which I am concerned is the ascension of the Prophet Muhammad through the seven levels of heaven to an encounter with God, known as his *Mi'râj* (ascension). The options this narrative offers imbue it with a distinctive potential for the author/storyteller, and include the following; the Prophet's seven entries to the levels of heaven offer the possibility of hierarchically arranged, symbolic interactions with other prophets or extraordinary angels; the splendours and greatness of heaven offers the possibility of dramatic strategies of exaggeration; the Prophet's witnessing of sufferers in hell enables the development of dramatic, didactically-oriented descriptions of the punishments awaiting wrong-doers; the heavenly steed Boraq invites fantastic descriptions of his appearance. I have chosen the *Mi'râj* as the subject of this paper for the reason that, as I hope to show, the just mentioned potential makes it prone to controversy in respect to the manner in which the narrative potential is to be interpreted.

Although the *Mi'râj*, at least in the Malay versions with which I am concerned, resists categorisation as a purely 'epic' text, it has much in common with that genre. In particular, the ascension has the nature of a 'mythic quest' by a heroic figure, and has become central to Islamic tradition for the reason that Muhammad returns from the quest with the obligation of the five *ṣalât*, dictated to him by Allah at the apex of the ascension. Furthermore, the distinction of the heroic figure is emphasized by the fact that he enters the presence of God during his quest, in the same way as epic heroes 'rub shoulders' with gods and supernatural beings. Hence the abstract dimensions of this paper may well be applied also to the epic *per se*.

The specific text-making context I will refer to in this chapter is the tradition of the reading of a religious narrative to a gathering, such as are commonly held to celebrate religious feasts or events of social significance by Muslims in the Malay world. This shall be referred to as the 'festive reading context' in this paper. The choice of narrative to be chosen for a particular occasion depends, of course, on the event or saint that is being celebrated, and also on the tradition of the region concerned. For example, the narratives concerning the revered personage of Sheikh Abdulkadir Al-Jaelani are popular in regions where the *Qadariyah* Sufi order has a strong presence (Drewes and Poerbatjaraka 1990). Other narrative readings are tied to particular events on the Islamic calendar, such as those describing the Prophet's ascension (*Mi'râj*) and his birthday (*Mawlid*).

The feast of the *Mi'râj* is held on the 27th day of the month of Rajab, and invokes two events from the Prophet's life, namely the *Isrâ'* and the *Mi'râj*, the *Isrâ'* being the journey of the Prophet to Al-Quds (Jerusalem) on the winged steed Boraq, the *Mi'râj* being the Prophet's journey from this mosque in Jerusalem through the seven levels of heaven, culminating in an audience with Allah at the highest level of heaven where Allah imparts to the Prophet the obligation of the $salât$, the five daily prayers.

First, a description will be given of a selection of *Mi'râj* texts, for the purpose of illustrating some characteristics of the *Mi'râj* narrative and the manner in which its texts are to be read. I also touch on the potential it offers for the use of the strategies of exaggeration mentioned above. Then, some eyewitness accounts of *Mi'râj* celebrations, written by the Dutch civil servant G.F. Pijper, are used to extend this description from the text to the context of the gathering. I will argue that a useful way of approaching these feasts and their texts is to consider them as reading events, in which particular conventions for interacting with written texts are accepted and implemented in a situation. Finally, I present a *fatwa* (legal opinion) from a magazine called *al-Imam*, published in 1906, that illustrates how, outside of the context of the festive gathering, *Mi'râj* narratives can be read according to a different set of conventions. This second context interprets the potential offered by the *Mi'râj* in a manner radically contrasting with that of our storyteller/author, thereby creating friction between the two readings.

Texts for Mi'râj gatherings
When I examined one of the Malay manuscripts of the *Hikayat Nabi Mi'râj* (the Narrative of the Prophet's Heavenly Journey), I noticed that the *hikayat* (in Malay, *hikayat* refers to a lengthy work in prose) is embedded between two other short texts.[i] The one preceding the prose narrative is illuminated and framed in a decorative box, while the one at the end is in the form of a *syair*, a very common verse form in the Malay world. It can therefore be said that the two embedding texts are formally as well as visually distinct from the main body of the manuscript.

In translation, the boxed text on the first page of the *Hikayat Mi'râj* reads:

> 'The prophet of Allah said to 'Abbâs, may Allah's favor be upon him, 'Oh 'Abbâs, whoever reads the narrative of my ascension or listens to it or writes it from beginning to end will obtain bounty from almighty Allah, praise be upon Him, and almighty Allah will forgive all his sins, just like a tree which loses all its leaves from its branches, so that not one remains. In this way will all a person's sins fall from his body.'

This statement is self-explanatory; by reading, writing and listening to the *Hikayat Mi'râj* we may obtain benefit from God. It is relevant to note that the text just quoted derives authority from being in the form of a ḥadîth. The ḥadîth literature is 'that which comprises all the sayings, deeds, and decisions of the Prophet Muhammad, His silent approval of the behavior of His contemporaries, and descriptions of His person' (Juynboll 1969: 4).[ii] In fact, the entire text of the *hikayat* is expressed as a ḥadîth, with the Prophet as the narrating 'I'.

The *syair* (poem) that is presented after the conclusion of the *hikayat* consists of thirteen four-line stanzas, including the following:

> 'When you read (this work), sing it with a melody / raise your voice up, do not hold back.
> Do not change any of its letters / to make your listeners happy.
> Do not read it amid conversation / speak with raised voice and eloquent tongue.
> All the listeners will then be happy / and will be touched deep in their hearts.
> Do not pause in your reading / until the end has clearly been reached.
> In one word are a number of meanings / to ensure it will reach the hearts of the listeners.'

> (Jikalau membaca lagu-lagukan / nyaringkan suara jangan ditahankan
> Hurufnya jangan dipertukarkan / supaya suka yang menengarkan
> Membaca jangan sambil berbicara / fasihatkan lidah nyaringkan sudah
> Segala yang menengar supaya gembira / ke dalam hatinya supaya mesra
> Membaca dia jangan berhenti / sehingga selesai adanya pasti
> Dalam sepatah kata beberapa arti / supaya yang menengarkan sampai di hati)

The two embedding texts clearly illustrate some prominent elements of the reading of the narrative of the *Mi'râj*. The text in the decorative box seeks to make us aware of the spiritual benefits of reading, listening to and writing the narrative. The concluding poem refers to the importance of its proper delivery, and emphasizes the deep engagement of listeners through the agency of the reader.

Turning to the content of the Malay texts of the *Mi'râj*, we readily notice the fantastic nature of much of their imagery. Take, for example, the following description of the Prophet's ascension to the second and third levels of the heavens found in Codex Orientalis 1713. The narrator is the Prophet himself:

'(On arriving at the second heaven) I met a massive angel sitting above a golden chair. I saw he had seventy heads, on each mouth he had seventy mouths. Each mouth had seventy tongues. On each tongue were seventy praises of Allah...(On arriving at the third heaven)...I saw a very large angel sitting on a golden throne, he had seven hundred heads and on each head he had seven hundred faces. On each face he had seven hundred noses and seven hundred mouths and one thousand four hundred eyes and ears, and each mouth had seven hundred tongues and on each tongue were seven hundred praises of Allah.'

This manner of engaging with the narrative potential of the *Mi'râj*, with its tendency to enlargment and exaggeration, is typical of many *Mi'râj* narratives. To mention just a few other instances: the levels of heaven are made of, respectively, copper, gold, brass, etc; the time required to make the journey between the levels is fivehundred years; and various rivers, including the Nile, have their source at the sacred tree located at the highest point of heaven.

A second, more recent Malay text relevant to this discussion is *az-Zahr ul-Bâsim* ('The Smiling Flower'). This work was published a number of times by Sayyid Uthman (1822-1914), a commercial publisher of Malay religious texts in Batavia.[iii] I refer here to the edition printed in 1896. Sayyid Uthman was in the business of publishing texts that were of relevance to the everyday lives of Muslims, including the proper method of reading the Quran, warnings against improper practice in religious acts, and instructions about the use of Arabic. Given the fact that the celebrations of the *Mawlid* and *Mi'râj* were so popular, it was only natural that Sayyid Uthman should also publish a book that could be used at both of these celebrations.

Az-Zahr ul-Bâsim contains the biography of the Prophet, to be read at the celebration of the *Mawlid*, commencing from the manufacture of a heavenly light passed to the Prophet Adam, which eventually reaches the Prophet Muhammad's grandfather. The Prophet's birth is described, along with events of his life such as the revelation of the Quran and the *Mi'râj*. The tale of the *Mi'râj* extends for approximately 30 of the book's 71 pages; it is complete with descriptions of the horrors of hell and the delights of heaven. In the introduction the regulations for the proper reading of the text (*aturan adab membaca*) are given; they are divided into four 'benefits' (*faedah*). Three of these open a window through which we can observe something of the nature of the festive reading context in Batavia at the end of the 19th century. As a matter of fact, the book has the character of a manual for the celebrations, providing the narrative for the purpose of loud reading, along with specifications for the holding of the event.

The first *faedah* concerns the proper environment for the reading of the work. The preferred locations for the celebration are specified; the presence of tables or chairs elevated higher than the reader is prohibited; mingling of the sexes is prohibited; odors offensive to angels such as cigarette and cigar smoke are to be avoided; fragrant odors such as those from incense and flowers are encouraged; and those present at the *Mawlid* reading should stand at the moment of the reading of the Prophet's birth (Sayyid Uthman 1896: 2-3).

The second *faedah* states that the translation into Malay was made so that people could understand the content of the Arabic *Mi'rāj* texts which were very common in the Malay world.

The third *faedah* is an exhortation directed to listeners; they should join in the recitation of an Arabic *solawat* (praise formula) seeking the intercession of the Prophet, his companions, and his family. The formula appears approximately every four pages in a prominent boxed frame; it is written in bold, enlarged script, and in translation it reads:

> 'Oh Allah, grant blessings and salvation to our master and intercessor Muhammad and his family and companions and make us among the best of his community and among those who gain his intercession by Your mercy, oh merciful of merciful ones.'

The narrative is not wanting in fantastic imagery. We read, for example, that the time required to travel between the levels of heaven is five hundred years (Sayyid Uthman 1896: 43). The Prophet's encounter with the heavenly gardens grants the author/storyteller the opportunity to engage in fantastic imagery and exaggeration:

> '(...) then He saw many broad gardens and a great number of trees of many varieties, including trees that are found in this world and those that are not. Their flower beds were of gold, silver and topaz, and all the leaves were of emerald and resembled silk, and their buds and fruits were like rubies and topaz of many shapes and flavours. And if any of the fruits or buds were picked, then at the same time a replacement would appear without any delay, and there is no limit on the amount of times this can happen. And if the occupants of heaven wish for music, then a gentle wind will come blowing upon the leaves of the trees of heaven, and they compete with each other with music and songs of a beauty never heard by human beings. And the messenger of God, peace and blessings of God be upon Him, also gazed upon a number of great rivers in heaven, some of them of water clearer than clear glass, and some of the whitest milk which never changed colour, and some of very sweet and clear honey, and some of very delicious *arak* (liquor) which does not cause drunkenness...' (Sayyid Uthman 1896: 55).

In summary, *az-Zahr ul-Bâsim* is a work specifically designed to be used in the celebratory readings of the *Mi'râj* and the *Mawlid*; the book's introduction and layout are to assist its users in carrying out and participating in the celebration. Its contents display the same penchant for fantastic imagery and strategies of exaggeration evident in the manuscripts of the *Hikayat Mi'râj*.

Mi'râj as reading event
Perceiving the festive reading context as a *reading event* recognises that, although written texts were central to the tradition, the written texts do not of themselves provide sufficient data for comprehending the conventions of the public reading of the *Mi'râj*. The different situation types in which reading events take place imply different strategies for interpreting the potential of the text. It is necessary, then, to extend our description from the text to the context of the festive reading.

We are fortunate to have descriptions of a number of *Mi'râj* celebrations from the first half of the 20th century. These were written by Pijper, who was from 1925 employed at the Bureau for Native Affairs (Batavia).[iv] The following is an excerpt from his observations of a celebration at a mosque in Batavia:

> 'Al-Zahr al-Bâsim is the most loved text, which men recite in tunes which are melodious, but apart from that unsophisticated. The readers take each other's place; a person who has been reading for a quarter of an hour or more hands the book over to someone else, so that in the passage of the night as many as ten or more men have had their turn at being the reader. The others listen to this in silence, but join into a chorus every time the reader arrives at the Arabic imprecation (*selàwat*, amongst the literate *solàwat*, the Arabic is ṣalawât) which appears repeatedly from pericope to pericope. (..) One of the reciters, being possessed of sufficient learning, explains difficult parts of the text in his own words. If they wish to finish the whole text in an evening, there is no time for digressions, but men gladly spend more than one evening on the *baca hikayat* [reading the narrative]' (Pijper 1934: 129).

The text read out to the gathering, however, was not necessarily fixed by the written text. The charismatic preacher could act as a mediator between the text and the gathering. Pijper observed the following celebration in North Bantam:

> 'The *Kijai* [religious leaders] usually do not just rattle off the text, but tell a story; it is perhaps for this reason that the *Mi'râdj* (the expression in North Bantam is *Mi'rat, Mèrat*) so strongly attracts the hearts of the people; they give descriptions, interpret and expand the sacred story of the heavenly journey, so that their expressive language captivates the old, the young, and the less religious. One arrives on the night of 27 Radjab in the local Bantamese *balai* (meeting hall), and observes around the lit-up place of

worship women and small girls leaning against the walls and standing before the opened windows. Inside sit the men and boys in a half-circle in rows opposite the Kijai, who has positioned three yellow cushions as a lectern for himself. Near him stands an incense bowl. Using the *ḥâshiyah* [commentary] of Al-Dardir as a basis, he describes in the local Bantam Javanese the fabulous features of Burâq, the mount with the bejeweled wings and the face of a woman of paradise. The *Kijai* will not hold back from comparing Burâq's speed with contemporary aeroplanes, and when he arrives at the description of the heavenly punishments, he will moralize about popular vices and gambling, lawlessness and neglect of religious obligations. While he has the floor, plates of dishes and side-dishes are endlessly being brought in and put down in the corner of the *balai* for the *hadjat* (feast) which will soon take place.' (op. cit.: 138-139)

Two characteristics of the reading event become apparent in this description: the reading serves a didactic function and, secondly, a deep engagement between the listeners and the narrative is established by means of the attractive performance by the reader. The tendency towards striking imagery in *Mi'râj* narratives now appears as a device in the service of these two characteristics: exaggerated imagery allows the creation of a text that is attractive and didactic. These are, arguably, defining components of the festive reading context, to which the character of the narratives used in them is, to some degree, traceable. Didactic goals and the creation of a deep engagement by listeners require a particular style of deriving meaning from written texts such as the manuscripts and the book mentioned above. The reader or reciter, and indeed the scribes of the manuscripts, utilized their potential for exaggeration and enlargment; this was the conventional method of deriving meaning from texts at the celebrations. The importance of closely examining the reading event is emphasised, in a different context, by Brice Heath, who uses the term 'literacy events'. This term implies that the ways of deriving meaning from written texts are subject to variation between cultural contexts. She writes:

'A key concept for the empirical study of ways of taking meaning from written sources across communities is that of literacy events; occasions in which written language is integral to the nature of participants' interactions and their interpretative processes and strategies (…) in such literacy events, participants follow socially established rules for verbalizing what they know from and about the written material. Each community has rules for socially interacting and sharing knowledge in literacy events.' (Brice Heath 1982: 50)

This model is useful, as it enables us to perceive harmony as well as logic in the particular set of interactions, interpretative processes and strategies evident in the celebration and the texts. Readers and listeners, all desiring Godly benefit, agree to follow certain conventions of signifying which give the events a unique narrative flavor. The need to edify and engage listeners encourages the participants to take advantage of the image-making potential in the religious narrative at hand, as well as in the narrating skills of the charismatic preacher/ storyteller, and perhaps also in local textual traditions.

Of course, the preceding discussion is by no means true for all celebrations involving readings; there was (and is) a wide variety of styles reading events, many of which do not follow the characteristics described above. The works I have discussed (with the exception of the one written by Al-Dardir) were written and read in the Malay language. It is not uncommon in the Malay world, however, for an Arabic text to be read, and in that case it is unlikely that participants would place great importance on the referential meaning of the text. What would be more important is completion of the reading of the text for obtaining spiritual benefit. Such an event would entail a different set of conventions for deriving meaning from the written text.

Interpretation outside the literacy event
The potential of the *Mi'râj* is inevitably interpreted differently outside the festive reading context. In 1906, shortly before Pijper was putting his observations to paper, and not long after the publication of *az-Zahr ul-Bâsim*, an unknown writer published his opinion concerning the narrative of the *Mi'râj* in the Singapore-based magazine *al-Imam*. *Al-Imam* was closely modelled on the Egyptian magazine *Al-Manar*, which first appeared in 1899 and reflected the social, religious, and political outlook of figures in the Middle East who were then engaged in a struggle with the 'conservative' religious institutions of their own communities. Kaptein provides a brief summary that includes many of the important features of this movement:

'The most prominent characteristic of this movement was the reaffirmation, in the light of modern requirements, of original Islam as it had been practiced by the pious ancestors (*al-salaf al-ṣâliḥ*). This original Islam was regarded as genuine and suitable for coping with the challenges of modern life. From this basic idea sprung a number of specific new developments, such as the rejection of the so-called *taqlîd*, the acceptance of the traditional authorities of the four schools of law (*madhhabs*) and their canonical interpretations. Instead of this *taqlîd*, the necessity of independent reasoning on the basis of only the Quran and Hadith (*ijtihâd*) was affirmed. Another major characteristic of this reformist movement was the rejection of many later Islamic beliefs and practices, which had not been observed by the *salaf al-ṣâliḥ* and were, therefore, to be eradicated.' (Kaptein 1993: 124)

Al-Imam was published in Singapore, a city where the Muslim community was exposed to a greater variety of influences than other metropolitan centers in the Malay world in that period, in part by virtue of its transit status for pilgrims. The journal's 'orthodox' religious outlook questioned the syncretism and eclecticism of indigenous religious life elsewhere in the Malay world (cf. Roff 1994: 43). One of its sections was reserved for the answering of questions sent in by readers; many of the answers have the form of a *fatwa*, which is a legal opinion given in response to a question seeking guidance on a matter of Islamic religious doctrine. The question that concerns me here was posed by a reader who was seeking guidance on the issue of the *Mi'râj*. His name is a pseudonym, Tâlib al-Hudâ ('Seeker of Guidance'), and the name of his place of residence, Muara ('Estuary'), is perhaps also not the genuine residence of the writer. The following is a translation of the question and part of the answer:

'The Question
The headwaters of the river Nile, which is in Egypt, are in heaven (*syurga*), which is found above the seventh level (of the heavens), as is mentioned in the *hadîth* of the *Mi'râj*. Now, Egypt is a nation in the land of Africa, and the land of Africa is surrounded by water in the way that an island is. The estuary of the Nile, therefore, is in Egypt or (in other words) on an island, and its headwaters are in heaven. This being the case, how can the headwaters be connected to the estuary, or how can the water flow from heaven to Egypt, especially when there is no watercourse hanging from heaven down to Egypt penetrating every layer of heaven (*langit*) until it reaches the surface of Egypt? Furthermore, from the earth to the lowest level alone is such a distance, how more extraordinary, then, is the distance to heaven (*syurga*) with its seven layers of the heavens (in between)?

The sun is in the fourth level, as is mentioned in the book *Sabîl al-Muhtadîn*. Now this fourth level is made of copper, the third of steel, the second from stone, and the first is of gold, and all of them are of a particular thickness, as is mentioned in the *hadîth* of the *Mi'râj*. This being the case, how is the light of the sun able to penetrate the earth when between the sun and the earth these four levels are shutting it off? Without even mentioning an object of that kind of thickness (as copper etc), if we block out the sun from the earth with a mere piece of paper the light of the sun is in no way able to penetrate the earth. How much more the case with a layer as thick as those, and in fact there is not just one of them?

It is obligatory to believe these two matters because of the books and *hadîth* that mention them, but I have not yet found a way that would lead to a wholehearted belief. This having been said, I here request that you assist me, dear sirs, in explaining each of these things so that I may understand them wholeheartedly.'[v]

The answer
The answer is that the land of Africa is one of the great landmasses and would be joined to Asia if the Suez Canal did not block the way. The Nile is a river in Africa. At its upper reaches it emerges from three lakes, all of

them within the African landmass. The distance between the place of its emergence and its mouth is 6,500 kilometers. In truth, Allah's decree has come to us in the Koran, *'Âlam tara anna Allâha anzala min as-samâ'i mâ'an fasalakahu yanâbî'a fîl-ard*. (Have you not noticed that Almighty Allah has brought down rainwater from the heavens and put it in the places where waters rise from the earth?).[vi] Indeed, the water of the Nile is from the waters I have just mentioned. Now, read and understand the following things:

Allah, the Exalted and Praised, ordered our master Muhammad, Allah bless him and grant him salvation, to give guidance to all humanity in all matters concerning their religion and to teach them all of His laws. In reality, a number of falsehoods were created by people who lied about the Prophet, Allah bless him and grant him salvation, like the falsehoods made by their predecessors about all the prophets who preceded him. The truth of the situation is that Allah, the Exalted and Praised, has formulated this religion with perfect care, praise to Allah!

Be aware that in truth not a single *hadîth* that stipulates the nature of the seven levels of heaven or describes how thick they are is sound. And most of the concoctions which are read by the storytellers (*tukang cerita*) in the story of the *Mi'râj* are manifest lies, such as, for example, those mentioned in your question. The result of this is that you are not obliged to believe in anything other than those things with a proof (*dalil*) which is rational (*'aql*) and agreed upon (*putus*), which is not imbued with any vagueness, or with the proof of being heard from the Prophet, Allah bless him and grant him salvation, (and) which correctly fulfills the conditions (*syurutnya*) of being *mutawâtir*. This means that the saying is related by several people for whom it was impossible to agree upon something contrary to common sense, such as the things which happen after death, about people rising from the dead and the delights of heaven and the tortures of hell and the accounting of all one's good and bad deeds and other things of this kind, rather than the matters of the hereafter which have been confirmed [155] by the impeccable one, may Allah bless him and grant him salvation. Not everything that is stated by all those know-alls or big-mouths wearing their big turbans or everything written by gullible people in their books which are completely unacceptable to rationality must be believed as part of the religion' (Anon. 1906: 150-155).

The answer concludes with an extensive description of the different levels of authority that should be given to different varieties of *hadîth*.

The method by which the writer of this *fatwa* interprets the potential of the *Mi'râj* reflects a mode of interpretation strongly evident in the Middle Eastern movement from which the Indonesian and Malay reformists derived much of their inspiration. From a theological perspective, its contents were not novel at the time the article was published; the process by which genuine Traditions are to be distinguished from false ones had been a major subject of Islamic theological scholarship since the second century Hijra (Encyclopaedia of Islam, vol. III: 23-24). Nevertheless, this *fatwa* bears the marks of its era in the sense that it touched on *hadîth*-related issues that were receiving great attention around the turn of the 19th century. Narratives such as the Malay manuscripts of the *Hikayat Mi'râj*, which presented themselves in the form of a *hadîth*, were the subject of heated debates in reformist circles. When the *fatwa* mentions 'the things which happen after death, about people rising from the dead and the delights of heaven and the tortures of hell and the accounting of all one's good and bad deeds and other things of this kind', it reflects the debate concerning the *isrâ'îlîyât*, which can be defined as Traditions and reports that contain elements of the legendary and religious literature of the Jews (Juynboll 1969: 121). Rashid Rida, the editor of *al-Manâr* and one of the significant figures of the reform movement in the Middle East, held a dire view of this corpus; for him, 'the pious forebears had not paid heed to the stories of Jewish and Persian converts, but had kept their religion clean from foreign influences' (Juynboll 1969: 122). *Al-Imam*, modelled on *al-Manâr*, was strongly informed by this sentiment.

Similarly, when the *fatwa* in *al-Imam* mentions 'storytellers', 'big-mouths' and 'know-alls', we are reminded of another dimension of the *hadîth* debate that was given specific recognition by Rashid Rida, namely the existence of narratives framed as *hadîth* but created by pious storytellers, *qussâs*, '[who] saw an easy profit by playing on the credulity of their audiences. Some of them were compelled to invent traditions through the urge to instill into their listeners awe and reverence towards the religion. Some people tried to gain the favor of sovereigns by fabricating traditions which might particularly please them' (Juynboll 1969: 100).

It is not only the process of distinction between genuine and false traditions that marginalises texts displaying fantastic and exaggerated textual strategies. When asked the question, 'how do I know what to believe?', the writer of our answer emphasises the importance of 'rationality' and 'common sense', both of which are clearly of less relevance to the process by which our storyteller engages with the narrative potential of the *Mi'râj* in the reading event.

Conclusion

To conclude, I refer to some observations made by Pijper in 1933 about the remembrance of the *Mi'râj* held by the Muhammadiyah, a reform-oriented movement with a strong vocation for education and modernization. The Muhammadiyah remembrance featured a parade of scouts and students, who arrived at an assembly hall where speeches and discussions were held. The speeches delivered at this gathering 'offered generally edifying, and also educational, historical and apologetic opinions about Islam; on this occasion the political ideals of Islam as well as purely religious ideals are touched upon' (Pijper 1934: 147). Although Pijper does not specifically state it, it seems the reading of the narrative did not feature in the event. The feast itself retained significance, but in accordance with the sentiments expressed by the writer of the *Al-Imam* article, the celebration ignores the opportunities for exaggerated and fantastic imagery offered by the narrative potential of the *Mi'râj*.

Above, I have presented the position of reformist scholars towards the narrative potential of the *Mi'râj* in the form of an article carried in a reformist journal, and cross-referenced it to the opinions of an influential Middle-Eastern reformist with a wide readership in the Malay world (Rida). Aside from the priority of distinguishing between *hadîth*, the arguments I have followed in this paper a more basic reason for the incompatibility of the reformist sensibility with the fantastic and exaggerated narratives. It is resistant to those narrative conventions for the reason that the conditions of the festive reading context, which lead the author/storyteller to use the conventions, were not present in the reformist *milieu* with the same prominence and authority as in the mosques and *balai* visited by Pijper. The reformists could not be expected to see merit in the *Hikayat Nabi Mi'râj* and *az-Zahr ul-Bâsim* because their context compelled them to a different interpretation. Although geographically proximate, they inhabited an altogether different context for the interpretation of the narrative potential of the *Mi'râj*.

NOTES

[i] The manuscript is KITLV 61, which was copied in Batavia in 1835.

[ii] In Goldziher's words, 'Through a chain of reliable authorities who handed down pertinent information from generation to generation, Hadith shows what the companions, with the Prophet's approval, held to be exclusively correct in matters of religion and law and what could therefore properly serve as a norm for practical application' (Goldziher 1981: 37-38).

[iii] More information about him is found in Kaptein (1997).

[iv] For biographical information, see Pijper (1977).

[v] The affected, naïve simplicity of the question suggests it may in fact have been an 'inside job', that is, it may have been composed by the staff of *al-Imam* in order to create an opportunity to publish on the topic.

[vi] This sentence is from the Koran (39: 21).

DEMISE AND REEMERGENCE OF *HIKAYAT SERI RAMA* – THE EPIC ADVENTURES OF A NON EPIC

Amin Sweeney

'It may well be argued that colonial print literacy created "the epics" in Malay, and that, in so doing, it effectively guaranteed their demise. While this seems to me to be a tolerably solid conceit, in a collection of papers which sets out to assess the effects of literacy on the epics in South and Southeast Asia, it may appear that my aim is to bring our deliberations to a swift conclusion. However, my now evident need to extricate myself from a potentially nasty situation should indicate that this is not my purpose.' These words might perhaps provide a rousing beginning to this paper, but any aptness is entirely coincidental, as they were written for another conference, held many years ago. I mention them here only to indicate that I have written an 'elegant sufficiency' by far on the colonial power politics of the term 'epic' and to provide assurance that I shall not be worrying the topic further.[i] Indeed, I really must stop writing papers which question the terms of reference provided by conveners! Let me simply refer to the words of Karim Traoré, a linguist from Burkina Faso, at a 1989 seminar here in Leiden. He and I were a tad bemused by the pious indignation of a European participant who insisted that Africans *must* have 'epics', as though to deny Africans 'the epic' would smack of discrimination. Karim Traoré's response was: 'No we don't have epic. But do you have...?' And he reeled off three or four genres of Mande storytelling.

In this paper, my guideline will be the e-mail message inviting me, which I received from Henk M.J. Maier last November, informing me: 'We are organizing a little seminar on: 'Epics: Demise and Reemergence', which, in short is about the question: what has happened to the tales that functioned as points of reference for communities and groups. In some nations/communities they are dead and gone, in others they are being re-created and play a certain role again – and for the first Indonesia is an interesting case *(Hikayat Hang Tuah, Ila Galigo, Hikayat Seri Rama* etc.); for the latter Western Africa (Mali, Gambia etc.) seems to offer examples.' For me, the key phrase here is 'tales that functioned as points of reference for communities and groups'. A comparison, say, of African oranges with Malay apples will not take us very far without an examination of function. I have found Eric Havelock's concept of 'epic purpose' very useful. He perceived the oral composition of the ancient Greek bard as a massive repository of useful knowledge, a sort of encyclopedia of ethics, politics, history and technology...' (1963: 27). Taufik Abdullah (1970) reached remarkably similar conclusions about the Minang *Kaba*, and he was clearly working independently of Havelock. I have argued that Havelock's comments concerning 'epic purpose' reveal much about the function of many Malay *hikayat* (written narratives, accounts), in that they served as a vehicle of general education; the plethora of material apparently extraneous to the tale was, in fact, the central point of such a *hikayat*, which was didactic; the 'tale' might function simply as the vehicle for this material. Havelock conceived the term 'epic purpose' because the composition he studied was a long 'heroic' narrative in verse, thus pertaining to the European genre 'epic'. Yet the term can be misleading, for the same purpose and function may be found in material which does not meet the accepted criteria of 'epic', as in many *hikayat,* which were composed in written prose and were often rather thrifty with the 'heroic'. The *Silsilah Raja-raja Berunai* and the *Sulalatu 'l-Salatin* come to mind here. The other side of the coin is that long 'heroic' narratives in verse should not be assumed to serve an 'epic' purpose merely on the basis of their external form, which tends to result from exigencies of oral composition: thus narrative is the primal way of organizing knowledge; verse is a vital way of programming that knowledge for survival. 'Heroic' tends to be a rather culture-bound notion but in this context the usage generally seems to refer to characters larger than life – a tad *'over',* to borrow an Indonesian term... This manner of portraying characters again appears to be a device for preserving knowledge in oral composition.

Henk M.J. Maier's invitation of November 2000 offered two carrots which the donkey writing this could not possibly refuse: *'Hikayat Seri Rama'* and 'demise'. I set to work. In April, I received a second e-mail from the conveners. The theme of the seminar had changed to 'Emergent Epics'. Perhaps political correctness had cranked in; 'demise' was out. It would not be nurturing to have participants warming to the topic of a dead epic; an epic which is no longer with us, a decidedly ex-epic, not an epic asleep nor in a coma, but very much an expired epic. Yet the donkey still claims two carrots, for he has chosen to write about 'the' *Hikayat Seri Rama.* This is a complex of chirographically-related manuscripts containing tales which parallel tales about Rama in India. It has thus been regarded as an epic merely because of its association with the *Ramayana*.[ii] And again, there are at least three hundred *'Ramayanas'* in India. But the good news is that the *Hikayat Seri Rama* complex is no epic and it is certainly not emergent. So its demise is still a valid topic!

Yet I confess to being a little puzzled by the terms 'emergent', 'reemergent' and 'demise'. How does one evaluate these developments? In the case of traditional Malay literature (i.e., manuscripture), it should be noted that it is scholars such as ourselves at seminars such as this who have been keeping those manuscripts on a life-support system simply by writing about them. This field of traditional Malay literary studies is still dominated by Europeans. After all, they created it. Indonesian university students of traditional Malay literature have little chance to express their own ideas unless they can quote a European, usually a dead one. In this context, the point is that anything written on the *Hikayat Seri Rama* in the 20th century by Malaysians and Indonesians has had but a very tenuous connection with 'Malay tradition' in the accepted sense.

In the field of Malay Studies, the mode employed and the stance assumed to study the 'tradition' have become very different from those adopted to study the scholarship of the tradition. But where does one end and the other begin? Paradoxically, the 19th century European scholars were in a sense less arbitrary: they could vent their spleen upon both scholarship and tradition. And 18th century scholars indeed treated much of the Malay tradition as scholarship in its own right, worthy to be heard, to be taken seriously, and disputed. By the 19th century, although scholars could offer pungent criticism equally of the tradition as of some of the scholarship about it, the tradition had been cordoned off, and scholarship meant Western scholarship. What Malay writers of the time had to say about the tradition was not considered either as part of the tradition or as scholarship; it was ignored. Maier (1988) draws attention to the British silence on Malay attempts to rewrite the history of Kedah to accord with new ideas on 'history'. Yet in the context of my comments on the reinterpretive tradition in Malay composition, we have in these attempts a major adjustment of the traditional schemata. Here is clear evidence of the continuity of the reinterpretive function, which had been so vital in aural Malay tradition. But the shift of medium from manuscripture to print caused a much more conscious struggle with the traditional schemata than in the past, when change could occur more imperceptibly, and the witnesses of the change – the older manuscripts – would eventually disappear.

Today, the average Western scholar tends not to revile the Malay tradition. It is bad for business! One is aware of the need to avoid imposing one's own norms on a tradition removed in space and/or time. But this has little bearing on the divide. In studying scholarship, different aspects of the critical faculties are brought into play; one applies a different set of criteria. One tends more to assume shared norms, and to feel oneself much more able to distribute praise and blame. The approach is much more evaluative, at least to some extent. This is perfectly acceptable up to a point. The problem with being so programmed to switch one's stance thus is that the scholarship is not itself seen to be part of the tradition and thus worthy of study also in this capacity. And I mean European scholarship as much as the scholarship of Malays and Indonesians. Furthermore, the exclusively evaluative approach still ensures that work judged inferior by 'international' standards is dismissed or more commonly simply ignored; and it is often such writing which tells us much about the perceptions of those who have not mastered the scholarly type of print-literate conventions required for, say, a university post. And, again, I am not referring only to Malay writers, for the unscholarly views – even by the standards of their time – of a minority of European 'effortless amateurs' such as Maxwell (1936) were fed back into the tradition. In addition, it is unwise to assume shared norms – a prerequisite for a fair attack according to the standards set for discussion of the Malay tradition – with our European predecessors of the 19th and early 20th centuries, for their society was very different from 'ours' or at least mine, and they existed in a very different noetic system. Perversely, that modern scholarship produced by Indonesians and Malaysians which is perceived by Westerners to be of 'international' standard is again not seen to be, or studied as, part of the Malay tradition.

When it is possible to provide an account over the course of nearly four centuries of how representatives of both the Malay and European systems have operated upon the same piece of writing, and when a critique over 350 years old is also available from the pen of a non-Malay Muslim scholar, who found himself in conflict with the Malay system, we have a useful case history of aspects of the interaction between noetic systems. Let me then tell you the tale of what we may label at this stage the Malay Ramayana. This is not a moral tale; there are no heroes, no villains; both Europeans and Malays were doing only what their respective systems had programmed them to do. Often, those actions were incompatible, or, indeed, in conflict with each other. And the meaning of an action, and/or the result of such action in one system might acquire a very different significance in the terms of the system interacting with it.

The rosy optimism of the last paragraph should be tempered with an icy draft of reality, for which I am grateful to Sirtjo Koolhof, whose observations to me on the *Ila Galigo* could well apply to the *Hikayat Seri Rama*. Essentially, we really know very little indeed about the fortunes of these tales in the past. Indeed, in the case of the *Hikayat Seri Rama,* while the relatively large number of manuscripts attests to a degree of popularity, I am at a loss to find any indication in writing that anyone ever found pleasure in the text! Of course, one might expect that such pleasure would have been expressed orally, thus ephemerally. A hint of this is found in the delight expressed to me in 1968 by Tengku Khalid, the last royal patron of the arts in Kelantan, for his manuscript of the *Hikayat Seri Rama*. He regularly read passages to *dalangs* (shadow-masters) of the shadow-play in search of material. Thus, as may be seen from the repertoire of Mat Ismail, material from the *Hikayat Seri Rama* flowed back into the realm of oral composition to be presented in the *Cerita Maharaja Rawana* (Sweeney 1972: 260-261)

It now seems appropriate to provide a word of explanation about the Malay Ramayana in a nutshell of conventional wisdom: there are more than twenty-five manuscripts of 'the' *Hikayat Seri Rama*, dating mainly from the 19th century, but the earliest originates from circa 1600. Scholars have established that 'the work' is not a translation of 'the Sanskrit Ramayana', but that the great majority of the motifs derive from Indian versions. It is wise at this stage to avoid identifying too closely with these findings, as I am concerned with collapsing the distinctions between scholar and 'tradition'. In looking at the 'adventures' of the *Hikayat Seri Rama,* I hope to cut through some of the cordons mentioned above.

The *hikayat* existed in a world of sound. It was intended to be heard. It was written to be chanted to a non-literate 'listenership', which would not expect to hear every word. And the writer would gear his composition to this situation. Appreciation of the qualities of the 'art' form *hikayat* was intended by the tradition to stem from experiencing the sound. The European, on the other hand, removed the manuscripts from the tradition with the aim of preserving them, silencing them in the process, and gave those manuscripts a new identity.

A *Hikayat Seri Rama* was acquired, it seems, by an English sea captain in 1612(?), probably from Aceh. It, together with a letter from Sultan Perkasa Alam Johan of Aceh to James I of England, came into the possession of Archbishop Laud, who presented it to the Bodleian Museum of Oxford in 1633. There it acquired a new identity: Laud B. 91, later changed to MS. Laud Or. 291. This also provided it with a new contract, which implied a new audience. The *Hikayat Seri Rama* had been intended to be heard: it had been intended to weave a spell of sound mesmerizing enough to communicate effectively its message. Laud Or. 291, however, was to be perused in silence and solitude. It had to wait nearly three hundred years for a serious reader, but museum time passes slowly; a manuscript in the Malay tradition aged much more rapidly. The norms of Bodleian time are reflected in the catalogue of Greentree and Nicholson (1910). Explaining in their preface why they have decided to produce the catalogue despite the small number of Malay manuscripts in their collection, they remark that 'the opportunities we have of acquiring additional Malay MSS. are so rare that a delay of centuries might not have seen any considerable increase in their number'.

While the aim of the Malay manuscript tradition was to update itself continually, and keep itself in the present, the European tradition was concerned with pushing that Malay tradition into the past. My juxtaposing of Malay concern with present beside European emphasis on past might seem to be implying that the Malay tradition was, in fact, more 'dynamic' than the European tradition that studied it. And yet this line of reasoning is no more absurd than the notion that the Malay tradition was – as has been commonly held by European scholarship – entirely static, or worse, that the abundant evidence available that Malay copyists changed manuscripts is to be interpreted as corruption and decline. And yet for those who saw the history of Europe as the glory that was Greece decline into the Dark Ages, this was the obvious interpretation, as is clear from the comparisons drawn between the Malay tradition and that of medieval Europe by 19th and early 20th century English gentlemen educated in the Classics. As I have indicated previously (1987), this was a valid parallel, but for other reasons than theirs: both were radically oral manuscript cultures.

European scholarship was little concerned with the progress of the tradition, for it was not seen as progress. So much of what we now perceive to be the result of development from orality to literacy was interpreted by European scholarship as regression. I need refer only to Kern's comments on the development of the *hikayat* style, or to Brown's attempts to halt the development of modern Malay, and force Malays to write (and even speak!) so-called 'classical' Malay.[iii] The notion of the pristine original led scholars to perceive Malay tradition in terms of a number of imagined archetypes, and to write histories of those non-existent archetypes. In the 19th century, history was, after all, considered to be the obvious way to classify knowledge of all types, just as the *hikayat* was seen by the Malay tradition to be the way to classify all manner of knowledge. Our problem now with this constant quest for originals is that scholars did not concern themselves with Malay writings as they were, but with how they ought to be or should have been. The reinterpretive work of generations of copyists was ignored or discarded. Obviously, such a concern with archetypes give rise to the notion of a static tradition, which Malay was not. If the scholars had been able to reconstruct those archetypes and project more appreciation into their understanding of them, we would have today also in Malay a more impressive and much earlier array of Great Books! It was left to Malaysia, many years after the idea of Great Books had lost currency in Europe, to create a rather sad list of *Buku Agung,* which essentially followed English taste (Sweeney 1980: 7).

The process of reinterpretation covered a wide spectrum of possibilities, ranging from merely updating the language, replacing obsolete words and structures with more current ones, to producing an entirely new argument. An example of the latter type of reworking is the *Sejarah Melayu,* which was reinterpreted to accord with the shift of power to the Bendahara line in Johor. To say that traditional Malay literature was schematic does not imply that the *hikayat* did not express a point of view. Schemata might be adjusted in various ways. The reinterpretation of individual manuscripts was part of the process of adjusting the schemata of tradition. Familiarity with those schemata of the tradition led to certain expectations. On occasion, we may find that those expectations are met on one level but not on another. Sylvia Tiwon's (1999) analysis of the *Hikayat Hang Tuah,* for example, argues that while this work appears highly formulaic on the level of word choice, radical, indeed subversive, adjustments are being made on the level of structure. And one may observe first hand in the oral tradition – viz. the Malay *wayang* (shadow-play) – that tight schematic control on one level may allow looser patterning on another level of composition (Sweeney 1987). In other instances, we are able to detect tensions between the schemata employed appearing in the form of apparent contradictions or inconsistencies. For example, in the work of Hamzah Fansuri, the writer at one point asks his audience – in the traditional manner – to change whatever does not meet their approval. In another passage, however, he insists on the Islamic procedure that his work should be copied faithfully. Obviously, when but one manuscript of a work exists, we cannot examine the progress of the reinterpretive function of the copyist. Internal tensions may, however, provide evidence of that function at work.

The European scholar also functioned as a copyist. There are few known instances of Europeans actually producing a calligraphic copy of a Malay manuscript.[iv] More often, Malay copyists were employed or the manuscript itself was acquired. Here, however, I am more concerned with the copying of manuscripts for print publication. The aim of this endeavour was to make the text available for *study* by a wide audience. Great store was set by accuracy in such transliterations. Changes were not to be made except, perhaps, where obvious 'corruptions' were found. Here, then, seems a clear major difference from the *modus operandi* of the Malay copyist, whose task was updating and reinterpretation. The European copyist, to the contrary, was concerned with preservation of the 'text', and this aim was, of course, in accord with European efforts over centuries to preserve physically the manuscripts themselves. One product of these concerted efforts was Shellabear's resurrection of Laud 291. Shellabear (1915) tells us in his preface: 'The complete text (...) is reproduced as closely as can be done by letterpress printing...The spelling of such a very old manuscript (probably the oldest Malay book in existence), is of great interest to students of the language, and has therefore been faithfully reproduced, even palpable errors of the copyist have not been corrected.' This undertaking was surely the diametrical opposite of what was done by the Malay scribe. At first sight, one might say that here there is no attempt to harmonize the text with contemporary conditions. Shellabear is concerned to preserve the discontinuities: we are forced to confront the archaic. Indeed, it is texts such as his, with the discontinuities resulting from extended dormancy, which created the notion of the archaic in Malay tradition. Here was a text bearing witness to a time long past which had escaped updating for hundreds of years. I have often referred to the homeostatic tendencies of Malay tradition, whereby much change occurs via the process of structural amnesia. Here in Shellabear's undertaking, perhaps, we cannot speak of homeostatis. But there is revealed a similar unawareness of creating change. For of course Shellabear was reinterpreting Malay tradition, and a certain consciousness of this is implied in his 'as closely as can be done'. Shellabear did, indeed, harmonize his text with contemporary conditions; he postulated an entirely new audience: a scholarly reader who was concerned with the peculiarities of 17th century Malay. Not merely was the text designed for easy visual retrieval; paradoxically, the visual cues for the reciter disappeared in the uniformly-printed letters of the text. And of course there is no more ornamental *'anwan* (title page), and this, as I shall argue, has resulted in a different interpretation and another switch of identity for the text.

The process of reinterpretation went much further in the work of other European copyists (and Malay scribes in European employ). Numerous letterpress texts of various *hikayat* appeared in both *jawi* and *rumi* script. In both, European format was introduced, with paragraphing and modern, European, punctuation. Transcription into romanized (*rumi*) script involved a further, more momentous mutation. Romanizing a Malay text requires one to establish the sound of each word. It is a process of inserting vowels and even choosing consonants. In the tradition, this was the reciter's task (a task first undertaken by the copyist, who is likely to have intoned the text while providing cues for the reciter), and a high degree of predictability – i.e., of 'formulaicity' – was needed for him to ascertain that, say k-a-m s-w-l was to be intoned as *kami sula* rather than *kamu sula, kami sulu* or *kamu sulu*. One thus needed a familiar context in order to be able to decipher the text. And the fact that there was this high degree of predictability made it unnecessary for the writer to adhere to a high level of consistency in his use of dots to distinguish letters, so that *nga* might have one dot or three, *ga* might have one dot, three or none. The expectation of continuity in the tradition, furthermore, was taken for granted. This is seen in the assumption that the reciter or future copyist would be familiar with the names of people mentioned in the text, despite the fact that the letters producing those names might have varying numbers of dots, and would know whether, for example, Rama's son was n-y-l-a-w-y, t-b-l-a-w-y or t-y-l-a-w-y.

The romanizer, if successful, deciphers the text once and for all. This process of disambiguating the text then makes redundant the disambiguating function of the *jawi* text itself. We then *read* it as redundancy. Similarly, the repetition so necessary for communication in a non-breathlessly-focussed tradition becomes redundancy for the *reader* concentrating upon every word.

I am not attempting to equate European reinterpretation with the homeostatic modes of Malay tradition, where the life span of manuscripts was short, and reinterpretations did not have their originals around for very long to bear witness to such changes. European reinterpretation – it might seem – involved not so much a change in the words or the argument of the Malay text, but a translation into a new medium: print. The text was rather repackaged for a new audience, and the new authorial contract was both implied in the packaging, and made explicit in the new author's introduction, usually appended to the text. And of course the manuscript was still preserved as witness.

That European reinterpretation involved only translation into the new medium is not, however, correct. What of the search for the original? Of course, before reconstruction of the archetype could be undertaken, there had to be a number of manuscripts available of 'a work'. My point is that scholars needed to perceive the existence of 'the work', of which the manuscripts were 'recensions'. The work existed not in the manuscripts; it was to be reconstructed from the best readings, and these were to be determined by the scholar. But even if only one manuscript were used, it was still possible to make corrections. In 1843, Roorda van Eysinga published a letterpress edition of a *Hikayat Maharaja Seri Rama*. Roorda van Eysinga had no intention of allowing 'palpable' errors to survive in *his* text. As it was 'too unclearly written for the typesetter, and with respect to the spelling so inaccurate, I have taken upon myself the heavy burden of recopying it and purifying the spelling', using the spelling system employed in his Malay grammar, 'which is considered to be the most pure by the best writers', by which he means the best writers of *his* time. Essentially, him! And the manuscript as witness? Well, actually, no one knows what became of it. I shall attempt to introduce some more innuendo on Roorda van Eysinga's work presently.

So the text itself might well be changed. Convention had it that the scholar was not changing 'the work'. He was correcting the manuscript in order to bring it closer to the original, and when he had a number of manuscripts, he could pursue this aim with a vengeance. Thus, although European and Malay copyists were apparently proceeding in opposite directions, both were, in fact, engaged in a similar task: making the best sense possible of what they read. The Malay scribe, too, made corrections. Mistakes were quite common, and correcting them was not the sole prerogative of the European scholar. And passages appearing obscure to the Malay copyist might well be clarified. One need only listen to the old reciter of *syair* smoothing out problems in the text by resorting to his or her own stock of formulas in order to realize that the copyist came to his text with a wealth of schematic alternatives to the material filling the slots of the text. He might have read or heard the reciting of other manuscripts; he is likely to have heard much from oral tradition. In this sense, the Malay copyist's task was also collating 'versions', even though he might have but one manuscript before him.

However, the European copyist was alone in the notion that his understanding of what made the best sense, of what was most logical and fitting, was also shared by the projected original author of 'the work.' Was it only copyists who garbled Arabic phrases, for example? And was not the scholar's criterion for 'good' Malay based upon his immersion in the written Malay of palace manuscripts dating from the 19th century? This is clear from Roorda van Eysinga's comment. It forms the basis of the normative attitude of Winstedt and Brown in the 20th century. The result of their projecting 19th century Malay far into the past led to their equating that Malay with Melaka Malay of the 15th century.

The reconstruction of the archetype remained largely an ideal; the Malay tradition proved to be a tough nut to crack. After all, it is no easy task to disinterpret the reinterpretation of centuries in a schematically composed literature, where a variety of dynamic material might fill the same slots. A simple example is provided by the *bangkitan Seri Rama* from the Malay shadow-play. I choose this advisedly from the oral tradition, for the principles of composition were similar to those of manuscripture, yet the dysfunctions become more quickly obvious. It was suggested to me by Hooykaas over thirty years ago that I might reconstruct the original form of this *bangkitan* (ritual run) from the many renderings I had recorded. Using philological principles, one could indeed recreate such a *bangkitan*, and its size would be so monstrous that it could never have existed. Half of the evening's performance would have been taken up with one enormous epithet! Hooykaas accepted my explanation with typical good grace.

An attempt was, however, made to reconstruct the archetype of the Malay 'version' of the Ramayana, but it was undertaken in German summary. By the time Zieseniss wrote, a clear understanding had jelled that there was 'a work', the *Hikayat Seri Rama*, found in several versions. Shellabear had already referred to Roorda van Eysinga's text and to Marsden's comments on another manuscript. And in the meantime, various articles had appeared concerning other manuscripts of the *Hikayat Seri Rama*. Now Malay tradition also referred to the titles of various *hikayat*. There was, for example, a mention of the *Hikayat Seri Rama* in the writings of Nuruddin ar-Raniri. So did both traditions consider it 'a work'?^{v} I would suggest that the European print-based expectation of the standard work differed considerably from the Malay perception of the *hikayat*. For the Malay, each manuscript *was* the *hikayat*. For the European, who might have at his disposal a large number of manuscripts, not merely from various places, but from different centuries, these manuscripts were but recensions of the 'real' text, which, for L.F. Brakel – an orthodox philologist – was a rather abstract concept; for him it was the *langue*, of which each manuscript was merely a *parole*. I would argue that the *langue* was a system of slots, and that the original text was but one more example of *parole*.

Zieseniss used not twenty-five manuscripts, but the two printed texts. These are clearly two schematically creative reinterpretations of an earlier interpretation or interpretations, and in trying to fit them together to construct an archetype, Zieseniss had little success, being forced by the contradictions and inconsistencies to conclude that the two texts, which we are able to demonstrate were chirographically related, derived from an oral archetype, which was clearly perceived by him to be some form of unwritten writing (Sweeney 1987: 30-31). Indeed such 'contradictions' may be found within the one text. These inconsistencies are typical of the orally-oriented Malay manuscript tradition, and are equally common in the stylized oral form. A case in point is the meeting for the first time between Seri Rama and Hanuman, which occurs twice in the same text (Laud 291). One copyist, armed with his alternatives, may include two fillers for one functional slot. A subsequent copyist may omit one of them or replace both of them with another. With a large number of manuscripts preserved and available, where each rendering is frozen, the scholar is presented with numerous intractable contradictions, which in the oral tradition would be smoothed out from performance to performance. There is a certain irony, furthermore, in the fact that Raffles MS. 22 does accommodate, more or less, the accounts provided in the two texts studied by Zieseniss, and this is further evidence that one need not seek oral archetypes in order to explain the development of the various accounts. But here, I am allowing Zieseniss to dictate the terms of the argument. The 'accounts' for Zieseniss are the sum total of the 'motifs', which are those elements that can be listed in summary and compared with Indian versions of the Ramayana. And the motifs tend to be reduced to a uniform level of importance. Indeed, those not found in Indian versions are presented as having little importance. I think particularly of the Muslim 'element.' I have long argued that tracing the origins of the 'motifs' will tell us little or nothing about the purpose of 'the *Hikayat Seri Rama*', or that it is a Muslim creation (Sweeney 1972). I would now go further and argue that the two 'versions' studied by Zieseniss advance, in fact, different arguments. Boiling them down into one version negates the *raison d'être* of both.

Traditional Malay literature placed great emphasis upon the genealogy. Many court compositions identify themselves as *silsilah* (Brunei), *salasilah* (the plural; Kutai), *sulalat* (offspring, descent, extraction; in *Sulalatu 'l-Salatin)*. Other court works aimed at eulogizing one particular ruler – e.g., *Hikayat Aceh, Misa Melayu* – commence with a genealogy providing the antecedents of that hero. And the great majority of other *hikayat* begin by introducing the hero via his antecedents. The pull of the genealogy is seen even in those works written at European initiative, such as the *Hikayat Nakhoda Muda,* and in the *Hikayat Abdullah*, the genealogy is of the protagonist who is also the writer. In the oral tradition, too, the genealogy is all important; the *dalang,* for example, demonstrates his identity from his genealogy, upon which attention is focussed in ritual drama. His hero is presented via his antecedents. And the shortest possible version of the basic tale will be the origins of the main characters.

The build up to the main protagonist is so pervasive in Malay oral and written tradition that the expectations of the listener are quite predictable. What, then, of the manuscript which, in 1633, became Laud 291, and subsequently 'Shellabear's *Hikayat Seri Rama*'? Let us attempt to break through the various postulations back to that of the scribe. Who, then, is presented as the protagonist? An examination of the treatment employed to produce the main character leaves little doubt but that Rawana is the recipient of that treatment. Even though the beginning of the tale is truncated, it commences with Rawana's early life, recounts his contract with God mediated by Adam, his gaining of sovereignty over four worlds, and his peace-making role in the war between Biruhasyapurwa and Inderpuringegara.

Whether the truncation was intentional or otherwise is irrelevant. Much has been made of the words *Patik membuang segala yang tidak baik* ('I discard all that is not good') which occur at the beginning of the text. Those who take the manuscript 'as is' interpret these words to be from the scribe to his patron, indicating that inappropriate material has been excised. Those who read the manuscript as a version to be corrected point to the fact that in other, longer, manuscripts, these are the words of Citrabaha indicating that Rawana must be exiled. To my knowledge, it has not been suggested that the scribe who produced Laud 291 could well have truncated his text deliberately at this point, producing a new meaning for the sentence in question. That would certainly fit the argument of the text, and should we not allow each manuscript to bear witness to its own time and place?[vi] The opening thus employs material designed to suit the motifemic slots structured for the introduction of the hero. There is, however, a tension between plot structure and character type, for the type is clearly not that of the typical hero. The writer thus creates enough common ground to achieve effective communication with his listening audience, but he only partly meets their expectations. Rawana is a good and just Muslim hero for the initial part of the text. But during that period, the expectation of the audience that this type will, in fact, revert to type is exploited to focus attention upon the morality of his actions. The refined young prince type hero does not offer these possibilities. He performs the functions allotted to heroes, and, indeed, in many of these he is simply the beneficiary of donors and supernatural helpers who do full justice to Vladimir Propp. In a tale concerning the breaking of a contract, he could not revert to type. Furthermore, in this tale, which creates a Muslim audience or one receptive to Islam but which is still conversant with Hinduism, an attempt to bend the character of Rama himself might lack persuasive power; the associations between Rama and Hinduism were too many, and Rama's character too well known. A radical switch might find the scribe indicted by his listeners under Anderson's law of self-correction!

After 141 pages of the *hikayat*, we are again presented with the machinery for producing a hero. This time, it produces Seri Rama, and, of course, he is the refined young prince type. As Rawana reverts to type and takes on the villain's role, Seri Rama assumes the mantle of hero, and his actions contrast with that of the villain. We might argue, however, that parallels are drawn between the childhood exploits of Rama and Rawana in order to demonstrate certain similarities: Rama's mistreatment of the hunchback brings to mind Rawana's bullying of his playmates, for which he was exiled to Serindip. Is Laud 291 then a *Hikayat Seri Rama* or a *Hikayat Maharaja Rawana*? One might say that this question already makes an unjustified presupposition. I would respond rather that it begins as a *Hikayat Maharaja Rawana* and becomes a *Hikayat Seri Rama*. Here again, we see the tensions. Ikram (1980) clearly feels it necessary to argue that the work is indeed the *Hikayat Seri Rama*: she notes that though the first page states that the *hikayat* is about Rawana, the conclusion tells us that 'this is a *hikayat* about Seri Rama', and she feels that the latter is *lebih tepat* ('more accurate') though without providing any reasons. I submit that this approach – i.e., judging which is 'more accurate', and the whole assumption that one has to make such a choice – merely glosses over the tensions which are the whole purpose of the work.

The opening contract of this work offers us a *Hikayat Maharaja Rawana*. The fact that subsequent sections of the book present other '*hikayat*' (accounts) of, for example, 'The Mad Buffalo' and 'Mulamatani', is irrelevant in this context. Scholars have, in the past, complained about the lack of data provided by Malay manuscripture, citing the omission of dates and the anonymity of authors. Very self-revealing complaints! The fact that the Malay text did not provide answers to the kinds of questions Europeans chose to ask does not mean that data were not provided on matters considered important by Malay tradition. A feature of most Malay manuscripts was the *'anwan*, an ornamental and illuminated first page (or first two pages: *verso* and *recto)*, which might be called the title page. I prefer to term it the contract page. The writing is usually confined to a much smaller area of the page than on other pages, and consists of a prolonged, descriptive title, containing the word *hikayat*, *syair*, etc., followed by the name of the protagonist. The *'anwan* of the present text reads:

> 'Ini hikayat yang terlalu indah-indah termasyhur diperkatakan orang di atas angin dan di bawah angin nyata kepada segala sastera perkataan Maharaja Rawana yang sepuluh kepalanya dan duapuluh tangannya; raja itu terlalu besyar ia beroleh kerajaannya empat tempat negeri dianugerahkan Allah Ta'ala [Dewata]: suatu kerajaan dalam dunia kedua kerajaan kepada keinderaan pada udara ketiga tempat kerajaan dalam bumi keempat kerajaan di dalam laut.'
>
> (This is an extremely beautiful account, widely known and spoken of by people above the (monsoon) winds and below the winds, manifest in the works of divination: the words about Maharaja Rawana with ten heads and twenty arms; this raja was very great: he obtained his kingdoms in four places, territories granted him by Allah the Almighty the *Dewata:* one kingdom in the world; second, a kingdom of the heavens in the air; third a kingdom located in the earth; fourth, a kingdom in the sea.)

The subsequent structuring of the tale demands, however, that this contract be modified. The tale does, indeed, become a *Hikayat Seri Rama*. Although our focus is upon Laud's text, it is worthy of note that this tension is reflected in other oral and written compositions concerned with Rama and Rawana. One need note only the existence of the *Hikayat Maharaja Rawana*, which is chirographically related to other *Hikayat Seri Rama* manuscripts, and parallels their content in Zieseniss's terms. Again, the complex of Malay *wayang kulit* repertoire has as its basic tale the *Cerita Maharaja Rawana*.

It is apposite at this point to look at the other *jawi* letterpress printing of the *Hikayat Seri Rama*: that published by Roorda van Eysinga in 1843. In view of the medium employed, it is surprising, perhaps, to note that Roorda van Eysinga has included an *'anwan*. It reads:

> 'Bahwa ini ceritera orang dahulu kala yang di negeri Hindustan seraya ini 'Hikayat Maharaja Seri Rama' namanya maka dipindahkan daripada surat naskhat oleh yang empunya dia iaitu Hakim Rurda pan 'Eisinga adapun kitab ini sudah ditera di negeri Breda pada perteraan tuan2 Berusi dan perseronya pada Hijrat 1258.'
>
> (This is a story about people of former times in the land of Hindustan, and it is named *Hikayat Maharaja Seri Rama*. It has been copied from the manuscript by the one who owns it, that is, Professor[vii] Roorda van Eysinga. This book has been printed in Breda at the printing house of Messrs. Broese and Co. in the *Hijrat* year 1258.)

Roorda van Eysinga's casting himself thus in the role of Malay copyist reminds us of the 18th century (and before) activities of the Dutch as writers of Malay literature (Sweeney 1987). The stance assumed in this preface, however, is European, not Malay: Malay copyists – if at all – tended to include their names and date of completion at the end of the work; only with print could one insert the date of completion at the beginning. And the stance of Malay copyist is assumed for the benefit of a Dutch audience. Indeed, when we reach the end of the *hikayat*, we find it is really the beginning of the book. The main title page is in Dutch; we read through the introduction and hit the end of the *hikayat*! In addition to this clash of conventions, we encounter a more basic disjuncture. From Roorda van Eysinga's other work, we know that he was not averse to embellishing his text. In his edition of the *Taju 'l-Salatin*, for example, he added his own poems matching the style of those occurring in his original text. The version of the *Syair Ken Tambuhan* published by De Hollander in 1856 was apparently based on a manuscript copied from a manuscript supposedly owned by Roorda van Eysinga, who translated it into Dutch in 1838. Roorda van Eysinga's manuscript is apparently no longer extant. This version of the *syair* is wholly atypical in that it ends with the death of the hero and heroine, producing a tragedy, as Roorda van Eysinga does not hesitate to point out. But in Malay terms, if the resurrecting of the hero and heroine is absent, the tale is incomplete. One may suspect that Roorda van Eysinga conveniently lost the ending to satisfy the European taste of his time. And even if this insinuation is unjustified, then the fact that Roorda van Eysinga selected this incomplete manuscript for his translation is equally valid evidence of his penchant for Malay literary engineering. It is possible, therefore, that in addition to correcting his *Hikayat Seri Rama*, he may have determined where it was to begin. Indeed numerous references to events earlier in the story only make sense after we consult other manuscripts which begin at an earlier point. Yet in advancing this view, I may appear to be caving in to the reconstructionists' scenario! My main point here, then, is that while Roorda van Eysinga felt himself entirely justified in improving his Malay manuscripts, and might thus seem to fit comfortably into the Malay tradition of reinterpreting his work to meet contemporary – here paradoxically European – norms, as far as Roorda van Eysinga was concerned, there was to be no reinterpreting of Roorda van Eysinga's own text! He emphasizes: 'Tegen het nadrukken van dit werk zal de wet worden ingeroepen, terwijl geene exemplaren als echt worden erkend dan die door den eigenaar geteekend zijn.' (The law will be invoked against any reprinting of this work; no exemplars will be recognised as genuine apart from those signed by the owner.)

It is unnecessary for me to prove that Roorda van Eysinga was responsible for choosing the point at which his *Hikayat Seri Rama* began. Indeed, there are other manuscripts which begin only with the antecedents of Seri Rama. What is of significance here is that in the Roorda van Eysinga version (and in those other manuscripts) the tensions I mentioned above are absent. We have a 'straightforward' *Hikayat Seri Rama*.

Elsewhere (1987) I have discussed at some length the implications for the study of Malay tradition of Havelock's ideas concerning Plato's rejection of the poets. When I first read Havelock's comments concerning the enjoyment and relaxation experienced by an ancient Greek audience as they were 'partly hypnotized by their response to a series of rhythmic patterns, verbal, vocal, instrumental and physical', I was struck by the fact that in 1968, I had written almost exactly the same remarks about the mesmerizing effects of the Malay *wayang* (Sweeney 1972). What could only be hypothesized about ancient Greek society was still experienced first hand in Kelantan and Patani. Indeed, a specific term, *angin* (literally: 'wind'), is used to designate this susceptibility to be overcome by the rhythmical spell of the *wayang*. Possession of *angin* is the most basic prerequisite for any prospective pupil of a *dalang*. One experiences one's *angin* first as a prickling of the skin, especially on the arms and at the back of the neck. *Angin* must be controlled; otherwise one may lapse into trance, and in ritual performances this inclination towards trance is encouraged, though the *angin* must still be subjected to certain controls. I had long noted that the mesmerizing effect of the *wayang* is the reason often given by orthodox Muslims to explain their hostility towards the *wayang*. Again, I was struck by the similarity with Plato's antipathy for the poets, which was, of course, no coincidence, considering the legacy of Greek philosophy in Islamic scholarship. In terms of *'akal* and *nafsu* ('rationality' and 'the passions'), the oral need to surrender oneself to the spell of performance smacks too much of *nafsu*. Only by detaching oneself from the performance – an option made possible by literacy – can the *'akal* gain ascendancy.

There was a close similarity of presentation and consumption between traditional Malay manuscripture and oral composition, and both employed the same basic principles of composition. Indeed, the 19th century description by Gibson (1855) of a manuscript recitation leaves no doubt that the performance of traditional Malay literature had the same mesmerizing effect as that of oral composition.

Ikram (1980) wonders whether the *Hikayat Seri Rama* was intended to educate or to entertain, and concludes that this is 'not yet clear'. It is my opinion that a distinction is being made where none existed in the tradition. In the oral tradition, it was necessary to mesmerize, to produce hypnotic pleasure in order to educate. Just as Plato – as argued by Havelock – rejected the traditional, i.e., oral mode of education, so too, did orthodox Islam oppose the radically oral pedagogy of many palace *hikayat* – i.e., those least influenced by *kitab* literature.[viii] I have often (Sweeney 1980) referred to the emphasis placed upon *faedah* ('profit', 'benefit') in Malay writing in which the ethos assumed is manifestly Islamic. I would argue that this is often the articulation of a reaction against the oral tradition. A case in point is the writings of Munsyi Abdullah, whose opinions are expressed in a very forthright manner, paradoxically the result of European influence. Many of his criticisms of 19th-century Malay society clearly reflect the impatience of a highly literate individual with an oral tradition, although he was obviously unable to articulate the problem in these terms. I would add that the distinction he continually makes between what is of *faedah* and what is 'false and futile' (*bohong dan sia-sia*) is a distinction between his level of literacy and the radically oral Malay tradition. What is of *faedah* is acquired as the result of study. That which is *bohong dan sia-sia* is heard 'along the street'. The *faedah* derives from *kitab* works such as the *Taju 'l-Salatin*; the *bohong* is found in the old court *hikayat*. Indeed, Abdullah clearly acquired much of his *faedah* versus *bohong* diatribes from such *kitab* works. The distinction between what is of 'profit' and what is 'soothing' made by Koster and Maier (1985) is a valid one, though these represent essentially two poles. The distinction should not, however, be seen simply as a criterion one may use to distinguish between genres, although it may be argued that 'genres' are a result. It indicates rather a clash – or to be less militant, and, perhaps, more accurate, an interaction – between systems: the traditional Malay oral and the Islamic literate. As writing displaced the oral tradition, and took over more and more the role of educating and the management of power, the oral tradition was increasingly left with the role of 'soothing.' And even this role was shared with written composition. It should be stressed, however, that merely accepting the idea of 'soothing' tells us little about the function of radically oral manuscripture or of oral composition in performance. Soothing was but one aspect of the manipulation of the emotions that was a central function of Malay literature and oral composition (Sweeney 1994).

It is not, perhaps, surprising, therefore, that one may perceive a divide between scholarly *kitab* literature, and the schematically composed, aurally-consumed, written palace literature. But there was interaction between the two, and attempts were made to bridge and even close the gap, so that the distinctions often appear to be more of degree than of kind. Tales regarded as *kitab* literature, too, were recited to listening audiences: the *Hikayat Amir Hamzah* and the *Hikayat Muhammad Hanafiah* are cited in the *Sulalatu 'l-Salatin* (*Sejarah Melayu*) as having been so presented. The *Hikayat Nabi Yusuf* is still chanted in Lombok. The Sufi scholar Hamzah Fansuri made use of the rhythms of the tradition in his *syair*, in order to expound his highly literate beliefs. Nuruddin ar-Raniri, an orthodox Muslim scholar from Gujerat, found enough *'akal* and thus *faedah* in the *Sulalatu 'l-Salatin* to quote it in his *Bustanu 'l-Salatin*. But he could not tolerate the heresies he descried in the works of Hamzah Fansuri. And perhaps Hamzah's penchant for weaving a spell of sound was a further reason for him to perpetrate one of the more dramatic examples of physical literary criticism in the tradition: the public burning of Hamzah's writings.

But here, I am merely setting the stage for Nuruddin's comments on the *Hikayat Seri Rama*. And these were comments which led even Winstedt into ribald comments on toilet habits, and caused Drewes to downplay the unsavory implications. For Nuruddin states in his *Siratu 'l-Mustaqim*: [ix]

'Bermula istinja itu wajib... maka istinja itu dengan air atau dengan batu atau barang benda yang suci lagi kasat yang dapat menghilangkan najis itu. Dan tiada harus bersuci dengan suatu benda yang dihormati pada syara' seperti tulang dan kulit yang belum disamak atau barang sebagainya, tetapi harus istinja dengan kitab Taurat dan Injil yang sudah berubah daripada asalnya dan demi(k)ian lagi harus istinja' dengan kitab yang tiada berguna pada syara' seperti Hikayat Seri Rama dan Inderaputera dan barang sebagainya, jika tiada di dalam(nya) nama Allah.'

(*Istinja* [cleansing oneself after bodily movements] is *wajib* [obligatory]... *Istinja* is with water or stone or anything which is clean and rough and able to remove the impurities. And it is not *harus*' to purify oneself with things respected in religious law such as bone and skin as yet untanned and suchlike, but *istinja* is *harus* with the Torah and the Gospel, which have changed from their original form. Thus also, *istinja* is *harus* with books of no worth in religious law such as *Hikayat Seri Rama* and *Inderaputera* and suchlike, if the name of Allah is not within them.)

Not surprisingly, Mulyadi was puzzled by the reference to skin and bone. However, Nuruddin's reservations about the use of skin and bone are explained by a passage in his *Bustanu 'l-Salatin,* for there it is stated that these substances were set aside as food for the jinn, who might not appreciate their dinners served à la mode.

'Dan sembilan orang daripada jin lalu dari sisi Ka'batullah. Dan pada suatu riwayat tujuh orang, maka didengarnya Nabi Allah membaca Qur'an. Maka ia pun datanglah. Demi didengar mereka itu Nabi Allah, maka masuk Islamlah mereka itu serta sembahnya: 'Ya Rasulullah, apa makanan kami?' Maka sabda Rasulullah, 'Akan makanan kamu tiap2 segala tulang yang sudah disembelih dan kulit keenderaan kamu.' Sebab itulah maka ditegahkan Nabi Allah istinja' dengan tulang dan kulit.' *(Kitab Bustanu 'l-Salatin*: I. 31-32)

(And nine of the jinn passed by the *Kaaba* of God. And according to one account there were seven of them. They heard the Prophet of God reciting the Qur'an and they approached. On hearing that this was the Prophet of God, they converted to Islam and humbly inquired: 'O Apostle of God, what is to be our food?' The Apostle of God decreed: 'Your food is all manner of bones [from animals] which have been ritually slaughtered and skin are your staples.' For that reason the Prophet of God forbade *istinja* with bone and skin.)

But what of the *Hikayat Seri Rama* and the *Hikayat Inderaputera*? It is painfully clear that Nuruddin did not appreciate these works. Yet this passage has produced some strange interpretations. And those interpretations are usually provided without context. Winstedt's remark that Nuruddin condemned the *Hikayat Seri Rama* 'to the lavatory', or that 'it might be used as toilet paper' is fairly close to the mark, but, provided without context, it has raised the hackles of many Malays, who explode that Malays do not use toilet paper! Johns follows Winstedt in seeing Nuruddin's remark as anti-Hindu, but perceives this 'violent antipathy to everything Hindu' as a reflection of Nuruddin's work 'as a polemist against the syncretists in India, for as far as is known, there was never any Hindu influence in Acheh' (Johns 1957: 35). That may be so, but it is highly probable that the *Hikayat Seri Rama* was found in Aceh, and Nuruddin's remark was directed at the *Hikayat Seri Rama* and, one should add, at the *Hikayat Inderaputera*, which was hardly very popular in India. Yet Drewes, while apparently accepting Johns's view that there was a clear connection between events in India and in Aceh, nevertheless opines: 'But is seems far-fetched to find an indication of his work as a polemist against the syncretists in India in his declaration that the Malay version of the Ramayana might be used as toilet paper. For this only means that since in the Ramayana the name Allah does not occur, the paper on which it is written may be freely used for that purpose. The same advice would have been given by the mildest of *faqihs'* (Drewes 1959: 284. Review of Johns). 'Only'?! Johns's view on the syncretists may well be far-fetched, but for Drewes to suggest that Nuruddin is merely offering mild advice – and that Nuruddin's choice of the *Hikayat Seri Rama* as toilet paper from among the innumerable substances which do not contain the name of Allah does not imply a condemnation but simply offers an interpretation of the law – is patently absurd. How would Drewes have felt if he were to learn that one of his writings had been singled out for such a fate? A similarly unacceptable interpretation of Nuruddin's comment is that it 'expressed his disapproval of works which did not mention the name of God' (Mulyadi 1983: 38). The inclusion of the name of God does not make the works any more acceptable to Nuruddin; it merely precludes their coming into contact with *najis* (the unclean). All these interpretations fail to appreciate Nuruddin's rhetorical ploy: he explains the rules on *istinja*. Then, assuming the stance of providing further exposition of the law, he proceeds overtly into specifics. And in choosing the area of texts, which are made of paper – a clean and rough substance – he is able to take a side-swipe at those of which he disapproves. It seems, furthermore, that Mulyadi misreads the word *harus,* giving it the modern Indonesian connotation of 'should.' Nuruddin uses the word in the context of *hukum,* where it carries the connotation of neither urged nor frowned upon.

If there is still any doubt about Nuruddin's intentions, then let us examine another passage, which gives an exhortation to all those who have children that they should not allow their children to be friendly with culpably ignorant people, those involved in performances, in gambling or cockfighting, or those who play the *rebana* (tambourine) or musical instruments, and continues:

'Dan jangan membaca hikayat yang tiada berfaedah, dari karena dalam hikayat itu terbanyak juga dustanya kepada memberi mudarat... Nescaya binasalah adanya dalam dunia dan akhirat, sebab nyata dustanya hikayat dengan rebana itu.'
(And do not read *hikayat* which provide no profit, for in those *hikayat* there is much falsehood which leads to harm... Without doubt they bring destruction in this world and the next, for those *hikayat* performed with the tambourine are manifestly false.)

We are told further that those who read such *hikayat* – *Hikayat Inderaputera* is given as an example – become infidels, and that people should read works which provide *faedah*, such as the *Bustanu 'l-Salatin!* This passage occurs almost verbatim in some manuscripts of both the *Bustanu 'l-Salatin*, also by Nuruddin, and one of the *Taju 'l-Salatin* (Mulyadi 1983: 23-25), which, too, was apparently produced in Aceh. Whether or not Nuruddin himself wrote this passage is largely irrelevant to the interpretation of Nuruddin's central thrust. The main antipathy here is towards *hikayat* which are performed with the *rebana*, and the concern is more with the performance than with the content of the work. This, too, seems clear from the context, where music in general is condemned. It is the *rebana* which produces those mesmerizing rhythms that demand a surrender to the spell of the performance, and allow the *nafsu* to gain ascendancy over the *'akal*.

The notion that Nuruddin's hostility towards the *Hikayat Seri Rama* is simply a reflection of the opposition between Hinduism and Islam is overly simplistic. Likewise, the idea that a Hindu Ramayana was given an Islamic flavor or 'colouring' has often been suggested – e.g., by Winstedt – but never argued convincingly. I shall return to this notion below. Such notions were given currency by the throwaway remarks of Winstedt that the *Hikayat Seri Rama* had to have the name of Allah to save it from the lavatory. Indeed, Winstedt views the use of *Allah Ta'ala* in Laud 291 as an attempt to save it from Nuruddin's injunction. It is tempting to make this link in view of the fact that both the future Laud 291 and Nuruddin were in Aceh in the early 17th century. But Laud 291 had left long before Nuruddin arrived, and the *Siratu 'l-Mustaqim* was apparently written before he came to Aceh. The notion, furthermore, that while Laud is physically the oldest text, it is the youngest recension – in view of this Islamic 'colouring' – arises mainly from the fact that Roorda van Eysinga's text does not contain the contract with Adam (see e.g., Winstedt 1958: 37). But Roorda van Eysinga's text starts at a much later point; all those texts which begin with Rawana do mention the contract.

It should be remembered that Laud 291 was produced in the period when the writings of Hamzah Fansuri and Syamsuddin were highly influential. The main thrust of Nuruddin's ire was directed not at the *Hikayat Seri Rama* and the *Hikayat Inderaputera,* but at the works of the two Sufi scholars. And, of course, the inclusion of the words *Allah Ta'ala* is highly unlikely to have been considered a way of saving a work from condemnation. Indeed, in Laud 291, the name of Allah has been repeatedly crossed out and replaced with *Dewata Mulia Raya*. The mention of 'toilet paper' was for Nuruddin a way of expressing his distaste. His method of actually dispatching books of which he disapproved was much cleaner: he had the available works of Hamzah and Syamsuddin burned.

It is clear that Hamzah was much more aware of the noetic system to which the *Hikayat Seri Rama* pertained than was Nuruddin. He did not write only *kitab* Malay; in his *syair* – I would repeat – he harnessed the rhythms and schemata of the radically oral Malay tradition. Rather than attempting to stamp out those rhythms, he exploited them for his own Islamic, literate ends. The Islamic device of using an originally Hindu story to introduce Islamic ideas, again via the rhythms and schemata of Malay tradition reveals a similar strategy. Although Barrett in an unpublished article (1963) did not use these arguments, he nevertheless arrived at a fairly similar conclusion: that the Islamization of the Ramayana in the Malay world was a Sufi achievement. For Nuruddin al-Raniri, the dogmatist from Gujerat, the exploitation of the oral aspects of the Malay tradition, whereby common ground might be created with a non-literate, listening audience in order to introduce new arguments, did not present itself as an option. For him, Malay was a learned language of Islamic scholarship.

It is worthy of note that the deletion of the phrase *Allah Ta'ala* in Laud 291 and the insertion of *Dewata Mulia Raya* by another hand does not indicate a move to make it sound more Hindu – a view which, anyway, contradicts the 'saving from the lavatory' theory. There is no evidence that *Dewata Mulia Raya* in the *Hikayat Seri Rama* referred to the Hindu triad, as Winstedt (1958: 37) holds, for the term was employed to indicate the God of Islam. (See also the *Hikayat Inderaputera*.) This is clear from the Muslim Terengganu inscription. And, it should be stressed, this was the *Mulia Raya* used by Hamzah Fansuri; it was not 'an epithet of the gods', as Drewes and Brakel aver (1986), but of God. And *Dewata Mulia Raya* is still used in the Malay shadow-play. This was believed to be a name of God during the time of the prophet Adam. And true to Muslim Malay tradition, the *Hikayat Seri Rama* was placed in the time of Adam, just as the *Hikayat Iskandar Zulkarnain* was located in the era of the prophet Ibrahim.

There is no evidence to suggest that the *Hikayat Seri Rama* stratagem was generally employed on tales deriving from Hindu times. A particularly simplistic view by today's standards – deriving from Winstedt, but still, it seems, the prevailing conventional wisdom (see, e.g., Mulyadi 1983: 39-40) – is that works were given 'Islamic colouring', or an 'Islamic veneer' in order to allow them to survive in Muslim times. There are two problems with this view: it does not take into account the homeostatic tendencies of Malay tradition, whereby the reinterpretive function of scribe and teller ensured that the material they produced was brought in line with current social conditions. That there is no surviving purely 'Hindu' literature is explained by this process of reinterpretation. Secondly, the yardstick so often used by European scholars for characterizing Muslim standards in the Malay world has been the writing of Nuruddin. And his forceful views have fitted in with their image of an implacable Islam suppressing the Malay 'literary spirit', an image which resulted from the traditional hostility and fear of Islam felt by Europeans since the crusades, a fear kindled anew and further fueled among colonial officials by the growth of pan-Islamism towards the end of the 19th century (Sweeney 1980). This also fitted in with the European view of the Malay as the perpetual underdog, as though submitting to foreign influences was the mark of the victim. It is true that orthodox, literate Islam was opposed to the mesmerizing oral tradition, but as the European scholars also found, that tradition was a tough nut to crack.

Although, unlike the situation of the oral composer in performance, the process of composition in the Malay manuscript tradition might not appear to involve performance, the writer and copyist worked with a maximum of auditory imaginings. Thus, an integral part of the chirographic skill was a knowledge of the principles of the chant. The composition was structured to be chanted, and the process of composition and copying apparently involved intoning the text. Yet although the text was composed of short sound bites to suit the rhythm of the chant, the principles of performing the text were transmitted orally.

The concept of transmitting a fixed text was well-known to Malay tradition. Malay was, after all, a major language of Islamic scholarship, and in Arabic great efforts were made to ensure that no sound of the Quranic text should be changed in the process of chanting or transmission. Vocalization guaranteed that there would be no ambiguity of pronunciation; and the science of *tajwid* ensured that the enunciation and interpretation should never vary. The centrality of the Quran in Arabic has determined the form of the written language to the present day, and one may argue that this has prevented the language of the Quran from becoming archaic. In Malay, texts in the *kitab* tradition might well be copied meticulously; some even employed vocalization. In the reinterpretive, orally oriented palace tradition, however, the scribe had little perceived need of vocalization, and there was no codification of the principles of enunciation. The processes of interpretation and reinterpretation, therefore, demanded a relatively high degree of continuity. If a copyist or a chanter were presented with a manuscript from a period much earlier than his own, or from a different geographical area, he might encounter problems interpreting it, though usually, his own stock of schemata might provide him with sufficient options, so that he could simply replace a word, phrase or passage with one of his own. And the copyist of *jawi* also had the option of merely copying the letters; he was not required to interpret the text as is the romanizer. It should be noted, furthermore, that manuscript Malay changed far less than did English print culture between 1600 and the 19th century. I would submit that the relative freedom of the copyist within his schematic constraints – and indeed the very nature of schematic composition – required a relative stability of the language.

It might well be argued that the reinterpretive function of the copyist, whereby the tradition was constantly updated, makes it impossible to provide evidence that discontinuity of transmission would make a text difficult not merely to reinterpret, but even to understand for those in the manuscript tradition. There is, however, the evidence provided by steles and gravestones – fixed texts par excellence – which, once inscribed, do not seem to have been read. In the *Hikayat Aceh*, for example, information on genealogies might well have been corrected by reference to the numerous available gravestones. But it was more important for one's writing to accord with what was said and heard in the writer's milieu. One finds no references to such inscriptions in the manuscript tradition. Scribes and chanters read and chanted manuscripts, not gravestones. It would seem, moreover, that once inscriptions lost their initial significance, they would be neglected, often buried, or used for other purposes, as, e.g., flagstones for mosques. When such inscriptions were 'rediscovered' by Europeans, local Malays literate in the *Jawi* script would find them difficult if not impossible to read, even though they were written in *Jawi*. And some such inscriptions, as, for example, those found on a number of gravestones in Patani where the Islamic calligraphy consists mainly of a complex of vertical lines, opaque even to the philologist specializing in such arcana, do not appear to have been written with the intention of being read. It seems that attention tended to be given by Malays to such inscriptions only after Europeans, in their search for antiquities, had focussed attention on such matters. And such inscriptions often acquired a magical significance.

This is the context in which we must view the apparent return of Laud 291 to the Malay manuscript tradition. Although Shellabear (1915) hardly postulates a Malay audience, there is no accounting for real audiences. We have seen the stance affected by Roorda van Eysinga of being a Malay copyist, and noted how that stance proves to be merely a European literary and copyrighted conceit. Shellabear surely did not expect that his printed text would be copied back into the calligraphy of the tradition. Yet in 1944, one Muhammad Ali did, in fact, accomplish this remarkable task. This new manuscript then apparently came into the possession of the Kedah royal family. Twenty years later, it was reintroduced in print as a manuscript of the Kedah royalty.

It is tempting here to see a reassertion of the Malay manuscript tradition. We might attempt to argue that the need to reinterpret and harmonize the manuscript with current needs led Muhammad Ali to copy laboriously the text of Shellabear (1915) rather than purchase the relevant back issue of *Journal of the Straits Branch of the Royal Asiatic Society* from the Royal Asiatic Society, Straits Branch. But times had changed; it was now the age of print. The nature of the copyist's task had changed accordingly. Reinterpretation of the Malay tradition continued apace, undertaken by both Europeans and Malays for their respective audiences. And increasingly, their efforts, and the audiences they created, overlapped. The European reinterpreters tended to ignore the reinterpretive work undertaken independently by Malays, which is where we may learn much of the Malay trends. They gave their attention mainly to the work of Malays whose activities had been initiated and directed by the Europeans themselves. Ironically, here, too, we see the Malay tradition surviving regardless. One may well ponder the possibility that had it not been for the European desire to preserve the old, to fix it, and disseminate it, the Malays might well have reinterpreted the old manuscript literature out of existence!

When we place our Kedah royal manuscript in the context of a consideration of the development of manuscript copying under European influence, not to mention the effects of colonial mass education upon the tradition, and the continuing reinterpretation of that tradition, we become aware that we must dismiss any notion we may entertain that the Kedah manuscript will throw light upon how pre-print manuscript culture would have dealt with the discontinuities involved in attempting to reinterpret a manuscript frozen for nearly 350 years. The copyist was a print-age man; even his copy book revealed this: the work is copied into an account book with a printed *jawi* running head indicating debits and credits (*masuk* and *keluar*)! He copied from a very clearly printed text, and could hardly have been blind to Shellabear's annotations. He was thus presented with a text which had, in a sense, already been updated. And, of course, by 1944, the tradition had largely been silenced; for then, *hikayat* were but rarely chanted. The acoustic aspect of the scribe's metier was dying, producing a cleavage between the acts of writing and chant. Works were copied in silence into silence. Muhammad Ali's transliteration reveals little tendency to harmonize the language to suit his own taste. The type and number of changes encountered are, in fact, similar to those in contemporary romanizations or, indeed, in the retyping of a text. Indeed, his work tells us no more about the modus operandi of the traditional scribe than does the work of a romanizer or typist. It gives the appearance of being more traditional only because of the copyist's choice of 'target' medium. He is proceeding in a counter direction to that taken by the romanizer, and, in fact, in copying into an older medium than that of his original, i.e., from typeset print to manuscript, his work is atypical of Malay tradition.

I have often drawn a parallel between the work of the palace scribe and the reciter of manuscripts. Both tended to adjust the language of the text to suit their own taste. I have found that the differences between the recitation of a *syair* and the text from which it is recited tend to be similar to the differences of word choice between a manuscript and its copy from the pre-print era.[xi] (Beyond the area of simple word choice, of course, the scribe had much more room to reinterpret further.) It seems likely that the copyist, too, intoned his text as he copied it, but the text itself does not tell us how it was intended to be articulated. One aspect of the reciter's task, therefore, was actually more similar to that of the romanizer, for both were required to interpret the pronunciation of each word in their text – or they could change the words, of course. Both had to supply the needed vowels. It is thus in the work of the romanizer that we are often able to detect discontinuity in the tradition when a text has been placed on ice and so remained unread and silent for a long period. And it is partly from the further adventures of the Kedah manuscript that we are able to observe the discontinuity resulting from the removal of Laud 291 over threehundred years previously. For the Kedah manuscript was to experience a further mutation after only twenty odd years.

But first, let us pick up the tale of Shellabear (1915), née Laud 291, who, in 1944, was in the process of being reconverted into a manuscript in modern *jawi* handwriting with no pretensions to calligraphic art on the equally unpretentious pages of an account book. And this was for the Kedah royal family! In 1957, Shellabear (1915) was romanized by Wahi bin Long for the Malayan Education Department. The intended readership for this publication was presumably those being educated by the department. The audience actually postulated, however, is somewhat ambiguous. The preliminaries are all in English, but the format is far from scholarly, except for the fact that the prefatory note to Shellabear's letterpress edition is slapped onto the beginning, still including the comment that 'even palpable errors of the copyist have not been corrected'. Some irony may be perceived in the fact that this comment, though referring to the supposed errors in Laud 291, are richly appropriate to the work of the romanizer. While the ambivalence of the audience postulated is perhaps an indication of the confusion attending the imminent end of the British *Raj*, my concern here is more with the interpretation of the tradition. It is palpably clear that this text presents a disjunction, which is not to say that the romanizer was aware of any problems. Unlike the philologist who studies 17th century Malay and attempts to understand the intricacies of the different methods of spelling, Wahi contextualizes the text in the language of the 20th century, but the gap is too great to bridge successfully. He is, furthermore, no longer able to bring to bear his own schemata of the tradition. And, unlike the *dalang* of the oral tradition, he has no dynamic material relevant to the Rama complex of tales which might throw light upon his text. Like many modern students in Malaysia and Indonesia who transcribe what they see, or hear from tapes, without perceiving any need for the result to be meaningful to them, Wahi simply romanized what he 'saw'. The process of copying had become a mechanical exercise, no longer a creative activity. A mechanical copyist of *jawi* may produce the required clone of his original. And this, after all, is what the European patrons had supposedly taught him to do. But even the most mechanically inclined romanizer is forced to interpret and supply the vowels needed in his copy. And for this romanizer, who was clearly not aware that in 1600 *jawi* spelling was very different – that, for example, *nga* might have but one dot and thus be identical with *ghain*, or that final vowels were usually omitted – the result is unintentionally very different from what was intended.

This, combined with a new feature: typographical errors, produces a text which, judged by the contract implied in the preface, does not fulfil that contract. Examples of problems, apart from general garbling and the production of pure gobbledygook, are seen particularly in the names of characters. Those familiar with the Rama tales know of Sang Penjelma, Anila, Anggada and Sugriwa. Here they have become Saghjalam, Anbala, Angkada and Surgiwa.

After an administrative liberation from colonialism, in 1957, our story enters another phase. Two trends became apparent in the print-era Malay reinterpretation of the tradition. The first trend, which involved a gradual but definite rejection of the tradition might seem to be at odds with the second, which was apparently concerned with preserving something of the tradition, though in a 'simplified' form. And of course, the European program: the preservation of the text in toto, which included both the physical preservation of the manuscripts, and the supposedly meticulous reproduction in romanized script, did not end with colonialism. In fact, these trends became compatible in Western terms, for they were subsumed by Western branches of knowledge; here, for example, 'history' and 'literature.' And although many ex-colonial European scholars chose to focus upon what was now 'classical' literature, Malays themselves struggled with their tradition to produce a new literature – by which I mean new forms of written expression; certainly not confined to *belles lettres*. It was the latter area, now singled out from other written expression as *kesusasteraan*, which gained much attention from Western scholars more focussed on 'literature' than philology, who judged it by international alias Western standards. The 'classical' acquired a new significance in the Malay context after the development of 'Malay Studies' at the university level. For Malays, too, it was now the raw material of philology. Once modern education had weaned them away from the oral habits of their tradition, they were in a position to study it! And the European ideal of physically preserving the heritage was successfully transplanted. A certain disdain for the *belles lettres* of the modern period was initially apparent from some of the ex-colonial scholars still teaching in Malaya, such as R. Roolvink, and only major pressure from Malay students ensured its admittance as a subject of study. And yet it is precisely in this area that one may perceive the continuity of the tradition, and the results of the struggle to achieve it.

But what of the reinterpretation of traditional manuscripts into texts suitable for visual consumption? I have observed that this process reveals an intuitive understanding of the need to make adjustments to meet the standards of a new medium. But what audience would such a composition postulate? It would not satisfy the seekers of the new knowledge, and it would not meet the requirements of those who had given the old manuscripture its new significance as philological text. However, a model had been given by colonialism: reading material for 'vernacular' schools. A number of such abridgements were thus prepared for use in schools. Producing textbooks, moreover, can be a highly lucrative enterprise. But apart from their role as reading material, and their attendant normative function of confirming values still embraced by those in authority, what was the point of such publications? They had lost the rhythms of tradition, which, though no longer heard, and no longer able to provide the intense pleasure of praxis still experienced in the oral tradition by the older generation of *wayang* aficionados, were still silently preserved in the old manuscripts.

We may now rejoin our royal Kedah manuscript, which had meanwhile been acquired by the Dewan Bahasa dan Pustaka, and we shall find ourselves involved in a minor exercise in unorthodox stemmatics. In 1965, the Dewan Bahasa dan Pustaka published a *Cerita Seri Rama,* which claimed to be a simplified romanization of the Kedah manuscript. The editor was Farid Onn.

Perhaps a little more innuendo will make this endless paper a tad more spicy. My only acquaintance with the Kedah manuscript is via the photographs of a few pages reproduced in Farid Onn's work. They are impossible to read without major magnification. The Dewan Bahasa dan Pustaka has no record of ever possessing the manuscript. Some thirty years ago, I asked Tengku Kasim, of the Kedah royal family and a patron of the arts, about the manuscript. He had never heard of it. Farid Onn claims that the manuscript was produced in 1924, but provides no evidence. The copyist gives 1944 as the date.

Farid Onn's text is part paraphrase, preserving some of the wording of the original, and part summary. The result is a work of modern Malay with some archaisms. Occasionally, an archaism – e.g., *tersebut perkataan* – is introduced in a place where it is not found in the original. Here we see the continuity of the tradition: the text is updated. A new element is the introduction of an archaic flavor. This again, paradoxically, constitutes a move to the present: it meets the expectations of a modern audience that an old text will sound old. Farid's work is a text in search of a genre. The illustration on the jacket seems to indicate that this is reading material for children. The introduction, however, is quasi-scholarly in that it provides a collection of formulas culled from colonial scholarship. And then we see one reason for the editor's choosing to use words no longer current. He appends exercises at the end of his book which test the reader's understanding of those words!

Sixty-six footnotes are provided. One might question the need for so many footnotes in a text which has been abridged into modern Malay. Yet it is reasonable to gloss geographical names such as Bukit Kaf; and the use and/or preservation of archaisms in the text is surely a legitimate antiquating device. Thus, words as *karar, ceteria, baiduri,* and *percintaan* (in the old sense) need a footnote. Closer inspection reveals that some quite common words familiar to any Malay schooled or not – e.g., *buyung, tidak berbahasa, medan, nujum, long* – are also glossed. And there is even a footnote explaining *mengusulkan* ('proposed'), yet this is a gloss on the editor's own language! I may be wordy, but I have not yet resorted to footnoting the words I use!

Perhaps most telling are Farid Onn's footnotes concerning *jawi* spelling. We are told that the *jawi* of *tua* in the text is *tuha,* yet the *tua* glossed is part of a sentence in modern Malay, and no glosses are given for other archaically-spelled words in the original. Notes providing *jawi* spellings of names are for some unknown reason confined to three pages (4-6), and one wonders at the necessity of providing the spelling of Jama Menteri and Sura Pandaki, which are quite unambiguous, while none of the dozens of less obvious names are glossed. And then there are a few footnotes claiming to compare the *jawi* spelling of the manuscript with 'the edition of Shellabear and Archbishop Laud', in which instances the spelling of the manuscript is replaced with that of 'Shellabear'. In fact, it is apparent that Shellabear's *jawi* text was not consulted. The editor has rather used Wahi bin Long's romanization, and his choice of Tabalawi and Wasi Wayan are forms found in Wahi Long's text, but not in the Kedah manuscript or Shellabear's *jawi* text. Indeed the Farid Onn text itself reveals the same discontinuity of the tradition found in Wahi. It also throws light upon the role of the footnotes. For Farid Onn has based his text upon Wahi Long, not upon any Kedah manuscript, which, if it ever existed, is itself a copy of Shellabear 1915. The spelling of proper names, for example, is simply lifted from Wahi, and the dozens of errors, including even transpositions of letters, are reproduced. Thus, again we find Saghjalam, Anbala, Angkada and Surgiwa. The footnotes are, in fact, an end in themselves. Farid Onn's text provides us with an intriguing exercise in futility.

This text, then, is a further development towards demise for the *Hikayat Seri Rama*. It also reveals the development of a new system, and therein it represents a step away from the colonial tradition, which was still espoused by Wahi Long. The new system preserves the façade of European scholarship, and the casual European observer may easily be deceived into seeing a system similar to his or her own. The new system emulates the formal aspects of European scholarship. The emphasis is upon form and appearance, not upon content. Herein lies the dilemma of the field. An emphasis on content would have to be the European notion of content, to which Farid Onn *et. al* pay unthinking obeisance. After all, any Malay attempts to develop the tradition had been disenfranchised. Malay attempts to lead the tradition from a strongly orally-oriented manuscript tradition into a print culture tradition were preempted by the colonial authorities. The result for the Malay tradition was fossilization.

Yet Malays were not passive recipients; scholarship became a passport. It was not an avocation, much less a vocation. The lifestyle of Hooykaas, living in a shed in his Hartford garden with no concern for material comforts, sheds some light on the pleasure of scholarship. This was an alien concept for many aspiring scholars in post-independence Malaya. For them, 'scholarship' became simply a career choice offering a bridge to remuneration, recognition and power.

With the advent of Western print-based mass education in the Malay world, the new medium was not simply superimposed on the old, radically oral culture. There was strong interaction, producing major tensions. Orality sought to appropriate literacy to its own purposes, for in oral terms, writing could be perceived as a super mnemonic device, which, ironically, was fatal for the oral tradition. And as the corollary of this, developing the new print literacy involved a major struggle with oral habits, for the need to fragment the formula was directly opposed to the oral concern to conserve wholes. I have remarked above that the approaches of Western scholarship of Malay tradition were incompatible with the practices of that tradition itself. And for a Malay to study his tradition in a 'scholarly' manner, he had, paradoxically, first to break free from its oral habits. Before the print-based thought processes of the scholar were interiorized, the Malay who would reproduce the procedures of that scholarship was forced to rely upon the formal patterns offered by various approaches of that scholarship. Some such approaches already supplied their own overall structure, such as editing or transcribing, which mainly involved following a series of clearly defined steps, and filling a number of ready-made, labelled boxes: 'the text', 'footnotes', 'bibliography', etc. Until the orally-oriented person has become privy to the thought processes which produced these models, he is unlikely to appreciate the inter-relationships, and his method will tend to be mechanical. The emphasis will be upon form rather than content or function; upon appearance rather than significance. The tendency still to compartmentalize and conserve wholes may result in the various steps completed becoming entities independent of one another.

In Farid Onn's case, the scholarly pattern is clear: select a manuscript, read and romanize, annotate, provide an introduction, append a sample of the text in facsimile. This was followed. One might wonder at the choice of the Kedah manuscript as the basis for the text. This was, after all, merely a modern transcription of the much more clearly printed text. Indeed the main point of studying it at all would have been to examine the work of a 20th century copyist, a task requiring comparative work with Shellabear's *jawi* text. Yet the only comparisons made were with Wahi's text, and the latter's readings were chosen over those of the manuscript, which were closer to Shellabear. Of course, Farid was not dealing with the Kedah manuscript or Shellabear's text. For his purpose was not to examine the details of the language; it was to abridge the text. A seemingly more obvious approach would have been to abridge Shellabear or a corrected Wahi Long. And of course, the text *is* an abridgement of Wahi Long. But the patterns had to be followed, even though this involved a convoluted and unproductive course of action. The scholarly posture demanded a manuscript and footnotes. The choice of this particular manuscript, furthermore, satisfied the new national heritage *topos*, for here was the appearance at least of a manuscript directly from the royal tradition – now one did not have to borrow one's tradition from the Sir R. O. Blanks of colonial society. And though one may find irony in this, the modern copy had, in a sense, been reannointed by the royal tradition. The only problem with that, of course, is that the Kedah royals had never heard of it!

In the matter of assuming a stance, the editor was able to adopt a ready-made ethos, which, in its turn, picked up a certain audience. As I have noted, this ethos presupposed work on a manuscript and scholarly apparatus such as footnotes. The introduction, which is a relatively toposized derivation of Winstedt, produces an audience familiar with English or one likely to be impressed by its use. The use of English includes quotations (without reference), terms, such as 'acculturation', and the placing of English terms in parenthesis to explain Malay usage, as, for example, 'conflict' to clarify the common Malay word *pertentangan* – again pointing to the predominance of form over function. But this employing of English in the Malay text is not merely a credentialling device; it reflects the continuing adjustment of the schema. The postulating of this scholarly Malay audience still shows signs of its English model.

But of course, the *intended* audience of Farid Onn's work was not a scholarly one. And it is here that we see the same type of ambivalence revealed in those texts produced earlier by the colonial authorities for use in vernacular schools but also for themselves. And this ambivalence was bequeathed to their Malay successors. The preface states that the work is intended 'especially for pupils studying old Malay literature', and this is confirmed by the presence of exercises at the end. But there is a disjunction between the scholarly treatment produced by following the predetermined recipe and the text itself. The modernized and summarized text is entirely adequate as an exercise in reading. But it is far below the needs of the serious student of the old literature implied in the exercises. This is further reflected in the fact that in order to provide questions considered appropriate to the student of literature, who is naturally expected to understand the language and style of that literature, the editor must supply three verbatim extracts from the original, for which there is a model provided by Longman's Malay Studies Series.

The setting for the final adventure of our *Hikayat Seri Rama* was provided by the dissertation of an Indonesian scholar, Achadiati Ikram, published in 1980. This date might seem to enable us to present her work as a chronological development in the growth of literacy in the Malay world, but this would ignore the fact that Ikram developed philologically very much in the Dutch tradition and speaks flawless Dutch.

If the casual observer of Farid Onn's piece just now could be persuaded to take a look at Ikram's volume he would – being much more savvy after the Farid Onn episode – experience a touch of *déja vu*. Yes, there is the form and the appearance. But once one looks at content, one experiences schematic overload. This adventure is a mechanistic ploughing through the motions.

A. Teeuw was Ikram's promoter, yet he seems quite uninformed about her dissertation. He states (Teeuw 1991: 214), with reference to the manuscript of the *Hikayat Seri Rama* to be chosen as the basis of her edition: '[She] convinced me as her promoter in Jakarta in 1978 that in this case too the best choice would indeed be to base the edition on a single, relatively old manuscript...' The fact is that Ikram made her choice of manuscript based on a misreading of one of Teeuw's own articles. In his article 'The History of the Malay Language' Teeuw states (1959: 150):

'That means that for the investigation of the history of Malay it is the age of the manuscripts that happen to have been preserved, which primarily determines the value of a given literary work and not the age of the text.'

I agree. He is addressing the *history of the language*. An example he gives of an old 'text' in a late manuscript is the *Hikayat Raja-raja Pasai*. The best-known example of the converse of this is the Laud manuscript of the *Hikayat Seri Rama*. The conventional wisdom, which has not yet been challenged, is that while Laud is the oldest manuscript extant, it contains one of the latest versions or texts. However, in her dissertation, Ikram chooses Laud on the basis of her misreading of this statement by Teeuw. She states: '(...) as has been advanced by Teeuw, the age of a manuscript is the one guarantee of the age of a version.' (1980: 84). Her reference is to page 151 of Teeuw's article, but this has to be a mistake.

The result is one more edition of Laud's text, already published by Shellabear and romanized by Wahi Long. Remarkably, unlike Shellabear, she provides no annotation of the text, though the text screams for annotation. Most of my colleagues involved with the *Hikayat Seri Rama* had assumed that Ikram would edit the Raffles manuscript. In his *Sastra dan Ilmu Sastra* (1984: 138), Teeuw avers that Ikram's dissertation is a structural analysis *(analisis struktur)*. Sorry, there is no structural analysis whatsoever, unless one counts a reference to Culler. Mainly, there is character-based description. The description provided, furthermore, is not based on a close reading of any text of the *Hikayat Seri Rama*. It is a simply an evocation of a generic Ramayana.

While the 'Epic adventures of a non epic' seemed to provide a catchy title for a paper, on reflection, I must confess that what is known of the adventures do not amount to very much! One can but dream of the times when the *hikayat* was chanted to the accompaniment of the *tambur*, causing at least enough pleasure in its listeners to warrant the joyless injunctions of Nuruddin ar-Raniri. Some idea of this pleasure could perhaps be gleaned from witnessing the delight of Kelantan *wayang* audiences watching the *Cerita Maharaja Rawana* forty years ago. Even then, few younger *dalangs* knew the tale. That too, has now gone, spurred on by the latter-day Nuruddins who rule in Kelantan with Talibanesque zeal, unaware that this tale likely played a role in the Islamization of the Malay world.

NOTES

[i] See Sweeney 1991.

[ii] Thus, while generations of Malay and Indonesian school children have been taught that the *Hikayat Seri Rama* and the *Hikayat Pandawa* are *epik*, in traditional Malay terms there are no criteria distinguishing them as such. They have been labelled 'epics' only because colonial scholars perceived them to be versions of the Hindu 'epics', the Ramayana and the Mahabharata, which again they had already classified as epics on the basis of a perceived similarity with Greek epic. If, accepting for the sake of argument that the Ramayana and Mahabharata are epic poems, it be proposed that the *Hikayat Seri Rama* and *Hikayat Pandawa* deserve the appellation 'epic' because they are translations of the Hindu epics, one must respond that they are neither translations, Hindu, nor poems.

[iii] See further Sweeney 1987: 116-117; 175-176.

[iv] I believe that van der Tuuk copied a manuscript of the *syair* of Hamzah Fansuri. Klinkert certainly produced a calligraphic 'enhancement' of Munsyi Abdullah's *Syair Kampung Gelam Terbakar.*

[v] See further Sweeney 1994: 40

[vi] Thanks, as always, to Ulrich Kratz.

[vii] Note: *hakim* is spelt h-k-y-m, not h-a-k-m (judge)

[viii] The word *kitab* in Arabic means simply 'book'. In Malay, only in the early 20th century, *kitab* acquired a religious significance. *Kitab* came to be identified with books on Islam. There then was seen to be a genre of *kitab* literature.

[ix] Printing by letterpress: Muhammad al-Bahri, Bangkok, Thailand (no date). See also Mulyadi 1983: 21, who cites this passage from a number of manuscripts.

[x] According to Islamic law, there is the *haram* (forbidden), the *halal* (lawful, permitted), the *sunat* (that which merits a reward *(pahala)*); the *makruh* (that which is frowned upon though not sinful); and *harus* (that which is neutral; one may do or not do what is *harus* according to one's choice. Mulyadi's translation of this passage is confused; she is drawn to the modern Indonesian meaning of *harus*. The result is her equating *wajib* with *harus*.

[xi] That is, before European colonial employers introduced new rules for copyists!

THE EMERGENCE OF BLACKFOOT STORYTELLING IN EDUCATIONAL PROGRAMS

Lea Zuyderhoudt

Introduction

In this paper I investigate the emergence of Blackfoot storytelling in educational programs and transitions in formal education in Blackfoot communities. I will demonstrate how the emergence of Blackfoot storytelling in educational programs is informed by Blackfoot intracultural dynamics yet facilitated by changes in external education policies. I will present data from archival research and fieldwork in Blackfoot communities in Montana (USA) and Alberta (Canada) in 2000 and 2001-2002.[i] The focus is on the Southern Piegan or Blackfeet of Montana, a Native American Nation that is part of the Blackfoot confederacy.

I will examine examples of contemporary storytelling and writing that coexist with older storytelling practices, to explore new ways in which present-day Blackfoot employ storytelling for educational purposes and to investigate how educational systems are being utilized to promote storytelling practices. Primary schools, high schools and local community colleges have recently come to play an important role in storytelling in Blackfoot communities. This is remarkable as they are part of an educational system that originated elsewhere and that has actively opposed indigenous storytelling practices in the past. The elders of Blackfoot communities play an active role in ensuring that storytelling in educational programs conforms to Blackfoot protocol. The emergence of contemporary storytelling practices in the context of formal education is thus informed by intracultural dynamics in Blackfoot communities as well as by changes in external educational policies. This process is comparable to processes elsewhere leading to the institutionalization or creation of epics.

Storytelling in educational programs has obtained a prominent place within the existing range of possibilities to communicate oral traditions and social memory. Recently, both Blackfoot and non-Blackfoot have labeled storytelling practices in educational programs as crucial for survival in present-day life. I will describe how storytelling was first countered and outlawed but later came to play such an important role in educational programs. Furthermore I describe how, despite being facilitated by new educational policies, these practices have remained embedded in local intracultural dynamics and governed by Blackfoot protocol. This shows the vitality of storytelling in contemporary Blackfoot communities.

Blackfoot education in transition
The Blackfoot are a confederacy that includes the Siksika, Blood and Northern and Southern Piegan (hereafter called 'divisions').[ii] The four divisions have a common ancestry, having split before the 17th century. The groups share a common history before and after colonization; they speak Blackfoot (a language of the Algonquin family), have similar customs and frequently intermarry. From 1855 onwards treaties were signed and reserves were created on historical lands, gradually ending nomadic life.[iii] This process has noticeably solidified local identities and attachments to the land.

Separate reserves augmented differences between previously mobile communities and created a new set of parallel but unique conditions for each division. Divided by the 49th parallel, the national border between Canada and the USA, the Blackfoot have been affected by different laws and assimilation policies on different sides of the border. This has lead to heterogeneity in the preservation of storytelling, ceremonies and language. In consequence, the Canadian Blackfoot have retained more extensive use and knowledge of the language, storytelling traditions and ceremonies (see Dempsey 2001: 620). In the 1990s such knowledge was increasingly shared among Blackfoot communities. Since 2000 the annual meetings of the confederacy have been reinstitutionalized, supporting further cooperation.[iv]

Educational systems of the Blackfoot traditionally have been family-based and difficult to trace for outsiders. Moreover, government officials did not recognize Blackfoot ways of education as beneficial for Blackfoot youth. As a result, they were promised schools 'for your children to be taught' in the Laramy treaty of 1855, although the Southern Piegan did not ask for this.[v] However, it took till 1872 for the first school to be opened at Teton River Agency. The capacity covered only a fraction of the population and according to the U.S. Commissioner of Indian Affairs 'none attended with any regularity' (Reports 1873: 252 in Ewers 1958: 269). Children were taken out of school to go on long buffalo hunts and on their return seemed to have forgotten all they had learned before. The impact of these schools was limited. According to the 1878 report of the Commissioner of Indian Affairs, of a population of twelve hundred children of school age, only twenty boys and thirty girls attended lessons for more than one month and only two learned to read and write (Ewers 1958: 283).

The importance of education in 'civilizing' indigenous peoples was increasingly stressed within the US government in the 1880s. Indian Agents sent by the US government found the lack of school capacity for Blackfoot youth problematic. Squeezing thirty-two children in a room literally intended for sixteen pupils hardly provided solace.[vi] In the 1890s the number and size of facilities for formal education increased. The New Holy Family Mission School opened up in 1890, followed by schools in Fort Shaw and Willow Creek in 1892. By 1894 three out of every four children of school age were in school. Judging from the reports of Indian Agents, missionaries were well aware that parents 'very much dislike to see their children taken away', and 'it remained hard to obtain children for the school and keeping them there' (Harrod 1971: 87).

The Curtis Act of 1898 was part of a trend in the US government's policy to use education as a means of assimilation. It extended the possibilities for keeping children in school, away from their parents. When the missionaries complained about attendance, the Indian Agent not only 'sent his police to apprehend the deserters, but he also held back the parents' requisitions for provisions from the government' (ib.: 88). Speaking Blackfoot and sign language in school was forbidden and cultural practices were outlawed. These oppressive policies had an enormous effect on the Blackfeet. In retrospect prominent Blackfeet such as Carroll Tatsey-Murray who was president of Blackfeet Community College have reflected on this period as follows: '... in order to survive, they discarded the old ways and sometimes ceremonial life. And in order to keep their children out of danger, they did not pass along their traditions' (BCC course guide 1994).

The communication of Blackfoot social memory and oral traditions across generations was also severely hindered by other assimilation policies. As part of these nation-wide policies, the U.S. Indian Agent Captain Lorenzo Cook prohibited the Sun Dance as well as drumming, stick games (gambling), 'Indian costumes' and cutting off fingers in mourning on the Blackfeet reservation in 1892. Six decades later Ewers, a non-Blackfoot scholar who was at that time curator of the Museum of the Plains Indian on the Blackfeet reservation, still could write down oral accounts of Blackfeet people on how Cook had seen to it that those that were caught building a sweat lodge or having cut off a finger in mourning were sentenced to thirty days in jail, and how he threatened to imprison women who made beadwork (Ewers 1958: 311).

Nevertheless storytelling continued to play an important role in Blackfoot communities and the content of the stories that were told apparently hardly changed. In 1982 Beverly Hungry Wolf, a writer from the Blood nation reflected on differences between contemporary stories and the stories that were transcribed by Duvall in 1909. She observed: 'They are about the same legends still told today, but in many cases more thorough' (Hungry Wolf 1982: 9).

After the Meriam Report of 1928, which revealed the 'deplorable living conditions of Native peoples in the United States', a trend towards governmental support for self-determination set in. In 1934 the United States passed the Indian Reorganisation Act that restored the power of the Blackfeet government and allowed for tribal schools. In 1935 the Blackfeet tribal business council drafted a new constitution that supported the institutionalization of tribal schools. The mission schools remained influential but the conditions under which pupils were taught improved, as children were allowed to go home after school and severe beatings became outlawed. However, curricula were still bound to state regulations, which hardly left any room for lessons in Blackfoot history and culture or storytelling.

The 1940s and 1950s were the 'Termination' period, which was characterized by the US government's attempts to discard treaties and jurisdiction that allowed for partial sovereignty of the tribes. The US government thereby tried to terminate Native American nations as legal entities. Education became a political tool again as educational responsibilities were transferred from the federal government to the state governments. Although hindered by educational policies Blackfoot educational initiatives were developed to promote storytelling practices in education. Schoolbooks were made to allow students to read stories but also to promote students to ask elders for stories. The available materials about those initiatives reveal a strong resistance to mainstream assimilation-oriented educational policies.[vii]

In the meantime the dropout rates remained high. In the 1950s only a quarter of the Southern Piegan who were eighteen and older held a high school diploma (Ewers 1958: 325). In the 1960s still only a small portion of the youth went to high school.[viii] Harrod, a non-Blackfoot writer who studied the role of the mission among the Blackfeet, related the high dropout rates to the strength of tradition that complicated the participation in schooling. 'Despite the traumas of the past,' he observed, 'the Blackfoot family still retained some of its traditional cultural wisdom', and the Blackfoot are 'burdened by the weight of their own past and by the pressures of white prejudice and discrimination'. (Harrod 1971: 160). Judging from contemporary oral accounts on the 1950s and 1960s by Chief Earl Old Person of the Blackfeet, the feeling of being caught between cultures was indeed thought to harm opportunities for young Blackfeet (Old Person 2001 and 2002 personal communication).

In the 1950s Ewers also sketched a gloomy picture of how only a minority of the people were 'full blood or wore braids', painted their faces, knew traditional crafts, were owners of medicine bundles or were participants in the Sun Dance (Ewers 1958: 328). Contemporary accounts, however, tell of how communities like Heart Butte and Starr School allowed for more thriving storytelling practices than Browning, due to their relative isolation.

The 1960s marked a gradual development towards a renewed sense of pride in being Blackfoot. Government policies were changing. In 1961 new laws allowed Native Americans to buy land and in 1969 steps were taken to involve Native American leaders in decision-making on education, healthcare and economic issues. In a conglomerate of processes of change, including the civil rights movement and the upsurge in ethnic awareness of minority groups, political momentum was created that increased possibilities for self-determination. As educational programs were no longer actively advocating assimilation, possibilities for transmitting Blackfoot knowledge in schools increased.

Efforts were made to support Blackfoot youth in identifying themselves with Blackfoot ways of life and not with what Harrod in 1971 described as the 'marginal limbo of the reservation'. Within Blackfoot communities notions like culture and heritage became defined as something that existed beyond the centers of clustered housing; it could be found in families and at religious and social events that supported regaining the old ways. The new Museum of the Plains Indian that was led by historian Ewers also emphasized the cultural heritage and developed programs for school children.[ix] Schools developed projects that trickled down to even the youngest children. The Browning Day Care Center, governed by the Methodist Church, stated in its goals that it intended to 'help the child regain its past, live productively in the present, and creatively in the future'.[x] Both the US government and the local Methodist Church thus developed new visions about the value of the historical and cultural heritage of the Blackfoot. While schools were still obliged to follow state curricula and could hence barely include storytelling in their educational programs, many initiatives were taken in tribal institutions in the 1960s and 1970s. In 1969 Browning High School students wrote their own textbook *Ethnography of the Blackfoot* under supervision of R. McLaughlin. This was the follow-up of an earlier mimeographed ethnography that had been written for educational purposes as well.[xi] For these publications students visited their own elders and asked them for information on history and culture.

In the early 1970s the Blackfeet Free School was established, a local initiative that, although not recognized by the state, allowed students to work towards their General Education Diploma. The School had the full support of the tribal business council that provided space and partial financial support; students earned a budget for the school by selling lunches to the community. Locally it was known as the 'Free School' as it provided free education and allowed adult students to pursue their own educational goals and to become involved in local cultural events. The school bus was used to take the students and their children to the Sun Dance grounds where they camped together. This marked a new era in Blackfoot education: students were supported and encouraged to partake in cultural events and ceremonies. Within state-recognized schools this was not yet an option.[xii]

Only from the 1980s onwards substantial room was created for Blackfoot studies and storytelling in school curricula. Although the Johnson O'Malley Act[xiii] allowed for tribal institutions to apply for 'money appropriated by Congress for the education, medical attention, agricultural assistance, and social welfare, including relief of distress, of Indians in such State or Territory' funds were initially used for relief of distress rather than for educational programs. Once education became the main focus, it generated the flourishing Johnson O'Malley Program on the Blackfeet reserve that developed extracurricular educational programs, such as the 'stay in school summer program'. In this program students are being immersed in storytelling, cultural activities and hands-on learning opportunities to increase their chances of returning to school in the fall with additional knowledge and skills.

In 1988 the American Congress declared: 'The federal responsibility for and assistance to education of Indian children has not effected the desired level of educational achievement or created the diverse opportunities and personal satisfaction which education can and should provide.'[xiv] This gave rise to a new set of more innovative educational laws that allowed for the inclusion of Blackfoot studies and storytelling practices in the curriculum, and provided financial aid for their development. These changes in educational laws further supported the introduction of storytelling practices in public schools. Time and money became available to let students partake in cultural events and put education in Blackfoot culture and language higher on the agenda. Initiatives of local cultural centers were integrated in the official curriculum.

Such changes in the law were important, as they made fieldtrips during school hours to important historical and cultural sites possible. This facilitated the students' attendance of the annual memorial of the Bear River massacre,[xv] making it a true community event.[xvi] Every year on the 23rd of January young Blackfoot go to this remote site on what is now called the Marias River to listen to stories from the elders on how their people used to live and what happened in 1870 when Colonel Baker almost entirely wiped out Heavy Runner's camp, killing 173 Blackfoot.[xvii] The students attend a ceremony and share a meal. For both elders and youth this proves to be a memorable experience. One of the organizers remarked that until recently 'many elders still only whisper their stories on the Bear River massacre' out of fear they would endanger the listeners by upsetting the Indian Agents. However, now young people are brought to the site, 'walk along the river and are allowed to pay respect to our ancestors'.[xviii]

Moreover, this opening up of a new context for communicating a dynamic corpus of textual and oral genres to young people in Blackfoot communities has led to the inclusion of a range of activities. Elders have come to schools to tell stories on history, culture and religion and to counsel students. They have come to talk about Blackfoot games, how to make and play them and what stories are connected to these games. Others are involved in making tapes for students to practice the Blackfoot language or teach arts and crafts, telling the stories that go with them.

Storytelling and protocol
Expressions of Blackfoot oral traditions and social memory have been transcribed by visitors to Blackfoot communities since the mid 18th century.[xix] Within a century the Blackfoot were considered to have 'excited more curiosity than any other of the native tribes of North America'[xx] and a growing corpus of publications that frequently make use of a selection of Blackfoot stories was established.[xxi] Since then, Blackfoot accounts have been used in descriptions and analyses of Blackfoot history and culture, in grammars and dictionaries, and in children's stories.[xxii] Today these transcribed accounts coexist with dynamic storytelling and writing practices of contemporary Blackfoot. Although storytelling has been deeply affected by the work of missionaries, formal education and assimilation policies, it continued to be important in upbringing, ceremonies and as a pastime, especially in the smaller and more

isolated communities. The existence of a rich ceremonial life including sweatlodges, sacred societies, bundles and the Sun Dance generated a multitude of storytelling events, especially after they were no longer prohibited.[xxiii]

Transcribed accounts and contemporary storytelling differ greatly in the format, style and the context in which stories are presented. These disparities became apparent to outsiders when Blackfoot interpretations of past and present gained a larger non-indigenous audience in the slipstream of increased interest in ethnic awareness.[xxiv] From the 1960s onwards multiple Blackfoot accounts were published, at first locally but later nationwide. These publications reveal differences between Blackfoot and outsiders in the way in which stories are to be communicated, presented and interpreted. Publications by Blackfoot and outsiders differentially tie into ongoing debates within Blackfoot communities on the authorization of storytelling and writing.

Within Blackfoot communities storytelling practices already became debated in the boarding school era. Students from boarding schools were barely familiar with Blackfoot storytelling protocol and customs. As customs and protocol were no longer self-evident for all community members, this set off a debate on how and to whom stories should be told. Moreover, for many families the boarding school era meant a temporary break with traditions. Especially towards the end of the boarding school era such breaks with traditions became an openly debated topic, because insufficient knowledge of Blackfoot ways of life was associated with social problems in Blackfoot communities.

The notion developed that storytelling can be utilized to help people to cope with the hardships of daily life. In order to help the youth reconnect to their local communities, Blackfoot health care and rehabilitation programs gradually started to incorporate informal teaching and storytelling. Simultaneously local projects were created in tribal institutions that aimed at supporting youth to make full use of Blackfoot knowledge in coping with the problems of daily life. Relationships between social problems and the lack of knowledge and experience with the Blackfoot heritage became hotly debated. The promotion of storytelling practices was found highly important, not only for the cultural but also for the physical survival of Blackfoot people. This generated innovative initiatives such as the Plains Indians Survival School (Calgary, Alberta) that support urban Blackfoot and other Native American youth in integrating their own cultural ways and stories into daily life. In these initiatives Blackfoot protocols on which stories are to be told to whom under which circumstances were found crucial.

The importance of protocol with regard to storytelling became clear when at the end of the 20th century a large portion of Blackfoot youth became educated in off-reservation schools. In these schools non-indigenous teachers, in an attempt to include Blackfoot studies, often used publications of non-Blackfoot such as those of Grinnell (1892) to contribute to their students' knowledge of history and culture.[xxv] Although many people argued this was a step in the right direction others argued this caused new problems. In 1991 Blackfoot elders came together to discuss social problems because within a six-month period there had been a series of suicides among young people in Blackfoot communities. The elders concluded that these deaths 'were a direct result of confusion about cultural identity and the young people's inability to cope with the realities of their communities' (Crowshoe and Manneschmidt 1997: 1). The youth had learned about personal power and traditional medicine from people and places outside their own culture that had neither the 'proper understanding nor the authority to talk on these matters' thus generating what elders have called 'cultural confusion' [...] 'Once they returned to the reserve and tried to implement these "unauthorized" teachings they were faced with rejection and obstacles which led to frustration, anger, depression and too often suicide' (ib.). The authority of storytellers, the context in which stories were told and the format and interpretation of stories thus became perceived as a matter of life and death.

The importance of protocols for storytelling draws attention to Blackfoot traditions and customs related to storytelling. Given the fact that storytelling is a crucial element in Blackfoot childrearing, informal education, ceremonies and systems of government, remarkably little has been written on storytelling practices. Renowned non-Blackfoot historians such as Ewers generally only provided a romantic description of how elders 'whiled away the long winter nights with storytelling' and how 'some of these stories were humorous, even vulgar: some were educational and inspirational' (Ewers 1958:160).

Fortunately, sporadic but invaluable observations in fieldwork notes, ethnographies and texts written by Blackfoot are available regarding which stories were told to which audiences. In 1954 Lowie described distinctions in popular and sacred versions of stories in his discussion of how Blackfoot owners of medicine bundles 'often explained the origins of the bundle of these sacred objects as the climax of a generally known story' and that 'there would thus be an esoteric and a popular version, the former is only known to a handful of bundle owners' (Lowie 1954: 126).

Contemporary Blackfoot writers make similar references as to how some stories can only be told in a certain context and should not be written down. Beverly Hungry Wolf, a member of the Blood tribe, wrote: 'Many were specifically adult legends, full of suggestive topics and tribal adventures. In keeping with our tribal traditions I cannot tell these legends in a public place, such as this book' (Hungry Wolf 1982: 136). Likewise Crowshoe, a North Piegan ceremonialist, proclaimed that his book Akak'stiman 'does not reveal sacred information known only to initiated ceremonialists' (Crowshoe and Manneschmidt 1997: 2).

The efforts of these writers show that although story writing fixes Blackfoot stories within alternative frameworks and opens them up to audiences outside the communities, care is taken to comply with the existing protocols on storytelling. Storytellers and writers ask advice of elders and the honorary council of elders who in cooperation negotiate these protocols. Local researchers as well as visitors from outside are asked to discuss their plans with the tribal cultural and historical preservation offices to ask permission for their projects. Although no formal procedure has yet been decided upon, violation of the rules can easily result in rejection from the community. Judging from audio tapes of public storytelling events that are present in the Blackfeet tribal archives and Blackfeet Community College, explicit references with regard to when and how which stories are to be told appear to have become an integral part of public storytelling practices.

Although formalized protocol is important, the evaluation and validation of stories and storytelling practices does not solely depend on protocols and authorization issues. With regard to storytelling and writing practices it is important to realize that the way in which one receives a story determines the value attached to it. Stories can come to Blackfoot in many ways. One can ask an elder or leader or another person for a story. Stories can be found in books, in the archives or on the Internet. One can also receive them through dreams, association or spirits. Stories can also come to a person without that person looking for them (in the same ways as described above). One may hear a story in a name giving ceremony or be presented with a story in the sweat lodge or at the Sun Dance. The way in which a story comes to a person is closely related to its perceived value and can determine to what extent the story (or parts thereof) are public, sacred or secret.

Finding appropriate stories for a situation can thus be an intuitive or spiritual process that is sacred and meaningful in a social context. Accordingly, protocols for storytelling relate to specific social contexts in which stories are to be told.[xxvi] For example, age groups had to buy themselves ceremonially into a 'society', thereby obtaining the rights to stories, songs and specific tasks. When a society would buy themselves into another they could transfer their society to a younger age group. This greatly structured storytelling practices within these societies. In 1997 Crowshoe stressed that it is a group endeavor to ceremonially buy the rights to take over a society, thus gaining 'their "right" to form themselves from dreams or a vision' (Crowshoe and Manneschmidt 1997: 25). Moreover, thereby the participants also 'accept incredible responsibilities by being knowledge carriers and ensuring through ongoing ceremonial practice the well-being of their community' (ib.: 20). An explicit social context was thus established that supported and regulated specific storytelling activities and designated knowledge carriers.

To this day the publication of stories connected to bundles and the filming of ceremonies are highly controversial and have stirred debates on the importance of protocol for storytelling. Stories about those who lost their luck after challenging the protocols or making mistakes are part of contemporary storytelling. This shows that the importance of contemporary storytelling can greatly transcend issues of reclaiming intellectual property and reveals current notions on what is sacred and secret. Moreover, it underlines the ongoing importance of protocols for storytelling and thus the importance of proper storytelling within educational programs.

Conclusion
For almost a century, federal and state laws and policies aimed at assimilation, using educational programs on reservations. Despite their devastating effects, local alternatives were developed within and outside of official educational curricula from at least the 1940s onwards.[xxvii] In the 1960s the possibilities for such initiatives increased due to changing educational policies. As a result a development towards integration of storytelling in educational programs set in.

While educational policies in the late 19th and early 20th century outlawed speaking Blackfoot and partaking in ceremonies and actively hindered storytelling, within a century local initiatives that promoted partaking in ceremonies and storytelling gained ground. In fact, new educational policies allowed for previously developed initiatives to be successfully instituted in public schools and promoted initiatives such as supplying school busses to visit the Bear River memorial. Changes in policies and educational laws in the 1990s have thus greatly supported the further development of Blackfoot educational initiatives and allowed for the inclusion of these initiatives in official curricula. These changes thereby promoted already existing developments towards the incorporation of storytelling in educational programs. The support for storytelling in education has thus provided new contexts for the communication of Blackfoot social memory and oral traditions and has added a new component to the existing spectrum of Blackfoot storytelling practices. Judging from the number of new initiatives that are currently being developed, a further inclusion of storytelling in educational curricula is to be expected.

Because storytelling is a strongly culturally regulated activity for which extensive protocol exists, developments towards institutionalizing storytelling practices for educational use required knowledge on how to comply with these protocols. The emergence of storytelling in educational programs has stirred local debates on how and to whom stories should be told. Protocols were increasingly made explicit in storytelling and writing and elders were frequently consulted. The implementation of storytelling in educational programs thus could be regulated according to Blackfoot protocols. Blackfoot writers of newly developed educational materials and literature, as well as storytellers visiting schools made sure to comply with these rules. This caused a selective emergence of Blackfoot storytelling in formal education. Protocols ensured that sacred and secret stories would only be told in a context that is appropriate from a Blackfoot perspective.[xxviii]

Due to the impact of intracultural dynamics educational programs became a platform for storytelling governed by Blackfoot protocols reflecting Blackfoot interpretations of what is sacred, secret and public. As unauthorized storytelling has been associated with suicides as a result of cultural confusion, the emergence of Blackfoot storytelling in accordance with Blackfoot protocol and regulations have become known as both a cultural and a literal matter of life and death, essential to the survival of the Blackfeet Nation. The impact of Blackfoot protocols on the emergence of storytelling in educational programs has not only provided a new platform for communicating Blackfoot knowledge. Storytelling in educational programs became an institution embedded in intracultural dynamics revealing the significance and vitality of storytelling practices in Blackfoot communities.

MATERIAL FROM BLACKFEET ARCHIVES, HISTORICAL AND CULTURAL PRESERVATION OFFICE

Blackfeet Community College course guide 1994-96 and course guide 2001-2002.
Brochure on annual meeting of the Blackfoot confederacy. Joyce Spoonhunter (2001).
Mission Statement Blackfeet Community College (1998).
Blackfeet Bilingual Teacher Training Report (1985).
Tribal Mission Statement. Blackfeet Archives Historical and Cultural Preservation Office (Year unknown).
Diverse manuscripts of the Blackfeet Heritage Program.

NOTES

[i] Research for this paper was made possible by grants from the American Philosophical Foundation and the Leiden University Fund. Special thanks are owed to Joyce Spoonhunter working at the Archives of the Blackfeet Historical and Cultural Preservation Office and Chief Earl Old Person for their support and cooperation, and to Jarich Oosten for feedback.

[ii] The confederacy as well as the independent divisions have been called peoples, nations and tribes.

[iii] The Blood (also Kainaiwa), the Northern Blackfoot (also Siksika) and the Northern Piegan live on reserves in Alberta, Canada. The Southern Piegan (also called Amska Pikuni, or Blackfeet) live on a reservation in North Western Montana, in the United States. The Gros Ventre have been part of the Blackfoot confederacy but separated from them in 1861 and will not be discussed in this paper.

[iv] Brochure written by Joyce Spoonhunter 2001, Blackfeet Archives, Historical and Cultural Preservation Office, Browning Montana.

[v] Governor Stevens' opening remarks in Partoll 1937: 3-6.

[vi] Ewers (1958: 308) referring to the Report of the Commissioner of Indian Affairs (1889: 223).

[vii] More information is available in the Archives of the Blackfeet Cultural and Historical Preservation Office.

[viii] Also see Harrod (1971: 160).

[ix] Archives Museum of the Plains Indian.

[x] Browning Methodist Church Files July 1969, Archives of the Blackfeet Cultural and Historical Preservation Office.

[xi] More information is available in the Archives of the Blackfeet Cultural and Historical Preservation Office.

[xii] At university level this was already the case. In 1973 a first Native American Studies Program was finalized by the University of Lethbrigde in cooperation with Blackfoot leaders like Leroy Little Bear (Niitsitapi 1970: 83). It offered 'specialized courses oriented toward contemporary Indian circumstances, interests and needs' offering degrees in Native American studies and teaching to Blackfoot students (Leroy Little Bear in Niitsitapi 1970: 92, 93).

[xiii] Sec. 452. – Contracts for education, medical attention, relief and social welfare of Indians.

[xiv] Sec. 450. – Congressional statement of findings.

[xv] In other publications also mentioned as 'Bear River Massacre' and the Massacre on the Marias River. See e.g. Bennett 1982, Dunn 1886.

[xvi] Being a student at the Blackfeet Community College in 2001 and 2002, I attended the event in 2002.

[xvii] Estimates vary from 124 to 173 see e.g. Bennett (1982) and Dunn (1886).

[xviii] Carroll Tatsey Murray interview Browning Public Television January 2002.

[xix] This is not to say that visitors by definition were welcomed see e.g. entry July 27, 1806 DeVoto (ed.) 1953: 437-440.

[xx] Dempsey (1978: 8) quoting from Governor George Simpson's Journal, 1841, March 24, 1841. Similar descriptions exist of other tribes.

[xxi] See Zuyderhoudt 2002: 157.

[xxii] Overviews are presented by Dempsey and Moir (1989) and Johnson (1988).

[xxiii] Long before the Native American Religious Freedom Act of 1996 many ceremonies were again openly performed.

[xxiv] For a more detailed description see Zuyderhoudt 2001.

[xxv] Especially Grinnell is a controversial writer as although his publications are valuable he has also played a problematic role in one of the major treaties through which Blackfeet lost access to part of their territory.

[xxvi] Gender-specific differences in the effects of these transitions on Blackfoot communities are described in Zuyderhoudt 2002.

[xxvii] From the period before I do not know of any initiatives but hardly any materials of this period are available in the Blackfeet archives.

[xxviii] This also has implications for researchers and writers outside Blackfoot communities. Honorary councils of elders and cultural offices have come to play a major part in the evaluation of projects of both Blackfeet and non-indigenous writers, and in procedures to get permission to conduct research.

WORKS CITED

Abaj Gêsêr Khübüün/Abaj Gêsêr Moguchij. 1995. Ül'gêr/Burjatskij geroicheskij êpos. Moskva, izd. Vostochnaja Literatura RAN (Êpos Narodov Evrazii).
Abdul Rahman Napiah. 1995. *Tuah-Jebat dalam Drama Melayu. Satu Kajian Intertekstualiti.* Kuala Lumpur, Dewan Bahasa dan Pustaka.
Abydalek, A. et al. (eds). 1995. *"Manas" Epos and the World's Epic Heritage.* Bishkek, Muras.
Afanou, F. and R. Togbe Pierre. 1967. *Catalogue des 'Cahiers William Ponty'.* Dakar, Département de Documentation of the IFAN, Université Cheikh Anta Diop.
Affandi, S. 1984. *Jaka Tarub and Nawangwulan. A Javanese folktale.* Jakarta, P.T. Rosda Jayaputra.
Ahmad, K. (ed.) 1966. *Hikayat Hang Tuah.* Kuala Lumpur, Dewan Bahasa dan Pustaka.
——, 1997. *Hikayat Hang Tuah.* Kuala Lumpur, Yayasan Karyawan & Dewan Bahasa dan Pustaka.
Anon. 1906. 'Soal-Jawab' *Majalah al-Imam* 1-5: 150-155.
——, 1949. 'La Ruse de Diégué' *Présence Africaine* 5: 796-809.
——, 1970. *Niitsitapi 'the real people' a look at the Bloods.* Standoff, Ninastakko Cultural Centre.
Arps, B. 1992. *Tembang in Two Traditions: Performance and Interpretation of Javanese Literature.* London, SOAS.
Asdar Muis, R.M.S. 2002a. 'Yang tersisa dari Festival dan Seminar La Galigo (1); Senirupa menggeliat di Tanah Garing' *Fajar online* 2-4-2002.
——, 2002b. 'Yang tersisa dari Festival dan Seminar La Galigo (2); Cucu Sawérigading tersisih di negerinya' *Fajar online,* 3-4-2002.
Aubin, F. 1996. 'La Mongolie des premières années de l'après-communisme: la popularisation du passé national dans les mass media mongols' *Études mongoles et sibériennes* 27: 305-326.
Aubin, F. and R. Hamayon. 2002. 'Alexandre, César et Gengis Khan dans les steppes d'Asie centrale' *Les Civilisations dans le regard de l'autre.* Paris, Unesco: 73-106 and 262-269.
Austen, R.A. 1969. *Northwest Tanzania under German and British Rule: Colonial Policy and Tribal Politics, 1889-1939.* New Haven, Yale University Press.
——, 1992. 'Tradition, Invention and History: the Case of the Ngondo, (Cameroon)' *Cahiers d'Études Africaines* 126: 285-309.
——, 1996. *The Elusive Epic: the Narrative of Jeki la Njambe in the Historical Culture of the Cameroon Coast.* Atlanta, African Studies Association Press.
——, (ed). 1999. *In Search of Sunjata: the Mande Epic as History, Literature and Performance.* Bloomington, Indiana University Press.
——, 1999. 'The Historical Transformation of Genres: Sunjata as Panegyric, Folktale, Epic and Novel' R.A. Austen (ed) *In Search of Sunjata: the Mande Epic as History, Literature and Performance.* Bloomington, Indiana University Press: 69-87.
Austen, R.A. and J. Derrick. 1999. *Middlemen of the Cameroon Rivers: the Duala and their Hinterland, c. 1600-c. 1960.* Cambridge, Cambridge University Press.

Bah, T.M. 1985. *Architecture militaire traditionnelle et poliorcétique dans le Soudan occidental du XVIIe à la fin du XIXe siècle.* Yaounde, Editions CLE.
Bai, G., Muraridan 'Kaviya' and Jogidan 'Kaviya' (eds). n.d. *Shakti Suyash.* Jaipur.
Bakhtin, M.M. 1981. *The Dialogic Imagination (Four Essays).* Austin, University of Texas Press.
Balzer, M.M. 1995. 'Introduction (Demography and the politics of identity in the Russian Federation)' *Anthropology and Archeology of Eurasia* 34-1: 4-10.
——, 1999. *The Tenacity of Ethnicity. A Siberian Saga in Global Perspective.* Princeton University Press.
Banham, M. and C. Wake, C. 1976. *African Theatre Today.* London, Pitman.
Bathily, I. 1936. 'Les Diawando ou Diogorames: Traditions orales recueillies a Djenné, Corientzé, Ségou et Nioro' *L'Education africaine* 25-94: 173-193.
Beissinger, M., J. Tylus, and S. Wofford (eds) 1999. *Epic Traditions in the Contemporary World- the Poetics of Community.* Berkeley, University of California Press.

Bekombo, M. 1993. *Defis & prodigues: La fantastique histoire de Djeki la Njambé. Récit epique dwala*. Paris, Classiques Africaines.
Belcher, S.P. 1999. *Epic Traditions of Africa*. Bloomington, Indiana University Press.
Benjamin, W. 1968. *Illuminations – Essays and Reflections* New York, Schocken Books.
Bennett, B. 1982. *Death, too, for The-Heavy-Runner*. Missoula, Missoula Mountain Press.
Berger, I. 1981. *Religion and Resistance: East African Kingdoms in the Precolonial Period*. Tervuren, Musée royal de l'Afrique centrale.
Blackburn, S.H. (ed). 1989. *Oral epics in India*. Berkeley, California University Press.
——, 1989. 'Patterns of Development for Indian Oral Epics' S.H. Blackburn (ed) *Oral epics in India*. Berkeley, California University Press: 15-32.
Blair, D.S. 1976. *African Literature in French*. Cambridge, Cambridge University Press.
Boyer, P. 1988. *Barricades mystérieuses & pièges à pensée: introduction à l'analyse des épopées fang*. Paris, Musée d'Ethnologie.
Brakel, L.F. 1976. 'Die Volksliteraturen Indonesiens' *Handbuch der Orientalistik III, Literaturen, Abschnitt 1*. Leiden and Köln, Brill: 1-40.
——, 1980. 'Dichtung und Wahrheit. Some notes on the development of the study of Indonesian historiography' *Archipel* 20: 35-44.
Brakel-Papenhuyzen, C. 2000. 'Arjuna's penance according to the Javanese tradition' Ch. Lokesh (ed) *Society and Culture of Southeast Asia. Continuities and Changes, Sudarshana Singhal Commemoration Volume*. Shata-Pitaka Series vol. 395l. New Delhi, International Academy of Indian Culture & Aditya Prakashan: 13-29.
Brakel, C. and S. Moreh. 1996. 'Reflections on the term *baba*: from medieval Arabic plays to contemporary Javanese masked theatre' *Edebiyat* 7: 21-39.
Bremmer, I. and R.T. Bremmer (eds) 1997. *New States, New Politics: Building the Post-Soviet Nations*. Cambridge, Cambridge University Press.
Brice Heath, S. 1982. 'What no bedtime story means: narrative skills at home and school' *Linguistics and Society* II: 49-76.
Brink, H. van den. 1943. *Dr. Benjamin Frederik Matthes; Zijn leven en arbeid in dienst van het Nederlandsch Bijbelgenootschap*. Amsterdam, Nederlandsch Bijbelgenootschap.
Brown, C.C. 1956. *A Guide to English-Malay Translation*. London, Longmans, Green & Co.
Brubaker, R. 1996. *Nationalism Reframed, Nationhood and the national question in the New Europe*. Cambridge, Cambridge University Press.
Bulbeck, D. and I. Caldwell. 2000. *Land of Iron; The Historical Aarchaeology of Luwu and the Cenrana valley; Results of the Origin of Complex Society in South Sulawesi (OXIS)*. Hull and Canberra, Centre for South-East Asian Studies, University of Hull/School of Archaeology and Anthropology, Australian National University.
Bulman, S.P.D. 1990. *Interpreting Sunjata: A Comparative Analysis and Exegesis of the Malinke Epic*. PhD thesis, University of Birmingham.
——, 1997. 'A Checklist of Published Versions of the Sunjata Epic' *History in Africa* 24: 71-94.
——, 1999. 'Sunjata as written literature: the role of the literary mediator in the dissemination of the Sunjata epic' R.A. Austen (ed) *In Search of Sunjata*. Bloomington, Indiana University Press: 231-251.
Burchina, D.A. 1990. *Gêsêriada zapadnykh burjat*. Novosibirsk, izd. SO RAN.

Calfchild, R. 1968. *Blackfoot legends*. Browning Montana, published by the author.
——, 1968. *Indian Version of Napiwa the Maker*. Browning, Montana, published by the author.
Camara, L(aye). 1980. *The Guardian of the Word*. Glasgow, Collins.
Césard, E. 1927. 'Comment les Haya interprètent leurs origines' *Anthropos* 22: 440-465.
——, 1936. 'Le Muhaya (l'Afrique orientale)' *Anthropos* 31: 489.
Chafe, W. and D. Tannen. 1987. 'The relation between written and spoken language' *Annual Review of Anthropology* 16: 383-407.
Charry, E. 2000. *Mande Music. Traditional and Modern Music of the Maninka and Mandinka of Western Africa*. Chicago and London: The University of Chicago Press.
Charton, A. 1934. 'Role social de l'enseignement en Afrique Occidentale Française' *Outre-Mer* 6: 188-202.
Chrétien, J-P. 1985. 'L'empire des Bacwezi: la construction d'un imaginaire géopolitique' *Annales ESC* 40: 1335-1377.
Cissé, A-T. 1988. *Le tana de Soumangourou*. Paris, Nubia.

Conrad, D.C. 1984. 'Oral sources on links between great states: Sumanguru, servile lineage, the Jaras, and Kaniaga' *History in Africa* 11: 35-55.
——, 1985. 'Islam in the oral traditions of Mali: Bilali and Surakata' *Journal of African History* 26: 33-49.
——, 1994. 'A Town called Dakajalan: the Sunjata Tradition and the Question of Ancient Mali's Capital' *Journal of African History* 35: 355-377.
——, 'Mooning Armies and Mothering Heroes: Female Power in the Mande Epic Tradition' R.A. Austen (ed) *In Search of Sunjata*. Bloomington, Indiana University Press: 189-230.
——, 1999. *Epic ancestors of the Sunjata era: Oral tradition from the Maninka of Guinea*. Madison, University of Wisconsin.
Conteh-Morgan, J. 1994. *Theatre and Drama in Francophone Africa*. Cambridge: Cambridge University Press.
Crawfurd, J. 1820. *History of the Indian Archipelago; containing an account of the manners, arts, languages, religions, institutions, and commerce of its inhabitants (3 vols.)*. Edinburgh: Constable. (3 vols).
Crowshoe, R. and S. Manneschmidt. 1997. *Akak'stiman: A Blackfoot framework for decision-making and mediation processes*. Brocket, Alberta, Keep our Circle Strong Project.
Curschmann, M. 2003a. 'Heroic Legend and Scriptural Message: The Case of St. Michael's in Altenstadt' C. Hourihane (ed) *Objects, Images and the Word: Art in the Service of the Liturgy*. Princeton, Princeton Universty Press: 94-104.
——, 2003b. 'Oral Tradition in Visual Art: The Case of the Romanesque Theodoric' M. Hageman and M. Mostert: *Reading Images and Texts: Medieval Images and Texts as Forms of Communication*. Utrecht (in press).
Cutter, C.H. 1971. *Nation-Building in Mali: Art, Radio, and Leadership in a Pre-Literate Society*. PhD thesis, University of California at Los Angeles.

Delafosse, M. 1912. *Haut-Sénégal-Niger.* Paris, G.P. Maisonneuve et Larose.
Delavignette, R. 1937. 'Le Theatre de Gorée et la Culture Franco-Africaine' *L'Afrique Française* 47-10: 471-472.
Detachement. n.d. *Detachement te Palopo, Verslag bevattende byzonderheden voor het patrouillegebied van opgemeld detachement over het verslagjaar 1 Januari-31 December 1930*. Nationaal Archief, Den Haag, KIT 1157.
Dempsey, H.A. 1978. *Indian Tribes of Alberta*. Calgary, Glenbaw Institute.
——, 1988. *Indian tribes of Alberta* Calgary, Alberta, Glenbow Institute.
——, 2001. 'Blackfoot' W.C. Sturtevant (ed) *Handbook of North American Indians*. Washington, Smithsonian Institution.
Dempsey, H.A. and L. Moir. 1989. *Bibliography of the Blackfoot*. New York, Scarecrow Press.
DeVoto, B. (ed) 1953. *The Journals of Lewis and Clark*. New York, Houghton Mifflin Company.
Diabaté, M.M. n.d. *Essai critique sur l'épopée Mandingue*. Doctorat de troisième cycle, Sorbonne, Paris.
Diawara, G. 1981. *Panorama critique de théâtre Malien dans son evolution*. Dakar, Sankore.
Diawara, M. 1997. 'Mande oral popular culture revisited by the electronic media' K. Barber (ed) *Readings in African Popular Culture*. Bloomington/Indianapolis and Oxford, Indiana University Press and James Curry: 40-48.
Dika Akwanya Bonambela, G.B. 1978. 'Jeki, livre de la connaisance profonde en Afrique' *Bibliographie des travaux realisés par le Prince Dika Akwa nya Bonambela*. Mimeograph, ONAREST, Yaoundé: 31-37.
——, 1985. *Nyambéisme: pensée et modele d'organisation des Negro-Africains*. Thèse d'État, Université de Paris VII.
Djajadiningrat, H. 1913. *Critische beschouwing van de Sadjarah Banten. Bijdrage ter kenschetsing van de Javaansche geschiedschrijving*. Haarlem, Enschedé.
Doumbia, P.E.N. 1936. 'Etude du Clan des Forgerons' *Bulletin du Comité d'Etudes historiques et scientifiques d'Afrique Occidentale Francaise* 19: 334-380.
Drewes, G.W.J. 1959. Review article of Johns, 1957. *Bijdragen van het Koninklijk Instituut voor Taal-, Land- en Volkenkunde* 115: 281-304.
Drewes, G.W.J. and L.F. Brakel. 1986. *The Poems of Hamzah Fansuri. Edited with an introduction, a translation and commentaries*. Bibliotheca Indonesica 26. Leiden, Koninklijk Instituut voor Taal-, Land- en Volkenkunde.

Drewes, G.W.J. and Poerbatjaraka., 1990. *Kisah-kisah Ajaib Syekh Abdulkadir Jailani*. Jakarta, Pustaka Jaya.
Dundes, A. 1980. 'The hero pattern and the life of Jesus' *Interpreting Folklore*. Bloomington, Indiana University Press: 223-261.
Dunn, J.P. 1886. *Massacres of the mountains: A history of the Indian Wars of the far west*. New York, Harper & Brothers.
Durán, L. 1995a. '*Jelimusow*: the superwomen of Malian music' G. Furniss and L. Gunner (eds) *Power, Marginality, and African Oral Literature*. Cambridge, Cambridge University Press: 197-207.
———, 1995b. 'Birds of Wasulu: freedom of expression and expressions of freedom in the popular music of southern Mali' *British Journal of Ethnomusicology* 4: 101-134.

(The) Encyclopaedia of Islam; New edition prepared by a number of leading orientalists. 1960-, Leiden, Brill.
Epanya Yondo, E. 1976. *La place de la litterature orale en Afrique*. Paris, Pensée Universelle.
Ewers, J.C. 1958. *The Blackfeet. Raiders on the Northwestern Plains*. London/Norman, University of Oklahoma Press.
Exner, M., 1998 'Ein neu entdecktes Wandbild des Hl. Christophorus in Altenstadt bei Schongau. Anmerkungen zur frühen Christophorus-Ikonographie' S. Böning-Weis et al. (eds) *Monumental. Festschrift für Michael Petzet*. Munich: 520-529.

Fachruddin, A.E. 2002. 'Colliq Pujié': pakar sastra Bugis yang terlupakan' *La Galigo International Festival and Seminar, Pancana, Barru 15-18 Maret 2002*: 6-9 [Also published in *Bingkisan. Bunga Rampai Budaya Sulawesi Selatan* 1999: 172-83].
Farid Mohd. Onn. (ed). 1965. *Cheritera Seri Rama*. Kuala Lumpur, Dewan Bahasa dan Pustaka.
Festival. 2002. *La Galigo International Festival and Seminar, Pancana, Barru 15-18 Maret 2002*. Ss.l.: s.n.
Freeman, J.E. 2000. 'Knowledge, secrecy, and the practice of senior womanhood among the Bamana of the Bèlèdugu (Mali)' *Mande Studies* 2: 115-127.

Gbagbo, L. 1979. *Soundjata: Lion du Manding*. Adidjan, Editions CEDA.
Gêsêriada: Fol'klor v sovremennoj kul'ture. 1995. Ulan-Udê, Ministerstvo kul'tury burjatskoj.
Gêsêriada: Proshloe i nastojascee SCHC. (S. Sh. Chagdurov ed.). 1991. Ulan-Udê, Ministerstvo kul'tury burjatskoj SSR. Burjatskoe otdelenie vserossijskogo fonda kul'tury.
Geysbeek, T. and J.K. Kamara. 1991. 'Two Hippos Cannot Live in One River: Zo Musa, Foningnama, and the Founding of Musadu in the Oral Traditions of the Konyaka' *Liberian Studies Journal* 16-11: 27-78.
Gibson, W.M. 1855. *The Prison of Weltevreden*. New York, Riker.
Goldziher, I. 1981. *Introduction to Islamic Theology and Law*. Princeton, Princeton University Press.
Greentree, R. and E.W.B. Nicholson. 1910. *Catalogue of Malay Manuscripts and Manuscripts Relating to the Malay Language in the Bodleian Library*. Oxford, Clarendon Press.
Grimm, W. 1957. *Die deutsche Heldensage*. Darmstadt, Wissenschaftliche Buchgesellschaft.
Grinnell, G.B. 1892. *Blackfoot lodge tales: the story of a prairie people*. New York, Charles Scribners' Sons.
Groeneveld, F. J. 1938. Memorie van bestuursovergave betreffende de onderafdeeling Palopo van den aftredenden Gezaghebber F.J. Groeneveld. [Nationaal Archief, Den Haag, KIT 1161/1-2.]

Hale, T.A. 1999. *Griots and Griottes. Masters of Words and Music*. Bloomington and Indianapolis: Indiana University Press.
———, 2002. 'Translating the African Oral Epic: The Example of the Epic of Askia Mohammed' *Metamorphoses* 10-1: 222-235.
Hamayon, R. 1981-1987. A series of five studies on Buryat epics, W. Heissig (ed) *Fragen der mongolischen Heldendichtung* I-V Wiesbaden, O. Harrassowitz (Asiatische Forschungen Bd 72, 73, 91, 101, 120).
———, 1990. *La chasse à l'âme. Esquisse d'une théorie du chamanisme sibérien*. Nanterre, Société d'ethnologie.

―――, 1993. 'Shamanism in Siberia: From Partnership in Supernature to Counter-power in Society' N. Thomas and C. Humphrey (eds) *Shamanism, History and the State*. Ann Arbor, The University of Michigan Press: 76-89.
―――, 1998. 'Shamanism, Buddhism and epic hero-ism: which supports the identity of the post-Soviet Buryats?' *Central Asian Survey* 17-1: 51-67.
―――, 2000. 'Reconstruction identitaire autour d'une figure imaginaire chez les Bouriates post-soviétique' J.C. Attias, P. Gisel et L. Kaennel (eds). *Messianismes. Variations sur une figure juive*. Genève, Labor & Fides: 229-252.
―――, 2001. 'Emblème de minorité, substitut de souveraineté. Le cas de la Bouriatie' *Diogène* 194, avril-juin 2001 (Recomposition des espaces post-communistes): 19-25.
Harrod, H.L. 1971. *Mission among the Blackfeet*. Norman, University of Oklahoma Press.
Hatto A.T. (ed). 1980. *Traditions of Heroic and Epic Poetry, vol.I*. London, Modern Humanities Research Association.
Havelock, E.A. 1963. *Preface to Plato*. Cambridge, Mass., Harvard University Press.
Heinzle, J. 1999. *Einführung in die mittelhochdeutsche Dietrichepik*. Berlin/New York, De Gruyter.
Heissig, W. 1973. 'Les religions de la Mongolie' G. Tucci, W. Heissig (eds) *Les religions de la Mongolie et du Tibet*. Paris, Payot: 341-517
Herbert, E.W. 1993. *Iron, Gender, and Power. Rituals of Transformation in African Societies*. Bloomington and Indianapolis: Indiana University Press.
Heringa, R. 1997. 'Dewi Sri in Village Garb. Fertility, Myth, and Ritual in Northeast Java' *Asian Folklore Studies* 56: 355-377.
Hocart, A.M. 1970. *Kings and Councillors*. Chicago, The University of Chicago Press.
Hoffman, B.G. 1995. 'Power, structure, and Mande *jeliw*' D.C. Conrad and B.E. Frank (eds) *Status and Identity in West Africa: Nyamakalaw of Mande*. Bloomington and Indianapolis, Indiana University Press: 36-45.
―――, 2000. *Griots at War. Conflict, Conciliation, and Caste in Mande*. Bloomington and Indianapolis: Indiana University Press.
Hollander, J.J. de (ed) 1856. *Syair Ken Tambuhan*. Leiden, Brill.
Hopkins, N.S. 1965. 'Le théâtre moderne au Mali' *Présence africaine* 53: 162-192.
―――, 1967. 'The Modern Theatre in Mali' *International Review of Community Development* 17-18: 169-88.
―――, 1972. 'Persuasion and Satire in the Malian Theatre' *Africa* 43-3: 217-228.
Humphrey, C. 1992. 'The Moral Authority of the Past in Post-Socialist Mongolia' *Religion, State and Society* 20: 375-389.
Hungry Wolf, B. 1982. *The ways of my grandmothers*. New York, Quill.

Ikram, A. 1980. *Hikayat Sri Rama; Suntingan Naskah disertai Telaah Amanat dan Struktur*. Jakarta, Universitas Indonesia.

Jansen, J. 1996. '"Elle connaît tout le Mande": a tribute to the griotte Siramori Diabate' *Research in African Literatures* 27-4: 180-197.
―――, 1998. 'Beyond Ownership: on the permission to perform the Sunjata epic' *Mots Pluriels* 8 http://www.arts.uwa.edu.au/MotsPluriels//MP898jj.html
―――, 2000a. *The Griot's Craft. An Essay on Oral Tradition and Diplomacy*. Hamburg, LIT Verlag.
―――, 2000b. 'Masking Sunjata-A Hermeneutical Critique' *History in Africa* 27: 131-141.
―――, 2001. 'The Sunjata Epic-The Ultimate Version' *Research in African Literatures* 32-1: 14-46.
Jansen, J., E. Duintjer and B. Tamboura. 1995. *L'épopée de Sunjara, d'après Lansine Diabate de Kela*. Leiden, Research School CNWS.
Janson, M. 2002. *The Best Hand is the Hand that always Gives: Griottes and their Profession in Eastern Gambia*. Leiden, Research School CNWS.
Jatta, S. 1985. 'Born musicians: traditional music from The Gambia' G. Haydon and D. Marks (eds) *Repercussions: A Celebration of African-American Music*. London, Century: 14-29.
Johns, A.H. 1957. 'Malay Sufism as illustrated in an anonymous collection of 17th century tracts.' *Journal of the Malaysian Branch, Royal Asiatic Society* 35-2.
Johnson, B. 1988. *The Blackfeet: An annotated bibliography*. London, Garland.
Lowie, R.H. 1954. *Indians of the plains*. Lincoln/London, University of Nebraska Press.
Johnson, J.W. and F. Sisòkò. 1986. *The Epic of Son-Jara: A West African Tradition*. Bloomington, Indiana: Indiana University Press.

Johnson, J.W., T.A. Hale, and S. Belcher. 1997. *Oral Epics from Africa: Vibrant Voices from a Vast Continent.* Bloomington, Indiana University Press.
Juynboll, G.H.A. 1969. *The authenticity of the tradition literature; discussions in modern Egypt.* Leiden, E.J. Brill.

Kaptein, N. 1993. 'The Berdiri Mawlid issue among Indonesian Muslims in the period from circa 1875-1930' *Bijdragen tot de Taal-, Land-, en Volkenkunde* 149: 124-153.
——, 1997 'Sayyid 'Uthman on the legal validity of documentary evidence' *Bijdragen tot de Taal-, Land- en Volkenkunde* 153: 85-102.
'Kavi Punjoji Barhat harvecam vircarit Chand Pabuji Rathaur rau' *Visvambhara* (1997) 29-3: 25-29.
Kennedy, R. 1953. *Field notes on Indonesia; South Celebes 1949-50.* New Haven, Human Relations Area Files.
Kern, R.A. 1939. *Catalogus van de Boegineesche, tot den I La Galigo-cyclus behoorende handschriften der Leidsche Universiteitsbibliotheek alsmede van die in andere Europeesche bibliotheken.* Leiden, Universiteitsbibliotheek.
——, 1954. *Catalogus van de Boeginese, tot de I La Galigo-cyclus behorende handschriften van Jajasan Matthes (Matthesstichting) te Makassar (Indonesië).* Makassar, Jajasan Matthes.
——, 1989. *I La Galigo; Cerita Bugis kuno.* Yogyakarta, Gadjah Mada University Press.
Kessler, C.S. 1992. 'Archaism and Modernity: Contemporary Malay Political Culture' J. Kahn and F. Loh Kok Wah (eds) *Fragmented Vision: Culture and Politics in Contemporary Malaysia.* Sydney, Allen & Unw: 33-157.
Kesteloot, L. (ed) 1971. *L'epopée traditionelle.* Paris, Fernand Nathan.
Kesteloot, L. and B. Dieng. 1997. *Les Epopées d'Afrique noire.* Paris, Karthala/Editions UNESCO.
Kerr, D. 1995. *African Popular Theatre.* London, James Currey.
Khadalov, P.I. and A.I. Ulanov (eds). 1953. *O kharaktere burjatskogo êposa Gêsêr.* Ulan-Udê, Doklady i materialy iz vystuplenij na ob'edinennoj nauchnoj 1953 sessii Instituta vostokovedenija AN SSSR i B-MNIIK, provedennoj 2-5 fevral'ja 1953 g. v gorode.
Khomonov, M.P. 1961-1964. *Abaj Gêsêr Khubun. Êpopeja (ekhirit-bulagatskij variant).* Ulan-Udê, Bur. komp. nauchno-issl. institut.
——, 1989. *Mongol'skaja Gêsêriada.* Ulan-Udê, Burjatskoe kniz. izd.
Khundaeva, E.O. 1999. *Burjatskij êpos o Gêssêre: svjazy i poêtika* Ulan-Udê, izd. BNC SO RAN.
——, 1999. *Burjatskij êpos o Gêssêre: simvoly i tradicii.* Ulan-Udê, izd. BNC SO RAN.
Kitab Bustanu 'l-Salatin. Bab yang Pertama. 1889. Singapura, American Mission Press.
Knight, R. 1984. 'Music in Africa: the Manding contexts' G. Béhague (ed) *Performance Practice: Ethnomusicological Perspectives.* Greenwood, Westport: 53-90.
Koolhof, S. 1995. 'Pendahuluan' M. Salim et al. (eds) *I La Galigo menurut naskah NBG 188 yang disusun oleh Arung Pancana Toa,* Jilid I. Jakarta, Djambatan: 1-49.
——, 1999. 'The "La Galigo"; A Bugis encyclopedia and its growth' *Bijdragen tot de Taal-, Land- en Volkenkunde* 155: 362-387.
Konate, S. 1973. *Le grand destin de Soundjata.* Paris, ORTF-DAEC.
Kone, T. 1970. *Soundiata.* Bamako/Niamey: Institut des sciences humaines du Mali/Centre régionale de documentation orale.
Koster, G.L. and H.M.J. Maier. 1985. 'A medicine of sweetmeats; On the power of Malay narrative' *Bijdragen tot de Taal-, Land- en Volkenkunde* 141: 441-461.
Kraj Gêsêra. 1995. izd. Naran.
Kul'tura Central'noj Azii. 1998. Ulan-Udê, Kniz. izd. Burjatskogo Nauchnogo Centra SO RAN.

Lalas, S. n.d. *Rajasthani sabd kos,* 4 vols. in 9 parts. Jodhpur, Rajasthani Research Institute.
Le Berre-Semenov, M. 2000. 'Le mouvement de conservation d'une ethnie en voie d'extinction, les Youkaguirs' S. Dudoignon (ed) *En islam sibérien – Cahiers du Monde russe* 41-2/3: 401-429.
Leshnik, L.S. and G.D Sontheimer. 1975. *Pastoralists and nomads in South-Asia.* Wiesbaden, Harrassowitz.
Leyden, J. 1811. 'On the languages and literature of the Indo-Chinese nations' *Asiatic Researches* 10: 158-289.
Lowie, R.H. 1954. *Indians of the Plains.* New York, McGraw Hill.

Maier, H.M.J. 1988. *In the Center of Authority: the Malay Hikayat Merong Mahawangsa*. Ithaca, Southeast Asia Program – Cornell University.
Matthes, B.F. 1872. *Aanteekeningen op de Boeginesche chrestomathie*. Amsterdam, Spin.
Maxwell, C.N. 1936. 'Light in the Malay Language' *Journal of the Malaysian Branch, Royal Asiatic Society* 14-3: 89-154.
McGregor, R.S. 1993. *The Oxford Hindi-English Dictionary*. Oxford, Oxford University Press.
McLoughlin, R. 1969. *Ethnology of the Blackfeet*. Browning, Montana, published by the author.
Minim. 2002. 'Minim, perhatian pada naskah "La Galigo"' *Kompas online*, 27 January.
Mohd, T.O. and A.H. Sham. 1978. *Warisan Prosa Klasik*. Kuala Lumpur, Dewan Bahasa dan Pustaka.
Monteil, C. 1929. 'Les Empires du Mali (Etude d'Histoire et du Sociologie Soudanaises)' *Bulletin du Comité d'Etudes Historiques et Scientifiques d'A.O.F.* 12: 291-377.
Moran, D. 1937. 'Le Théâtre Indigene en Afrique Occidentale Française' *Revue bleue* 17-18: 573-576.
Mulokozi, M.M. 1983. 'The Nanga Bards of Tanzania: Are They Epic Artists?' *Research in African Literatures* 14-3: 283-311.
——, 1986. '*The Nanga Epos of the Bahaya: a Case Study in African Epic Characteristics*. Dar-es-Salaam, PhD, University of Dar-es-Salaam.
——, 1997. 'The Last of the Bards: The Story of Habibu Selemani of Tanzania (c. 1929-93)' *Research in African Literatures* 28-1: 159-172.
Mulchand, P. (ed). 1991. *Chand Rau Jaitasi rau (Vithu Sujai ru kahiyau)* Bikaner, Bharatiy Vidhyamandir Shodh Pratisthan.
Mulyadi, S.W.R. (ed). 1983. *Hikayat Indraputra* (Bibliotheca Indonesica 23). Dordrecht, Floris.
Mumford, W.B. and G.St.J. Orde-Brown, 1936. *Africans learn to be French: A Review of educational activities in the seven federated colonies of French West Africa, based on a tour of French West Africa and Algiers undertaken in 1935*. London, Evans Bros.
Mundy, R. 1848. *Narrative of events in Borneo and Celebes, down to the occupation of Labuan: From the journals of James Brooke, Esq., Radjah of Sarawak, and Governor of Labuan, together with a narrative of the operations of H.M.S. Iris*. London, John Murray.
Mutembei, A.K. 2001. *Poetry and AIDS in Tanzania: Changing Metaphors and Metonymies in Haya Oral Traditions*. Leiden, Research School CNWS.

Namsaraeva, S.. 1998. 'Khambo-lama: karma Rossii-v postojannom bespokoistve' *Kommersant-Vlast* 7-259: 50-52.
Namzhilova, M.N. 1988. *Üligery khori-burjat*. Ulan-Udê, Kniz. izd. Burjatskogo Nauchnogo Centra SO RAN.
Napiah, A.R. 1995. *Tuah-Jebat dalam Drama Melayu. Satu Kajian Intertekstualiti*. Kuala Lumpur, Dewan Bahasa dan Pustaka.
Nas, P.J.M. 2002. 'Masterpieces of Oral and Intangible Culture' *Current Anthropology* 43-1: 139-148.
Naskah, 2002. 'Naskah "La Galigo" perlu masuk kurikulum' *Kompas online*, 20 March.
Newbold, T.J. 1839. *Political and Statistical Account of the Straits of Malacca, viz. Pinang, Malacca and Singapore, Vol. I and II*. London, John Murray.
Newton, R.C. 1999. 'Out of Print: the epic cassette as intervention, reinvention, and commodity' R.A. Austen (ed) *In Search of Sunjata: the Mande Epic as History, Literature and Performance*. Bloomington, Indiana University Press: 313-327.
Niane, D.T. 1959-61. 'Recherches sur l'Empire du Mali au Moyen Age' *Recherches africaines: Etudes Guinéennes*, Part 1: 35-46 (1959), Part 2: 17-36 (1960), Part 3: 31-51 (1961).
——, 1960. *Soundjata, ou l'épopée Mandingue*. Paris, Présence Africaine.

Olthof, W.L. 1941. *Babad Tanah Djawi in proza. Javaansche geschiedenis loopende tot het jaar 1647 der Javaansche jaartelling*. 's Gravenhage, Nijhoff.
Osman, Mohd. Taib and A.H. Sham. 1978. *Warisan Prosa Klasik*. Kuala Lumpur, Dewan Bahasa dan Pustaka.
Oyler, D.W. 2002. 'Re-Inventing Oral Tradition: The Modern Epic of Souleymane Kanté' *Research in African Literatures* 33-1: 75-93.

Pallas, P.S. 1995. *Khram Gêsêra. Poseshchenie Kiakhty. Puteshestvie po Burjatii cherez Selenginsk i Udinskij ostrog v 1772 godu*. Ulan-Udê izd., Naran.

Patrouille-actie. s.a.n.d. *Daf. 1 P Patrouille-actie Palopo*. Nationaal Archief, Den Haag, KIT 1157.
Pareanom, Y.A. and A. Syarief. 2002. 'Mencari jejak La Galigo' *Tempo* 31-6 (8-14 April): 69-72.
Partoll, A.J. (ed) 1937. 'The Blackfoot Indian Peace Council' *Montana State University, Sources of Northwest History* 3: 3-6
Paula R. (ed). 1991. *Many Ramayanas. The Diversity of a Narrative Tradition in South Asia*. Berkeley, University of California Press.
Pelras, Ch. 1996. *The Bugis*. Oxford/Cambridge, Mass., Blackwell.
———, 2002. 'Pendahuluan siklus La Galigo yang tak dikenal' *Kompas* 5 April.
Pennacini, C. 1998. *Kubandwa: la possessione spiritica nell'Africa dei Grandi Laghi*. Turin, Il segnalibro.
Person, Y. 1968. *Samori-Une révolution dyula*. 3 volumes. Dakar, Editions IFAN.
———, 1977. 'Samori: construction et chute d'un empire' Ch-A. Julien et al (ed). *Les Africains* (I), Paris, Editions JA.: 249-286.
Pigeaud, Th. 1967-70. *Literature of Java. 3 vols. Catalogue raisonné of Javanese manuscripts in the Library of the University of Leiden and other public collections in the Netherlands*. The Hague, M. Nijhoff. (3 vols).
Pijper, G.F. 1934. *Fragmenta Islamica; Studien over het Islamisme in Nederlandsch-Indie*. Leiden, E.J. Brill.
———, 1977. *Studien over de geschiedenis van de Islam in Indonesia; 1900-1950*. Leiden, E.J. Brill.
Poinsot. 1997. *Sur la route romane: l'église Saint-Pierre et Saint-Paul et le canton de Rosheim*. Strassbourg.

Quénum, M 1946. *Légendes africaines*. Rochefort, Editions A Thoyen-Theze.

Raffles, Th.S. 1817. *The history of Java*. London: Black, Parbury and Allen/Murray.
Ramanuyan, A.K. 1991. 'Three-hundred Ramayanas. Five Examples and Three Thoughts on Translation' Paula Richman (ed) *Many Ramayanas. The Diversity of a Narrative Tradition in South Asia*, Berkeley, University of California Press.
Ras, J.J. 1992. 'The Babad Tanah Jawi and its reliability: questions of content, structure and function' *The shadow of the ivory tree. Language, literature and history in Nusantara*, Leiden, Vakgroep Talen en Culturen van Zuidoost-Azië en Oceanië, Rijksuniversiteit te Leiden: 174-214.
———, 1992. 'The genesis of the Babad Tanah Jawi. Origin and function of the Javanese court chronicle' *The shadow of the ivory tree. Language, literature and history in Nusantara*. Leiden, Vakgroep Talen en Culturen van Zuidoost-Azië en Oceanië, Rijksuniversiteit te Leiden: 243-258.
Ratnu, B.P. 1996. *Suva Uday Samsara*. Dasauri, Published by the author.
Rehse, H. 1910. *Kiziba, Land und Leute: eine Monographie*. Stuttgart, Strecker and Schröder.
Ricklefs, M.C. 1972. 'A consideration of three versions of the Babad Tanah Djawi' *Bulletin of the School of Oriental and African Studies* 35: 285-296.
Roff, W.R. 1994. *The Origins of Malay nationalism*. New Haven/London, Yale University Press.
Roorda van Eysinga, P.P. 1827. *De Kroon aller Koningen van Bocharie van Johor*. Batavia.
———, 1838. *Radin Mantri. Eene Romance naar een Indisch Handschrift van Ali Musthathier*. Breda.
———, 1843. *Geschiedenis van Sri Rama Beroemd Indisch Heroisch Dichtstuk*. Amsterdam.

Sabatier, P.R. 1977. *Educating a Colonial Elite: The William Ponty School and Its Graduates* PhD Disseration, University of Chicago.
———, 1978. "'Elite' Education in French West Africa: The Era of Limits, 1903-1945" *International Journal of African Historical Studies* 11-2: 247-267.
Sadji, A. 1936. 'Ce que dit la musique africaine' *L'Education africaine* 25-94: 119-172.
———, 1985. *Ce que dit la musique africaine*. Paris: Présence africaine.
B. Sakariya (ed). 1984. *Muntha Nainsi vircita. Munhta Nainsi ri khyat, Vol. III* Jodhpur, Rajasthan Oriental Research Institute.
Salim, M., F.A. Fachruddin Ambo Enre, N. Rahman, S. Koolhof and R. Tol. 1995. *I La Galigo menurut naskah NBG 188 yang disusun oleh Arung Pancana Toa*. Jakarta, Djambatan.
———, 2000. *La Galigo menurut naskah NBG 188 yang disusun oleh Arung Pancana Toa*. Makassar, Lembaga Penerbitan Universitas Hasanuddin.
Salleh, M.Hj. 1986. *Cermin Diri-Esei-esei Kesusasteraan*. Petaling Jaya, Fajar Bakti.

Samad, Ahmad, A.1981. *Sejambak Kenangan (Sebuah Autobiografi)*. Kuala Lumpur, Dewan Bahasa dan Pustaka.
Sayyid Uthman, 1896. *Az-Zahr ul-Bâsim*. Batavia, published by the author
Saxena, L.L. 2000. *The Bhils of Rajasthan*, Jodhpur, Rajasthani Gromthagar.
Schoenbrun, D.,L. 1998. *A Green Place, a Good Place: Agrarian Change, Gender, and Social Identity in the Great Lakes Region to the 15th Century*. Portsmouth, NH: Heinemann.
Scholem, G.G. 1974. *Le messianisme juif. Essais sur la spiritualité du judaïsme*. Paris, Calmann-Lévy.
Schulz, D.E. 2001 *Perpetuating the Politics of Praise. Jeli singers, Radios, and Political Mediation in Mali*. Cologne, Rüdiger Köppe Verlag.
Sears, L.J. and J.B. Flueckiger. 1991. *Boundaries of the Text-Epic Performances in South and Southeast Asia*. Ann Arbor, Center for South and Southeast Asian Studies, University of Michigan.
Seitel, P. 1999. *The Powers of Genre: Interpreting Haya Oral Literature*. New York: Oxford University Press.
Seitel, P. n.d. *Haya Epic Ballads*. Unpublished manuscript.
Shaharuddin b. Maaruf, 1984. *Concept of a Hero in Malay Society*. Singapore, Eastern Universities Press.
Shaktidan Kaviya, Dingal ke Aitihasik Prabandhkavya (sanvat 1700 se 2000 vi). 1997. Jodhpur, Scientific Publishers.
Sharif, Z., and J.H. Ahmad. 1993. *Kesusasteraan Melayu Tradisional*. Kuala Lumpur, Dewan Bahasa dan Pustaka.
Sharma, C.S. and S. Bhil. 1998. *Rajasthan ke kala evam Sanskriti*. Jaipur.
Shellabear, W.G. (ed). 1915. 'Hikayat Seri Rama' *Journal of the Straits Branch of the Royal Asiatic Society* 71: 1-285.
Sidibé, M. 1929. 'Les sorciers mangeurs d'hommes au Soudan Français' *Outre-Mer* 1: 22-31.
——, 1959. 'Soundiata Keita, héros historique et légendaire, empereur du Manding' *Notes africaines* 82: 41-51.
——, 1977-1978. *Veillée avex le vieux Mamby Sidibé*. Bamako, Ministère de la jeunesse, des sports des arts et de la culture.
Sidikou, A.G. 1997. *Recreating Words, Reshaping Worlds: The Verbal Art of Women from Niger, Mali, and Senegal*. The Pennsylvania State University, PhD thesis.
Smith, J.D. 1980. 'Old Indian, The Two Sanskrit Epics' A.T. Hatto (ed) *Traditions of Heroic and Epic Poetry, Vol.I*. London, Modern Humanities Research Association.
Smith, J.D. 1989. 'Scapegoats of the gods: The Ideology of the Indian Epics' S.H. Blackburn (ed) *Oral epics in India*. Berkeley, University of California Press.
——, 1991. *The Epic of Pabuji, a transcription, translation and study*. Cambridge, Cambridge University Press.
Stein, R.A. 1959. *Recherches sur l'épopée et le barde au Tibet*. Paris, Presses Universitaires de France.
Street, B.V. 1987. *Literacy in Theory and Practice*. Cambridge, Cambridge University Press.
Stroganova, E. 1999. 'Millenarian Representations of the Contemporary Buryats' *Inner Asia* 1-1: 111-120.
Sugiyo, T. 1984. *Jaka Tarub. Cerita rakyat dari Jawa*. Bandung, penerbit Alumni.
Sulastin Sutrisno, 1983. *Hikayat Hang Tuah-Analisa Struktur dan Fungsi* Yogyakarta, Gadjah Mada University Press.
Suripan, S.H. 1993. *Cerita Kentrung Sarahwulan di Tuban*. Jakarta, Departemen Pendidikan dan Kebudayaan.
——, 1993 *Pantun Kentrung*. Jakarta, Yagasan Obor Indonesia.
Sweeney, A. 1972. *The Ramayana and the Malay Shadow-play*. Kuala Lumpur, National University of Malaysia Press.
Sweeney, A. 1973. 'Professional Malay Storytelling: Some Questions of Style and Presentation' *Journal of the Malaysian Branch, Royal Asiatic Society* 46-22: 1-53.
——, 1980. *Authors and Audiences in Traditional Malay Literature*. Berkeley, Center for South and Southeast Asian Studies.
——, 1987. *A Full Hearing: Orality and Literacy in the Malay World*. Berkeley, University of California Press.

——, 1991. 'Epic Purpose in Malay Oral Tradition and the Effects of Literacy' J. Flueckiger and L. Sears (eds) *Boundaries of the Text: Epic Performances in South and Southeast Asia.* Michigan Papers on South and Southeast Asia, 35. Ann Arbor, University of Michigan. 141-161.
——, 1991. 'Literacy and the Epic in the Malay World' J. Flueckiger and L. Sears (eds) *Boundaries of the Text: Epic Performances in South and Southeast Asia.* Michigan Papers on South and Southeast Asia, 35. Ann Arbor, University of Michigan: 17-29.
——, 1994. *Malay Word Music.* Kuala Lumpur, Dewan Bahasa dan Pustaka.

Taju 'l-Salatin. – see Roorda van Eysinga, 1827.
Taib Bin Osman, M. 1976. 'Classical and Modern Malay Literature' *Handbuch der Orientalistik III, Literaturen, Abschnitt 1.* Leiden/Köln, Brill: 1-40.
Tan Sooi Beng. 1993. *Bangsawan – A Social and Stylistic History of Popular Malay Opera* Singapore, Oxford University Press.
Taufik Abdullah. 1970. 'Some Notes on the Kaba Tjindua Mato: An example of Minangkabau Traditional Literature' *Indonesia* 9: 1-22.
Teeuw, A. 1959. 'The History of the Malay Language' *Bijdragen van het Koninklijk Instituut voor Taal-, Land- en Volkenkunde* 115-2: 138-156.
——, 1984. *Sastra dan Ilmu Sastra.* Jakarta, Pustaka Jaya.
——, 1991. 'The Text' J.J. Ras and S.O. Robson (eds). *Variation, Transformation and Meaning.* (Verhandelingen 144). Leiden, KITLV Press: 211-229.
Tiki a Koullé, P.C. 1987+1991. *Les merveilleux exploits de Djeki la Njambè.* Douala, Collège Libermann.
Tishkov, V. 1997. *Ethnicity, Nationalism and Conflict In and After the Soviet Union, the Mind Aflame.* London, Sage Publications Ltd.
Tiwon, S. 1999. 'Breaking the Spell; Colonialism and Literary Renaissance in Indonesia' *Semaian* 18. Leiden, University of Leiden.
Tod, J. 1972. *Annals and Antiquities of Rajputana or the Central and Western Rajput States of India, vol. I (1829)* London, Routledge and Kegan Paul.
Tol, R. 2002. 'Pengembaraan La Galigo ke Washington DC; Memperkenalkan Husin bin Ismail' *Kompas* 5 April.
Tounkara, M. & Barrie, P. 1988. *Le Monde Malinke de Kita des Années 1910.* Bamako, Editions Jamana.
Tracey, H. n.d. *'Tanganyika. Nyoro/Haya/Zinza.' Sound Recording, Roodepoort, Transvaal, Union of South Africa: AMA, Sound of Africa Series.*
——, 1952. 'Recording Tour in Tanganyika by a Team of the African Musical Society' *Tanganyika Notes and Records* 32: 43-48.
Traore, B. 1958. *Le Theatre Negro-African et ses fonctions sociales.* Paris, Présence africaine.
Traore, K. 1999. 'Jeli and Sere: the Dialectics of the Word in the Manden' R.A. Austen (ed) *In Search of Sunjata: the Mande Epic as History, Literature and Performance.* Bloomington, Indiana University Press: 171-188.
Trigano, S. 1997. 'Les deux Messies d'Israël' C. Cohen-Boulakia and S. Trigano (eds) *Figures du Messie.* Paris, Collection Cerisy: 11-22.

Ül'ger Alamzhi Mêrgên Khübüün Aguj Gookhon Düükhej khoër / Burjatskij geroicheskij êpos Alamzhi Mêrgên molodoj i ego sestrica Aguj Goxon. 1991. Sostavil M.I. Tulokhonov. Novosibirsk, Akademia Nauk Sibirskoe Otdelenie.

Unknown. 1906. 'Soal-Jawab' *Majalah al-Imam* 1-5: 150-155.

Vanchikova, C.P. 1998. Mongolojazychnye obrjadovye teksty kul'ta Gêsêra. *Kul'tura Central'noj Azii,* 111-144.
Van Helden, A. 2001. *Een halve eeuw UNESCO – Idealisten en ideologen, intellectuelen en boekhouders.* Den Haag, Nationale Unesco Commisie.
Veldhuisen-Djajasoebrata, A. 1984. *Bloemen van het heelal. De kleurrijke wereld van de textiel op Java.* Amsterdam, A. W. Sijthoff.
Voorhoeve, P. 1951. 'Van en Over Nuruddin Ar-Raniri' *Bijdragen van het Koninklijk Instituut voor Taal-, Land- en Volkenkunde* 107: 353-368.

Wahi bin Long (romanizer). 1945. 'Hikayat Seri Rama' (romanized version of Shellabear's 1915 text). Singapore, MPH.
Wake, C. 1984. 'Preface' *Theatre Research International* 9-3: 166-168.
Warner, G. 1984. 'The Uses of Historical Sources in Francophone African Theatre' *Theatre Research International* 9-3: 180-194.
W.E.C. International. 1990 [1988] *Mandinka-English Dictionary*. Fajara, Literacy Department The Gambia.
Weiss, B. 1996. *The Making and Unmaking of the Haya Lived World*. Durham, Duke University Press.
Westphal-Hellbusch, S. 1975. 'Changes in the Meaning of Ethnic Names' L.S. Leshnik and G.D. Sontheimer (eds) *Pastoralists and nomads in South-Asia*. Wiesbaden, O. Harrassowitz: 116-138.
Will, R. 1988. 'Die epischen Themen der romanischen Bauplastik des Elsaß' in F.J. Much (ed) *Baukunst des Mittelalters in Europa: Hans Erich Kubach zum 75. Geburtstag*. Stuttgart: 323-336.
Wilks, I. 1999. 'The History of the Sunjata Epic: A Review of the Evidence' R.A. Austen (ed) *In Search of Sunjata: the Mande Epic as History, Literature and Performance*. Bloomington, Indiana University Press: 25-58.
Winstedt, R.O. 1958. 'A History of Classical Malay Literature' *Journal of the Malaysian Branch, Royal Asiatic Society* 31-3: 1-261 (Revised version of Winstedt 1939).

Yoms, Tom and the Star's Connection. n.d. *Pona-Pona-Ditaki-Wayame-E'Wake* Douala, Fotso-Kamague and Music Store.

Zemp, H. 1966. 'La légende des griots malinké' *Cahiers d'Études africaines* 6-4: 611-642.
Zhamcarano, C. 1913-1931. *Proizvedenija narodnoj slovesnosti burjat. Obrazcy narodnoj slovesnosti mongol'skikh plemen. Teksty* I, Petrograd 1914; III, part 1, Petrograd 1918 & Leningrad 1930, part 2 Leningrad 1931.
Zhukovskaya, N.L. 1992. 'Buddhism and problems of national and cultural resurrection of the Buryat nation' *Central Asian Survey* 11-2: 27-41.
——, 1995. 'Religion and Ethnicity in Eastern Russia, Republic of Buryatia: a panorama of the 1990s' *Central Asian Survey* 14-1: 25-42.
——, 1997. *Vozrozhdenie buddizma v Burjatii: problemy i perspektivy. Issledovanija po prikladnoj i neotlozhnoj etnologii n°104*. Moskva, Inst. etnologii i antropologii RAN.
Zieseniss, A. 1963. *The Rama Saga in Malaysia*. Singapore, Malaysian Sociological Research Institute. (translation of *Die Rama Sage unter Malaien, ihre Herkunft und Gestaltung*, Hamburg, 1928).
Zuyderhoudt, L.M. 2001. 'The Immigrant and the Indian' in *Inro@ds*, Volume 1, number 1 (http://www.inroads.umn.edu).
——, 2002. 'Engendering Blackfoot Histories' B. Saunders and M.C. Foblets (eds) *Changing genders in intercultural perspectives*. Leuven, Leuven University Press.

MANUSCRIPTS

Universiteitsbibliotheek Leiden LOr 3186, Sejarah Jipang. 1255AH/1839 AD (article Brakel-Papenhuyzen).
Rajasthani Research Institute (Chaupasni), Ms.402 Pabuji ra duha (article Kamphorst).
Rajasthani Research Institute (Chaupasni), Ms.402 Pabuji ra pravara (article Kamphorst).
Rajasthan Oriental Research Institute (Jodhpur), Ms.5470 Pabuji ro Chand Meha Vithu ra kahi (article Kamphorst).
Codex Orientalis 1713 of the Legatum Warnerianum, Library of Leiden University. Hikayat Nabi Miraj. (article Millie).
KITLV 61, Library of the Koninklijk Instituut voor Taal-, Land- en Volkenkunde; Hikayat Nabi Miraj. (article Millie).

SOUND RECORDING

Body, J. and Yono Sukarno 1997 'Jemblung. Narrative traditions of Java.' PAN 2048 CD (article Brakel-Papenhuyzen)

CONTRIBUTORS

Ralph A. AUSTEN is Professor of African History and co-chair of the Committee on African and African American Studies at the University of Chicago. His current research focuses on the political economy and cultural dimensions of European overseas expansion, the Atlantic Slave Trade in African and African-American memory, and the historical development of African oral and written literature (focusing on the Mande region of West Africa). Publications include: *African Economic History: Internal Development and External Dependency* (1987), *The Elusive Epic: the Narrative of Jeki la Njambe in the Historical Culture of the Cameroon Coast* (1996), *In Search of Sunjata: the Mande Epic as History, Literature and Performance* (1999) and (with Jonathan Derrick) *Middlemen of the Cameroon Rivers: the Duala and their Hinterland, ca. 1600-ca. 1960* (1999). Contact: wwb3@midway.uchicago.edu

Clara BRAKEL-PAPENHUYZEN is attached to Hebrew University, Jerusalem. She was educated at the University of Leiden, Monash University, Melbourne, and at Institut Seni Indonesia/Universitas Gadjah Mada, Yogyakarta. She holds a PhD from Leiden University with research on the ritual Bedhaya dances of the Courts of Central Java. She did extensive research and practice of the Performing Arts of Asia, with special emphasis on Indonesia and India. Current research projects deal with Dayak dance and music in Sarawak, and with oral traditions in North Java and North Sumatra. Contact: clara.brakel@wolmail.nl

Stephen P. BULMAN is Head of History at the Newman College of Higher Education in Birmingham, England. He holds a PhD from Birmingham University. His dissertation was a comparative survey of variants on the Sunjata epic. He is currently researching oral traditions concerning Sumaoro Kante and Susu as well as preparing a text edition on Sumaoro legends. Contact: s.p.bulman@newman.ac.uk

Michael CURSCHMANN taught at Princeton University, USA, from 1963. Professor emeritus, 2002. He is a Fellow of the Medieval Academy of America, and a (corresponding) Member of the Bayerische Akademie der Wissenschaften. Research interests and publications in German, Latin and Scandinavian literature 12th to 16th centuries; oral and written forms of communication; late-medieval/early modern music; literature and the visual arts. In preparation: *Wort-Bild-Text. Studien zur Medialität des Literarischen in Hochmittelalter und früher Neuzeit.* Contact: micur@Princeton.edu

Roberte N. HAMAYON, anthropologist and linguist, is Professor at the Ecole Pratique des Hautes Etudes (Sorbonne), in the 'Religious Studies' section. She conducted fieldwork in Mongolia and Siberia since 1967. In 1970 she founded the Journal and Center for Mongolian and Siberian Studies, located today at the EPHE (Sorbonne). Her most recent publications concern shamanism, among them: *La chasse à l'âme*, 1990; *Taïga, terre de chamans*, 1997; *The concept of shamanism: Uses and Abuses* (ed. with H.-P. Francfort), 2002; *Chamanismes* (ed.) PUF, 2003. Contact: roberte.hamayon@ephe.sorbonne.fr

Nienke van der HEIDE holds an MA in Anthropoloy from Utrecht University. She now is a PhD student at the Amsterdam Research School for Social Sciences, University of Amsterdam. She spent two years in Kyrgyzstan to conduct fieldwork. She is currently finishing her PhD dissertation. Contact: nienepien@hetnet.nl

Jan JANSEN is Associate Professor at the Department of Cultural Anthropology (Leiden University). His main fields of interest are Mande oral tradition and socio-cultural changes in West Africa. He is the co-editor of *African Sources for African History* (published by Brill, Leiden). Contact: jansenj@fsw.leidenuniv.nl

Marloes JANSON currently is postdoc at ISIM (Leiden). She lived with the griottes, female bards, from a Mandinka community in eastern Gambia for more than a year and was trained by them as an apprentice. From this perspective she describes in her PhD dissertation (Leiden, 2002) the daily life and concerns of the griottes, their skills, their techniques for learning the profession, their means of subsistence, their relationships with their male counterparts, and their patronage networks. Contact: Marloes.Janson@12move.nl

Janet KAMPHORST is affiliated with the Research School CNWS (Leiden University) and presently completes her PhD dissertation on the oral and written Pabuji tradition of western Rajasthan. At the heart of her research is the story of the 14th-century Rajput hero Pabuji Dhamdhal Rathaur, a medieval warrior who is now worshipped as one of the many folk gods of North-west India. Working together with several Rajasthani poets, singers and performers, she aims to answer questions about the manner in which the present and the past are related in the Pabuji tradition. Her findings demonstrate how divergent, local histories relate to the modern historiography of the region. Contact: jankam65@hotmail.com

Sirtjo KOOLHOF is librarian at the Royal Netherlands Institute for Southeast Asian and Caribbean Studies (KITLV) in Leiden. He was an editor of *La Galigo menurut naskah NBG 188* (Jakarta 1995, Makassar 2000). Currently he is writing a PhD thesis which will contain a text edition and translation of an episode from the *La Galigo* epic. Contact: koolhof@kitlv.nl

Henk M.J. MAIER is Luce Professor of Southeast Asian Studies at University of California, Riverside (USA). He has widely published on Malay literature and language and translated a number of modern Malay novels into Dutch. Contact: hmjmaier@hotmail.com

Julian MILLIE is an Australian researcher currently completing doctoral research at the Research School CNWS, Leiden University. He completed his masters thesis at Monash University, Melbourne, on a work of classical Malay literature, the Syair Bidasari. The product of that research is currently being published in the Bibliotheca Indonesica series of the KITLV, Leiden. His doctoral research concerns traditions seeking the intercession of Sheikh Abdulqadir al-Jaelani in West Java. Contact: julianmillie@hotmail.com

Amin SWEENEY was born in London, is a Malaysian citizen, taught in Malaysia and California. He now resides in Indonesia and Malaysia. He writes on Malay and is completing a project to publish the works of the 19th-century writer Munsyi Abdullah. Contact: AminSweeney@aol.com

Lea ZUYDERHOUDT is a PhD student at the Research School CNWS (Leiden University). She holds an MA in history (Leiden University), an MA in cultural anthropology (Leuven, Belgium) and has studied Native American Studies at the University of Minnesota, USA. Since 1995 she has done extensive fieldwork in Blackfoot communities. Her PhD research focuses on Blackfoot perspectives on the past as expressed in oral and written accounts and investigates how these are part of Blackfoot intra-cultural dynamics and at interplay with non-indigenous writings on Blackfoot history and culture. Contact: L.M.Zuyderhoudt@let.leidenuniv.nl

Literatur: Forschung und Wissenschaft

Karl-Heinz Stoll
Die Interkulturalität afrikanischer Literatur
Chinua Achebe, Cyprian Ekwensi, Ngũgĩ wa Thiong'o, Wole Soyinka
Die englische Sprache in Afrika, die literarischen Medien Roman und Drama sowie die Themen der afrikanischen Literatur sind Ausdruck kultureller Pluralität. Der Beitrag postkolonialer Literatur zu unserem Orientierungswissen besteht in ihrem Potenzial sprachlicher und inhaltlicher Desorientierung als Voraussetzung einer Emanzipation von eurozentrischen Vorurteilen. Das Buch geht ein auf die englische Sprache als Medium wirtschaftlicher Globalisierung und kultureller Fragmentarisierung. Dann werden anhand der Eigenarten von Sprache, Handlungsführung, Introspektionen und mythologischem Ideengehalt die Werke der vier bedeutendsten schwarzafrikanischen Autoren exemplarisch als „Dazwischen-Literatur" interpretiert. Zielgruppe sind Anglisten, Afrikanisten und alle, die sich für die Rolle von Kultur in unserer globalisierten Welt interessieren.
Bd. 1, 2003, 400 S., 30,90 €, br., ISBN 3-8258-6698-x

Literatur – Sprache – Medien
Schriftenreihe des Kollegs der Promovierenden des Fachbereichs 07 der Universität Hamburg
herausgegeben von Prof. Dr. Knut Hickethier, Prof. Dr. Wolfgang J. Meyer und Prof. Dr. Johann N. Schmidt

Anil Kaputanoglu; Nicole Meyer (Hg.)
„Nur das Auge weckt mich wieder ... "
Erinnerung Text Gedächtnis
Im Wechselspiel von Repräsentation und Umdeutung ist uns mit literarischen Texten ein wichtiges kulturelles Medium des Erinnerns gegeben – ein Medium, das durch verschiedene Formen und Verfahren des Erinnerns das Erinnern unterlaufen und verschieben oder das Erinnern selbst beizeiten bis an die Grenze der sprachlichen Darstellbarkeit führen kann. Der vorliegende Band erprobt in unterschiedlichen Erkundungen diese vielfältigen Möglichkeiten literarischer Texte, am kulturellen Entwurf eines Gedächtnisses sowie einer Erinnerung teilzuhaben.
Bd. 1, 2003, 360 S., 25,90 €, br., ISBN 3-8258-5529-5

Christian Maintz; Oliver Möbert; Matthias Schumann (Hg.)
Schaulust
Theater und Film – Geschichte und Intermedialität
Seit der weltweiten Etablierung des Kinematographen zu Beginn des 20. Jahrhunderts werden die Beziehungen zwischen Theater und Film kontrovers diskutiert. Im Mittelpunkt solcher Debatten stand zunächst vorwiegend die Rivalität zwischen dem traditionellen und dem neuen Medium; die jüngere Forschung rückt demgegenüber eher Verbindungen, Übergänge und Interdependenzen ins Blickfeld. Der vorliegende Band versammelt neun Beiträge, die solche intermedialen Relationen behandeln: Sie reichen von der Theater-"Verfilmung" über wechselseitige formästhetische bzw. strukturelle Beeinflussung bis zur Frage der Kompatibilität theoretischer Modelle.
Bd. 2, 2002, 304 S., 25,90 €, br., ISBN 3-8258-6208-9

Peter Brandes; Michaela Krug (Hg.)
Übergänge
Lektüren zur Ästhetik der Transgression
Im Phänomen des Übergangs kreuzen sich Raum und Zeit. Als ein Phänomen der Öffnung destruiert und schafft er komplexe Konstellationen von Innen und Außen, Gegenwart und Vergangenheit, Differenz und Identität, Heimat und Fremde. Im ästhetischen Arsenal von Gesellschaften sind diese Übergänge nicht nur in unterschiedlichen Bildern und Motiven archiviert, sondern die damit einhergehenden Schwellenerfahrungen werden selbst zur ästhetischen Produktivkraft. Die Beiträge dieses Bandes erkunden die literarisch und filmisch inszenierten Überschreitungen von topographischen, zeitlichen und sprachlichen Begrenzungen sowie von Geschlechter- und Gattungsgrenzen.
Bd. 3, 2003, 184 S., 17,90 €, br., ISBN 3-8258-6900-8

Literatur – Kultur – Medien
herausgegeben von Peter J. Brenner (Universität zu Köln)

Peter J. Brenner
Kultur als Wissenschaft
Aufsätze zur Theorie der modernen Geisteswissenschaft
Krisendiskussionen gehören zum Alltag der deutschen Geisteswissenschaften seit ihrer Entstehung. Es besteht aber Anlass zu der Vermutung, dass im vergangenen Jahrzehnt sich reale Entwicklungen vollzogen haben, die zu einem gravierenden Strukturwandel geführt haben – in eins mit dem krisenhaften Strukturwandel der Universitäten und

---

LIT Verlag Münster – Hamburg – Berlin – London
Grevener Str./Fresnostr. 2 48159 Münster
Tel.: 0251 – 23 50 91 – Fax: 0251 – 23 19 72
e-Mail: vertrieb@lit-verlag.de – http://www.lit-verlag.de

des deutschen Bildungssystems.
Die hier vorgelegten Aufsätze von Peter J. Brenner, entstanden zwischen 1989 und 2002, analysieren diesen Wandel. Sie setzen sich mit den universitären Organisationsformen der Geisteswissenschaften ebenso auseinander wie mit den aktuellen, kulturwissenschaftlich, interkulturell und kulturanthropologisch orientierten Grundlegungsdiskussionen.
Bd. 1, 2003, 272 S., 19,90 €, br., ISBN 3-8258-6021-3

Nicola Denis
Tartuffe in Deutschland
Molières Komödie in Übersetzungen, in der Wissenschaft und auf der Bühne vom 17. bis zum 20. Jahrhundert
Diese umfassende komparatistische Studie macht es sich in fünf Teilen zur Aufgabe, die Mechanismen der *Tartuffe*-Rezeption in ihrem chronologischen Gang durch die Jahrhunderte zu erfassen und deuten. Molières weltbekannte Komödie ist, in Deutschland wie in Frankreich, immer auch Gegenstand weitreichender Umdeutungen geworden. Alle zu Wort kommenden Interpreten, ob Übersetzer, Gelehrte, Regisseure, Schauspieler oder Autoren, prägen dem Text zeittypische, aber auch persönliche Lesarten auf und bieten dem Rezipienten einen Tartuffe mit mehreren Gesichtern dar. Die wohl berühmteste literarische Parabel der Verstellungskunst erhält sich so auch im Gang durch die deutsche Literaturgeschichte ihren schillernden Charakter: die Fabel der Scheinheiligkeit, gespiegelt im Illusionscharakter der Bühne, wird wie nach wie vor lebendige Herausforderung Molières an sein Publikum begriffen.
Bd. 2, 2002, 552 S., 79,90 €, br., ISBN 3-8258-6022-1

Eva-Maria Ernst
Zwischen Lustigmacher und Spielmacher
Die komische Zentralfigur auf dem Wiener Volkstheater im 18. Jahrhundert
Seit der Antike ruht das komische Potential der europäischen Komödie in der Hauptsache auf den Schultern einer Zentralfigur, die für das Wiener Volkstheater eine unbestrittene Bedeutung erlangte, so dass sich alle Vertreibungsversuche à la Gottsched als wenig fruchtbar erwiesen. Die vorliegende Studie widmet sich unter sozial- und kulturgeschichtlichem Gesichtspunkt den mannigfaltigen Bemühungen von Wiener Theaterleitern und Autoren des 18. Jahrhunderts, für die Gestaltung der komischen Zentralfigur innerhalb der aktuellen poetologischen Diskussion gültiges Konzept zu entwickeln. Gegenstand der Betrachtung ist dabei vor allem die Entwicklung der komischen Zentralfigur von einem episodisch auftretenden, passiv-komischen „Lustigmacher" zu einem aktiv-komischen „Spielmacher" nach Art antiker Dienerfiguren.
Bd. 3, 2003, 328 S., 29,90 €, br., ISBN 3-8258-6730-7

Franka Marquardt
Erzählte Juden
Untersuchungen zu Thomas Manns „Joseph und seine Brüder" und Robert Musils „Mann ohne Eigenschaften"
In dieser Untersuchung der beiden wohl wichtigsten Romane der deutschsprachigen Literatur zwischen 1930 und 1945 geht es nicht, wie in der literaturwissenschaftlichen Antisemitismusforschung sonst üblich, um „das Bild des Juden" bei Thomas Mann oder Robert Musil. Vielmehr unternimmt die Arbeit den Versuch, das Erzählen von Juden, Jüdinnen und Jüdischem jenseits der imagologischen Ebene in literarischen Texten zu fassen und in seinen narratologischen, strukturellen und diskursiven Verflechtungen mit den Beständen der Tradition zu beschreiben. Das Ergebnis ist überraschend: Thomas Manns vermeintlich biblischer Roman erweist sich als viel stärker mit dem Ballast der traditionellen Judenfeindschaft behaftet als Robert Musils Riesenfragment, in dem genau diese Tradition nicht fortgeschrieben, sondern aufgebrochen wird.
Bd. 4, 2003, 416 S., 29,90 €, br., ISBN 3-8258-6805-2

Literatur – Theater – Medien
herausgegeben von Prof. Dr. Holger Sandig (Erlangen)

Silke Buss
Fernando Pessoa auf europäischen Bühnen
Theaterwissenschaftliche Analyse der Werke *Faust, Der Seemann* und *Der anarchistische Bankier* und elf szenischer Realisationen
Fernando Pessoa gilt als der bedeutsamste portugiesische Dichter unseres Jahrhunderts. Daß er auch für das Theater schrieb, ist wenig bekannt. Dennoch haben sich in den letzten Jahren verschiedene Regisseure in Europa seiner Werke *Faust, Der Seemann* und *Der anarchistische Bankier* angenommen. Ob es ihnen in ihren Inszenierungen gelungen ist, tatsächlich das Stück und nicht den charismatischen Autor auf die Bühne zu bringen, untersucht diese theaterwissenschaftliche Arbeit. Elf Produktionen aus Deutschland, Frankreich, Spanien, Österreich und der Schweiz werden auf der Grundlage einer vorausgehenden Textanalyse untersucht, wobei das Entstehen des jeweiligen Theaterkunstwerkes von der Idee bis zur Rezeption verfolgt wird. Ihre Nähe zu den Inszenierungen verdankt diese Studie einer reichen Bebilderung sowie zahlreichen

L IT Verlag Münster – Hamburg – Berlin – London
Grevener Str./Fresnostr. 2 48159 Münster
Tel.: 0251 – 23 50 91 – Fax: 0251 – 23 19 72
e-Mail: vertrieb@lit-verlag.de – http://www.lit-verlag.de

Zitaten von Regisseuren wie Christoph Marthaler, Aurélien Recoing, Brian Michaels und Moisés Maicas.
Bd. 1, 2000, 584 S., 35,90 €, br., ISBN 3-8258-4518-4

Donata Kaman
Theater der Maler in Deutschland und Polen
Ausgehend von den theoretischen Vordenkern: E. G. Craig, R. Wagner, A. Appia untersucht diese Studie eigenwillige Theaterarbeit von Malern, die ihren Visionen ein Bild verleihen. O. Kokoschka, W. Kandinsky, O. Schlemmer und ihnen gegenüber die Nachkriegsgeneration der polnischen Maler: T. Kantor, J. Szajna und A. Woron setzten ihrer jeweiligen Zeitgeisterfahrung ein optisches Zeichen im Theater. Alles in allem kommt die untheatralische Theatralität der Kunst mit dem 20. Jahrhundert auf einen überraschenden Weg, der doch schon in der Kulturgeschichte seit M. Grünewald und H. Bosch als Bilderszenario seelischer und gesellschaftlicher Katastrophen vorgeahnt war.
Bd. 2, 2001, 328 S., 25,90 €, br., ISBN 3-8258-4747-3

Studien zur englischen Literatur
herausgegeben von Prof. Dr. Dieter Mehl
(Universität Bonn)

Christa Jansohn
Zweifelhafter Shakespeare
Zu den Shakespeare-Apokryphen und ihrer Rezeption von der Renaissance bis zum 20. Jahrhundert
Bd. 11, 2000, 448 S., 35,90 €, gb., ISBN 3-8258-5133-8

Axel Stähler
"Perpetuall Monuments"
Die Repräsentation von Architektur in der italienischen Festdokumentation (ca. 1515 – 1640) und der englischen court masque (1604 – 1640)
Bd. 12, 2001, 584 S., 35,90 €, gb., ISBN 3-8258-5142-7

Anne-Julia Zwierlein
Majestick Milton
British Imperial Expansion and Transformations of *Paradise Lost*, 1667 – 1837
Bd. 13, 2001, 512 S., 65,90 €, gb., ISBN 3-8258-5432-9

Astrid Laupichler
Lachen und Weinen: tragikomischkarnevaleske Entwicklungsräume
Interpretationen zu Shakespeares Problemstücken und Romanzen
Bd. 14, 2002, 432 S., 35,90 €, gb., ISBN 3-8258-5824-3

Christa Jansohn (Hg.)
In the Footsteps of Queen Victoria: Wege zum Viktorianischen Zeitalter
Das viktorianische Zeitalter gehört zweifellos zu den interessantesten und gleichzeitig vielschichtigsten Gebieten der englischen Literatur. Der Band versammelt 16 Beiträge, die anläßlich des hundertsten Todesjahres der Königin Victoria im Rahmen einer Ringvorlesung am Centre for British Studies in Bamberg gehalten wurden. Die in deutscher und englischer Sprache verfaßten Beiträge renommierter Forscher und Forscherinnen sollen einen Einblick in die verschiedenen Gebiete des viktorianischen Zeitalters geben.
Der Band ist in folgende Abschnitte unterteilt: 1. Cultural Memories, or Images of Queen Victoria, 2. Science, Society and Victorian Culture, und 3. Reading and Writing in Victorian England. Eine ausführliche Bibliographie rundet den Band ab und soll zur weiteren Beschäftigung mit dem viktorianischen Zeitalter anregen.
Bd. 15, 2003, 352 S., 25,90 €, br., ISBN 3-8258-5884-7

André Schüller
A Life Composed
T. S. Eliot and the Morals of Modernism
"The modern literary critic", T. S. Eliot wrote in 1929, "must be an 'experimenter' outside of what you might at first consider his own province; [...] there is no literary problem which does not lead us irresistibly to larger problems."
The present study follows Eliot's principle and situates his literary and critical work in a wide context that reveals manifold links between aesthetics, ethics, politics and epistemology: the historical context of early-twentieth-century idealism, vitalism and pragmatism, especially the intensely political Bergsonian controversy, and the modern context of the philosophies of Charles Taylor, Michel Foucault and Richard Rorty. 'Knowledge', it argues, was verbalised in the modernist age, individualised into the *act* of 'knowing', an act with motives and goals, and thus introduced into the realm of ethics – a process central to twentieth-century thought. Eliot's poems especially, constructed as "a life composed", a literary lifetime linking composition and composure, ponder the virtue of precision, the sins of pride and "mental sloth", the temptation of prejudice and the need for conviction. Decidedly tentative, Eliot's poems solve the problem of morally significant literature. In a century of suspicion, they ask the crucial question of where one should start to rely.
Bd. 17, 2002, 368 S., 24,90 €, br., ISBN 3-8258-6362-x

LIT Verlag Münster – Hamburg – Berlin – London
Grevener Str./Fresnostr. 2 48159 Münster
Tel.: 0251 – 23 50 91 – Fax: 0251 – 23 19 72
e-Mail: vertrieb@lit-verlag.de – http://www.lit-verlag.de